Rounding the Bend

The Life and Times of Big Red

David H. Roper

ISBN: 0985650133
ISBN 13: 9780985650131
Points East Publishing, Inc.

For the real Big Red, and the real
Grampy, who inspired this story

Next to the wound,
What women make best
Is the bandage

JULES-AMÉDÉE BARBEY D'AUREVILLY

TABLE OF CONTENTS

December 12, 2014

I'd just finished shoveling my driveway and was in the midst
of ducking from another of my daughter Mai Linh's nicely-placed
snowballs when a FedX truck pulled up. "Package for Daniel Ha
Roan," the man said. "Requires a signature." I signed while Mai
Linh jumped gleefully at the sight of a package. "Oh, Daddy, open
it, open it."

"It's probably nothing, honey. Some boring legal stuff," I said.

Mai Linh grabbed a corner of the package in her snowy mit-
ten. "Well, at least can I open it? Please? Maybe there's something
really special in there."

It bore a name I didn't know, but it came from a special place
I long remembered. I let Mai Linh open it. "Oh, gobblesmack,"
she said. "It's only a big old beat-up notebook." She handed me
the package. "Daddy, I'm going inside for cocoa. Maybe play with
Jiminy Cricket. Come in and have some cocoa too, Daddy." And
off she trotted.

Inside, clipped to the notebook, was this letter:

12/10/14

Dear Cubby,

I hope you get this.

I'm not sure how to begin this letter. I'm not even sure if I should call you Cubby or Danny or, now that you're certainly a grown man, perhaps Dan. But Cubby is what Orca (Red) called you, so that's how I know you.

Red's great spirit left his body on December 6. I was with him. I was his nurse at a veterans' home in Minneapolis. I only knew him for a short time, but on one very special day and night in November I spent some of the most profound hours of my life with him. He took me downriver, through Monkey Rudder Bend. Then he took me aboard Cirrhosis of the River, the houseboat you knew so well. It was there, on a snowy, late fall evening that he shared his heart, his soul, and his remarkable story with me.

Red wanted you to have his things, including this notebook. He told me that if anybody could make some sense of his life, it would be you.

I think, in many ways, his life made perfect sense. Cubby, I have read this notebook; I think Red would have wanted me to. Anyway, he wanted you to have it, along with his gold bracelet, his memories board, and his antique waffle iron collection. (I can ship all these to you once I figure the best and safest way.)

I know much of what you two went through together long ago; and I know those times were as vivid in Red's mind as if they happened yesterday. There's a lot Red didn't say to me. But he said it in this notebook. I also know, from reading your letter sent to him via The Waffle Palace, that you wanted to make peace, that you finally understood that what he had done back then was best for your Grampy at the end. Red and I found your letter just a few weeks ago, unopened and pinned to the schedule board in the kitchen of The Waffle Palace. Hard to believe, but it was dated August 8, 2013. Finally finding out how you felt was tremendously important to Red.

Cubby, everyone has a unique story and every story is important. And every story should be told, because, really, we're all connected. That's what I believe anyway. As in the sacred song of the great whale, there's a message carried within each of us, woven into our soul, that we need to share. Deep down I believe Orca Bates knew that his message was that he made the world a better place even if his song was, to some, as peculiar and mysterious as the whale's.

At the end, when he was delirious, he mumbled something about heading for Cloud 23. Then he asked for his son. "Does he have a son?" the doctor attending to him asked. "No," the home's administrator answered, "no family". But that was the wrong answer. The right one is here, in this notebook. So cherish it, Cubby, as you cherish those you love.

In spirit,

Wihopa Webster, aka 'Toddy'

I

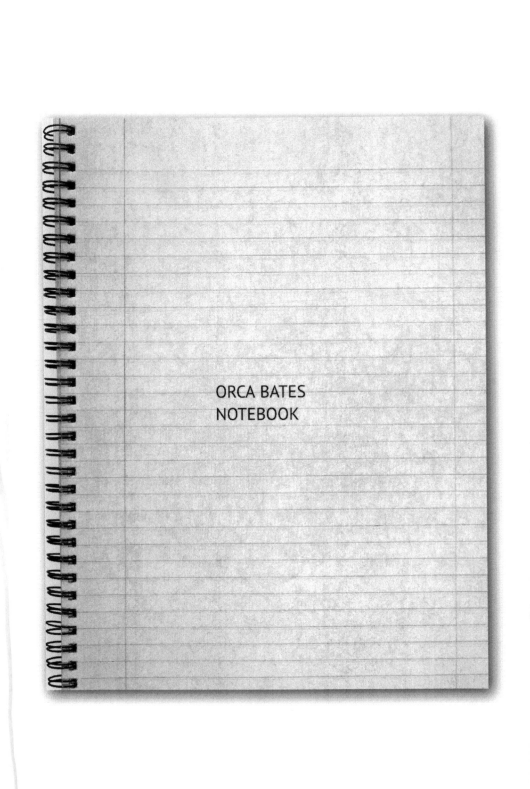

ORCA BATES
NOTEBOOK

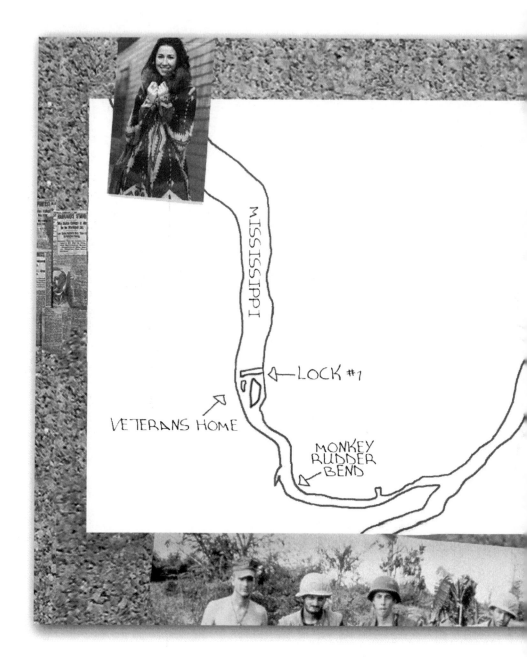

MISSISSIPPI

←— LOCK #1

VETERANS HOME ↗

MONKEY
RUDDER
BEND ↙

1

2014: GROUNDED OUT IN AN OLD SOLDIERS' HOME

Toddy gave me this notebook and said I should write in it. I ain't real literate, but hell, with only 26 letters in the alphabet, I figure even I can build something here just by moving them letters around just right. Anyway, Toddy promised that it would be good for me. Told me some religious guy said, "If the pain of your story ain't transformed, then it'll get transmitted!" I don't wish to transmit my mess of a life to nobody. It's a little late for the transform part, I figure, but I'm gonna write this now just to get things down and maybe figure out some stuff before I go.

I'm sixty-two years old, about forty pounds overweight, got more miles on me than a well-used taxi, and what's brewing inside this body is probably six of the seven leading causes of death. So if you somehow get ahold of this notebook of mine, and for some stupid reason you keeps reading, don't worry: it'll probably be a short read. I'm writing it for myself, not you, but if the spirit moves you, stay aboard. You never know what's around the bend.

My name is Orca Bates; most call me Big Red. Before this place I'm in now, I lived under the Wabasha Street Bridge in St. Paul, Minnesota, floating in the current of the Mighty Miss in a houseboat named *Cirrhosis of the River*. Not the name I would of chose; Webb off the towboat *Elsie Mae* come up with that one, talked me into it, thought it was funny. Cirrhosis—he should know. Can out drink Larry and Retch in his sleep, Webb can. And those two can drink!

Anyway, my real name came after a whale when my daddy first saw me. Twelve pounds eight ounces at birth. Had to swim hard just to get out. Been swimming hard ever since.

River men like to say that most of their money goes to women and booze, and the rest gets wasted. In my case, the women and booze brought plenty of trouble. Both of them is likely what caused me to land here in this veterans' home for the hopeless, as I like to call it. Cubby—and he went to college—would call this 'a real irony' 'cause now it's me that's stuck in one of these places instead of Grampy Joe. But more on all that later.

Daddy was a river pilot, too. He weren't around much. Hard to believe, actually, that he was even there for me being born. I think I got a lot of my problems from being downstream of the old man — that stream being the women and booze. The women part, well, I just can't help it with women. I said to Cubby once during some quiet thinking time on board *Cirrhosis*, "Ever think about the fact that every single one of us come from a woman?" Cubby cracked something like, "Real profound," but I just continued with my theory, saying, "So we're all part woman then, ain't we? Every one of us that got here also got rejected; rejected from a woman's body. Thrown out, if you get my drift. Pushed out and pulled out. Big hairy hands in rubber gloves holding those cold steel tongs around our soft, tiny heads." Well Cubby, he just rolled those almond-shaped eyes of his. I continued. "Now what's profound here, Cubby, is that after that happens, we males spend the rest of our lives trying to push our way back in." Anyway, I just love women: they feel good, they're squishy and they smell good. I guess the way I am with women is maybe a big part of my life story 'cause it shows my character, which is something I got a lot of, 'cause a lot of people call me one.

So here I am, way up on a mud bank, my props churning but this old barge of a body ain't going nowhere. I been asking myself, "How you going to back out of this slough, Red?" You'll need full astern. But power's down. River's dropping. And the crew here ain't much help. I hear there's 91 of us wrecks in this place. Most from some war, I figure. This old soldiers' home goes back almost to the Civil War. They got dementia care, rehabilitation, spiritual services, and what the brochure says is 'domiciliary care' which is a 'home-like environment for homeless veterans' (that'd be me). Well, this big old place, from the outside, looks like something from some Stephen King movie—crumbling brick, four levels, a bunch of turrets like in some old castle, and one big old leafless oak tree out front that looks like it ain't got nothing to live for. From the outside looking in, this place is not what you'd call a welcoming sight. But looking out from my room, what they got for me here is one thing does me better than all of those rehabilitation services: the Miss. If I look out my little window and there ain't no leaves on the trees, I can spot her flowing by. That'd be about Mile 847 of the Mighty Mississippi, I do believe.

2

A BOTTLE IN FRONT OF ME OR A FRONTAL LOBOTOMY

I ain't been a good resident; more like a mad, cooped-up, oversized rodent. I'd been here only a few days, and they put me on my second nurse. First one couldn't handle me. And the second one—she's the one I call High Falutin' 'cause she's all full of herself—making assumptions and judgments without knowing or caring a whit about me or where I come from. Seems to me the emptiest folks is always the ones that are full of themselves. High Falutin', by the way, is the name I gave her 'cause it's an old river term referring to steamboats with tall smoke stacks and fancy flutes. Tall stacks gave those big hot embers from the boiler fire a better chance to burn out before floating down and reaching the deck. The way most steamboats ended their days was by burning up from those embers. Fluting was that wire mesh at the top, kind of a fence to break up the bigger embers into small pieces. But on high falutin' boats it's all fancy and decorative, which don't serve no purpose that I can see. Well, anyway, I'd about had enough of being told by this nurse with tall stacks how to eat, how to sit up in bed, and why I had to keep my robe on and tied tight and proper like. So one day I told her she was a life-sucking, negative bag of annoying hell. Maybe I come out too straight with it, but I figure that if you're going to use words to get to the point, well then choose them words that do just that. So they put me on some sort of probation. Anyway, I do believe what I said worked good as Falutin' didn't seem to want much to do with me after that. Good, I thought. Just leave me alone, sitting by my window, maybe listening to Dylan or Hank Williams, and looking at the Miss.

Well, don't you know it, but the next day my door pops open and this new nurse comes breezing in, all cheerful like. She picks up the chart from the end of my bed, and damned if she don't say, "Wouldn't be a bad day to be on the river, would it, Mr. Orca Bates?"

"And just who might you be, young lady? And how'd you know about me and the river?"

"I'm Wihopa Webster. I checked you out; word has it you were kind of a legend on the Mississippi. Anyway, I heard that you were having a hard time settling in here and I –"

"Well, I got two questions: What the hell kind of name is that? And are you anything like those last two barges of coal dust I had for nurses?"

But man, she don't miss a beat: "And I have two questions for you. The name Orca? What kind of a name is that? I know. But do you? And are you really, really as mean as you sound?"

"Even meaner, Missy Hopa. And you should know about how dangerous orcas are with you, I bet, being Eskimo and all."

"I'm actually Sioux."

"Sue's better; that's a name I can get my arms around."

"Sioux—as in the Native American tribe. And it's Wihopa, W-I-H-O-P-A, not Hopa."

"Indian name, huh? What's it mean?"

By Jesus, if she don't blush right up.

"It means 'pretty' or 'astonishing woman'."

Ain't that the truth, I'm thinking. But what comes out of my mouth is: "Well, that name don't sound so pretty. Sounds like we're all hoping for something."

She puts down the chart and looks at me. "Maybe we are. So what do you like to be called?"

"Call me anything but late to dinner."

"Seriously, let's talk about your name now. Orca: the whale. You should take that as an honor, a badge to live for and live by. In my culture the whale spirit animal is the earth's record keeper for all time. As a totem, the whale teaches you about listening to your inner voice, understanding the impact your emotions have on your everyday life. In fact, the whale spirit animal actually *requests* emotional rebirth."

"Well, last time I looked, little lady, I weren't no whale, though I talked to one years ago. No, I was just named after one. And that weren't my doing. And this rebirth stuff I don't buy. I was born once, from what I can tell, and once is all you gets."

"Well, just as the whale must surface to take a new breath, so must you, Orca. I believe it's important for each of us to observe the hurt and resentment inside, but not to jump on it and give it energy; we need to let go of it, put it on a boat, and let it float down the river. If resentment or hurt is your regular meal, you're filling your plate with fast, cheap food. And we all know that's bad for your health."

I just scratched my head. "Fast food on a boat. That's me alright. You know, Wihopa, all this talk is making me hungry. But then again, I'm *always* hungry."

Next thing she does is she looks behind me.

"Are those all your things?"

"All my worldly possessions," I say. "Piled up and waiting for some dumpster." She moves over by my room's fake wood, industrial-strength metal closet and looks at something leaning against its side.

"What are all these old metal contraptions?"

"That's my antique waffle iron collection."

"You collect waffle irons? Wow, that's unusual."

"Why not? Folks collect weirder stuff than that: umbrella cover sleeves, sugar packets, nails, back scratchers, soap bars, and even airline barf bags."

Then she moves right on to look at some more of my stuff.

"What's this? Is this your memories board?" she says, looking at my old cork board.

"I can't remember."

"Well, try."

"Just some old newspaper clippings."

She leans closer to one of the clippings. "Is that your dad and son?"

"No, that's Grampy Joe and Cubby."

"Oh, wow, your grandfather."

"No it's not. Listen, it's a long story. And it's private, which is something that ain't in great supply around here."

"Look, I know you're having a hard time settling in, but I thought I could give you…"

"You thought you could give me what? A foot bath? Wash my feet like you're Jesus? Give me a 'therapy talk'? Give me a better pillow for my chair? That it? Listen little lady, what I need and what's inside me nobody but me can see. And you don't want to look inside me, 'cause that ain't a pretty sight. So I guess what I need is one of them frontal lobotomies."

Well, I figured that would do it like it usually does when I speak my mind. Finish her off. But she don't flinch, just gives me some cute dimples and one of them Mona Lisa half smiles. "Well, you're in luck, Orca Bates. Frontal lobotomies are on special here this week."

Now, here's what I'm thinking: You ain't never faced up to the likes of a rig like this, Red. What you got here in front of you is one hot toddy, like that old river drink made with a baked apple in a mug of heated rum. There ain't a human on earth that don't like that. And by Jesus, for the first time in months and months I felt my own half smile, along with pieces of the old Big Red, like a spring river melt, start flowing back from some cold place way upstream and around the bend.

"As for your 'special', Hot Toddy—and that's my new name for you, by the way—I think I'll hold off on that. Right now I do believe I'd like a bottle in front of me, and if that don't work maybe then I'll get me one of your frontal lobotomies."

So that's how me and Toddy got rolling. I may be stuck in here, but now I know I got two prime visuals. I got the view of the Miss, and I got Toddy. Like a fine towing vessel on the Miss, whether she's moving upstream toward me, or headed away around a bend, it's all good. I get to look at that sweet face and them dimples around that smooth skin of hers as she smiles when I call her Toddy. And when she walks away it's just fine, too, what with that long silky black hair of hers swinging back and forth across the waistband of those tight white stretch nurse pants. She's got an ass like a Studebaker, Toddy does. Built for comfort, not speed. And she don't make assumptions, like them other nurses. She's curious, too. Really seems to want to know about me and the river life. You got to love someone who's curious. She even says she thinks she knows why there ain't much of a filter from my brain to my words; says she studied it a little in nursing school and that it might be a mild case of what they call Assburgers. She says these folks sometimes don't take in things right and ain't real good at reading people, or don't react right to the looks on their faces, and then they say the wrong thing. I'm not sure I'm buying that, but if it is Assburgers, then—along with me having what Toddy calls 'an intimidating presence' at 6'3" and 290 pounds with a big red beard and pony tail—I could see how some folks thinks of me as a handful.

3
NOT TO SOUND POETIC OR NOTHIN', BUT LIFE IS LIKE A RIVER

Not that it matters anymore, even with having Toddy around. Inside this home for the hopeless is where the river ends for me, most likely. Not to sound poetic or nothing, but my life, like that 2340-mile journey of the Miss, is flowing away into some big gulf, carrying with it all I picked up along the way. It's been a lot of miles, and everything in my mind is swirling around in a current of churned-up thoughts of people and places and things that happened. Some of the worst thoughts I try to stay away from; but I know they're living there, just under the surface, and can pop up most any time, like those deadheads—them partly underwater river logs. Those things can sink you. At night, spotting them is almost impossible until it's too late. Anyway, I ran some bends too hard, hit my share of snags, and ran aground here and there in this life. Momma would have said, "you should have just learned from it—like you done on the river—then life might have been better for you."

Funny how it all works—what happens at the end of the lifeline—ain't it? Seems most of us gets a good enough start. Fresh start, I guess you could say. (This all makes me think of Cubby and *his* life. I'll tell you about him later.) Anyway, we're an open book, a tiny baby, completely helpless to everything, with no control over nothing, don't know good from evil and got no plans for the future except to scream for food. I probably screamed for food—lots of it. Someone must have been good enough to pick me up, maybe to stop my screaming. Someone must have cared. Really caring, I think, should be a person's number one job.

Anyway, my fresh start soured pretty quick. Daddy was always off on some line boat, pushin' barges on the Miss or the Illinois rivers, sometimes downstream as far as the Gulf. Best times for me was right when he first got home. All I wanted him to do was throw a baseball with me. Never any good at it, but I always loved that game. Now, since I'm getting close to the end of my game, I wonder if they got baseball in heaven. Guess I'll find out soon enough, like those two lifelong friends who wondered about it and agreed that whoever got there first would come back and let the other know. First guy died; so he comes back to earth and says, "Good news and bad news. Good news is they *do* have baseball in heaven. Bad news is I seen the lineup; you're up to bat soon."

Anyway, Daddy would be gone for thirty days—thirty days on and then he'd come home with thirty days off. That might sound okay, but I came to learn that that life don't settle the self much, if you get my drift. What I mean is, Daddy, like all of us river men, got himself two identities in that life, whether he liked it or not. On the river, especially hooked to a big tow and against some bad current, the world goes by at about two or three miles an hour. You can stare at the same tree stump just about forever, thinking about something over and over. You wonder where the river stories come from? They come from all that idle time: time in the pilothouse, time in the galley, time waiting to lock through, time waiting for a busted lift bridge, time waiting for a crew change. Plenty of time. Just waiting. People aboard get plenty close when the world moves that slow. And the other world, the one on the bank, that one's so close you can see it, hear it, and smell it. But you can't touch it. Like your life, it's just going by, with a lot of stuff just out of reach. In the daytime you might stick your head out of the galley and spot a yellow school bus on a river road, maybe watch some kids run along the river bank to school, maybe wonder about your own—if you was lucky enough to have some—wonder who's raising them, where they are right now. Then other thoughts barge in, and you try to push 'em back as you know they ain't no good for you. Like at night, when there's less to do and less to see, you might get to wondering about the woman you left ashore—wondering what she's doing, if she's warm in bed, and if anyone's in that bed with her. Them thoughts can get out of control. Them thoughts can crush a man. Out on a line boat, it's like you're in purgatory. The other world, the one you come from, you sometimes just ache for it. And then, when you get back ashore, everything's new. Even Daddy seemed new when he got ashore. Everybody'd want to hear all about his adventures. Even Momma. Then there was things she had for him to fix around the house. And then there was me and my baseball glove and playing catch. But after a few days with Daddy around, me and Momma would get back into our routine and go about our lives the way they was when he was away. So Daddy would start meandering down to the riverbank by the St. Paul Barge Company. One time after school I seen him standing there on the bank, just staring out at a line boat headed south. About then he had twenty or so days left 'til he went back. Hard to get hired for a shore job for just twenty days, so he starts meandering somewhere else—over to The Slough, the old river bar in South St. Paul, and drinking heavy. That's when the trouble would really start. But that's an old story then, ain't it?

4
SOMETIMES YOU ARE THE WIND-SHIELD, SOMETIMES YOU ARE THE BUG

Anyway, Daddy just kept on drinking and I just kept on eating—mostly it was all them waffles Momma and me made. Hell, when you pop out into the world at almost 13 pounds you got a lot of body to feed from the git go. I needed to stay at the front of the food line just to survive. When I reached sixth grade the next tallest kid in my class only came up to my armpit. Along with that, God gave me a big appetite and a big mouth to go with it. And not just for eating. I used my mouth to speak my mind to just about everybody in sight. Got away with it mostly, because I was so big, and getting bigger. One bad side of being so big is people think if you're big you can't be smart—though they don't dare say that to your face. As a big guy, I have always noticed and worried about the little guy. A lot of little guys learn to hang in the shadows, keep to themselves, and are always looking ahead for a way out of a bad situation. But sometimes, like a bear tracks a fish, they get stalked and caught, even when they're careful and hanging in the shadows. I always fig-ured—even way back—that maybe I was put on earth this big because it was my job to protect the little guy. Like that Walter Collins in high school. He was this freckle-faced, red-headed mouse of a kid who sat across from me in homeroom. He slunk into the room, sat down quick, and stuck his nose in a book, hoping to miss the attention of these two punks named Harlan and Max. I bet that kid wished he was invisible. But they had Walter's number, and kept nailing him with spitballs shot through those plastic straws from the cafeteria. Poor kid didn't have a chance and he sure wasn't going to rat on them to our 100-year-old homeroom teacher, Miss Giles. I just rolled my eyes at Harlan and Max, but it bugged me. It was one snowy winter in South St. Paul that year, and I began thinking that—in addition to spitballs—snowballs (or maybe even ice balls) would likely be headed Walter's way on his walk home. So I took—and here's a big word that Cubby would like— 'preemptive' action after school one day. I waited for the day Harlan got detention, which wasn't a long wait, and holed up in this hallway alcove by all the lockers. The alcove was dark, set-in about six feet, and led to a door that went to the janitors' space. I had figured on having my little chat with Harlan instead of Max, as he was the ringleader. Dealing with the both of them at once was not something I cottoned to, though I do believe it would have been no problem for me. I didn't worry about the janitors; they never showed their faces once the principal left the building. They just stayed back behind that door playing cards. I know because my daddy was friends with two of them. Well, sure enough, Harlan moseyed by.

"Hey, Harlan, got a minute," I said as I stepped out from the dark.

He jumped a few inches, figured out it was me, then looked real suspicious.

"Kind of in a hurry, Orca."

"No, really," I said, gesturing him over to where I stood in the shadows. Then, when he came closer, curious, I slowly moved around him so he was inside and I was now outside, blocking his exit from that little alcove. "I been thinking, maybe you and Max should leave that little Walter kid alone. You know, cool it with the spitballs."

"What's it to you? What're you, his bodyguard or something?"

He shouldn't have said that.

I just looked at him and cocked my head. "Who's *your* body-guard, Harlan? 'Cause it sure ain't me. And you're going to need a real big one to stop me from using that plastic cafeteria straw of yours to shove a spitball the size of New Jersey up your ass."

Well, the very best thing that Harlan could have done right then he did: he didn't say nothing. Just nodded and left. I bet that to this day that Walter kid is wondering why all the spitballs suddenly stopped coming his way.

5

NITROGLYCERIN VS. VIAGRA: ONE HARD CHOICE

Anyway, back to this veterans' home. I'd be lying if I said I was getting on all right in this place, even with Toddy coming into the picture. She's trying her damnedest to get me involved with the home's social activities—things like word game, read aloud, story telling, bingo, ring toss or cookie bake. "Toddy," I said, "excuse my French, but are you shitting me?"

"Orca, it's a good thing to get involved. You have a lot to give, and so do the other residents."

"Toddy, I don't know that many words, so I ain't playing that word game. Reading aloud is for first grade—the best two years of my life, by the way. And bingo, that's for old ladies. Ring toss is, well, it's what a couple wives have done to me so it ain't exactly a favorite activity. And cookie bake? Cookie bake? If Retch or Webb ever caught word that I was baking friggin' cookies in some home for the hopeless, well, that just wouldn't go down right around the river."

"Tell me about your image."

"You'll just have to use your imagination, Toddy."

"How do you see yourself?"

"I do believe I can see myself just fine, with me being this big and all."

"No, really."

"We're not going there, Toddy. Remember what I said? None of this touchy feely psychology stuff."

"Well, what about going on one of the home's field trips then?"

"Field trips was in second grade."

"What about telling stories of your river experiences to some of the other veterans? Maybe during our beer & pizza night? I'd sure love to be there for that one."

Poor Toddy, she just didn't get it. What I needed was simple: just to bust out of here. Like Grampy Joe done years ago. I laughed to myself. What I also needed was a young me and a Cubby to help me do it like we helped Grampy. (Cubby, who was one of them English majors, once told me this part of the story is something called 'fore-shadowing' because I'm sort of telling you, but then again I ain't.)

Then I told her I had one hell of an idea.

Toddy smiled, cocked her head, pushed back some of that shiny black hair of hers, and looked at me kind of funny.

"You know, I love them dimples, Toddy."

"Orca."

"Call me Red. Everyone calls me that."

"I like Orca."

"Okay. So my idea is a field trip. I do believe I'd like a field trip."

"That's terrific. I'll get a copy of the home's field trip schedule."

"This would be a special kind of exclusive field trip, Toddy. Real customized like."

"I don't think..."

"This would be special for you too, Toddy. You can be my chaperone and all."

"For me to go as part of the...well, it has to be officially..."

"Let's just call it an outing, then. Not a field trip."

"An outing where, Orca?"

"Toddy, how'd you like to face up to 400 feet of grain barges, get behind the sticks of 2000 horses of Cat diesel, and drive through Monkey Rudder Bend?"

"You want me to do what? If that's a proposal, Orca, you'll have to get down on one knee."

"This is better than marriage, Toddy. And having been there a couple times, I do believe I'm an authority on that subject. On this special customized field trip—I mean, outing—you gets it all: your curiosity satisfied about me and the Miss, the chance to meet real river men like Retch and Webb, and have a real life experience on the river."

Deep down, I figured this outing was never gonna happen. Why would such a hot, smart nurse half my age want to spend her day off pushing barges with a bunch of rough-edged river rats? Then I figured: maybe Toddy thought this river outing would fix me. Nurses like to heal people. Maybe this outing was gonna be my own special form of penicillin. Anyway, by Jesus, she finally said yes, telling me she also had her own special reasons why she wanted to go; something about her ancestors way back living just below Monkey Rudder Bend on Pike Island. But before we left, we did hit a few snags, mostly 'cause of my behavior, I guess. And also, Toddy was taking all these precautions for when we left the home; like making sure I didn't forget to take my nitroglycerin pills with me. They're for my heart. Tiny little pills in a tiny little bottle.

I remember back a while how I got these pills. My doctor, who I think is maybe younger than Moses but not by much, said I'm supposed to put one under my tongue if I feel them chest pains I get from time to time; says that may continue to happen to me during stressful activities such as walking up stairs or sexual intercourse. I can't for the life of me figure how one tiny pill inside my giant body is going to do one lick of good. Kind of like putting one grain of sugar in a cup of coffee and expecting something sweet to happen. Plus, the doc said I shouldn't be taking 'erection-enhancing medicines' at the same time because that could cause a 'life-threatening drop in blood pressure'. I just scratched my head, all confused, and asked him: "So if I take this Viagra stuff to allow me to stay hooked up for a while, and then I get a heart attack while really driving hard through a bend, so to speak, then I *shouldn't* pop one of them nitros to stop my heart attack 'cause they both at once might kill me?"

"Yes," he said, "due to a sudden and dramatic drop in blood pressure."

"But if I'm *already* having the heart attack, then what's the difference?" Well, here's where old Moses looked at me all confused. But I just continued: "I do believe if I'm in the saddle and have a heart attack then that blood pressure of mine, especially at the fulcrum of the tow—you know, the point of all the action—well, it's going to drop pretty damned quick on its own." That put the old doc back on his heels, and then he just looked down and started fiddling with his stethoscope and not saying nothing. So I just decided to close out the conversation as we weren't getting nowhere. "So anyway, Doc, I think I'll skip the nitro; that way I got a better chance of keeping up the blood pressure so I can stay hooked up right until the very end."

6

THE END OF CIRRHOSIS:
FLUSHED OUT WITH FOUR ACES

Once Toddy was satisfied I was prepared for the outing, I went ahead and called Webb's house to see if he knew when the *Elsie Mae* might be coming through Lock & Dam #1. Had to borrow Toddy's phone to do it, as the phone company and I been having a long-term disagreement about my bill. They said I needed to 'make payment arrangements'; so I proposed an arrangement: when I had money I'd give some to them. That didn't fly and I just couldn't accept their version, which had something to do with me paying them something right away. I did tell them that I was a big customer (and that weren't no lie) and I told them that it seemed I wasn't buying nothing but air anyway, so why charge for that? Anyway, my phone line's still deader than Elvis, though she does fire up and I can get my numbers off it. Turns out Webb was off working a big line boat on the Illinois River. So I called Retch's cell and got nothing. Then I called his house and got his wife. She told me he was working the *Elsie* while Webb was gone and I could most likely reach him right away on the VHF. I had my handheld portable right there by the window all plugged in because what I did most since I got in this place was listen to the pilots down below me on the Miss. Range is about five miles line of sight, and with us being in the home way up on the hill maybe even more. I guess I was kind of eavesdropping, listening to my old life just flowing by below me, listening to chatter from my pilot friends about their kids, their deckhand problems, their wife problems, river currents, snags, diesel engines and people and animal sightings along the river bank.

So I transmitted; gave Retch a try on channel 69, hoping he was scanning that channel, which was our old chatting channel. "*Elsie Mae, Elsie Mae.* You on there, Retch?" I knew he'd know my voice. Lots of river men know each other's voices better than they know their wives' voices; hell, some of them probably talk to each other more than to their wives. It's funny, but sometimes you can go years and years on the river and talk and talk to a guy but never know what he looks like. You know all about him, his life and his problems, and you picture him looking one way, maybe big and fat and all assertive and then you finally meet, maybe in some river bar, and he's this little skinny quiet guy.

"*Elsie* on 69, I gotcha fine, Red."

"Retch, I was wondering if you'll be locking through #1 sometime this week. I got a friend would like to see the river and ride a tow."

"Later in the week, Red. Any friend of yours is a friend of mine, old buddy. Tell him to wear boots. Maybe we can get some work out of him."

"It ain't a 'he', Retch. It's a lady. Well, a nurse, kind of. See, I'm not getting on too good lately and she's helping me along and I want to show her the river life."

"Well, tell her to wear boots anyway, Red. And I do hope she's something to look at; I'm getting mighty tired of staring at these two Louisiana river rats they give me for deckhands. Plus, all them nude sunbathers around Shelton Island is now gone away along with the hot weather, so something hot on board would be good right now."

"I gotcha fine, Retch. And so does she, 'cause she's standing right next to me and listening pretty good."

"Well, that takes care of that then. Now she knows what to expect. Anyway, I've got some switch work down in South St. Paul, then a run up the Minnesota to Cargill grain terminal, than down to South St. Paul again, then back up the Miss to Minneapolis to grab some empties, then locking down at Lock #1 with the empties back to South St. Paul. Should be at #1 about Wednesday afternoon, most likely. How about I call you when things get real definite. I think I still have your cell number, Red, unless it's changed."

"Well, Retch, me and the cell company had a little falling out, so can you just call me on 69? I'll have it on all Wednesday morning."

"Sure, but where you living now, Red; you know, since you lost her?"

"I'll fill you in once we're aboard, Retch."

"Gotcha fine, Cappy. *Elsie Mae* going back to Channel 16 and standing by."

I signed off and turned off my VHF, and was feeling pretty good, at least 'til Toddy leans toward me, acting in that Florence Nightendale-nurse kind of caring way.

"Tell me about your loss, Orca," she says. And Jesus, if she doesn't right then put her soft little hand on my arm.

"My what?" I says, kind of gently so as to not scare her into taking away that hand from my arm.

"I heard Retch say, 'Where are you living since you lost her, Red?' It's not my business, I guess, but I just hope it wasn't, you know, a wife, lady friend or, God forbid, a child."

"Worse than all that, Toddy." Then I see all that sadness and confusion get bigger and them dimples flattening out along with that spirit of hers. "*Cirrhosis*," I say. "I lost *Cirrhosis*, Toddy. To Webb, as a matter of fact."

"You lost her to Webb? Who is she?"

"*Cirrhosis of the River*."

"*Cirrhosis of the River*?"

"My houseboat, Toddy. My home. Lost her in a card game that kind of got out of hand. But fair and square. I ain't denying that. I was in deep: I'd bet my Dodge Power Wagon 5.7 liter hemi truck, all my cash, and a promise of my next two paychecks, which I hadn't even earned yet. But I had four aces. Four aces!

— 31 —

Only two hands beat four aces Toddy, and Webb ain't lucky or much of a card player—at least before that night—and he ain't much of a bluffer either. So I raised him with the title to *Cirrhosis*. Anyway, Webb looked all shocked, then shook his head. 'Red,' he says—and excuse my French, Toddy—'that's your fucking house you're betting'. I just looked at him for a while. Stared at him, really. 'That's my bet Webb,' I says. Webb looked over at Larry and Backin' Jack, the other two that was in the game but had long since folded.

"You know I love this houseboat, Red."

I just said, all steady like, 'Your call, Webb'. And he calls me."

"He called you what, Orca?"

"No, that's a card thing, Toddy. Means 'show me what you got, 'cause I ain't going no further.' So I put down them four aces, watching Webb's face the whole time for any sign of something. Then, even in the weak light of that one lamp behind Larry, I could see the color coming back into Webb's face, and it reminded me of one word: flush. And that's just what he had."

"But four aces is really good, right?" Toddy says, all helpful like.

"Good. But not good enough, Toddy."

7

BLIND BIRD WATCHERS AND GREAT BEHINDS: TODDY'S GOT IT ALL FOR ME

Since we had a few days 'til Retch's call Wednesday morning, Toddy figured it would be good to try to get me socialized. I told her right off that I don't take to talking about war experiences and I don't like hearing about 'em either, and seeing that this place was all full of just those people, this didn't look like a promising idea.

"I just want you to start with Gil. Jim Gillson," she says. "He never talks about the war, and pretty much keeps to himself. He's a lot older, about 80 I think, and blind from a war incident in Korea, but I think you'd really like him, Orca. He's a huge fan of Elvis, as I know you are. Sings Elvis songs all day long. He has amazing hearing and can even identify a bird by its faintest call."

"So you want a 'keep-to-himself', 62-year-old gimped-up wreck like me to hang around with a 'keep-to-himself', 80-year-old Elvis-impersonating blind bird watcher. That it?"

"Pretty much. Trust me on this," Toddy says. And then she puts that soft little hand on my big hairy arm again; lays it right over my gold bracelet. I think to myself: If she keeps doing that I'll hang around and do anything with anyone she wants. Just name the activity and the person. Just as long as you keep that hand on my arm, Toddy.

"Tell me about this, Orca," she says, lifting up her hand and looking down at my bracelet. "It's the biggest gold bracelet I've ever seen."

"That's $8000 on my wrist," I says. "Unlike women, it has always stayed with me. Never comes off. Never. Except when I'm dead; then I'm passing it on to someone special if I ain't broke; or, if I'm still broke, to someone responsible enough to get me buried and then pay off any of my debts. Actually, this and that pile of junk by my closet there is all I got. I ain't exactly a—what do them finance yuppies call it? —yeah, a 'high-net-worth individual'."

"But where did you get such a bracelet? Did you have it made?"

"Let's just say it got left to me at the very last minute."

"Kind of an inheritance?"

"No, had to do with something I tried to do for somebody."

"That's really nice, Orca. Tell me about it."

"That's no-no land, Toddy. You're playing therapist again, and that's one of them places we don't go. So, let's go over to you instead. How'd you ever land in this place, having to deal with the likes of folks like me? Lots of better places for being a nurse, I do believe."

"I found this through the Native American Initiative; it helps with careers for health-care workers who are Native American. I grew up on a reservation in Northern Minnesota and always wanted to become a nurse, so I applied for a scholarship and came down here to school in the Twin Cities. That's how the nursing started. My grandfather served in the Vietnam War. I was only five when he left. I loved him very much. He was given the name 'Little Warrior'. My mother told me he felt a calling to serve. A lot of Native Americans do, despite our history with the United States government. Anyway, he didn't come back. Years later, when I completed nursing school, it just seemed like an honorable thing to do my nursing in a veterans' home. A way to honor my grandfather."

"Kind of a downer place for you to work, seems to me. You know, all us wounded, washed-up wrecks, waiting to die, with nothing else to do but play bingo and drool over your great behind."

"I don't appreciate that comment, Orca."

"About the bingo?"

"No, the 'behind' part."

"What, you don't appreciate having a great behind, Toddy? Why in the name of Jesus would anybody not appreciate having a great behind?"

"Well, it's rude and sexist."

I just gave her a great big smile and then she said, "But we'll just write that off as your mild Asperger's kicking in."

"Toddy, you know in your heart that great behinds, at least on women folk, account for a big part of why we're all here on this earth. You know that those behinds and other key visual parts are what spurns the drive that leads us to that great act that leads to reproduction. It's human, for crissakes."

"We're not talking about this. And it's 'spurs'."

"What about 'spurs'"? I asked. But before she could answer, I just kept going. "I guess you got a point there, Toddy," I said. "On the right person spurs might help move the act along faster, I reckon. Or you could use them if you was into one of them sadomachino things."

Toddy looked away from me for a bit. Looked at the blank white wall for a while. Then she looked back at me and took a deep breath through her nose. "Orca, I don't know if you're really sharp and just playing with me or if you're..."

"What? Stupid?"

"No, Orca—trying to be difficult. Anyway, it 'spurs' on the act, not 'spurns'. Spurns means 'reject'. Orca, maybe we should get away from the carnal side of things."

"What's carnal?"

"Your feelings about my rear end, for one thing."

"So, it's bad to have these carnal feelings?"

"I suppose not. Certainly it's human nature. You just don't outwardly express those things."

"Jimmy Carter did, and he was the President of the United States. Said he had 'lust in his heart'; I read it in a *Playboy* interview years ago. Looked at the centerfold first, of course."

"Well, I bet that didn't do him any good politically, Orca."

"So you mean I got to suppress these carnal feelings?"

"Best to keep them to yourself."

"Then how in God's name, if all of us in here did that, would you ever find out you have a great behind? Especially being that you yourself can't see it."

At that point Toddy took herself another big sigh.

"Let's change the topic. What makes you tick, Orca? I mean, what really makes you happy?"

"Your behind, Toddy."

"No, seriously. Really, can you be serious for once?"

"The only things I'm serious about are rivers, food and women."

With that, she got up and said she had some paperwork to finish and she was off. But about ten minutes later she came back and dropped off three things: the new schedule of the upcoming talks in the home, the list of field trips, and a book called—and I'm not shitting you on this—*Thriving on Broccoli*.

8
EVEN ANTS GOT A LEG UP ON ME

I chewed on that 'happy' question of Toddy's for some time. I thought about that morning mist, like some big ball of floating cotton, that can roll in over the green meadows around Lake Pepin, Wisconsin, sixty miles downstream. I thought about quiet nights aboard *Cirrhosis*, sipping on a cold brew while talking to young Cubby about his dreams and plans for the future. I thought about sitting down with the boys at The Slough river bar after a tough run down through Monkey Rudder Bend, and just laughing and telling stories. I thought about my 1980 Dodge Power Wagon, the only brand new thing I ever owned. And I thought about Lillimore.

"To answer your question, being good, maybe, is what makes me happy," was what I finally said when Toddy came back. Surprised myself when I said it.

"Like good at pushing barges? I hear you're great at that."

"Yeah. Spent my life pushing things around and up and down. Like some dumb ant dragging crumbs around a sand pile."

"I bet you pushed those crumbs better and faster than most of the other ants."

"Truth is, Toddy, the whole thing takes about the brains of an ant. It's not like being a surgeon or research scientist or in some other fancy job."

"Don't jump all over ants, Orca."

"I don't jump on 'em. Just stepping on 'em does the trick."

"Maybe you should think twice about that. You know, ants are much more like humans, or vise versa, than you think. They farm, raise aphids as livestock, launch armies into war, use chemical sprays to alarm and confuse enemies, capture slaves, engage in child labor, and exchange information ceaselessly."

"So now even the ants are smarter than me."

"No. But did you hear about the experiment to find out if they count their steps?"

"You're playing with me now, Toddy."

"No, really. Some scientists trained a bunch of ants to walk across a patch of desert to some food. When the ants began eating, the scientists trapped them and divided them into three groups. They left the first group alone. With the second group, they used Super Glue to attach pre-cut pig bristles to each of their six legs, essentially putting them on stilts. The third group had their legs cut off just below the "knees," making each of their six legs shorter. After the meal and the makeover, the ants were released and all of them headed home to the nest while the scientists watched to see what would happen.

The regular ants walked right to the nest and went inside.

The ants on stilts walked right past the nest, then stopped and looked around for their home.

The ants on stumps fell short of the nest, stopped and seemed to be searching for their home.

It turns out that all the ants had walked the same number of steps, but because their gaits had been changed—the ants on stilts walked with giant steps; the stumpy ants walked in baby steps—they went exactly the distances you'd predict if their brains counted the number of steps to the food and then reversed direction and counted the same number of steps back. In other words, all the ants counted the same number of steps back!"

"Huh. Ant legs. I could never get Super Glue to stick to much of anything," I said.

Toddy just shook her head and smiled at me for a while.

"You know, everything and everyone has a purpose, Orca. That's what I believe anyway. The surgeon fixes people. The research scientist searches for ways to make the world better. The towboat pilot transports grain to places that need it to feed people. Some of those people eat the grain and grow to become surgeons, scientists, and river towboat pilots. Ants march on. And the cycle continues. Nothing is greater than anything else. "

"There's got to be more to it than that. I see these little houses with the used car out front and the kids running around, and I think 'That's it?' That's the goal? Just to make *more* people who live in *more* little houses with used cars and more kids?"

"That's life, Orca. The world over. Little houses or little huts, or big McMansions or tin shacks and little kids. That's it. Create and do good things."

"Well, I ain't created nothing, Toddy. Not even kids."

"But you've done good work."

"A couple of times, maybe. Way back. All I got now is some memories."

"Way back? What were they, Orca?"

"Someday, Toddy. Maybe someday. Not now."

"Well then, now is either the time to make new memories or enjoy the ones you have. Rewind the tape. Play it over again. Think about it. Maybe fast forward through the bad parts. Or maybe play them too. And learn from them. Or make new tapes."

"The only tapes I like to replay are Elvis and Dylan," I said.

And then, by Jesus, if Toddy doesn't start singing to me; she looks me in the eyes, runs her hand through that long, silky black hair, and launches right into my favorite song. And she does it in the prettiest darn voice I ever heard.

> *Oh, I miss you Nettie Moore*
> *And my happiness is o'er*
> *Winter's gone, the river's on the rise*
> *I loved you then and ever shall*
> *But there's no one here that's left to tell*
> *The world has gone black before my eyes.*

And these bad luck women stick like glue
It's either one or the other or neither of the two.

When you're around all my grief gives 'way
A lifetime with you is like some heavenly day.

Well, this was about the first time yours truly didn't know what to say. It hit me straight in the gut. I just sat there, and looked out the window toward the Miss. Then Toddy took the pressure off.

"I heard you singing it by the window, Orca. A few times. I loved the melody and was intrigued by the lyrics. So I googled some of the them, found out it was Dylan, and downloaded the song on my iPod. Learned the whole thing. But when I heard you sing it, you sang the name 'Lillimore'; when I read the lyrics, it was 'Nettie Moore'."

"I do believe I know that, Toddy."

"Oh."

"Just doing some substituting, that's all. Anyway, what are you meaning about 'making new tapes'?"

"It's about making new again; about how the world, unlike in that song, doesn't have to go black before your eyes."

"Hell, it's just a song, Toddy."

9

ME IN YOGA PANTS: A REAL STRETCH

"May I tell you a story, Orca? It's about my grandmother, my unci, which is the Lakota Sioux word for grandmother. She was a great artisan, like many Sioux; skilled at beadwork, quillwork, carving, pipe making, drum making, flute making, and leatherwork of all kinds. These are crafts that have been handed down from generation to generation. Just as you pushed barges, my grandmother pushed beads on a string. She did intricate work with great pride and reverence. When I was little, she blessed me with a spirit guide to look over me. She told me I was a very special little girl and the spirit guide would show me the way. But really, I think my spirit guide is my unci. Anyway, when she was very weak and dying she began her most elaborate work: a brocade vest and striped trousers with a bone white buckskin jacket decorated with fringe and amazing quillwork. She went at it with all the enthusiasm of a young girl. I'm sure it didn't even occur to her that she wouldn't live to finish it."

"Well, my daddy used to say, 'don't start something you can't finish."

"That is exactly wrong, Orca. You see, her last work, like the wind and the sun and the rain, was all part of the cycle of this world. To truly be alive isn't about finishing. It's about continuing, restarting, growing."

"I'm all done growing, Toddy."

But I tried to think some more about what Toddy was saying: all this spirit guide business and everything being as important as everything else; you know, pushing barges and beads being as good as being surgeons and scientists. But I was just going up current with it all, too loaded down with sixty years of questionable cargo, to make much headway. So I just said, "I don't understand even one speck of a grain of dust about what you said."

"Have you heard that saying, 'Life is not a dress rehearsal', Orca?— it's not about reaching the end of some life race by being a headliner with all these accolades or certificates or a fancy career; those things get buried with their owners. I think it was Maya Angelou who said, 'People will forget what you said, people will forget what you did, but people will never forget how you made them feel.' I mean, in your heart, Orca, when you remember someone in your own life, what is it you remember that's most important to you?"

"What I know, Toddy, is I've said things to some of these people that made them feel pretty bad. And I bet these folks will never forget how I made them feel. Folks I care about seem to get all used up and then go away."

"When you have folks you care about, Orca, it's best to love them. And care for them. And fix them when they're broken. And heal them when they're sick."

"The only things I can properly care for seem to be towboats and their big Cat diesels. I listen good to them. Know when they're not feeling right."

"Well, you should think on this," she said, and then she got up and started to walk out of the room. Truth be told, watching Toddy walk away was always a mixed bag, especially on her yoga class days, 'cause it meant she was leaving my presence, but it also meant I got to watch her walk away in them tight yoga pants. But this time she stopped at the door, then turned back and looked at me.

"You like yoga pants, Orca?"

"Depends who's in 'em."

"What if you were?"

"Why, Toddy, I do believe—and this is supposing it were even humanly possible for me to push this body into some yoga pants—that there could only be one thing more visually horrifying to the civilized world."

"And that would be?"

"Me in one of them Speedo swim suits."

"Well, sweat pants then."

"For what?"

"For yoga. Well, it's called 'gentle yoga'. There's a class here. Some of the other guys go and they like it. Meets Tuesday mornings. Look, trust me on this, Orca. I know it's a stretch, but you'll end up thanking me. It's actually really good exercise."

"I don't do exercise, Toddy. If God wanted me to bend over, he would have put food on the floor."

"Well, your body will feel better. Everyone swears by it. I promise."

"Just like them yoga pants would be on me, it's one real stretch getting me to do ANY of this, Toddy. You'd have a better chance getting me to attend a prayer meeting for transgendered Baptists."

"Orca, you make me smile. Where do you come up with this stuff?"

"Me? Where do *you* come up with the idea of a 290-pound, washed-up, out-of-shape gimp getting some benefit from crossing his legs all funny, chanting 'home' over and over along with a bunch of over-the-hill nursing home residents including, I bet, some blind birdwatcher named Gilbert? Give me one good reason for me doing this Toddy."

"Well, I'll be teaching the class."

"Then how about we start with a private lesson?"

"No, it's a group thing only, Orca. And it's Gillson, not Gilbert. And it's om, not home. "

"Not that I *have* ever and *will* never need to know this, Toddy, but just what is it about this om business?"

"Om is an affirmation of the divine. Om is the sound that was made when the whole universe was created. Om is thought of as a "word of power," so chanting it before and after a yoga class is believed to produce a profound effect on the person chanting, and in the world. When the spirit passes through the veil and goes beyond thinking, the spirit is liberated from the three states of consciousness and we achieve enlightenment."

"Are you shitting me?"

"No, I'm not *shitting* you, Orca. Really. It's so."

"So, yours truly is going to let some spirit fellow pass through me so as to let me achieve enlightenment? That it?"

"Will you try? You might enjoy it!"

"No."

"You are being stubborn, Orca Bates. If you are going to live here, you should really try. Try to get involved. Try to make some friends. Get a hobby. Because I tell you one thing for sure: Sitting around here looking out that window won't do you a lick of good. And if you can't help yourself, then I can't help you either."

And damned if right then Toddy doesn't turn and head out the door again, saying something I couldn't quite hear.

"Toddy," I said. "I didn't catch that."

Toddy stopped in the hall and turned to me, her hands on her hips. "I swear, you could pick a fight with Santa Claus."

"Then bring him on. He never did me a lick of good either. Though, now that I think of it, he does know where all the naughty girls live."

"And the outing on the river is off, Orca. If you won't help yourself, then I can't work with you."

And then she was gone.

10
THIS BROKEN TOW IS WORSE THAN GOUT

I got to being even more bottled up inside myself after that. Now, like that last nurse High Falutin', Toddy didn't come around much. When she did she acted real formal-like and so did I. It was like we broke our tow; cables snapped from the towboat, and all that power was still there but suddenly no good. No connection. And all that valuable cargo was just drifting away downstream. What you going to do, Red? Watch it float down river until it grounds out or takes out the Omaha Railroad Bridge? No. You got to cable back up, got to steam down to the drifting cargo, round up, face up, and stop this from being a disaster. On the river this would hardly phase me; grab them throttles and the steering sticks, and do what you know. But different with people, though—for me, anyway. Don't know why, but I never got built with those skills. Can rescue barges, not relationships. I freeze up when it matters most with people I care about. Or shoot my mouth off at them. Go figure, I thought to myself. Or maybe don't go figure. Maybe just sit and stare out toward the Miss, and think about why I got this way.

11

IF YOU ARE WHAT YOU EAT,
THEN I NEED TO EAT A SKINNY
PERSON

After a while I got to thinking about Lil again. Which got me to thinking about the old days, in the 1960s. Which weren't no surprise 'cause that's about all I thought about anyways. For a little while it seemed like Toddy was filling up that space, and I was making some headway into the future. But now we was disconnected, and I figured I'd just as well throttle back and drift downstream, back to Lil and the Waffle Palace.

It all came to be, me and Lil, because of waffles. I been loving waffles since I was little, though I guess I was never really little. Momma said I could push down close to a dozen waffles by the time I was ten. Some of my best memories are making waffles with Momma in the kitchen of that second floor apartment in South Saint Paul. Daddy didn't want to have nothing to do with this, though most of the time he was away down south on some line boat anyway, so it was just Momma and me. It was then we done the most talking. Over the years we cooked up more than 20 waffle recipes: lemon, apple sauce, cinnamon, buttermilk, banana, coconut, sourdough, even butterscotch and peanut butter and jelly. Momma would put on her apron and then help me with mine, one with different colored cupcakes on the front that said "Bakers Club". When we got to cooking the batter I'd try to stick my nose in the steam for a good smell, and Momma would squeeze my neck gently and tell me to be patient. One morning, when the first batch of some mighty fine raised waffles was done and I was carefully drizzling some real maple syrup that I got for Christmas into each little square box, Momma got real philosophic-like.

"Men are waffles, Orca. You should know that. That's where most men live and think—in those little square boxes in the waffles. But they only live in one box at a time."

Momma told me this was called compartmentalization. Well, this was all too much for me at 10 —I'm still trying to hook onto this thought at 62. I began to think Momma was headed 'round the bend, going all mental on me, and I got real worried. "You're talking funny, Momma," I said, but then she continued:

"This is a good time to talk about the difference between men and women, Orca," she said, giving the batter another stir. "It's about seeing the big picture."

I said to Momma, "If men are waffles, living in waffle squares, then what are women?"

She smiled at me and lit a cigarette, which I never liked 'cause the smoke ruined the smell of the waffles. Also, she seemed to smoke more than eat, and I always figured that the cigarettes were what made her so skinny. Daddy, too. It's a wonder I came out so big, with Momma being so tiny and Daddy just a lick of a man himself. I figured maybe I was adopted, but Momma said 'no', that I was made the old-fashioned way. Anyway, she thought for a while and then got up to stub out the cigarette in the sink. She stood there for a while, looking down at the pan soaking there with the pasta remains from last night's supper. Then she said, "Women are spaghetti." This had me real confused. It wasn't until years later that Cubby told me about these things called 'medifors' that I began to understand.

Anyway, Momma continued.

"Well, Orca, waffles are like men, at least to a woman, I think. We need them because we're hungry. They start out as a great idea for the beginning of the day. Oh, the batter is often lumpy at first, even with the right ingredients, but with the right amount of effort things can be smoothed out, and then in the cooking they even get steamy and more appealing. But when you're cooking them, they need to be watched very closely. If they're undercooked, they're kind of yucky and fall apart when you lift the cover and look inside. And if you leave them alone too long, they get crusty and sometimes go to pieces. Waffles are tough. A burnt waffle will leave a bad taste in your mouth."

"What about the boxes?"

"Men operate in one little square at a time, like the syrup you carefully drizzled into each little box. That's how men think. They don't understand that the other boxes are all connected, all part of the whole. Women do; that's why they're like spaghetti."

Momma could see I was pretty confused.

So she said, "Let me give you an example, Orca. We'll use Daddy's love of trucks as an example. Let's say we're out on errands, driving down Cahill Road in Inver Grove and we pass by that big Cub Foods supermarket. In the parking lot Daddy points out his dream truck, that Diamond Blue 1956 Ford F-100 he's always talking about. When I see that truck in front of Cub Foods, I start to think about the groceries I need to pick up for the family, which makes me think about the Sunday dinner with Daddy's family that's coming up, which makes me think about church school activities that morning, which makes me think about regular school, and your fifth-grade teacher. And this goes on and on, one thought wrapped over and under another one. Just like spaghetti. Now we're a mile down Cahill Road, past the grocery store, and my head is spinning with all these thoughts. But your Daddy? Still thinking about one thing: that Diamond Blue 1956 Ford truck. That, Orca, is why men are waffles and women are spaghetti."

Anyway, since I figured that when I turned into a man I was going to be one of the waffle species, it made sense to make waffles my hobby. Learned a lot. Did you know that August 24 is National Waffle Day in the U.S.? That was the date the U.S. patent was given to Cornelius Swartwout, the inventor of the waffle iron, in 1869. Yeah, waffles go way back. I wonder if Swartwout was a big guy. Anyway, in addition to collecting recipes and cooking waffles, I got to collecting waffle irons, both antique and modern ones. I found them at yard sales, in appliance repair stores, and even at the dump. General Electric made electric irons as early as 1918. I have a 1919 G.E. model in my collection. Also got a Griswald Oval No. 8, a Superlectric Twin Model 750 from the 1920s, and a Manning Bowman 5050 Twinover. The oldest irons were made of two hinged iron plates connected to two long wooden handles. Some of the early irons had plates made with special imprint patterns—instead of them square little boxes—like family coats of arms, religious symbols, the State of Texas, and silver dollars.

Anyway, my favorite is the raised waffle. Nothing better or smoother in this world (except for maybe a pair of Caterpillar 3508 diesels). Here's the recipe I use today. I'll try to give it to you like I'm one of them fancy chefs appearing on those TV cooking shows. Here goes:

> First, you need yourself a half cup of warm water (I use half a coffee mug, 'cause that or a can of beer is usually what I got near me most of the time—the mug works just as good as them fancy measurers. I ain't never been much for this precise measuring business...always wondered who came up with all these amounts...like you're gonna break out in hives if you put in that extra quarter cup of water. I've been cooking the way I've been living my whole life, eyeballing things and adjusting my way through, though maybe I should have measured better. Anyway, then you take one of them packages of dry yeast, a couple cups of warmed milk, a stick of butter, melted, a teaspoon each of salt and sugar, two cups of flour, two eggs, and a pinch of baking soda. Here's another example;

what the hell's a pinch? If you're a tiny woman with thin, tiny fingers, that's one amount; if you're Orca Bates with fingers the size of a bratwurst, then that's another amount. Go figure. So now you throw all this in a <u>big</u> mixing bowl, because that batter is going to rise like a bad snow melt on the river. Add the water and sprinkle in that yeast. Let it sit for five minutes. Then you got time to take a leak or crack another beer. Then add the milk, butter, salt, sugar, and flour to the yeast mixture and beat it like a borrowed mule. I still use Momma's old hand-rotary beater, made out of steel; not those cheap plastic ones with fake chrome finish that break easier than a ten-cent condom. Anyway, cover the bowl with plastic wrap and let stand out overnight at room temperature. If you have a cat, then put either the batter or the cat in the cupboard 'til morning. Go have another beer, take another leak, and hit the sack.

In the morning, just before cooking the waffles, beat in the eggs, add the baking soda and stir until well mixed. Don't be nervous, but the batter will now be thinner than an Amish phone book. Pour about ½ to ¾ cup batter into a very hot waffle iron (actually, forget that ½ and ¾ bullshit); just pour it in until it's about to spill over. Bake the waffles using my special technique: after the time it takes for a couple of slurps of coffee, lift the top of the grill real lightly and slowly, peek under, and see what you get for resistance; when that waffle is ready to come out, you'll feel it, like a loose tooth. Anyway, now's the time to sit and enjoy your waffle. Bone appetite.

1 2
SWEETER THAN ANYTHING YOU
COULD POUR ON A WAFFLE

When that northwest wind blows from downtown St. Paul across the Wabasha Street Bridge and the river, it shoots right down the avenue and into the side of the St. Paul Waffle Palace. On a good day, when the windows in the kitchen was open, that waffle smell came out and landed on me like ducks on a Junebug. Funny I never stopped before, since I was hungry every day after school, but I always figured, why go in? There ain't no way you can mass produce a waffle that's any good, to my liking anyway. But this particular day I was hungrier than a bear in spring. Plus I had a few bucks in my pocket, so I went in. First thing I saw as I passed through that smudged-up glass door was that this was probably one of them franchised places where everything was the same, whether in St. Paul or San Paolo. There was about a dozen little chrome-backed things that didn't seem to know whether they was chairs or stools, and each one had a red vinyl seat atop a single round black metal leg. Now I wasn't sure of two things: if I could even fit onto one of those things and if that black pole leg was going to hold me if I did.

In the middle of all those stools was a lady with glasses and a white sweater sitting with her purse in her lap, hanging on to it like it held the keys to Fort Knox. Then there was a skinny guy in a cheap shiny suit sitting by the cash register at the end. He was talking to the waitress, who turned and nodded at me 'cause I had stopped and was standing by the door, trying to figure on where to sit or whether to go in at all. She had a pen tucked over her right ear and most of it disappeared into some of the longest and prettiest wavy red hair I'd ever seen. She'd tied her hair in a ponytail but I imagined what it would look like if she let it all loose. She weren't much older than me—probably still in high school. The skinny guy in the cheap suit kept bending her ear, but she kept glancing my way. Finally she turned to me and said, "Don't be shy; there's always room for one more." The skinny guy chuckled and put down his coffee, saying, "Yup, even for somebody who looks like he might be more than one."

He gave a cocky little laugh that started to sting like usual when folks poked at me for being big and all. But instead of laughing along with him, that waitress gave me a look that just came out of nowhere, one that was sweeter than anything you could pour on a waffle. The first thing that look did was make my heart glow like a light stick. Then my mind turned down my glowing heart and turned up this thought; this girl can't be *that* perfect if she's taken a shine to the likes of you, Orca Bates.

Finally I went over to one of the booths and sat down, as I didn't like the thought of me on one of them stools. The skinny guy was still slobbering all over her, but she turned around and poured a glass of water and headed my way. I could see the skinny guy taking in his good view of her rear end from his spot by the cash register at the head of the line of stools, and I guessed I knew why he was sitting there and I bet he sat there a lot. She put the water down and reached into her apron pocket for an order pad. Her being so pretty and up close like that got me real nervous, so I grabbed for a menu and, like an idiot, didn't open it but just looked at the giant waffle picture on the cover. Under the waffle it said, 'over 2,000,000 served since 1961'. I tried to picture what 2,000,000 waffles looked like, but I weren't getting nowhere with that.

"Know what you'd like then?" she asked.

"I bet you have waffles here, right?"

"At The Waffle Palace?"

"Yeah, just saying, you know. I wondered about the different kinds you got."

"They're listed there, on the right inside page if you open up the menu." Then she looked over her shoulder at the skinny guy. "I'll just give you a minute and be back, okay?"

So I began my looking at what was supposed to be all those waffles, but I was surprised to see that there was only two kinds: plain and pecan. What kind of a waffle palace has just two kinds of waffles? I put down my menu and looked over toward the waitress and the skinny guy. The skinny guy was showing her some kind of paperwork, but when I raised my arm I got her attention and she came back to my booth.

"Made up your mind?" she asked.

"Not much there for my mind to make up. You only got two kinds of waffles?"

"That's right, but lots of toppings."

"No raised waffles even?"

"No, I never even heard of a raised waffle."

"Well, I'll have two of each kind of what you got then."

She looked down at her order pad. "Um, that's *four* waffles? 'Cause they're pretty big and usually one is..." Then she looked at me. "Okay, four it is."

I sat there drinking my water, wondering if maybe the Waffle Palace's waffles were so good that they only needed two kinds to please their customers. I figured I'd know soon enough. Either way, I was ready to eat just about anything when the waitress came back empty-handed.

"I just wondered if you wanted the cook to maybe make two and then another two after a few minutes, just so some don't get cold?" she asked.

Damned if that weren't thoughtful of her. But I said, "No, just bring 'em on all at once. I'll be past number one and two before three and four even get to think about cooling off. Food don't have a chance of long term survival around me. Maybe that's why they named me after a whale." Well, that got her to laughing pretty good.

And then she said something that messed with my heart and my brain again. "You must be, Orca? You go to Central, right?"

"You *know* me?"

"Well, not really. I mean, I heard something really cool about you, that's all. From my friend Holly."

"Me? You did? You sure?"

"Holly makes you sound like you're kind of like Superman or Zorro or the Lone Ranger or something."

"Well, guess I should have worn my mask and black cape. You know, disguise myself when I comes in public places like this so no one recognizes me. Leave my horse outside, of course."

"You're funny."

"Maybe. But I am confused. I don't think I even know anybody named Holly."

"She's Walter Collins' sister."

"The little red-headed kid?"

"Yeah. Holly said word got out about you standing up for him; somebody heard Harlan tell his buddy Max about how they best cool it on Walter for a while, and that Orca almost destroyed him in the hallway for messing with Walter."

"I guess being big comes in handy once in a while. Better keep eating waffles."

"Well, I bet your waffles are ready. I'll go see. By the way, my name's Lil."

Well, I got to feeling pretty good. And I knew I'd feel even better once I dug into them waffles. But I'm sorry to say that weren't true. When Lil came back with the waffles, I dove in right away, going back and forth between the pecan one and the plain one. Didn't do any toppings 'cause I wanted to concentrate on two things: the outer crust and the inner core. You want a thin, but crisp crust for sure, and an inside that ain't all raw and doughy. It's all about the batter. Got to build it right from the beginning. Kind of like raising somebody right, I guess. Not to sound too technical, but waffles have a higher liquid-to-dry ingredient ratio. (This ain't me being all professor-like. I read this in one of my cookbooks.) When this gets out of whack, you get yourself a waffle that ain't right on the outside and even worse on the inside—probably like the skinny guy at the counter. You got to have a batter that's just right, thick but pourable. Well, these waffles here at the Waffle Palace tasted like old cardboard on the outside and wallpaper paste on the inside. I ate them anyway, but it weren't easy. Then Lil came back, all smiling.

"Guess you liked them."

"Well, let's just say I got a new name for them for the menu: 'Awful Waffles'. I do believe they are the worst waffles I've ever had. Though I ain't had two million yet, I've had a lot."

She leaned toward me like she was going to whisper something, and kind of cupped her hand over her mouth. "I *never* eat them. Ever since the new cook, and some new franchise recipe rules, they've gotten even worse. Please don't tell my boss I said this. I need this job."

"Well, what I'd tell your boss is that if it weren't for you, this place would be emptier than a hermit's address book."

She gave me this big smile and blushed up good. By Jesus, almost by accident, I said probably the coolest line in history. Right from my own little brain and out of my own big mouth. It weren't no line though. It were the truth. The princess of The Waffle Palace, that's what Lil was.

13

SAVING THE PRINCESS AND THE PALACE

As you might guess, I started to eat at the Palace a lot, due to me having gone around the bend over Lil and all. Besides the fact that I couldn't stand the rest of the world being stuck with eating another two million of those awful waffles, I knew I'd have to push down a few more myself in order to be near Lil. Maybe I shouldn't have worried though, 'cause it seemed the world was starting to stay away from the Palace's waffles on its own. Other than the guy in the shiny suit and an occasional trucker, business looked to be pretty steady...steady terrible.

I worried that Lil would either lose her job because the place would go under, or she'd quit because of bad tip money. That would leave me grounded out, up a dry creek, with no way to see her. Unless I asked her out. And I knew I'd never dare do that, even though Momma always said to me, "if you don't ask, then the answer is always 'no'." I do believe that if Lil did say 'no', I'd be like a giant balloon with a pin stuck in my heart. So I knew I needed a plan, something more than just going in there, making small talk, and eating waffles. I also wanted to get closer to shiny suit guy so I could hear what he was saying to Lil, and maybe find out what all the paperwork was that he kept showing her. But I didn't dare risk fitting into one of them dumb chairs at the counter; it'd be embarrassing not to fit and even worse to get stuck.

That's when I thought about that pay phone on the wall pretty close to the counter. I figured I could look busy pretending to make a couple of calls instead of just sitting there alone at the booth. And then I could listen in on cheap suit guy. So that's what I did. Turns out he was pushing some kind of insurance on Lil for her to push on her parents. I got to listening pretty close. He was asking Lil lots of questions: How much life insurance do you think your parents have now? How much are their lives worth? How good do you think your dad would feel knowing he was protecting the family if something happened to him? If he had a way to protect your dear mother forever from the financial horrors of widowhood for just a few dollars a month, he'd probably want to know about it right?

"It's amazing," he said, "but this costs just about what a couple of pizzas a month cost, and provides the ultimate in security and peace of mind. I bet your dad's a clean liver too, Lil, which in my business means he's a good risk, so the premiums are even lower."

Anyway, I stood there during my fake phone call, just listening away. Maybe I got to listening too hard; the cheap suit guy seemed to pick up on that and he looked over at me and said, "Hey Waffle Boy, anybody on the other end of that line? Come on over here; I got a waffle joke for ya." So I just hung up and went over; didn't even bother to say a fake goodbye. "You ever hear this one," he says:

> "So one day, a mother and her two boys, Timmy and Tommy, are riding in their car on the way to church. Timmy leans over, smacks Tommy across the head, and Tommy yells out, 'Ouch, you fucking wanker!' Later that day in church, the mom goes to talk to the priest, and says: 'Father, my boys just won't stop swearing and I don't know what to do.' The priest says 'Well, have you tried smacking them?' She says 'No, doesn't the church look down on that?' The priest says 'Well, yes, but in some cases we'll make an

exception.' The next day, the two boys come down for breakfast and she asks Tommy what he wants to eat. Tommy says "Well, gimme some fucking waffles.' The mom backhands Tommy so hard he flies out of his chair and lands against the door. Shocked and terrified by this, Timmy becomes very quiet. His mother turns and asks him what he wants for breakfast, and he says, 'Well you can bet your sweet ass I don't want no fucking waffles!'

About then cheap suit guy starts laughing pretty hard at his own joke, slapping his knee. "Pretty good one, huh?" he says to me and Lil, who kind of stands there, half smirking, half embarrassed.

"Well," I said, "what I know *ain't* good is swearing in public or in front of a young lady." Lil smiled and then she looked down.

The guy just shook his head a few times. Then he said, "It's *part* of the joke, dummy. You *have* to swear."

Well, I'd about had it by then—which don't take much with me—and I said, "And also, that's stupid; little kids don't talk that way to their mothers."

The guy shook his head some more and said, "Why don't you go back to your booth and eat some more waffles."

"Well, I can do that, but I just have a couple insurance questions for you."

"You need insurance? That'd be one big policy." Then he starts laughing again.

"Not for me; this being that my momma is kind of sick and all."

"How sick?"

"Breast cancer."

"Oh, sorry kid. That's rough. Well, I'd need to know a lot more, but I'm sure I could get her into some term life. My name's Schloggle. Art Schloggle, by the way."

"What's term life?"

"Well, it's for a fixed period of time."

"You mean, a period of time before she dies or all the time until she dies?"

"It could be for a shorter term. She may not be in the 'preferred life' customer category. Look, there's a lot to discuss. Have one of your folks call me sometime later, okay?"

Then he got up, handed me a business card, and put one hand on my upper arm like he was shaking hands, but with my bicep. I don't like strangers touching me, so I stepped forward pretty quick and he let go pretty quick. "Not in the 'preferred life' category? I don't understand," I said. "So my Momma don't have a 'preferred life'? Why would you guys sell life insurance if it ain't good 'til the end? 'Cause I don't..."

"Kid, I gotta run."

"Seems like a racket," I said.

After he left and Lil went into the kitchen, I went over to my booth and sat down, feeling all confused and sad. Then Lil came by and stood next to me.

"Hey, sorry about your mom. You want some cocoa or something?"

"Sure. Thanks. Guess I kind of scared your friend away."

"Boy, you sure get right to the point on things."

"It's stupid. It's a problem I got. I just say stuff to people. All kinds of stuff. I just thought insurance for my mom and all would somehow...help. I dunno. Just stupid."

"Well, I'm sure your mom is wonderful."

"Yeah, she's my Jiminy Cricket."

"Your Jiminy Cricket?"

"Yeah, that Disney character. He was one of my favorites. Momma used to read books to me a lot when I was little; books with Jiminy Cricket in them. He was kind of Pinocchio's conscience. And he warned kids to steer clear of dangerous stuff."

"And Pinocchio's nose grew when he told a lie."

"Yeah. I'm figurin' that's why that insurance guy has a long nose."

"Let me get you that cocoa. I'll grab some for both of us. It's time for my break anyway."

When she got back with the cocoa and a couple of napkins and sat down opposite me in the booth, I felt on top of the world, like I had just climbed a mountain. I mean, she didn't *have* to sit down with me. I didn't even ask her to sit down with me, though I can't tell you how many times at night I sat in my room and tried to figure a way to get her to do just that.

She took a little sip of the cocoa and whipped cream, then wiped her lips with the napkin. "Does your mom have a good doctor?" she asked.

"I guess so," I said. Then I just sat there like a dummy and stared at my cocoa.

"I'm sure she'll be fine," Lil said, and was quiet for a minute. "So, anyway, what's your dad do?"

"Towboats. He's a towboat pilot for Shetland Barge in St. Paul. He's away a lot, which ain't a bad thing. What's your dad do?"

"I'm not sure, exactly. Works in an office in Rosedale."

"Home every night though?"

"Pretty much. You going to work on the river after high school?"

"Well, not being exactly college material, I'll probably start decking—that's a deck hand—after graduation."

"Maybe you could become a great chef? You know, work in some fancy restaurant in St. Paul or maybe even New York."

"Yeah, a great big chef. That would be me alright. But that takes school, too. And that takes money, which is in short supply in my family. What about you? There must be life beyond The Waffle Palace."

"I might go to school to become a cosmetologist."

"Wow, you got to be smart for that, I bet. That like astronomy? Studying stars and stuff?"

"I think that's cosmology, but you're close. This is beauty treatments for hair and skin and putting make-up on women."

"Well, the way I see it, you don't need any of them things."

Then she laughed pretty good and kind of threw her head back.

"Well, that's the nicest compliment I've had since...Well, anyway, this cosmetology is about giving other people beauty treatments."

"Well, sign me up then. I'll be your first customer. If you can make me look good, then the rest of the people in the world will be a piece of cake."

She laughed pretty hard again, wiped her lips on her napkin, got up and then started to pick up the cocoa cups to take back to the counter. "Two things, Orca," she said. "I think you're much smarter than you think." About then this guy came in from the back of the restaurant, and Lil got to moving faster, looking down and fiddling with the cocoa cups. "Look, I got to go; it's my boss" she said, kind of under her breath.

"Wait," I said. "What's the other one?"

"The other one?"

"You said there was two things."

She looked up from the cups. "Well, the beauty thing; you know that 'beauty is only skin deep' saying? Well, it's not, that's all. Beauty's much deeper," she said as she turned away and headed for the counter. Then she said something else. It was kind of muffled by her steps, but it sounded like: 'At least on you'.

And then she was gone. I picked up that napkin of hers 'cause her lips were right on it, even if they was only lipstick lips. I folded it up real careful like, stuck it in my pocket, and headed home to see how Momma was doing.

14

THE ONE THING THAT'S SCARIER THAN LOSING YOUR MOMMA IN THE SUPERMARKET

Anyway, Momma wasn't gettin' better. Funny thing was that she seemed like she was worried mostly about me the whole time when I figured she should be worrying about herself. First they found this lump and they took it out. I figured that would be that. Kind of like taking out a splinter from your finger. Or taking the lumps out of that raised waffle batter I love so much. Smoothing things out and looking forward to the next morning. But Momma said that the doctor told her it got into these lymph node things, and she drew me a diagram of what he told her about these nodes and also about these four stages.

I tried my hardest to understand and try to figure how I could help. I thought about how I should have studied harder, especially science, so then I could have been a doctor and helped her myself. But all I saw in that diagram was what looked like a river chart that Daddy once showed me, with a bunch of Mississippi tributaries. So mostly I just stood there, kind of paralyzed. Or asked Momma if she wanted some more water. Then asking her again. She would just smile back at me and say I should not worry, but maybe go do some homework or find a friend and go fishing in the river. But I was afraid to leave. Momma said me being big and strong was good, but this time I had to be strong somewhere else. I didn't know how to do that.

Daddy just kept making excuses, saying he was sorry he was away so much, but that's the way it was. I ain't sure how sorry he was, really. Seems as if being sorry after it's too late is about the easiest thing a person can do. Let's you do the bad stuff and then wiggle out at the end.

Anyway, when the end of that last stage come along, and Momma was in the hospital in one of them beds with a crank on the end so she could sit up, she said this to me:

"I know it's hard, Orca. But do good works. It makes all the difference."

"Work hard, Momma?"

"No, that's different. But do that too. But also do some things you can be really proud of, no matter what else goes wrong with your life. That way those things can be your shining stars, always up there for you to look at." Then she smiled at me and squeezed my hand. "Do that for me, will you?"

"How do I know what those things are going to be, Momma?"

"It'll be like hooking a fish. You'll feel it for sure. You'll just know. Your heart will tell you. And your conscience. Like Jiminy Cricket. Remember Jiminy Cricket, Orca." Then she closed her eyes.

It felt like Momma's body fell into a giant whirlpool, spinning away and slowly disappearing. I wanted to put my great big hands around that little crank at the end of the bed and crank and crank and crank, faster and faster, until she was well again. But I just stood there, holding her hand, thinking about being little with Momma and thinking about her reading to me, and thinking about where I'd find my conscience if Jiminy Cricket wasn't around anymore. And I squeezed Momma's hand harder, but it didn't squeeze back.

15

ENGLISH, MATH AND WESTERN CIVILIZATION IS GOING TO HAVE TO GET ALONG WITHOUT ME

Suddenly school was even less interesting than even before Momma died. I just didn't see the point of it anymore. Even though Momma said work hard, this wasn't the kind of work I was made for. Studying stuff—stuff like French and algebra and western civilization—mixed with me about as good as oil and water. The two weren't ever going to mix.

Daddy stuck around for a while after I lost Momma. He was between jobs he said, all done working on that line boat down on the Illinois River. So he was around the house, though mostly he was out. I figured that 'out' meant over at The Slough, drinking. So he weren't much good to me. Actually, I weren't much good to me either. I mostly sat on the couch and stared at the television. Daddy would go out around noon, wearing that oil-stained Caterpillar hat of his, jeans and a blue-checked flannel shirt with big fake pearl-looking buttons. One day he stopped and looked at me. He was looking pretty much in need of either a few aspirin or a quick drink. Then he shook his head and kind of sneered at me. "You know, Orca, probably you ain't going to amount to nothing because of school, so you best pick up a trade and get your fat ass off the couch."

I looked up at him and said, "You ever think about planning a memorial or something for Momma? 'Cause that's what *I've* been thinking. I been thinking about *her*. And Father Porter has been calling."

"You know I got your momma cremated. That's what she wanted and it's all paid for. By me." Then he jabbed his finger a few times into his chest. "And I been busy since then and I don't know them church people the way your momma does. Or did. Why don't *you* do it? You're the one doing all the moping. And when you're done doing that why don't you go down to Shetland Barge and talk to Bobby Driscoll about decking on a tow or at least being a shop monkey for him. You might learn something more valuable than eating waffles. Bobby knows me from when I did some trip piloting on the *Frank Hastings* for him. He just might hire you. It's time you started contributing something around here; pay for all the food you been eating."

After he left I picked up the phone and called Father Porter back. We had a meeting the next day and picked a date for Momma's service; he said he'd pick the music and prayers 'cause I didn't really know anything about that. He said he could get it in the newspaper and that's how people would know to come, 'cause everybody reads those notices.

Then I went home and decided to drop out of high school. I figured that if you drop out of something, you got to land somewhere else.

16

TWO DEVILS AND ONE ANGEL IN ONE CHAPEL

It seems odd, but there's a little red devil next to me. I'm sitting here alone in the last row of this chapel. The little devil is sitting in the lower corner frame of a stained glass window, which is just to the right of my pew. You would think there would be angels or pictures of Jesus and other holy stuff, not a little red devil. I'm sitting away from the others, way in the back, in case I cry. Father Porter wanted me to sit up front with family members. I can't see if Daddy has shown yet, and we're about to start.

From where I sit, I see the backs of many heads, but no faces. Faces show so much about character; I do believe I've learned that much.

Father Porter is up now. I think them Catholic priests have to play it by the book, talking about how Momma would be in the warm bosom of God's heavenly paradise, how we should not let ourselves feel sad (are you shitting me?), or that death is unfair, because Momma is in the kingdom of heaven now, and it ain't our place to question God's plan. Finally, he got himself back down to earth, down to the real world, and talked about the little bit he really did know momma, about how she was helpful in this or that church activity, and kind of putting in a plug for some of the events she helped run for the church fundraisers. Almost like he was recruiting a replacement for Momma.

I close my eyes, put my head back, and take a deep breath. I'm fuming inside, but I'm also at peace. How's that possible? On the one hand, I feel like I should charge the pulpit, look up to God and ask for Momma back. Yet next, when I open my eyes, I'm looking at the ceiling and feeling kind of peaceful knowing one fact for sure: that Momma isn't hurting anymore. The chapel is a V-roofed building, and the ceiling looks like an upside down boat, with exposed planks, ribs, and a roof beam like a long keel. Floating up to heaven. That's the deal, I think. If she hasn't already gotten up there in the clouds, I'm thinking that Momma is probably looking back at me from inside that brass urn up on the altar.

Father Porter is done. How much could he possibly say? *I* should be the one speaking. I could go on forever about Momma and all the good she done for me, teaching me stuff about standing up for other people, stuff about men living in little waffle boxes and women being spaghetti, and stuff about listening to my conscience, doing good work, and some other things she said just before she died. Well, thinking that gets me to crying pretty good. Quite a sight, a big guy crying. That's why I'm alone in the back. Still, I look away, to the side. I look over again at that little red devil in the window next to me. You stay away from my Momma, I mouth to him. Right then a gleam of light catches the corner of my eye. The light comes in through the main door of the chapel, and along with it a person; it lights up the girl with the prettiest wavy red hair in the whole wide world. And by God, like an angel landing in my pew, if she don't sit right next to me, close enough that I can smell that shampoo she uses to make that hair so nice. Then you know what she does? She hands me a Kleenex.

Just then there's a rustling in the front row and, sure enough, Daddy is there, and he gets up to speak. He's looking down now as he rises, doing his best to seem real sad and thoughtful like. But I know this guy better than any of the others; what he's really thinking is 'How do I look?'. I catch his quick glance to check out his own reflection in the mirrored part of a stained glass window as he goes by. I look over again at that little red devil next to me. There's two of you in here now, I think to myself.

Then Daddy goes up to the side of the alter and then walks up to the podium. He's wearing his only suit, a cheap one like that insurance guy Art Schloggle wears. But Daddy's not selling nothing. At least not to me. Well, I guess I don't know what to expect when Daddy gets up there. Funerals is new to me. And I think maybe new to Daddy too, judging by his delivery. I don't know why, but his speech is stuck in my memory, maybe because it was so short and so bad. I ain't never heard a eulogy, but I know enough that they're not supposed to be about the person giving it, but about the one that's dead. So here it is—but you'll have to use your own imagination about Daddy's mumbling and zero eye contact with anyone in the chapel:

Hello. I been thinking about what I ought to say, and I guess I've had time to think, being in the pilothouse a lot all these years, away a lot from the Mrs. due to all that responsibility of pushing barges filled with millions of gallons of hazardous cargo by your houses at night while you're all sleeping. My own daddy had himself a few accidents, but I'm glad to say I haven't had one. Probably learned from his mistakes.

Anyway, Orca's mom was a good girl. I got no complaints. I guess maybe her main skill was feeding Orca. And we can all see how good she was at that. [I guess the old man thought he was Johnny Carson or somebody, but nobody laughed.] *And my pushing barges put food on the table anytime they needed it. But it's a lonely life, churning along at 3, 4, 5 miles per hour, day after day, so close to the river bank and civilization you can hear it and smell it. But bills need to be paid, so that's what I had to do. Funny, I was saying that to Herb, one of my deckhands, just the other day. We was coming up river, headed back to St. Paul, and I said I missed so much 'cause of my job, and now I had even more responsibility what with taking care of Orca and all.*

Anywho, I guess we should all get on with it. That's what Orca's mom would have said, maybe. Like I was saying, she was a good girl. Really took good care of Orca, 'cause she knew he needed it. So I'll close by saying thank you for listening.

I look over again at that little red devil next to me. I ain't betting my soul on this, I mouth to him, but my money says that was the shittiest eulogy in the history of funerals.

Well, hearing Daddy speak, at least it stops my crying. I grab a glance at Lil. She's looking down, her eyes closed. Must be praying, I figure. Then I notice she has a little white purse and an orange cardboard box by her. The box says '*The Waffle Palace...Over 2 Million Served*'. I slide over closer to whisper something to Lil, even though it's hard for me to whisper 'cause of my deep, gravelly voice, but I try. "You brought *waffles* to Momma's funeral?"

"No," she whispers back, "it's a gift for you."

"You know the last thing I want or need is a Waffle Palace waffle, Lil. Them things is dead on arrival even when they're fresh and hot, much less cooped up in a box in a hot church."

"It's not waffles," she whispers.

"Well, I need to go. I can't deal with Daddy up close right now. Let's go out before the others."

So we went out that same door that Lil come from. She had her dad's Chrysler Valiant and I climbed into the passenger seat. Lil smoothed her pretty black dress when she got in, first under her and then on the top once she got seated. Real ladylike. "Let's go down to that park by the houseboat marina," she said. "It's peaceful. You can open your present there."

I didn't say nothing while she drove along the left bank of the river through a couple of tough St. Paul neighborhoods, by a power station and the old concrete plant, and then up and over the St. Paul High Bridge, which must be more than a half-mile long across the Mississippi. Then we followed the River Road, which is real woodsy all of a sudden and passes by some of the abandoned and closed-up sandstone caves, which go way deep into the bluffs. I been in a couple, and heard that a handful of kids been killed by carbon monoxide in there. Then we drove down river some more until we got to the Harriet Island park, which is near the houseboat colony. I still didn't feel much like talking, even though my heart was beating right out of my big huge chest 'cause of Lil coming to Momma's funeral. We parked and walked over to some swings, and Lil put down the Waffle Palace box on a picnic table. I sure did wonder what was in it. Lil sat in one of the swings. I didn't know if I was supposed to push her, but I did know I was going to do those little swings a favor by not sitting in one myself. So I just stood there like a dummy while Lil swung a little bit. Like in one of them romantic movies, I so wanted to put my hands gently on her back and push her, but I was scared she'd tense up on me and I couldn't take another horrible thing on this day. What would Momma say to do? I wondered.

"So what's next, Orca," Lil said finally.

"I dropped out of school, Lil."

"What? You can't..."

"I can't do school. So I figure I should do something I can do."

"And what's that?"

"Maybe Shetland Barge."

That made Lil stop swinging. She stood up and smoothed her skirt. Then she shook her head.

"Oh, Orca, maybe don't get started with that. Maybe break away from what your dad and grandpa did."

"Where should I break to?"

"What about the chef career we talked about?"

"More school and money."

"Well, look, I had this idea a while ago and didn't bring it up to you, what with your mom and all, but here's what I'm thinking. My boss has to do something pretty amazing pretty quick at the Palace or you and Art Schloggle will be the only customers left."

"And *we're* only there because of you, Lil."

She blushed up and I swear her hair and face was now one same rosy glowing color.

"Well, here's my idea: I bet no one on planet earth makes such an amazing waffle as you do, Orca; it's just that nobody knows that! Why not start making them at the Waffle Palace? You'll be a hero, business will boom, I'll make great tips. It will all be good. Then, when the newspapers pick up about these amazing waffles and all these people coming from all over to taste them, and some culinary guy hears about it, and you get a scholarship at one of those fancy cooking institutes..."

"I thought you said they had to cook according to that franchisor company recipe, all standardized and everything, or your boss would lose his franchise he bought for the St. Paul store."

"Well, no one needs to know. At least not at first. And then when word gets out he can contact the franchise company and get them to change it."

"But ain't that cheating? Breaking the rules. They must have a reason they want to use that awful recipe if they sold two million of them."

"Well, they're not selling them here. Anyway, at least think about it. And then I can ask my boss." Then Lil went over to the picnic table and picked up the Waffle Palace box. "Anyway, speaking of Waffle Palaces, you should open your present. And I promise it's not a waffle," she said. She laughed and threw her head back and them red curls, all clean I figured from that shampoo I smelled in the church, well they just danced in the sunset. Lots of stuff I don't notice, but I sure noticed that.

Well, I didn't know what to make about the idea of getting a present for my Momma's funeral, but I went over to the picnic table and sat down next to the box, on the other side of the table from Lil. I wanted to sit with her, on the end, on her side, but I figured I'd turn the whole table up in the air like a seesaw if I did, which has happened to me before at picnics.

"Go ahead, open it."

"Okay, as long as there ain't one of them awful waffles inside."

And so I opened it. And it was the second time I cried that day. But this time I didn't care if it was just Lil or if the whole world was walking by and seeing this big lug crying, 'cause when a person does something so good and so true and so thoughtful like that, none of them inhibitions inside a body has a chance. And when Lil put her soft pink hand on my big hairy arm, my heart was smiling right through my chest.

What was in the box was a rubber toy, about six inches tall, with a blue top hat, an orange vest, and yellow shoes.

It was Jiminy Cricket, resting gently on a bed of Waffle Palace napkins. Taped to his vest was a small handwritten card. It said,

Always let your conscience be your guide.
— Jiminy Cricket

17

A Sad Soul Gets Two New Soles from a Good Soul

I hated ever taking any of Daddy's advice, but I knew, with me cut-tin' short my education, that there would be much better money working the barges than anywhere else. So I headed over the Waba-sha Street bridge which crossed the Miss, rolled myself over the guard rail on Kellogg Boulevard, took a short cut down the river bank, and lumbered across the rickety steel walkway that led to the Shetland Barge Company wharf barge. The company office and shop is all on one barge, set between the county jail and a law book publisher. Prisoners and law book makers gets the best view of the river. Go figure.

I opened the wharf barge door and walked in, the wind slam-ming it shut behind me. Bobby Driscoll was bent over the short block of an 871 Jimmy. He was holding what I knew was one of them bore wear gauges. I knew this and I knew about 871 engines from hanging around the towboats that Daddy drove when I was a young kid—plus I'd helped with a couple short block rebuilds in my engine shop class during my junior year in high school. The engine was up on some skids by the shop door. Bobby straightened himself up and reached for a shop rag. He had on blue-and-white-striped coveralls and a Detroit Diesel hat. Bobby was a big man himself, and I knew from river talk that he was a good guy but you didn't mess with him either.

"You're Frank Bates' boy," Bobby said.

I nodded and stepped closer.

"Dropped out of high school, I hear."

I nodded again.

"What you want to do that for?"

I just shrugged. About then I began figuring that this interview wasn't going too good, and I better say something.

"Kind of liked my engine shop class," I mumbled, looking over to the side of the shop and then down at the 871 on the floor, "so I thought working around the real thing might be good."

He kept wiping his hands on the rag, looking at me and then at the 871, and then back up at me again. I knew he had something in mind 'cause he looked at me the way that high school offensive line coach looked at me when I lumbered onto the field on tryout day. "Well, maybe someday you could learn your way around an engine, but what I need now is someone big and strong on deck, someone who can lift heavy cable when we're switching tows, but is also sure-footed enough not to slip on an ice-coated steel deck and end up crushed between two 200-foot steel grain barges and drowned in the river."

I looked down at the shop floor and then looked up at Bobby. "I'd prefer to drown, and then be crushed, in that order, if I have a choice," I said.

Bobby smirked. "You look like a solid kid," he said. Then he shook his head a little. "But I had some problems with your daddy, you know."

"Yes, sir. I bet."

"Oh, and sorry about your mom, kid."

"Me too."

"Maybe when you get done grieving and all, you should go back to school."

"Maybe."

"You know that saying, Orca—it's Orca, right?—that once you wear out one pair of boots on the river, you never get off. River gets into you by then, flowing through you like blood in your veins.

You try to get off the Miss for a while, and, well, like blood leaving your veins, you start to feel like something's wrong, feel weak, like you're bleeding out." He threw the rag onto the workbench, and shook his head. "Never seen anyone ever really get off. Oh, sometimes they'll try some shore or river job like dispatcher at Cargill Grain or even welding barges ashore at Twin City Barge. But they ain't the same after that, always drifting down to the river bank and staring out at the tows going by." He reached back and scratched his neck. "I guess it's cause them tows they're watching, they're always going somewhere, and those guys that went ashore, well, they ain't anymore."

I just stood there like a dummy, but I knew I should say something. "I'm strong," I said. Bobby looked at me. "I guess that's pretty obvious," I added. "And I ain't like my daddy."

"Well, I'll give you a try, Orca. Shifts is 12 hours, pay is $18 per shift. That's $1.50 an hour. You can start for one shift as an extra man, just watching and learning, so you're up to speed for the next twelve-hour shift."

"Thanks."

"And get some good boots."

As I headed toward the wharf barge door, he said, "Hey, Orca, ain't you forgetting something?" I turned and cocked my head before he continued. "You know, like maybe asking me what day you start and what time?" He just shook his head and smiled. "Anyway, meet for Friday morning 6 am crew change here at the wharf barge at 5:30; you can hitch a ride on the company pickup with Larry and Pudge. And Geb is the trip pilot that day. You'll be doing your crew change at the stump; you know the place, just above Monkey Rudder Bend? You'll be on the *Shula B*. I'll tell the boys you'll be riding along."

"Thanks, I know the spot," I said. I felt really good for the first time in a while, and most of it was because Bobby was giving me a new start I guess. I always heard Bobby had a heart, that he was a good soul when folks was down and out. I turned to leave again, but then Bobby walked over to the supply wall behind the 871, saying, "I just thought of something, Orca. I'll bet you'd fit right into Blister's boots. He didn't last long working for us, pretty big and strong, but way too lazy for this kind of work. And too lazy to ever come back for his boots, I guess." He looked them over pretty carefully, turning them upside down and inspecting the soles. Then he shook his head. "He didn't even last long enough to break them in. They're not cheap ones either; pretty good boots for the job. Take them home with you and try them on. If they fit you'll save yourself twenty or thirty bucks."

"Thanks."

"But remember," he said, "They wear out pretty quick."

I headed for the door again, then something bugged me. I stopped and turned back to Bobby. "Is Blister that guy's real name?"

"It's a nickname, Orca. Everyone on the river gets one sooner or later."

"How'd he get 'Blister'?"

"'Cause he only appeared after the work was done."

"Oh," I said, and went out the door. I ain't that fast but on the way up the river bank I figured it out. And then I had my first laugh in a real long time.

1 8

THE ONLY BUSBOY BIGGER
THAN A BUS

Being a busboy at the Waffle Palace paid one dollar an hour, and even with my D- grade in old man Halverson's basic math class, I could still do the figuring that that was a full one third less than my river pay. And it weren't no fancy chef job leading to training at that Gordon Blue place in Paris either. But it put me close to Lil, and it was part of her plan to get me in position to do some cooking of real waffles to replace them cardboard Frisbees they called food. So I finally met with Lil's boss, the guy who owned the franchise. His name was Wally Swade, kind of a nervous little man with a thin mustache and the biggest comb-over I ever did see. He always wore a white-collared shirt with a breast pocket stuffed with a plastic pocket pencil protector and a lot of red and black pens. Most of the time he was so nervous that when he put one of them pens away in his breast pocket, he usually missed the protector a couple of times, so his shirts had lots of red and black pen lines on them. It was like some little kid had used the shirts to draw on. I wasn't the best choice for a busboy, of course, being nearly as big as some of them booths and having a hard time reaching and sliding in to clear their plates. But busboy help was hard to find, I guess, and Lil told Mr. Swade that she could vouch for me as reliable and a hard worker.

Of course Art Schloggle was still a regular, popping up every so often in his maroon Corvette and nosing around Lil like a hungry muskrat on the river bank. He ignored me, especially 'cause now

I was just a lowly busboy instead of a customer, and I soon realized that Lil was not tired of his attention or his car. During her break one day he took her outside to show it to her, and I watched through the Palace's glass door as she got into the passenger seat. Schloggle got behind the wheel, and it looked like he turned on the radio and they listened for a while. I could see Lil's curls just bouncing away. Hell, I didn't even have a car, and it didn't take me long to figure I was going to lose this race, if it was a race at all. Schloggle had to be ten or twelve years older than Lil, and I could tell she was taken by this older, slick insurance salesman and his shiny souped-up convertible. I knew what he wanted, even if Lil didn't, and it weren't the chance to honor her all the days of her life, either. The whole thing made it too painful to work there, so I decided to quit, thinking that I was better off with just the river decking job with Bobby Driscoll. At closing time, and right before I was going to tell Mr. Swade I was quitting, Lil came up behind me as I was taking off my Waffle Palace apron by the time clock. I could tell she was excited.

"Jimmy went home sick suddenly, and Mr. Swade's not here to fill in for him tomorrow, Orca. This is your big chance," she said. "You can step in and cook. You can make your magic batter at home tonight and bring it in tomorrow. I can help you in the kitchen; I know where everything is, and I can handle other short order stuff. Tomorrow's usually our slowest day, but we only need to try this on a few customers. Mr. Swade doesn't even have to know Jimmy's not coming in."

"I don't know, Lil. I was just thinking of quitting."

"No, no, no, Orca. Not now! This is what we've been waiting for; don't you see? It's great for both of us. And even if it backfires, well, we weren't going to last much longer anyway." Then, damn if she didn't put her hand on my arm again. "Look," she continued, "tonight get that amazing batter of yours together, and I'll meet you here an hour before opening tomorrow."

I thought for a minute. If I quit, or if I stayed and got fired for being a busboy who made himself the cook and changed the recipe, well, it wouldn't matter much either way. Plus, it would help Lil.

And so I did it. That night I whipped up my very best batter, and a lot of it, too! I met Lil bright and early. Between the two of us we was like a team, and I sure liked that.

I noticed right away that everybody that was coming in was ordering waffles and not much else, which was strange to me, since people had begun avoiding Waffle Palace waffles like they was hemlock, or whatever that stuff was that killed that Romeo guy. It was a small but steady crowd that morning, mostly regulars who had somehow hung on despite the waffles. Now they was all ordering waffles.

When Lil leaned her pretty face over the stainless steel order shelf between the back counter and the kitchen, I said "What'd you do, Lil, offer each of these guys a kiss if they ordered one?" Well, that weren't the right thing to say, but things just come pouring out of me sometimes. Now, I don't pay much attention to people's looks, but I sure saw Lil's; it weren't a good one, and Lil just ripped down the order slip, grabbed the plate and headed to one of the booths with it. But I still couldn't understand how the word could have gotten out so quick. It just didn't make sense. Then she came back with another order, put her hands on her hips, tilted her head, and said, "Since you asked, I told them that this waffle recipe was brand new today, and they got a free next breakfast if they didn't absolutely love these waffles."

"Jeez, Lil, you did that?"

She grabbed the plate with the double order of two raised waffles I'd just made, and said, "Yes, Orca, because that's what I think of your waffles."

And so it went. Nobody claimed a free next breakfast. And nobody stopped eating my waffles. And Lil was right all along. Not about me ever going to that Gordon Blue place. And not about me becoming a famous chef. But she was right about my waffles and about her tips increasing and about me becoming the cook, part time, along with Jimmy.

The cooking times was good, but the best time was when me and Lil had our breaks. The break room was in the back of the kitchen and had a small table and a pretty good-sounding radio. We'd sit there with our cherry cokes, listening to pop radio on WDGY, talking and laughing about our two worlds: mine the one alone in the back wrestling with eggs, bacon, and batter, and Lil's in that weird human one out front.

"Man, Peterbroke had a bad fight with his wife again," Lil said.

"Drowning his sorrows in my waffles, huh?" I said. I knew the guy she was talking about, the trucker with the Peterbilt hat. He came in most every day when he was back from a road trip. I could see him at his favorite seat through my order shelf window. We named him Peterbroke, 'cause he looked like a pretty broken trucker.

"I don't know why he tells me this stuff, Orca. Why would you tell a teenage girl you barely know about personal stuff like that? It's creepy."

"He needs to tell somebody, I guess."

"Well, he was stabbing at his waffles like he had some other target in mind."

That got me to thinking of them custom waffle molds I'd been reading about in my waffle club newsletter. I thought it would be a great idea for the Waffle Palace. Special waffles to celebrate special customers or special holidays. Special waffles to cheer folks up. Special waffles for loyal customers. So I said to Lil, "I'm thinking of getting some custom waffle molds cast for our irons. Like one for that angry trucker, maybe with a smiling semi-truck cab and grill."

"Wow, you can do that?"

"Well, I can send away a drawing and get the molds done."

"Oh, my gosh, that would be hysterical. And maybe you could make one for Miss Stinky. You know her, that sweet little old lady who reeks of cheap perfume and prays before she eats your waffles."

"No need to pray with my waffles; it was that old recipe that would kill you; folks should have prayed for survival every time they ate one. Maybe I could make a special one for Miss Stinky too. Maybe one that says, "God loves you."

"Perfect. Oh my gosh, did you know that she takes your waffles home? She puts the leftovers in her purse."

"Probably feeds them to her cats. All little old ladies have lots of cats."

"Boy, she was *really* jolly today. Did you notice?"

I shook my head.

"Well, anyway," Lil continued, "I found out why. Remember me telling you a while back about that broken side mirror on her old car, how she said it was just hanging off her car door about to drop? She was terrified because she thought she couldn't afford to fix it, and that the police would come and take away her car registration. She was praying for a miracle, she told me. Well, yesterday when she came in she was ecstatic. She said it *was* a miracle. The mirror was reattached. You'd think her dead husband had come back to life she was so happy."

I thought of Momma. Then I said, "Well, that'd be a whole lot nicer than a fixed car mirror."

"By the way, have you been feeling okay lately?" Lil asked.

"Why you asking me that?"

"That was a long bathroom break that I covered for you the other day."

"I'm fine."

"Orca, the bathroom door was open a foot the whole time."

"You peeking on me, Lil?"

"There was no one even in the bathroom. But then when I looked through the front window I saw this real big kid fiddling with a mirror on a customer's car."

"Well, it was an easy fix, Lil," I said.

"You're too much, Orca. You're going to heaven. You know that, don't you?"

I just looked down and fiddled with my cherry coke glass. Right about then Lil popped up from her chair. I was hoping and praying that she was going to hug me. But she headed for the radio on the counter. "Oh, my gosh! It's The Monkees! It's *I'm a Believer!*" She turned it up and started to sing along and dance all around the little break room. I'd never seen Lil like that. She knew every word.

I thought love was only true in fairy tales
Meant for someone else but not for me.
Love was out to get me
That's the way it seemed.
Disappointment haunted all my dreams.

Then I saw her face, now I'm a believer
Not a trace
Of doubt in my mind.
I'm in love, I'm a believer!
I couldn't leave her if I tried.

I thought love was more or less a given thing,
Seems the more I gave the less I got.
What's the use in tryin'?
All you get is pain.
When I needed sunshine I got rain.

Then I saw her face, now I'm a believer
Not a trace
Of doubt in my mind.
I'm in love, I'm a believer!
I couldn't leave her if I tried.

I didn't know what to make of it, except that I knew that song was about me. And maybe about Lil, too. Right then she twisted and twirled closer, and reached out her hand to me.

"Come on, Orca. You must know the mashed potato dance. Shake it up!"

Well, ain't no human on this planet wants to see Orca Bates "shake it up". But I did stand up, which was something I guess.

"Come on, Orca. Shake it," she said again, dancing away.

Instead, I rolled it, which was the best I could do, kind of rocking back and forth, caught like a barge in a cross current.

19
MONKEYING WITH A GOOD IDEA

Since I was now kind of a savior to Mr. Swade and even to Lil, I was figuring that maybe I should at least stick with the pain of Schloggle being around, and go down fighting for Lil instead of just fading away during all of his monkey business. I knew I had to do something really special. And then it hit me like a ton of bricks: the Monkees. Lil's favorite band was on its 1967 tour and coming to Minneapolis. Tickets would probably be a whole week's paycheck, but this was a no-brainer. My biggest fear was that I wouldn't be able to get up the courage to ask her. But then I knew she would never say no, no matter who asked her, because it was a once-in-a-lifetime opportunity. So I went ahead and bought the tickets. I also went out and bought a cool shirt; well, as cool a shirt as I could find in XXL size. It was paisley, all yellow and purple, with a big collar like the Monkees wore, and along with it I bought some bell bottom pants.

Funny, though, how things can turn on you just so sudden like and change your life, like those stories about how overnight the river makes a cut-through in a sharp bend and the next day you wake up and your house is located in the next county. Maybe if I had this ticket idea even a day earlier, or had bought the tickets and then asked Lil even a day earlier, it all would be different. But I waited and waited and waited until I thought the moment was just right, which turned out to be back by the punch clock at the end of a good shift. I stood behind Lil at that time clock, smelling that shampoo in her wonderful hair, holding the tickets in my big sweaty paw. I think Lil sensed something and she turned.

"Is everything okay, Orca?"

I just stood there, smiling like a dummy, and then handed her the tickets.

She blushed right up. "That is sooooo sweet, Orca." But she seemed more nervous than excited, and I couldn't make no sense of that at first. She looked down and mumbled, "But I'm already going."

First I just shrugged and looked over and stared at the schedule board behind the time clock. Then I looked away from her and wiped my eyes.

"Hey," Lil said. "Maybe we can see you there. That would be fun."

I knew that weren't going to happen. Even a dummy like me could figure out who the 'we' was.

20

COLD BEER FOR A BIG HOT BEAR
IN A SANDSTONE CAVE

I really felt like punching out that time clock after this happened. I was so bottled up inside I thought I'd explode. But I just walked out of the Palace, trying to take the high road and telling Lil I hoped she'd have a good time, but that I didn't want to use the tickets except with someone who really loved the Monkees. And that weren't me, to tell you the truth. Knowing I could easily scalp them and get my money back didn't make me feel any better. I was too down.

It was still really hot outside when I went out the back door of the Palace, and this didn't do the steam that was building inside me much good. I didn't want to go home to the apartment 'cause there weren't no air conditioning. So I headed down to the river. But even down there it was windless and hot. Then I thought of them sandstone caves. Then I thought of beer, cold beer. Beer for one big hot bear who was going to sit in a sandstone cave to cool off and do some thinking about his future. I knew there was always a couple of six packs that Daddy kept in reserve in the refrigerator. He'd be out drinking at The Slough by now, so I could go home and take one. He probably wouldn't remember whether he had one or two sixers in there anyway when he got back, and maybe I could replace it later if I could get one of them older decking guys from Shetland Barge to buy for me.

I grabbed the beer and my big six-volt flashlight, put them both in the small lunch cooler I took with me on the barges, and headed off, walking down to the river road and hoping I could hitch a ride on that two-mile stretch to the caves. But on the river road, which as I said before was kind of remote and woodsy, people in cars got nervous about stopping 'cause of the kind of characters that drift down that way. Most of the folks going to the caves have their reasons: they're running from something, or hiding from something; they're kids wanting to explore the caves or party in one; or they're teenage couples looking for a remote place to go parking, 'cause you can drive up right under them bluffs by the cave entrances. Oh, the cops swing by once in a while to check on things. Those cave entrances keep getting boarded up, but the kids just keep tearing them boards right down; and if they're really closed up good, the braver kids find these vent hole entrances up the hills on the bluffs, and use ropes to lower themselves down. I've seen one or two of those vent holes they've used, with the old ropes still hanging down in, tied to a tree at the other end. But mostly the cops seem to like to park there, so they can take their naps. Anyway, I'd have to get lucky that someone would recognize me and pick me up. And my luck wasn't running too good lately. But I did get lucky, and damned if it wasn't my new boss at Shetland, Bobby Driscoll, who picked me up. I felt kind of stupid, him seeing me walking by myself and carrying a cooler along that woodsy river road that pretty much leads to nowhere except the caves. I knew I had to think quick, which ain't my strong suit. So I just said the truth, which was it was damned hot out, we didn't have no air conditioning at home, and I liked nosing around in the caves. What I wanted to say was that I was really mixed up. I wanted to say that in the worst way. And I come close to saying it to Bobby, because there was something about him I wished I had in my old man.

"Not really safe in them things, Orca," Bobby said.

"I'm staying close by the entrance, Bobby, and I got a flashlight in this cooler."

"And maybe a beer or two?"

"Maybe that might be," I said.

"Well, you take care, and we'll see you tomorrow bright and early for crew change," he said, and he let me out right by a place called Carlson's Cave. Carlson's wasn't that popular 'cause it wasn't that deep or interesting, which was fine by me as I was only looking for a cool quiet place to think a bit, not an adventure. No one seemed to bother too hard about closing off the entrance and, like a tired, hot and angry bear, I lumbered on in. Shining my light around at all the graffiti on those light brown sandstone walls, I read some spray-painted messages from other teenage brains, like *South High Bites the Big One*—clever stuff like that. There was an old metal chair in there, a good, wide rigid one—them folding ones don't work for me—and I sat down close by the entrance. I didn't really need my flashlight, but I left it on anyway, shooting up at that rounded ceiling, to signal to anybody else coming in that someone was already there so go find your own cave.

The first beer went down pretty quick, and that beer, mixed with the cool air started to put me calmer for a bit. But then my thoughts got all jumbled, swirling, like some Mississippi backwater whirlpool. I pushed down two more beers while thinking about Momma, and what she'd say about what to do about everything with Lil and The Waffle Palace, and Shetland Barge. But mostly I couldn't stop my mind from thinking about Lil with that con-man Schloggle. I kept picturing them at the concert, Lil all excited and jumping up and down, and then Schloggle putting his skinny arms around her, and then later Lil getting into his Corvette, her face all flushed from the excitement of the concert, and then them going back to his apartment...

Well, that's when I had to change the channel on my thinker before the picture got too dark. So I turned to the future and thought, well, screw it, maybe I'll just be a hermit from now on. Stay away from love. Work the river, maybe work my way up to line boat captain someday, ship out down south, maybe a month on and a month off, buy myself a houseboat, get a couple of loyal kitty cats, come home to the boat between trips, play some poker with river friends, and maybe do my drinking at The Slough. Just like the old man. Well, that wouldn't be Momma's plan, that's for sure. But it would keep me from getting hurt again. No, Momma would say: Don't feel sorry for yourself, keep moving ahead no matter what. Rise above it all. Do good work. But I'm just too damn stupid to figure out how to do all that. And what's that mean, 'rise up above it all'? Put on a cape and fly around and save people? That'd be a sight. I looked around me. Here I was, a seventeen-year-old big fat kid sitting in a rusty chair, drinking beer alone in a cave on a late August Saturday, trying to figure it all out and 'rise above it all'.

I cracked the fifth beer, like I was going to find the answer at the bottom of the can. But what I found were more pictures of Schloggle and Lil. This was turning into a bad movie shot in a dark cave. I had to get out.

2 1

TANGLING WITH A CHEAP-SUITED MUSKRAT

It was dusk, almost dark, when this bear came out of hibernation. And I was a hungry one, ready to eat most anything that came my way. I was even madder when it dawned on me that I'd probably have to walk all the way home since no one was going to pick up a hitcher in the dark. It looked like nobody was around as I stumbled down the sandy slope in front of the cave entrance and started toward the river road. But then I heard the faint sound of music near the trees by the far end of the small turnaround space. Some couple's there parking—wish it were me, I thought. Even though I was in a pretty angry mood, I didn't want to scare them, so I headed out over by the other side of the turnaround. That's when I heard a girl's voice say 'no'. Then I heard 'Please, no!' Then, louder, I heard 'I said NO!'

I changed course right quick. I would have done that for anybody, I reckon. But also, I knew that voice. I knew that voice from during the day and I knew that voice from my dreams at night. And as I got closer, I knew that Corvette convertible. Schloggle had his arms wrapped around Lil, and was pulling her onto his lap in the driver's seat. I don't think either one of them saw me coming. I didn't say nothing, just ran over, reached out, picked him up by the collar, straight out of his seat and, like I was throwing a medicine ball, heaved him fifteen feet in the air. He landed in a half-dead juniper bush. I just stood there and looked at him.

"Oh, my God, Orca, what are you doing?" she hollers.

"Stopping him."

"Stopping him? He wasn't..."

"You said 'no', then 'please no', then 'NO'. You was begging him to stop hurting you, Lil," I said, my voice all raspy and winded.

"No, no, he wasn't really...I mean..."

And then, like I said earlier about the cops coming to Carlson's Cave for naps, well, right then was nappy time for a St. Paul police officer, and he pulled in just as old Schloggle was picking some of them thorny juniper stems off of his head and from out of his torn shirt. Even in the near darkness I could see that his forehead was already starting to show a big red lump, and he didn't waste no time hobbling over to the safety of the police car.

"That big guy there, he...he tried to kill me," he squealed as the cop opened the patrol car door. "You just missed it officer, didn't he, Lil. It's A&B, A&B," he said as he looked back and forth at Lil and the cop.

"You alright young lady?" the cop asked.

"I don't know what happened. I don't know. We were sitting here and Orca came out of nowhere. It's just confusing," she said.

"You know this boy?" the cop asked Lil.

"Yes, sir. We work at the same restaurant."

I knew right off by what Lil was saying that she weren't interested in righting the whole thing for me by playing the victim role and having me be her savior. No, I knew that I was one dead bear. In fact, I was so disgusted that I didn't say nothing. Just stood there, looking at my feet and shaking my head.

And so I got arrested for something, and it weren't for protecting Lil. Maybe it was going to be assault and battery (which I found out was the A&B that Schloggle kept screaming about). A&B—those are two letters I didn't see any of at grade time in high school, I thought to myself. Well, I finally might get a couple.

Being put in jail was like going from being a fish in the ocean your whole life to suddenly being dropped into a goldfish bowl, people staring in at you while you move 'round and 'round with nowhere to go, almost bouncing off the bars and walls, waiting for someone to come by and save you. Maybe them goldfish get used to it, but not this big whale. I can tell you this: if you wants to know the meaning of freedom, get yourself put in jail. Any dignity you once had gets left outside the jail door. Plus, when you're like me and you didn't do nothing wrong, then it's even worse.

But I wasn't the only goldfish in there. There was an Indian kid. Even younger than me. Long black hair down to his shoulders; he could have passed for a girl from the back. He sat on the bunk at the corner of the cell, his hands on his chin, just staring at the floor. He didn't say nothing to me, and I didn't say much to him either for some long while. I weren't in no mood to discuss the weather or about cops being especially mean to Indians, or me being wrongly put in jail. Finally, though, I got scared of the silence, 'cause it let my mind get filled up with all the bad things that had been happening—losing Lil, losing Momma, maybe losing my new decking job 'cause now I'd be missing my very first day. So I started talking to the Indian kid. All I could think of saying to him was what they always said in them prison movies. So I said it, "What you in for?"

The kid dropped his left hand from his chin and turned to look at me. I ain't much at noticing stuff but that kid had the brightest blue eyes I ever did see. I can sure remember that. I didn't think Indians even had blue eyes.

"Open bottle," he said.

"You shittin' me? They put you in here for an open bottle?"

"That and other stuff. Plus, I'm a minor."

"Well," I said, "I sure can't stand it in here."

"Safer than the street," he said. "You gettin' bailed out?"

"I doubt it. Momma is dead, Daddy is off drunk somewhere, most likely, and I ain't got a lot of friends with bail money."

"So what you in here for?"

"That's a good question. The guy I threw into the bushes is saying assault and battery."

"Then you're screwed, man."

"Well, it weren't assault and battery, I got to tell you. It were the opposite. I was trying to protect somebody."

But about then the kid started to lose interest, like he'd heard too many excuses all his life, and put his hands back under his chin and took to sulking again. Nobody said nothing for a really long time. So I got to thinking about getting out, and that got me to thinking about them Perry Mason episodes on TV with that Raymond Burr guy playing Perry Mason and him saving all them wrongly accused folks. I wondered if there weren't some real lawyer guy who could do this for me. I got to picturing old Schloggle in the court room and my lawyer guy firing questions at him 'til he folded up like he was full of bullets. I had Lil there, too, sitting in the back, realizing that I was really the hero and not the bad guy, and then the judge frees me and they take Schloggle.

"Your Momma die a long time ago?" the Indian kid says, kind of quietly.

"No, just happened," I said. But I didn't want to talk about that, so I changed the subject. "What's your bail?"

"A hundred bucks," he said.

"Won't your parents put it up for you?"

"They don't know I'm here. My mom said she'd put me in some juvenile delinquent home place if I ever got busted again. So if I ever get out, I ain't going home. And I ain't going to the JD place either."

"Where you gonna go then?"

"Well, they leave the side door open at the Sacred Heart Church in South St. Paul. I can sleep under the benches there. I done it before."

Then that Indian kid stood up and walked over to my side of the cell. He smiled just a little. I remember that because he never smiled before.

"One morning I woke up in there. Opened my eyes to this pair of old lady legs, legs with them, you know, them thick brown nylon stockings old ladies wear. Lady was kneeling right beside me while

I was sleeping under the pew. The bottom of one of her shoes was flat against the side of my face."

"I believe that would wake me up real quick," I said.

"Man, you should have seen the look on her face when she saw me, like I was some rat climbing out of a heating vent in the floor under the pew. I thought she was gonna die on the spot. Right there in front of me and God. Then she kept calling me 'child' and asking me why I wasn't sleeping at home. So I told her. Then she asked me if I ever stole anything or hurt anybody. I said 'no,' and then she said I could stay at her place 'til I made things right and until I found Jesus. But I said I weren't looking to find nobody, and I was fine here and then she asked if I would pray with her. I said 'no,' and then she asked if it were all right for her to pray for me. I said 'yeah'. I figured there couldn't be no harm in that."

Seemed to me that that was more talking than that kid had done in a year's time. He may have thought so too, 'cause he headed to the other side of the cell and sat down, putting his hands back under his chin. I just shuffled back and forth in front of the jail door for some time, leaning my head on them bars, being like that goldfish, just bumping here and there, trying to find a way out. After a while that got pretty old, so I just stretched out on that hard cot and tried to sleep.

Well, I did get out. Got out in the morning. Got out 'cause Lil bailed me out. I figured what she bailed me with was tip money from Waffle Palace customers (probably including Schloggle), but I didn't ask. After I collected my cooler and flashlight that they kept from me while I was in jail, we went outside and sat in Lil's dad's Valiant.

Lil was in her Waffle Palace waitress uniform. "How'd you get off work in the middle of morning rush?" I asked her.

But it was clear that Lil was none too happy about making small talk, and she didn't bother to answer my question. Instead, she said "Orca, I know you did what you thought was right. And that was sweet. But it was different than you think."

I just shook my head when she said that. I sat there, looking away from her and out my side window at nothing in particular.

"I was just trying to slow him down," she continued.

"I love you Lil, that's all," I said, still looking out the window. It just poured out of me like waffle batter onto a hot iron. Only there weren't no sizzle on the other end. There weren't nothing coming back from Lil, so finally I turned to look. She was looking down, her hand was squeezing her forehead, and she was crying. "I love you too, Orca, but in a different way. You need to understand that. Both ways are good."

"Art Schloggle ain't no good for you Lil," I said.

Lil started the car.

Nobody said nothing after that.

22

BACK TO THE PRESENT: THE ROUGH DIAMOND SAVES THE BLIND BIRD WATCHER

Anyway, as I was staring out my little window in this veterans' home for the hopeless and thinking about what a heap my life had become—what with losing Momma and Lil way back, losing *Cirrhosis* in that drunken card game, losing my towboat license 'cause of health issues, losing a couple of wives 'cause of drinking and being away too much down river, losing Cubby 'cause of what I did to Grampy in the end, and now, I reckon, for losing Toddy—well, I got to thinking about just jumping out. I hoisted myself out of the chair and leaned toward the window, but either it was too small or I was too big. Jesus, Red, I said out loud, you're even too big to kill yourself. Right about then I saw this red-checked hunting hat and a wheelchair rolling along the side driveway, moving kind of fast, maybe even out of control. I lifted open the window enough to get my head out and looked around the corner just as the wheelchair rolled over the embankment and disappeared. Oh, shit, I said out loud, and headed down the back fire stairs and out the side door. Some alarm went off when I opened it but I just kept going. My knees ain't too happy after sixty odd years of being stuck carrying 290 pounds, but I worked my way down to the bottom of the ravine. What I found was one crumpled wheelchair along with that 80-year-old Elvis-impersonating, blind bird watcher that Toddy wanted me to be friends with.

"You okay there, partner?" I said after catching my wind.

"I think so. Thank you. Thank you. I'm glad someone found me. I just had to get out here to get closer to the sound. It would be rare this late in the fall, but I swear I'd heard the characteristic four-tweet sound of a Prothonotary warbler."

"Well, I been known to travel many a mile for a glimpse of a beautiful woman, but never to listen to a silly bird. Look, let's get you picked up and maybe I can also fix your wheelchair."

"Okay. I think I'm fine. The wheelchair kind of protected me when it tipped over."

"Well, let's go careful anyway," I said.

"I'm Gil. You're Orca, right? I can tell by your diction and your raspy voice."

"Don't know about my diction, but that's me, partner. And call me Red."

And then I picked him up like a baby, and carried him up the embankment. Those bad knees were really overloaded, but I guess the rest of my body still had the horsepower for the job 'cause we made it. And there at the top was Toddy and a couple of them big staff guys.

"What have you done to him, Orca Bates?" Toddy asked as she ran toward us.

All I wanted to do was put Gil down and then get off my feet, but I also figured I'd get ready to duck fast when she tried to wallop me.

"What he did was save me, Miss Wihopa," Gil said to Toddy.

And that were that. In Toddy's mind, I went from someone who last week she said would pick a fight with Santa Claus to what she calls me now— 'The Rough Diamond'. I ain't sure where she's going with that, but I think it's another of them 'medifors' that Cubby taught me about way back, meaning it means something else than what it is.

23
SQUEEZING THE SHAMAN: ONE OF MY NEW LIFE GOALS

So I found out that Toddy is one of them shaman people. They're all about magic. I guess I'm not surprised, the way she talked about whale spirits and that I should be sending my emotions down river on a boat. I don't quite know how I'd get them bad emotions out of me and aboard, but maybe that's the shaman's business. Anyway, I know she's a shaman 'cause I went to her talk last night. Was just curious, I guess. I stayed in the back, half hidden behind that sliding curtain they put up to divide the room from the wretches that either want to learn something or look at her fine behind, and those that don't. I have to admit, I was mostly wanting to get out of my room and also add to my collection of Toddy visuals. I didn't expect to learn nothing.

Anyway, here's about how it went. Old Gil was right up in the front row in his wheelchair—now all fixed by me, I might add. Don't know why he was so close, seeing as he can't see nothing and has that super charged hearing that would probably let him hear Toddy from the other end of the building. Could be he wanted a sniff. Being a blind guy, I bet his smeller is pretty good, too. And Toddy does smell good, like clean sheets and oranges. Toddy had on some kind of pants suit, like that Clinton lady always wears, but on Toddy things look different; even a bad pants suit don't have a chance at hiding those curves of hers. Shaped like a Coke bottle,

Toddy is. Well, here's what I heard from my half-hiding position at the back of the room.

Today I'm going to speak about a subject many have heard of but perhaps know little about. It's called shamanism. I'm not going to get into my personal story too much, which was a quest I went on for three days when I was young, but I want to show you what I've learned from my people in the hope that you can use some of this to make your lives more balanced and rich. Someone once told me that it's good to begin a serious talk with something funny. But how do you say something funny about something as sacred as shamanism? Well, there once was this shaman who chose to walk the world barefoot, which caused his feet to blister a thousand times over. He ate only bugs and berries that he found in nature, which caused him to became very frail. This diet also caused him to be plagued with horribly bad breath. He was known as the Super Calloused Fragile Mystic Hexed by Halitosis.

Well, all them wretches that loved Toddy laughed their sorry little asses off. I thought it was pretty damned stupid. Then Toddy got all serious.

To begin, shamanic beliefs and practices have attracted the interest of anthropologists, archaeologists, historians, religious studies scholars, and psychologists. Hundreds of books and academic papers have been written on the subject. Shamans are intermediaries or messengers between the human world and the spirit worlds. Shamans are said to treat ailments and illnesses by mending the soul. Alleviating traumas affecting the soul or spirit restores the physical body to one of balance and wholeness. To me, shamanism is energy. And life is energy. And life is magic. And magic is in every inhalation of life. Energy is never destroyed, only recycled. That means there is always a fingerprint left behind. Native Americans, Vikings, ancient Celts, Aborigines...all the Old People of the Old Ways had old-school psychic chutzpah. They didn't have the science to explain stuff as we do today. But does that make their wisdom any less significant? We all feel energy in different places, from parts of nature, from a particular person or animal, even from the sky. We know it's there but, like the wind, we can't see it or touch it. So why do we doubt the spirit world? Why do we doubt things that are unexplained?

About then, good old Gil raises his hand. "Miss Wihopa," he says, "where do you get all *your* energy? You seem to have it in abundance." I hear some chuckles and Toddy smiles and laughs too, looking down a little and shaking that long shiny black hair.

In my case, as funny as it may sound, I get energy from big old trees. Flashes of a past life will come back when I'm alone in the woods. Old trees tell me stories, not with a human voice, but in a spiritual way. When I'm having a bad day and tired of the material life, I go and stand with my back against an old tree, and all that negativity disappears into the ground. In a short time I feel refreshed!

That's about when yours truly let go of the curtain and headed back to his room. All this spirit business was giving me a headache. Plus, I didn't want no one to see me showing an interest in this stuff. What if word got out to the river. Probably worse than being caught baking cookies.

The next day Toddy stopped by my room. She had that amused Mona Lisa smile on.

"Have a restful night last evening, Orca?"

"'Bout the same as usual, little lady."

She picked up my bib overalls off the floor, folded them in half, and put them on the top of my dresser.

"You know, I ain't a little kid," I said.

"No, you're more like a teenager. Little kids pick up their clothes." Then she turned to the window, opened it a crack, and looked out. "You left before I talked about the whale spirit," she said.

"Left where?"

"You're too big to hide behind a curtain, Orca Bates."

"Okay, you got me. But I been thinking, Toddy. After we do this outing down the river, what do you say we head out into the woods at Fort Snelling State Park and lean against a tree together?"

"It's a solo thing with the trees and me, Orca."

"Okay, two trees then?"

"You're incorrigible."

"Is that good?"

"No trees, Orca. But I will take you up on your river outing offer."

I just smiled, along with my heart. "You won't regret it, Toddy. And you'll be safe, even when we drive Monkey Rudder Bend. You'll be with me."

"That's the only part that makes me nervous—your monkeys—not the bend."

2 4

THIN ICE, LOCKS AND THOSE
DAMN BUTTRESS DAMS

I got back in touch with Retch and was able to figure a time that would work for us to get aboard *Elsie Mae* at Lock and Dam No. 1, Mile 847.9. It's between Minneapolis and St. Paul, just upstream of where the Mighty Miss and the Minnesota rivers meet. The dam used to be owned by the Ford Motor Company, which ran a hydro-electric power station there. Plenty of river current in that spot. Right below is Monkey Rudder Bend. On one side of the locks, to the east, there's an overflow dam—we river guys calls it a buttress dam or spillway.

The spillway is what really scares us river pilots, especially a cub pilot making his first run out of a lock chamber. He pictures losing power, or breaking his tow somehow just upstream of the lock chamber and spillway when the river's really running hard, then getting caught sideways, then the current shoving him over to the spillway, and then, well, it ain't good. Picture a couple of 195-foot barges and a towboat going sideways over Niagara Falls, only on a smaller scale. Actually, even after forty-odd years, I still gets a little scared near a lock and dam, mostly the overflow dam part, 'cause of something that happened way back in my early river days. But, like with what happened in 'Nam, I ain't going there.

And I sure won't say nothing to Toddy about the bad sides of this river work. Wouldn't want to scare her out of our big outing. But I guess about here's where I ought to say something about all this towing business. Towboats don't actually tow barges; they push them. Pushing barges, for a pilot, is 99% boredom and 1% terror. The 1% part includes pushing barges with a million gallons of gasoline through steel bridge spans in a fast-running river in the middle of a city in the dark of night. It ain't for those with weak hearts, especially when the head of the tow can be stretched out a couple of football fields in length ahead of you.

I believe that the largest tow ever pushed on the Miss was 72 barges: eight barges wide by nine long. A barge is 195 feet long by 35 feet wide, so you can do the math on that one, 'cause I can't. Them big tows is pushed by line boats up to 200 feet long with about 10,000 horsepower. Crew stay aboard 24x7 for 28 days, then they're off for 14 days. The smaller harbor boats, like the ones moving barges up and down short distances between South St. Paul and Minneapolis, are only about 55 feet long. These boats, like the *Elsie Mae*, can work 24x7, mostly bustling around to get the loaded grain barges all lined up in St. Paul for the big line boats to hook up to and take down river as far as New Orleans for the grain to be loaded on ships. It's one long trip—there's 27 locks they need to go through on the Upper Miss alone. The trip all the way down river is 2000 miles and can take 20 days at three miles an hour. Imagine driving your car 2000 miles at 3 miles an hour! Or worse, spending all that time with some chatterbox sitting next to you the whole time. On a towboat, a deckhand can leave the pilothouse if the captain is a chatterbox, but a captain can't go anywhere. No, when the captain has a deckhand who talks like he's been vaccinated with a phonograph needle, he'll tell him to shut up right quick.

The *Elsie Mae* is big for a local harbor towboat—75 feet long, 114 ton, two big 3508 Cat diesels, three decks, and painted white, red, and white from top deck down. The white pilothouse on top is the smallest deck, but big enough to hold me and a couple deck hands, with room left over to shoot plenty of bullshit. It's got windows all around and usually a long bench seat behind the captain's chair. Crew sometimes hang out on this bench, smoking, drinking coffee, and telling lies with the captain. Lots of stupid stuff and once in a great while something kinda profound gets said. This pilothouse is where most of the action is:—steering controls, throttles, radios, search lights, and a microphone connected to a loud hailer to yell at the deck crew, who can be standing 400 feet away from the pilothouse when handling lines at the head of the tow. If the crew don't like the captain, their only other choices for hanging out is on the first deck, either in the engine room or in the galley, which is right next to the engine room's screaming diesels. The second deck, which is a sleeping cabin, can't be used by crew when they're on duty. When it's nice out, some crew just climb out onto the tow and sit or sleep on the barge decks.

The plan was for Retch to be locking through at Lock 1 around 2 pm and end up in South Saint Paul at about 4:30, so me and Toddy was going to drive her car down river to the St. Paul Barge Company office barge, leave it there, get in the company's double cab pickup with the new crew, and drive back up river to Lock 1 to meet the *Elsie* for crew change. That way we'd have a car waiting for us downstream at the end of the day.

After arranging things with Retch, I headed out of my room to find Toddy. I didn't have to go far. She was walking down the main hallway, headed back from her yoga teachin, when I caught up with her. Because of them quality rear end visuals, I took my time catching up, sneaking along as best I could with my 290 pounds and bad knee.

She was holding that yoga mat of hers, the one with all that Native American design stuff on it, and she had on this new pair of matching yoga pants with all these tree shapes and flying thunderbird patterns and zigzags and bright colors. "Jesus, Toddy," I said, "If that rig you're hooked into don't brighten my life. You look like the tastiest Easter egg I ever did see."

"You like them, Orca?"

"I like anything on you or nothing at all. You know that, Toddy."

"Careful. That's one. Remember, two demerits and the outing's off."

"Well, that's what I come to tell you, Toddy. Just talked to Retch. We're all set for Wednesday. We'll be meeting the *Elsie* at 2 o'clock at Lock 1."

"Well, you'll be on thin ice until then. One demerit left."

"Anyway, it's only two days. I can keep my mouth shut for two days. Oh, and you should dress real warm. River can be chilly."

"Thank you. I'll dress appropriately."

"Well, don't show up in that outfit, or..."

"Or what, Orca?"

"Not going there, Toddy, 'cause I smells another one of them demerits if I do."

Even though I knew the pilothouse would be heated, steel towboats with steel decks, even in November, can be colder than a whore's heart, and I knew Toddy would want to step outside the pilothouse for two reasons. One would be to get a better look in Fort Snelling State Park for all them native animals. The other would be to get away from Retch's cigarette smoke and the sweaty and diesel-soaked clothes of them deck hands, who would surely be planning to sit close by Toddy. Few things is certain in life, but one is that river gossip moves faster than a fat kid at a cake buffet, and the Wednesday crew of the *Elsie Mae* would all know by now that female visuals and some sweet new odors was coming their way.

On Wednesday at noon I headed out of my room, wearing my old blue Carhartt jacket and carrying my handheld VHF radio. I waited for Toddy by the edge of the parking lot. I was right about it getting cold. I put my hands in my pockets and looked up at the sky. My mind took me back a ways. Those ain't like Cloud 23. Them's bad weather clouds, I thought. In this part of the world, even in November, winter can sneak right up and pounce on you. Could be snow coming tonight. Glad we're doing this outing now, I thought.

Right then a dented red Subaru Forester backed out of a parking space and stopped right beside me. On the rear window was a big decal; it said NATIVE AMERICAN PRIDE, with a feather on top and an arrow on the bottom of the words.

I opened the squeaky passenger door and leaned down. There was Toddy, looking as good as a stack of 100 dollar bills on my side of a poker table. She had on a tribal print pea coat with a fur collar, black leggings, and a pair of tall black leather boots. I stepped back and took in the whole scene, thinking how Retch was going to owe me one for this visual. "You need new sneakers, Toddy," I said. Toddy looked at me, and then looked at her boots.

"They're rubber soles and grip really well; they should be fine on the barge," she said.

"No, your tires, Toddy—them sneakers is almost bald."

"Okay, Orca. 'Sneakers' huh? Never heard that. Well, here we go, bad sneakers and all. Slide right in."

"Slide ain't the right word, Toddy. I don't slide in too good in these things. 'Jam' yourself in might be a better way to say it." I should have told Toddy how unbelievably cute she looked. That's what I should have done. Instead, by way of a compliment, I said this: "Forester? You got a Subaru *Forester*, Toddy? Them's for... You ain't one of *them* kind of women, I hope. Man, that would sure be a waste for the males of this world."

"That's a demerit. That's two now. Two and you're out, remember?"

"Now wait a minute, little lady, you said no go if I got two *before* we left. Technically, we've already left."

"I'm not gay. And there would be nothing wrong with that if I were."

"I'm just sayin'..."

"You've said enough."

Then she shifted into first gear and off we went down the hill.

"Stick shift, huh? You can drive a stick?"

"I can do a lot more than you've ever dreamed of, Orca Bates."

"Well, I'd like to dream about that."

I was in trouble again. But then, seems I'm always in trouble, and the rest of the time we didn't say nothing, except for me giving her directions until we got to the Saint Paul Barge Company.

2 5
KEEPING MY HEAD WHILE
DRIVING THE TOW

When we pulled into that gravel lot just above the ramp to the office barge, there was old Skid, pulling hard on the stub of a cigarette and leaning on the St. Paul Barge Company's crew cab pickup,

"Jesus, Skid, you still decking?" I said, sticking my head out the Forester's side window.

Skid flicked the cigarette into a muddy puddle by his feet.

"Still going, Red. What choice I got?"

"Well, you could die. At least, you *looks* like you could die."

"You always know just the right thing to say, Red."

"Well, I'm just sayin' maybe you should take it easy after all these years."

"So, you ready to go, Red? If you are, I'll get Butane."

I just nodded, and pulled myself out of Toddy's car as Skid headed for the office barge ramp.

"Hey, Toddy, you looking so pretty and all, well, can I borrow your phone and take your picture, just for posterior sake? My phone don't work."

"I know," she said, and handed me hers. "And it's 'posterity'; 'posterior' means...well, anyway, that fellow is named "Skid?" Toddy asked, as she got out of the car and started buttoning up her coat. "That's his name? And butane? What do we need butane for? Heat?"

I fiddled for a while with Toddy's cute little camera phone and snapped a fine shot of her standing there by the shop.

"I'm betting Butane's a deckhand, Toddy. He must be new on the river; a greenhorn. But Skid's been around a long time."

"I figured that from your dialog. Is Skid his real name?"

"Nobody's got a real name on the river, Toddy. Skid's name came 'cause he's always slipping and sliding on the barge decks. Amazing he's made it this far. Somehow he always seems to skid to a stop before he goes over."

Right then the office barge door slammed and I turned toward the ramp. Some beanpole of a guy in blue-and-white striped coveralls headed toward the company pickup. He had the narrowest head I ever did see, like it'd been squished by a vice, and what sprouted straight out of it was this flaming orange hair that looked like fireworks on the 4th.

"You Butane?" I asked.

"How'd you guess?"

"Just a long shot."

Toddy looked over at me and smiled. "And Retch? Do I want to know where he got *his* name?"

"Well, I ain't one to speak despairingly of somebody, but you might just think of the word 'wretched' to get your answer."

"Disparagingly."

"Huh?"

"The word is 'disparagingly'.

"No, I think the word for Retch is 'wretched'.

"No, when you said...oh, never mind, Orca."

Me and Toddy sat in the back part of the crew cab. It was a tight fit, which was fine by me. Toddy and me was knee to knee as Skid took the wheel, Butane climbed in, and we headed upriver along Shepard Road, up Cleveland Avenue South, and across the Ford Parkway to cross the Miss and pull up to Lock & Dam #1 to meet the *Elsie*. In the parking lot I could see Retch lining her up at the right bank lock wall.

"Is that the *Elsie Mae*?" Toddy asked.

"Yup, that's Retch moving her in pretty nice. He's a little out from the wall, but going okay. They'll be tied off in no time, then we'll climb onto one of his empties, then down from that onto the *Elsie*. The old crew will take the truck back to the office barge downstream."

"I'll be walking on one of those barges?"

"Well, yes, that'd be right, Toddy. Unless you skid and fall off, then I do believe you will be swimming in the lock chamber instead of walking on the barge. But don't worry, in that event I will gladly jump in after you, making the water level rise right quick in that chamber, and that will float you up onto dry land. Kind of like the two of us getting into a bath tub together."

"I think I'll pick drowning in the lock chamber then."

"Suit yourself, little lady. But, remember, I am your knight in Carhartt clothing, always here to serve, protect, and save you."

Then I just stared out at the tow, at *Elsie*, and at the black smoke from them twin exhausts, and listened to the sweet sound of them 3508 Cat diesels.

"You miss it, don't you, Orca?" Toddy said right then, putting her hand on my arm.

"It's only been a year since 'cause of my health I lost my towboat license, Toddy, but I miss it so much I can taste it."

"Well, the best thing about memories is making them. So let's make some more today."

Like Momma and Lil way back, Toddy could say just the right thing at the right time. What she said kind of got me, and made me look upriver, away from her, and rub some wet from my eyes, being real discreet like. Then, still looking away, I thought to myself, I'm starting to love you so much I'm bustin' out of myself. But you're too good. Too good for me, Toddy.

Toddy had no trouble getting aboard the barge and onto *Elsie*. It was yours truly, what with the weight and the bad knee, that had the problem. Toddy was careful not to help me along though. I reckon she knew to leave me and my dignity alone in front of these river folks. We walked along the barge deck and climbed down the steps that are welded to *Elsie's* pushing knees, which were up against the stern of the first barge. I took Toddy down the main deck walkway and we stuck our heads in the galley and then the engine room. Toddy grabbed onto one of the latches on the big steel watertight door leading into the engine room and looked in. "Pretty cool," she yelled over the sound of the engines.

"Yup, but mostly pretty hot," I said. "Let's head to the stern and climb the second deck ladder. I'll show you the bunk room; then we'll climb one more ladder up to the pilothouse and you can meet Retch." When we got to the second deck, I grabbed the handle to the bunk room door and then stopped. "This ain't the Ritz, Toddy," I said. "More like a man cave gone bad. You sure you want a look?"

"Maybe I should just use my imagination."

So we made our way to the pilothouse. On the way I began to worry about Retch. Or about what Retch might say. I turned back to Toddy. "Just a warning, Toddy," I said. "Retch is a little rough around the edges."

She tilted her head, put her hands on her hips and smiled. "And what are *you*, Orca? Smooth as a baby's bottom?"

"You got a point there, Toddy. Just sayin'. That's all."

Retch was barking orders out through the microphone of his loud hailer to his new crew out on the tow when we stepped into the pilot-house. "Fuckin' Butane," he said, to no one in particular. Then he turned to me and Toddy. "Oh, my company has arrived," he said. Then he bowed at us like we were friggin' counts or something.

"How they hangin', Retch," I said. "Been a while."

Retch smiled, showing us them few remaining yellow teeth of his; most either got knocked out or rotted out, I figured. Hell, you could kick a field goal through what was left. And then there was that scar. Somehow, I'd forgotten about that scar. It curved across his cheek and down to the corner of his mouth like somebody got only halfway through trying to carve a big pumpkin grin.

"Retch, this here is Toddy," I said.

Toddy stepped forward and stuck out her hand. "Actually, it's Wihopa. Orca, ah, Red, calls me Toddy."

"Well, whatever you calls yourself, nice to meet ya," Retch said. Then, after checking out Toddy pretty good, he looked over at me. "Lot of catching up to do, huh Red?"

"No doubt about that. River's running pretty good, Retch. All that rain we been having up north this month has done it. How's your schedule?"

"We're good. No need to push it hard through Monkey Rudder."

I cocked my head and looked at him. "You gettin' more cautious in your old age, Retch? More like Backin' Jack?"

"I ain't you, Red. Nobody's you."

"I'll take that as a compliment."

"Take it any way you want. Maybe *you* should drive this tow through the bend then, Red?"

"I'd *drive* her through Retch. You know that. No flanking through, like some old man in a wheelchair."

Retch thought for a minute, then stepped out of the pilothouse and checked how much lock water was left to drain before the doors would open and we'd head out. "River's running pretty hard to be driving the bend," he said. "Even for you."

"Excuse me, could one of you translate?" Toddy asked.

"Well, Toddy, it's like this," I said. "It's possible to *drive* two empties, instead of flank them, through Monkey Rudder, by going real fast and using that speed to keep your steerage. Kind of like in a Minnesota winter when you gets into a car skid. A scared rookie driver will brake to slow down. But then he'll lose his steering. Same thing here. If you flank the bend, you're going slow, like stepping on the brakes, so you're losing steerage thrust on your rudders, and also you're pulling back against the tow by reversing your engines to keep the towboat over in slacker water so you can let the current in the middle slowly carry them barges partly through the bend. Then when they've straightened out, you put the hammer down, and power through the rest of the way. It works, but it's slow. But when you *drive* the bend, Toddy, it's the opposite—full speed, balls to the wall all the way, giving you lots of steering thrust on your rudders, and making great time. Like them Olympic bobsleds on the television."

"But how can something so long and straight turn in a bend, no matter how fast it's going? I mean, if the tow is longer than the bend, well..."

"You'll never make it on the river, Toddy," I said. She started to look all hurt and sad before I continued. "Because you're too smart and curious for the likes of us, little lady. You're right. But I'll tell you: with this here particular bend, you *can* drive it with under 500 feet of total tow length. With two barges and *Elsie*, we're 465 feet; that's cutting it closer than two roaches on a bacon bit, so your line ups at each part of each bend has got to be perfect. Perfect."

"So then flanking is safer?" Toddy asked.

I looked over at Retch, and he smirked at me.

"Depends on who's driving," I said, looking back at Toddy. "Flanking is easier. And slower. And takes less skill." I looked downstream, toward the bend. "Flanking is for pussies, Toddy."

"But it don't take less skill, Red," Retch said.

"Much less skill and much less balls, Retch," I said.

"What if somebody is coming the other way when you're doing this, this driving the bend business?" Toddy asked.

"That's one big problem," Retch said.

"What's the other?"

"You don't make the bend, and you drive 400 feet of tow weighing 3000 tons into the bank and into whatever's on the bank."

"Oh, dear," Toddy said.

"Yeah," Retch continued. "I figure Red's about the only one left that can drive this bend and make it through when the river's running hard."

"Maybe," I said, feeling pretty good for once, feeling pretty alive.

"Red, why don't you take the sticks once I gets us down by the woods and out of sight of the lock tenders. No one will know, and I could use a break."

I smiled at him. "You ain't nervous about the bend today, Retch, because..."

"I ain't scared of nothing Red. You know that."

"So you ain't scared of me driving this bend?"

"If it gets me to my beer at The Slough any quicker, I'll take that chance."

About then Toddy hopped up on the bench seat at the back of the pilothouse, looking excited, like it were kickoff time at the Super Bowl. She chose a good spot. It got her up higher, and gave her good viewing through the front, side and stern windows as *Elsie* and her tow slid past the little scrub island below the dam and the head of the tow began to reach the woodsy area of Minnehaha Creek. About then Retch turned to me. "All yours, Cappy," he said, and stepped outside onto the side deck of the pilothouse.

Man, it felt good to take them sticks again. I throttled up right away, feeling all the power I knew was in them 3508s.

"What's all that shaking and black smoke?" Toddy asked, looking up through the rear window.

"That's kind of the diesel engines' version of letting off steam. I got her up to full power and I suspect the rings is bad; that's why she's giving off all that black smoke. It's been a tough life of pushing a lot of weight. Both for me and them engines, Toddy."

My mind flashed back through some heavy shit I'd pushed myself through over the years.

"Orca, you have your nitroglycerin pills with you like I asked, right?"

"Hell, Toddy, this is what my heart *needs* right now, not what's going to strain it," I said, as I moved the steering arms just a tad so as to start lining the whole tow up tight along the left bank to get my first approach just perfect. Just then Retch came back into the pilothouse, looking pretty tensed up. "You want one of my nitroglycerin pills, Retch? Looks like you could use one," I said.

"You're awful close to the left bank, ain't you Red?"

"Got to be, Retch. Got to be to get my line up for the first bend."

"You're hooked up pretty good on them throttles, too. She's really shakin'."

"3508s love running hard and hot. You know that, Retch."

"I'm just sayin'..."

"Look, Retch, you want to take her through, or you want *me* to take her through?"

"The way you got us hooked up and lined up now, what choice we got?" Retch said, shaking his head and heading back out to the side deck, slamming the door behind him.

"Ya see, Toddy," I said, "the thing about driving a bend is thinking ahead, sticking to your plan, and not losing your cool. The head of the tow is like one of them wide receivers in football, running out ahead way before the quarterback even gets ready to throw the ball, and then finally he does, and throws it high in the air, still nowhere near where that wide receiver is at that moment. But he knows there's a plan—he knows that boy is going to turn and end up under the ball. So it's like what's going on right now, where I'm aiming the head of the tow straight for the trees on the right bank, and it all looks like a disaster brewing unless you knows what I'm up to. But Retch, for all his years on the river, can't see it."

Damned if Retch don't right then come shooting back into the pilothouse.

"Jesus H. Christ, Red, you *got* to back her, at least to slow us down when we hit."

"We ain't going to hit, Retch," I said. "You got to have faith." And I turned back and looked at Toddy on the bench seat behind me. "Faith. Right, Toddy?" I said.

"Faith does not need to push the river, because faith is able to trust that there is a river. The river is flowing. We are in it."

"What, Toddy? That shaman stuff?"

"It's a Richard Rohr quote. He's a great teacher."

About then what I did was start singing, which is something I does when things gets a little heated up in my heart, especially now with Toddy right behind me. It was a Dylan song that come to mind and out my mouth while I was driving that bend:

> *Spirit on the water*
> *Darkness on the face of the deep*
> *I keep thinking about you baby*
> *I can't hardly sleep*

We didn't ever hit, and we *had* to be that close to the bank, 'cause I knew the second bend was the toughest, and I wanted every foot of floating space near that right bank to line up to make the last bend. And that we did. Sweet Jesus, it all felt so good, and I jumped into that last Dylan verse:

> *You think I'm over the hill*
> *You think I'm past my prime*
> *Let me see what you got*
> *We can have a whoppin' good time*

I looked over at Toddy, figuring she'd be—what's that big word that Cubby told me once – yeah, 'swooning' over me. She sat there on the bench, legs crossed, with one hand gripping her knee.

"Orca," she said, leaning forward, "Is there a ladies' room on this boat?"

Now this were a development I hadn't thought about. "Well, Toddy," I said, "I wouldn't call it a ladies' room exactly; 'basic facilities' would be more like it. And I can't speak for its condition."

"Anything's fine," she said.

"Remember you said that, little lady. It's off of the galley. I'll call Skid on the handheld. He can come up and show you the way." Toddy nodded. "You'll be safe with Skid. Just don't hold his hand, in case he slides over."

After Toddy and Skid left, I opened the pilothouse door to see why Retch hadn't come back in. He was leaning on the third deck railing, looking mighty pissed and relieved at once. "Come on in, Retch," I said. "You'll freeze your balls off out there." Retch came in and seemed pretty riled up still, not saying nothin' at first. I figured he'd be all happy with the time we was making, and be thinking about his early beer at The Slough.

"You're fuckin' lucky this time," he said finally.

"Screw you, Retch."

"Showin' off for some Injun squaw."

I let go of the sticks, turned and put my face up real close to his, and jabbed my finger in his chest. "Retch, what you going to do, blame a whole race of people 'cause thirty years ago you got your ugly face slit open and your stupid white ass kicked in a gang fight with some Indians in South Minneapolis? That it?"

"What the hell is up with you, Red? I do you a favor and bring you and your... your guest... aboard, and you get all righteous with me, like some mealy-mouthed liberal."

"Maybe I am getting righteous. Something wrong with that? And Toddy, by the way, has forgotten more than you ever learned. She's told me lots; can read folks and the earth like they're newspapers. The whole newspaper, not just your fuckin' sports page. You might listen to her and maybe learn something important for once in your sorry ass life."

Retch flicked his cigarette out the port side door. "You've gone around the bend, Red."

"No argument there, Retch."

"I'm going to take a leak."

"Figured you was all done with that," I said. "Figured you pissed in your pants in that first bend. But if you're going to the head, you'll have to wait. Toddy's in there."

"Well, I'll piss over the side then," he said, and headed out.

26
TODDY THINKS ABOUT THE ORIGINS OF THE EARTH, WHALES, THE EAST AND SALVATION; I THINKS ABOUT SUPPER

We was coming along the right bank under Fort Snelling now, and it seemed Skid and Toddy was beginning to be gone a long time. I figured maybe she weren't feeling good, and the condition of them 'facilities' on board weren't likely to help. But right then the door opened and there was Toddy.

"You all right, little lady? You been gone a long time."

"On our way back from my adventure in your facilities, I was telling Skid about our native history in this area along the river."

"You lived around here?"

"No, but my people did. A lot has happened on this stretch of the river, Orca."

"Funny, all these years, back and forth, up and down, I never thought about that. Good thing you're so curious, Toddy, 'cause I reckon you can stuff lots of important things in that pretty head of yours."

"It's more than just curiosity; this area right here is part of my heritage, and the earth around it belongs to all of us, so it's very important."

"Well, that being Fort Snelling, and it being a state park and all, I guess it do belong to all of us. Other than the fort, all I ever figured was in that park was trees and swamp, and, if we got lucky going by, maybe some topless ladies lying by the river."

"Well, in there are lakes, white-tailed deer, fox, woodchucks, turkeys, coyotes, turtles, and snakes. And spirits."

"Hell, Toddy, I thought I was going to show you around *my* world, and here you knows more about it than me."

"It's our world; and I bet I don't know more or less than you. Just different; plus, you're busy when you're coming through here, Orca."

"No, that ain't it, Toddy. I got as much time to be curious as the next person."

"Orca, just as you wanted to come back to your home here on the river and show me your knowledge and talent, I wanted to return to this same area to get close to where my people came from. That's one of the reasons I wanted to come on this outing. And maybe show you something, too. You see, way back, Mdewakanton Dakota Sioux lived in this area. In fact, this area where the Mississippi and Minnesota rivers join is thought to be the place of origin and the center of the earth."

"Seems Indians was always everywhere first. So, what the hell, why not start the whole earth. It's got to start somewhere, right? So why not with them empty-walkintowns."

"*MD WA CAN TON*".

"Yeah, them. Why not them?"

"Well, it didn't turn out so well, and—Orca, I think you should go to the right or left quickly—there's something in the water straight ahead!"

"Toddy, you just leave the driving to me. Give me this one thing to be better at than you. Anyway, I can't see nothing; where you looking?"

"You and I can't see it, but..."

"Magic, huh?"

"If you look carefully over there, you can see the head of a deer swimming toward the other bank. It changed course dramatically, as if it had encountered something large underwater."

"Like maybe a sunken tree? Well, I can't turn this rig that fast, Toddy; we'll have to cross our fingers." And by Jesus, if she weren't right. One of the biggest deadhead logs I ever did see—it was more like a whole tree—banged and slid along my tow. Coulda played hell with my rudders and props. "Hell, Toddy, you sure do notice stuff," I said. "That would have got me good."

"It's all about living in the moment, being aware, trying to pay attention. To everything. Everything is connected to everything else, I believe. Just like that deer and that tree and us on this tow. We're all born of nature and part of nature, part of a web of life."

"Well, you saved me from what would have been one really mad Retch. Wouldn't have helped my river reputation none either."

We went on for some time not saying nothing, just looking. Then Toddy spoke up.

"Orca, I should tell you that I have, well, this message from the universe."

"Well, hell, Toddy, that's got to be mighty important then. You going to share it?"

"It's not like that. It's a kind of vibration."

"Could be bad shaft alignment or loose engine mounts on them big Cat diesels below us, Toddy. That'll do it every time."

"No, this is spiritual, Orca. My spirit guide keeps telling me that I've been chosen to be your spirit guide."

"Well, you're doing pretty good at that so far, little lady. Mind telling me what these vibrations is like? If they're good, I should get me some."

"They're clues: the whale, the east, salvation."

About then I figured Toddy was maybe going 'round the bend on me. I can do about as much kooky stuff as the next guy, but where Toddy was going was pretty far out there, I figured.

"Did you ever go east, Orca?" she asked.

"Like the East Coast?"

"Well, yes. And even farther east?"

"I been even farther, Toddy. I been so far east that the only other direction I could go was back west."

"Like Vietnam?"

"I been there. We don't talk about that, Toddy. You know that," I said, just as Retch come up the steps and into the pilothouse. He was still giving me the cold shoulder, but for some reason that didn't bother me like it used to. "You want to take her through Omaha Bridge, Retch?" I asked.

"Might as well," he said, and so I moved away from the sticks and let Retch take *Elsie* the rest of the way home.

Me and Retch didn't say much of nothin' after that.

27

STEAKING MY CLAIM: SUPPER AT THE SLOUGH WITH TODDY

"I suppose this is a silly question, but are you hungry, Orca?" Toddy asked as we walked over to her car.

"Hungry enough to eat the balls off a fast-running bull, Toddy," I said.

Toddy shook her head slowly and smiled. "Couldn't you just say 'I'm really hungry'?"

"In the olden days, back when I was a teenager, that's just what I woulda said, but Cubby, he taught me to put in some visuals and shake some spices onto my words. You know, give 'em some character."

"They're certainly spicy. Orca, you mentioned Cubby when we first met, and…"

"I did?"

"Yes, when we first met in your room at the home."

"Well, I been forgetting things a lot lately. Hell, I've already forgotten how many times you told me you loved me and called me a sex magnet."

Toddy just got in the car, shaking her head some more. I squeezed into the front seat as she fired up that rice burner's tiny engine and popped it into first. Then she stopped. "Oh, I just remembered; there are snacks in the back that I'd brought for you and the crew, but like a dummy I never took them out of the car when we got here. They're behind me, Orca, in a cooler on the floor behind my seat. Help yourself."

"Don't mind if I do," I said, and reached around behind Toddy's seat to grab that little Playmate cooler. It reminded me of the one I had when I first started decking, after I dropped out of high school, the one with the tricky top where you had to find that secret button. I opened it up and looked in. "There's no food in here, Toddy," I said.

"Really? There has to be. I filled it."

"Nope, nothing Toddy, only celery sticks, carrots, what looks like some pieces of stale-looking pancakes, and a plastic container with something kind of yellow-brown and all mashed up inside. What is this stuff?"

"That's hummus. It's good for you."

"Sounds like one of them big military cars that them friggin' yuppies is driving these days. Anyway, how could something that looks like that be good for me?"

"It's a dip. You dip the carrots, celery sticks and pita bread into it."

"No, Toddy. I will not do that, at least not until I'm starving on some desert island and even then not 'til I know what's in this hummer stuff."

"Hummus. It's a Middle Eastern food made of chickpeas, olive oil, garlic, tahini, lemon juice, and salt. You might actually like it, you know."

"Nope. I'm taking my chances on that desert island," I said, and that seemed to do it, 'cause Toddy put her car back in gear and we headed out. I figured I must have hurt her feelings and all, what with me not appreciating nothing. But I couldn't find the words to say something right. Same old story. Couldn't find the words. Her shoulders started to shake like she was going to sob or cry and I started to feel even worse, but then she turned to me, and I saw that the shaking was from her laughing. "So where do we find a fast-running bull?" she asked.

"Closest place is The Slough. It's been a while since I been in there; used to go in quite a bit when I was working the river. And my daddy, hell, he wore a hole in most of the bar stools in that place. Anyway, I don't have to worry about him now. And I reckon the steaks and walleye is still good."

"Well, because this has been such an interesting day, Orca, this meal's on me."

* * *

"Jesus H, the place is packed," I said as Toddy rolled into The Slough's parking lot. "Park in that handicapped place right there Toddy. Them spots is always right up front and handy. That's why they give 'em that name."

"I'm not handicapped."

"Sure you are. You're with me, ain't you? That's one hell of a handicap."

"I'll let you out by the door, and then find a legitimate place," Toddy said.

"Hell, no. I ain't gonna get left by the door like some gimp. Who's gonna protect you as you walk across this dark parking lot?"

Then Toddy did something that hit me smack in the heart. She stopped, turned off the car, and leaned right up to me, straight faced, all steady like and staring. It was like she was just knowing everything, like that daily llama guy.

"You would, too. Wouldn't you?" she said.

"Would, too, what?"

"You would protect me. Or you'd die trying. Wouldn't you?"

My heart was going so fast I wanted to reach into my pocket for that little bottle of nitro pills. "Hell, Toddy," I said finally, "I got to eat, and with you buying supper for me and all, I got to get you safely into The Slough, don't I? It's just like that evolution guy said, 'survival of the fittest'."

"Darwin."

"Yeah, him."

The Slough is actually one of them things they calls a supper club in the Midwest. But it ain't a club 'cause anybody can get in and go in. It's one level and made to look like a cabin, with fake log siding on the front. The other side is for the function hall, with cheap-looking shingles, like they run out of that fake log shit and got a deal on the other stuff at Home Depot. It's got a couple small windows, one with a neon Grain Belt beer sign. There's also a big sign out front that sits on top of a long metal pole. On the sign it says *The Slough Supper Club -- Casual Dining and Drink*, and under that is a giant martini glass tipped sideways. Out front of that sign, on a little trailer, is one of them mobile signs where you can change the message. Me and Toddy stopped and stared at it. It said:

Bacon is red,
Steak can be blue
Poems are hard
eat here.

Toddy started chuckling.

"Pretty shitty poem, Toddy," I said. "Sounds like something that I woulda wrote. It don't even rhyme. Owner must have told some kid bartender to make a sign to drum up business. Kid couldn't do it."

"Orca, it's funny. Don't you..."

"Steak ain't even blue, Toddy."

* * *

When we got inside, there was a line of folks waiting in front of that podium thing; behind it was this nervous looking little hostess. "Maybe we should try somewhere else," Toddy said.

"Don't you worry, little lady, once we slip her a C-note, all will be good."

"What's a C-note?"

"A hundred dollar bill."

"You have a hundred dollar bill?"

"No. But I did once."

"Well, she looks pretty frazzled. Let's try someplace else."

"I don't know, Toddy. I got my heart set on a big pile of steak and potatoes in this place. Let's just hang on a few minutes and see," I said. When we got up to the podium thing I could see what Toddy meant; that hostess—name tag said her name was Heidi—was more nervous than a turkey in November, holding her clipboard, looking this way and that, running her hand over the top of her head. "Good evening," I said, all formal like. She looked up at me and Toddy.

"How many? Two?"

"No, no. Not two—46. A busload of forty-six seniors in wheelchairs. They're out of the bus, in the parking lot now. Getting kind of cold out there. Anyway, we called ahead. Talked to the manager. Manager said it'll all be fine and Heidi would take care of it."

Toddy kicked me in the shin about when that little missy was looking like she was gonna put a steak knife into her heart. Then Toddy leaned in to her. "He thinks he's funny. He's not. And we can go someplace else. So sorry."

Heidi looked mighty relieved. "No, no. If you're just two, I can do that. It seems that all the others waiting are parties of four or more. I can put you in the corner, over by that window and fireplace."

And so me and Toddy got our own table under the window with the neon Grain Belt sign and in front of the fake fireplace, which had a plug coming out of the side of it; and them fake logs, which looked like painted-up plastic, glowed in the middle like they was radioactive. "Wonder what forest you find them logs in, Toddy?" I said. About then I spotted that big table filled with them free cruddy trays and a giant loaf of bread with orange cheese oozing out the middle. "I think I might grab me some of them cruddy trays, Toddy. You want some?"

"Crudités. And no thank you. Orca, why did you DO that?"

"Do what?"

"Do that to that poor girl?"

"I was helping her, Toddy."

"Helping her?"

"Yeah. Cubby said once that 'everything is relative' and I knows what that means."

"What?"

"See, I didn't have that C-note for her, but I knew that little lady needed some relief real bad. So I had to make some relief."

"What are you *talking* about?"

"I figured she needed to see how much worse things could really be. So I showed her. Pure genius, that's what I'm thinking it was. Something that genius guy with the long white hair sticking up woulda done."

"That's Einstein. Theory of relativity. And that's different, Orca. So you showed her how much worse things could be?"

"Yeah, made her all better. Mostly." Then, before the old me could catch myself, I said, "Kind of like what you been doing with me."

Toddy leaned toward me, looked me in the eyes, and put her hands under her chin.

"I do hope I'm being helpful, Orca."

"Dinner and a pitcher of beer is a big start, Toddy," I said, all nervous, knowing even as I said it that it weren't the right thing to say. The right thing to say, what I wanted to say, what my heart wanted to say, was that I loved that she cared. Like Momma. Like Lil. Like Jiminy Cricket.

Of course, right then this young waitress comes by. Why is it that them waiters and waitresses always show up at the worst possible times? I remember when Denise, my first wife, and me was splitting up. We was in a restaurant at a little table just like this and she were madder than a Montana bobcat, sayin' she never loved me, that I wouldn't give her no children, that I was always barging around, never making enough money, and never home. She was so mad she was spittin' the words at me. She was boiling, no 'seething'—that's a good word for it. Cubby used it a few times way back, about how he felt about what they done to Grampy. And then, sure enough, this waitress come sashaying by, tilting her head and grinning from ear to ear, just overflowing with pleasantness, and she says, "And how are WE doing this evening?"

And Denise, looking like that girl in *The Exorcist*, eyes wide, with spittle now dripping down her chin, turns to the little creature and says, real loud,

"AND HOW THE FUCK DO YOU *THINK* WE ARE THIS EVENING?"

Yup, that Denise, she was a wild one.

Anyway, the waitress that me and Toddy had didn't have the best timing either, but maybe that was just fine; maybe her coming by right then kept me from saying something that wouldn't have come out right anyway.

I ordered The Slough's large pitcher of beer.

"I'm sorry, Orca, I don't drink beer," Toddy said.

"I suspected that, Toddy. This here pitcher is for me, if you don't mind. But I'll bet you'll want yourself a white wine."

Toddy looked at the waitress and said, "I'll just have soda water and lime, thank you." After the waitress left Toddy said, "I don't drink, Orca."

"You got yourself a problem? Well, I knows lots of people that does. And I got no beef with that."

"No, it's because of a number of things. One is that a lot of Native Americans have an enzyme deficiency, so our bodies usually break down ethanol into water and acid way slower than other races. Because of that, our risk of alcoholism is greatly increased."

"So the Irish, they must have bucket loads of this enzyme?"

"No, I think they simply drink more because they want to and their culture has set high alcohol consumption levels as kind of a 'standard'."

"Well, I don't want nothing to mess with that good brain of yours, Toddy."

"Thank you, Orca."

So, after I got done with a pile of meatballs and gravy, which I soaked up with some big hunks of bread filled with that Velveeta cheese, I was ready for the main course. Even though the prime rib, which the menu said was 'two huge pink slabs surrounded with hunks of white fat,' looked pretty tasty, I stayed with my plan of having a big steak. When the waitress come by again to take our order, Toddy asked her why such a big crowd tonight, and she said there was this high school reunion going on in the function hall. South St. Paul High, she said.

"Well, I'll be," I said. "Went there myself. Partly anyway."

"It's the 45th!" the young waitress said, like she were imagining the Stone Age, with a cave packed full of Fred and Wilma Flintstone types.

"Anyway, I'll have the big man's prime sirloin, two baked potatoes, and creamed corn to get me rolling," I said. Toddy ordered the chef's salad.

"Did you come in here often after work, Orca?" Toddy asked.

"Many a time, Toddy. See that round table over there? That's where me and my crew would stake our claim. I remember this tiny waitress we had one time; I think it might have been day one on the job for the little lady. She come by, all nervous in the face of us nasty river men, like we was gonna shanghai her, put her in the bilge, and take her away down river. Well, I just took that tiny hand of hers in my giant paw, and put into it a C-note, and said, "Sweetie, I want you to fill the top of this round table with Grain Belt beer bottles 'til you can't see the top no more. Then kindly go away, 'cause we don't want no interrruptin' as we got some cards to play and some stories to tell, and it's been one long day on the river."

"That was sweet...in your own special way, I guess," Toddy said. Then she excused herself for the ladies' room. Now here's where I wants to go on record that yours truly stood up when Toddy got up.

Momma told me once that that was a sign of respect for a woman, so I figured I'd try it out and see what happened. But nothing happened, except that I felt like an idiot. I stood up. Toddy headed off to the ladies room. And then I'm just standing there, all alone by my seat, everybody staring at me, but I got nowhere to go but back down in my chair again. Momma said something about this being chivalry, but I couldn't figure that; I didn't protect nobody and I weren't wearing no armor, even if we was sitting at a round table. So I kind of looked around me like a goof and sat back down. But then I didn't have nothing to do but sit there, so I got up and went back to the cruddy tray table (though I took it kinda light this round, so as not to spoil my appetite). I finished a few more meatballs and still no Toddy back from the ladies' room. Since us men is mostly the ones with the beer-filled bladders, I always wondered why the ladies' rooms had lines outside when men's rooms—except at hockey and baseball games—is usually like a morgue. Now, I knows that men got a lot less to do in the restroom, plus we do things quick. We goes in fast 'cause we're filled with beer we held too long, and straight to the urinals, unzip, stare straight ahead at the wall 12 inches from our noses, re-zip, run about three drops of water over our hands, maybe try a quick look in the mirror to see if something is stuck between our teeth, and head on out. And we don't talk to nobody. Ever.

Women is different. I figure they go in there for lots of reasons and this is why it takes so long: I bet it's 'cause they need to get some time away from the boring guy they're with. They need to check their hair and makeup, they need to talk with total stranger women about them same men they're getting away from—or about their clothes or where they got their lipstick—and then, maybe, just maybe, they need to take a leak. And then, if they got some one-piece jumpsuit on or that panty hoses stuff, well, the leak part is a real time sapper. Yup, as much as I loves women, I'm glad I ain't one.

When Toddy came back I could tell she was all excited about something. I stood up again, figuring that chivalry rule must be for both going and coming.

"Orca, I was chatting with the nicest lady, Julie, in the ladies' room, and told her that you were in the same high school class but didn't know about the reunion, and that you were right out here in the dining room. I gave her your name. She didn't go to your high school, but her husband did, and she's going to see if he remembers you."

I kinda looked down and shook my head. "Toddy, it ain't my class. It ain't my class 'cause I didn't finish. That's why I weren't invited. No sense in me being there," I said, and stabbed at my last meatball.

"Maybe you should go into the function room after we eat?"

"No."

"Well, the best way to rekindle..."

"No," I said again. But I felt bad deep down, what with all these things Toddy was trying to do for me, so I said, "Thanks, Toddy. I'm getting ready to move on, not go back. And right now what I'd love to move on to is the big man's prime sirloin, if it ever gets here."

"Here she comes now," Toddy said, smiling and getting up from her chair. "And I think that must be her husband with her."

I figured I'd better stand up again, 'cause Toddy did and apparently we was having company.

"Hello, again," this tall, blond-haired lady said, reaching out and shaking Toddy's hand. Then Toddy turned to me. "Orca, this is Julie and..."

"Oh, and this is my husband Walter," Julie said and they both stepped a little closer and smiled. This Walter guy, a little guy, kind of bowed his head at Toddy but was mostly looking at me, and was kind of lit up all over, like he'd just found the daily llama, right here in The Slough. I reached out and shook his hand. "I'm Orca Bates," I said.

"I know. Believe me, I know," the little guy said. He looked over at his wife and they both smiled at each other.

"We was in school together?" I asked. "Sorry, been a long time."

"We were in homeroom together, freshman year. If it weren't for you I think I never would have finished school, would have dropped out," he said. Then he shook his head. "Maybe worse."

Right about then his wife chimed in, all gushy like. "You stopped those two bullies who had been making his life miserable since junior high. Every time we talk about high school he brings that up. Everything changed for the better after that." She put her arm through Walter's, and leaned against him.

Walter kind of bit his lip and then reached out again and shook my hand. "You don't forget stuff like that. Ever," he said.

It all came back to me right quick after that, and I said "You know, something always puzzled me about that. I never told nobody what I did."

"Well, it got out. Everybody knew. And that was good enough for me. All the way through the rest of high school nobody bothered me. I came out of hiding, out of my shell, and senior year was great. So thank you," Walter said. I just looked down at the carpet and smiled. "But something always puzzled me, too," he continued. "What was in it for you? I mean, why'd you do it? You hardly knew me; I was just this nerdy scared little red-headed kid one row over in homeroom."

I thought about that for a while—kind of a long while. Everybody looked at me, expecting an answer. But I couldn't find the words. The words I was thinking though was that I knew what he was going through 'cause it's just as hard to be really big as it is to be really little.

Then Toddy looked at me, all proud like, and said, "Orca saves people. It's what he does."

* * *

It were turning into one of the finest days, and now nights, for me in a real long time. First, driving that bend, then Toddy saying that compliment and being all proud of me and all, and now in comes the big man's prime sirloin. Done just perfect. I got to eating away, with Toddy munching along on her rabbit food. I started thinking about them two bilge slugs, Harlan and Max. I put down my fork, just temporary, and said, "Just for the record, Toddy, I never laid a hand on either one of them bullies."

"I believe you Orca. I was wondering, though, since we're into the past, can you tell me a bit about this Cubby fellow you keep mentioning?"

"Cubby was my roommate, well, my tenant, about a million decades ago, on board *Cirrhosis*. He was a college kid, from out east, going to school in St. Paul. He needed a place to live, liked things that float, and answered my ad. I was done with having wives, pretty broke, lost the house to Lenore, and had been living on *Cirrhosis*, which I bought for four grand when I was flush from a long tow job on the Illinois River. She was just a steel hull, fifty foot or so, with a wood frame house on her. Built the insides myself. Not bad, actually. Anyway, I figured some cash rent would give me the pocket money I needed and I could stay under Lenore's radar. So I put an ad in the St. Paul paper; it were pretty good. Said something like:

> Want real romance living? Live on *Cirrhosis* the houseboat under the bridge on the Miss near downtown St. Paul. $125 (cash) a month. I lives there to but I won't bother you none. You gets a good roof (tarred it myself), own room with pretty tight window, some electricity (comes and goes). Good wood stove (wood included). No flush toilet (but good porta potty; need to take turns dumping it). P.s. girls is fine, either having them aboard or being one, I don't discretionate. Also, I'm a waffle connasewer, so I makes great waffles for all on board.

"That ad *worked*?" Toddy said.

"It got me Cubby. He was the only one to apply though."

"Why is a kid from out east going to St. Paul for school?"

"He said he really needed to get away from some stuff out east. Switched to college here." As soon as I said that I remembered some mighty important stuff I'd left in the storage bilge on *Cirrhosis* after I lost her in that card game. I knew Webb was downriver working that line boat for at least another few days. I knew where the key was. And I knew I had to get that box of stuff.

"Toddy," I said, I need to get some of my stuff off of *Cirrhosis*. Mind if we stop on the way back?"

"I'd love to see it, Orca. But I thought it wasn't yours anymore?"

"It ain't, but Webb don't have no problem with me going aboard."

So we headed out of The Slough. I wondered if I'd ever put eyes on the place again. Well, I was thinking, this was a good way to end it, and me and Toddy stepped outside.

"Oh my, Orca, it's snowing. Big huge flakes. How wonderful."

"Hold on to my arm there, Toddy," I said. And we headed out to the car, and then down to the river.

28

Opening the Floodgates One Snowy Night on Cirrhosis

Even when the flowers was blooming in May, Grouchy's Marina weren't no spring picnic. And now, in November, with everything cold and dark and the trees like skeletons, the place felt more like a floating tenement row than a marina for pleasure boats. There was about twenty of us living aboard when I was last here on *Cirrhosis*. Most of the houseboats looked more like giant floating boxes patched together out of plywood, pressboard, aluminum, and steel, and tied to rickety, rusty, and rotten wood-planked docks that ran along the muddy right bank of the Miss.

Most of us ended up living here for a bunch of reasons: divorce, drugs and alcohol, debt, mental illness, or from just being a social misfit. There was a few true river rats or romantics that loved living afloat, and we was all mixed in with some real river rats, though mostly they minded their own business, staying in the water by the riverbank. When I was last here on *Cirrhosis* my neighbors were a non-talking hermit nicknamed 'Meltdown' on the *Broken Promise*, a couple of hard-drinking towboat pilots on the *Tom Thumb* and the *Beaver*, and an over-the-hill playboy on a sagging houseboat named *Puss E*.

Mostly we was a core group. Once in a while there'd be a new arrival, usually in the form of a lady friend moving in with one of us, sucked in by the romance of it all in the summer. But that didn't last. We were what Cubby called 'a static bunch'; most of us and our houseboats didn't go nowhere, our motors long ago frozen up from lack of care or money to fix 'em. And the occasional lady friends broke off sooner or later, drifting away to find better neighborhoods and better men. Then we was back to each other. This was okay — until winter. Then our bunch of misfits pulled even more inside ourselves, taking cover in our flimsy frozen-in boxes, hiding from the whining north wind, and praying that the heaving, grinding ice wouldn't spring a weld in our hulls, and cause us to go down when the spring thaw came.

"Watch your step there Toddy," I said as we worked our way along them rickety wooden stairs that led down the steep bank from the parking lot. "Hang on to the railing; probably smarter than hanging on to me."

"It's not very well lit," Toddy said.

"Nothing's very well anything around here, even though this place used to be run by one of the kindest river men I ever met. Named Gordy. Always smiling. Always a hello."

"Why is it called Grouchy's then?"

"That's what folks call Gordy. It's his marina."

"Yes, but if he is always cheerful..."

"Things don't make a lot of sense down here Toddy," I said as we got to the bottom of the stairs and headed down the marina docks toward *Cirrhosis*. Toddy put her arm through mine and held on tight. The river hadn't frozen hard yet, not even in the quiet water near the bank, and the docks was narrow and slippery and rocked and tilted (especially on my side) as we walked.

"That's the *Puss E*," I said. "Looks like she's got one foot in the grave. That guy owns her must be one old playboy by now." There was a blue light inside, lighting up one of them cheap velvet paintings of some nude woman, that was hanging on the wall over a giant couch.

"Why the name?"

"Oh, come on, Toddy."

"He likes cats?"

"You're playing with me now, Toddy. I know you are. Anyway, hang on tight. And we should look down, not ahead." But then I stopped, breaking my own rule, and looked at a few of these unlighted docks ahead, with all that snow piling up steady on them slippery planks. "You know, now that I think about it, maybe I should help you back to the car and I'll go back to the boat and get what I need. This ain't a place for a lady, snows really coming down, it's gettin' cold, and you not bein' safe down here..."

"I'm safe with you, Orca. And I'd like to see the boat."

We kept going down the docks. I knew *Cirrhosis* was tied up at the very end, almost under the Wabasha Street bridge, which crossed the river from South St. Paul to downtown St. Paul. We was doing fine until we spooked a couple of ducks that was under one of the dock sections. Toddy jumped up, then landed pretty hard and slipped. But I still had her arm and kept her from falling all the way.

"Oh, dear. I think I twisted my ankle Orca." She balanced on one leg. "I shouldn't put weight on it."

"Well, don't hop Toddy. Too slippery."

"Is there perhaps some ice on the boat? I should ice it."

"Probably plenty of ice cubes for Webb's cocktails," I said, and then, before really even thinking about it, I said, "Put your arm around my shoulder, Toddy."

"I can't reach your shoulder, Orca. You're too tall."

So I did one of them deep knee bends like they does on them TV exercise shows and got down to Toddy's level. My bad knee weren't too happy about this. Once Toddy had her arm around my shoulder, I reached down under her knees and picked her up, bridal style. She gave a little chirp. "Don't you worry none, Toddy," I said, "I'm carrying you to safety, down the aisle of Grouchy's Marina and over the thrushhold into the safety of *Cirrhosis*."

It was probably the first time in history a person with a sprained ankle started laughing. That done my heart real good.

I put Toddy down real gentle like and bent down and felt around for the key. Sure enough, it was still right there on the cup hook I'd screwed onto the back of my old barbeque grill, which sat there on the front deck, 10,000 burgers later.

"Don't worry, Orca," Toddy said when I started to pick her up again. "I can hop over that 'thrushhold'." I opened the door, which stuck a little like it always did, and felt around 'til I found the lamp I used to keep on the dashboard by the old steel steering wheel, and, fingers crossed, switched it on. "We got power, Toddy," I said. "That's a real good thing. Means we got heat too, most likely." I held the door as Toddy hopped inside. "Plop yourself right down on that couch," I said. Toddy looked at the couch with suspicion. It did look different. I remembered it used to have black and white stripes but now there weren't much white there. Must be the dirt filling in the white stripes over the years, I figured. "Don't worry; nothin's gonna bite you Toddy," I said. "Them bugs that live in that thing always go south for the winter." Toddy hopped over and sat herself down on the end that didn't have no holes, while I turned on both them old electric space heaters.

"Oh, my, it's really pretty cozy in here. And there's a steering wheel and controls right in the living room," Toddy said.

"That'd be true, Toddy. This used to be a noble vessel that actually moved and went places. I could drive *Cirrhosis* right from my living room couch. Now how many folks can say that! Everything's all froze up now, though: controls, steering, and both them Ford 302 engines in the stern. If you could walk, I'd give you the tour, but you can see most of it from there. I bought this boat when it was named *Wylie's Ark,* and was owned by an eccentric St. Paul millionaire who just loved puttering around on it and having a place to go to get away from his business world. He never bothered to finish the inside, just had a big empty room with an old wood stove in the middle. The front deck had the same barbeque grill; back deck had a big stack of firewood next to the engine room hatches. Wood stove, gas engines. Even Wylie couldn't insure it; and he owned an insurance company! Anyway, after I got the boat I separated the big room into this here living room and two small bunkrooms. Also made a little room for the head and space for a big water storage tank for the winter when there weren't no fresh water on the docks. Used to carry water in five gallon jugs down here from the marina office. Anyway, I insulated the walls, finished everything in knotty pine and cedar— still smells good, don't it?—put down this brown shag carpet, and built this little kitchen with that fake butcher block counter stuff. And I had myself a new house!"

"I'm impressed, Orca. You're pretty handy," Toddy said as she looked around. "I've never seen windows like this."

"They came with the boat. Wylie told me they was old windows from Minneapolis street cars they was scrapping. Weren't too tight, so, like I see Webb done here, I used to tack plastic over the outside of each one in the winter."

"That must have made your world opaque," Toddy said, and smiled.

"I don't know what that word means, Toddy."

"It means cloudy, blurred, non-transparent."

"Well, it made my world warmer."

"Yes, I understand, I was just making a ... no, that's good Orca. I got it."

"Well, you just relax and warm up while I gets to looking for them ice cubes. Then I'll look for that stuff of mine," I said and made my way to the kitchen area, opened that mini-fridge and found a plastic tray of cubes in the little freezer part, leaning against a half-eaten Dove bar. "Got the ice cubes, Toddy; I'll wrap 'em in a towel," I said as I pulled them out.

"Thank you. I think I'll need your help on something else," she said. "Could you help me remove my boot from this bad foot?"

I got all nervous right then, but brought the ice pack I'd made and handed it to her. "I don't know, Toddy. You know I'm a big, strong, clumsy guy, and I don't want to hurt you none. I just don't want to hurt you none."

"We'll go slow. The boot's all unzipped. You just need to pull it straight down and slowly." Then Toddy leaned back on the couch and stretched her foot out. I got down on my knees on the rug and picked up her bad foot like it were a glass slipper. But I just couldn't pull.

"It's only a slight sprain; you won't break my foot, Orca."

And so I started to pull the boot off, real careful, like I was delivering a baby. I felt Toddy wince, and I looked up at her. There was tears flowing from them beautiful eyes of hers, and I stopped 'cause this hurting was taking me deep into some place I don't go.

"Keep going, Orca; the boot's coming off. I'll be fine. Trust me. Keep going. I trust you."

'I trust you' is what broke the dam. For a long time I'd been keeping them words dammed up from the rest of my daily thinking, locked away in the back of my head. They wasn't allowed to come out because they was hooked onto some real bad memories from when some other folks trusted me, and I let them down. But this time, when Toddy said them, with her in that pain and all, and 'cause of the way my heart now was with her, well, I couldn't stop them. They jumped right out and surged over me, broke the dam, and the bad stuff poured out. I just started sobbing and sobbing, like some big blubbering whale, my head bent down on my big heaving chest, and I rocked away, back and forth, back and forth.

I felt Toddy's hand on my head, rubbing it softly. It was like that hand made them inside feelings turn into words, and out they spurted, like pus from an infected blister.

"People died 'cause of me, Toddy. Died 'cause of me," I kept saying, my eyes shut, while rocking away.

And then I heard singing:

Wani wachiyelo Ate omakiyayo
Atay nimichikun
Oshiya chichiyelo
Wani wachiyelo Atay omakiyayo
Wani wachiyelo Atay

And then Toddy sang it again. And again. After that she starting saying this prayer, rocking away with me, her hand still stroking
my head:

> *Great Spirit,*
> *whose voice I hear in the winds*
> *and whose breath gives life to all the world, hear me.*
> *I am small and weak.*
> *I need your strength and wisdom.*

I don't reckon I know how long this went on, but it all got welded
into me, that song and them chanting words. Finally I stopped
sobbing, but I couldn't look up.

Toddy was quiet for a long time. Then she said, "Do you know
the "Tale of Two Wolves," Orca?"

I shook my head and kept looking down.

"A grandfather is talking with his grandson and he says there
are two wolves inside each of us that are always at war with each
other. One of them is a good wolf that represents things like kind-
ness, bravery, and love. The other is a bad wolf, which represents
things like greed, hatred, and fear. The grandson stops and thinks
about this and then looks up at his grandfather and says, 'Grandfather, which one wins?' The grandfather quietly replies, 'the one
you feed'."

I looked up at Toddy, my eyes wide and staring right into hers.

Toddy stared back. "You're good, Orca Bates," Toddy said.
"That's what I know. And we'll stay right here until you know it,
too."

I rubbed my eyes dry on my shirt sleeve. "Might be a little late
for all this, Toddy," I said.

"It's never too late, Orca. Remember when we first met and I
told you about my spirit guide... my unci... my grandmother, how
she began her most elaborate quillwork when she was very old and

knew she would never finish it? And when I said nothing is ever finished, only a continuation? Look at today, Orca. Look at today! Things happened for the good, things you didn't know would happen. You know, I love this saying: 'We are born in one day. We die in one day. We can change in one day. We can fall in love in one day. Anything can happen in one day'."

"So what do we do, Toddy?"

"We go back."

"Back to the veterans' home?"

"Back in time."

"I don't know, Toddy, I never told anyone any of this. And it's all dark back there."

"We're going to turn on some lights. There's a time and a place for everything, Orca Bates. Now it's time for you to tell me your story."

"Then you got to tell *me* something, Toddy. Something about you."

"Fair's fair, Orca. What would you like to know?"

"How about why you're down on this boat in a snowstorm, alone with someone with my past and with someone you haven't known for even two weeks."

"That's better explained after I hear about you. Okay?"

Then I got up off the rug, which weren't easy. "Well, Toddy," I said, "I think I'm gonna fire up the wood stove. If we're going back in time, that's gonna take a while. Might as well make things good and comfortable."

"No argument there," Toddy said, pulling her coat tighter around her.

"Orca, believe me, you just turned a huge corner already by not shutting me out on this."

"Then maybe we can do that one-day-fall-in-love-stuff, too, Toddy."

"Let's get you to love yourself. From there it gets easy. And Orca, is there any tea on the boat?"

"Tea?"

"Yes. Or something hot."

"Hot, Toddy?"

She smiled. "Well, it fits the name doesn't it?"

"You know, now that I think of it, Webb does like iced tea in the summer; should work just fine as hot tea. After I fire up the stove, I'll have a look."

I headed out the stern door to the back deck wood pile, hoping there still *was* a wood pile. First I thought the door was stuck. I pushed harder and it gave way slowly. What was pushing back on it was snow. Lots of snow. We ain't going nowhere, I thought as I looked at the buried docks. There was plenty of wood at least, and I grabbed a big armful, and some sticks from the kindling box, and headed inside. I figured I'd better tell Toddy about all the snow, but something inside made me hold off, and I started setting up the newspaper, kindling, and three logs into that wood stove. It all was like riding a bicycle again, 'cause I'd done this stove so many times before. She was a fine old stove, and she fired up real good, and was soon crackling away and drawing good, even with that wind outside. I felt proud of the work I'd done on rebuilding that stove pipe and weather shield.

I began to search the cabinet for some tea. I moved a few cans of Dinty Moore beef stew and a box of powdered donuts, and sure as shootin' there's a box of Lipton iced tea bags. Things was warming up and I was feeling better.

"Before you know it, Toddy, you'll have your tea and it'll be hotter in here than noon in June," I said. "And maybe I can find my favorite mug for you here in the cupboard. I left most everything behind when Webb took over the boat. The mug says 'Rounding the Bend' on it and it's got a picture of a narrow stretch of the Miss with the sun lighting up them clouds real nice. Really loved that thing." I looked and found that Webb had quite a collection, but I couldn't find mine, so I just reached in and grabbed a couple of his.

"Tea for two, Toddy," I said when all was done, and handed her a cup. She started shaking her head and giggling.

"Didn't I make it right?" I asked.

"No, it's what it says on my cup. Did you see this? She held it out to me:

Life is Not a Fairy Tale
If you Lose your Shoe at Midnight,
You're Drunk.

"Yeah, Webb ain't much of a romantic, " I said. "Just a regular working stiff." I got to thinking about him now owning *Cirrhosis*, and how my life might be different now if it weren't for that one card game. I looked down at my mug. The top line of the writing said,

Harleys Don't Leak Oil

The bottom line were pretty worn away, but I could still read it

They Mark Territory.

I pulled up that old rocking chair I'd left aboard, and lowered myself into it. "This was my momma's," I said to Toddy, "I should bring it back to the veterans' home."

"Absolutely. I wonder if it will fit in the back of the Subaru," Toddy said.

"The problem with rocking chairs, Toddy, is they're like this houseboat; they rock, but they never gets you anywhere. Momma rocked in this. Right up until the end."

"Rocking is good, and it does get you somewhere. In thought. And it's calming," Toddy said. I sat there, thinking about Momma, holding my tea. The old *Cirrhosis* moved a bit, heeling from a gust of that strong November blizzard I knew was lurking outside.

"Tell me about Cubby," Toddy asked.

"It's going to take more than that one cup of tea, Toddy."

"As I think you know by now, I'm pretty patient."

"Well, I knows you're pretty—we'll see how patient."

II

2 9
THE ODD COUPLE IN GROUCHY'S MARINA

I said to Toddy, "I told you about how Cubby answered that ad of mine. And how I needed a tenant 'cause Lenore left me. Did I tell you about Lenore?"

"Your first wife. The one from *The Exorcist*?"

"No, this would've been my second wife. Anyway, Cubby told me on the phone that he was a college kid, and I figured that would be okay, even though he was young enough to be my kid, if I'd ever had one. I told him to come meet me down here at the boat, and right on time there's this knock on the door and standing in front of me is this Oriental kid."

"Asian."

"Huh?"

"Orientals are rugs."

"It's too late to enlighten me Toddy."

"Not so much."

"Anyway, he didn't talk like one of them... like one of them Asians. Talked real good English. Like he were born across the street. Seemed like a real nice kid, real serious like, and I figured he'd be just right. Plus, he was my only applicant."

"That's odd; you'd think applicants would swarm to the boat from that ad of yours, Orca," Toddy said, shaking her head and smiling.

"I know, Toddy. But you never know about the general public, even when they gets a deal like I was giving 'em. Just makes you scratch your head, don't it. So, anyway, Cubby's real name was Danny Roan; I named him Cubby 'cause that's what we calls green-horn or rookie pilots on the river—I just thought it stuck nice on him. Like Toddy does on you, Toddy."

"Thank you, Orca. How long ago was all this?"

"Must have been nearly twenty years ago. Cubby moved aboard at the end of August, right before school started. Was in his last year of college; he was gonna graduate that coming spring."

"He came out here just for the last year of college? I wonder why? Did he know anyone?"

"Just said he needed a change. He had a good friend from his high school days who was now in college and living in the Twin Cities. The friend said Cubby could room with him. So Cubby transferred and moved out here, but in the meantime the guy had got himself a girlfriend, and she'd moved in. So Cubby was outta luck for his housing. That's when he saw my ad. Anyway, that first day when Cubby came to the boat to look things over I showed him what would be his little room. "It's real cozy like; you might have to step outside to change your mind, but you got room to sleep and read," I said. Showed him my room too, which weren't much bigger, so he'd feel things was pretty fair. I still remember the look on his face when he saw my big Cheryl Tiegs poster. You know that one, Toddy?...The one with her in that red bathing suit and them nipples just popping right out like..."

"That's fine, Orca."

"Sure is fine, Toddy. So here's how it went from then on:

* * *

I told him right then he was free to decorate his room any way he wanted; maybe get his own poster of a Chinese girl in a bathing suit.

'I'm not Chinese,' Cubby told me, as he started to open the door to the head. 'Is this the bathroom?'

'Sort of; I've been meaning to get to that,' I said as he opened the door and looked into the tiny room.

'What do we do about showers?'

'Right up the street is an athletic club. I ain't much for working out, as you might have figured, but there ain't no rule says you have to work out if you're a member, so we just use the club for its shower facilities. Membership is real cheap.'

'That's okay,' he said. 'I really want to live on the water. I think living on a houseboat would be so cool. Also, if it's okay, I'd like to put up a picture of my grandfather's sailboat. And I'd like to try to get a small desk in here. I have a lot of studying to do this last year. I'm shooting for the kind of grades I need to get into a good law school.'

'So you'll be being pretty quiet then?' I asked.

'Studying doesn't make much noise. And I'm not too social; I only know one person out here so far. But I guess I was wondering: How would it be on your end? I mean, it's a pretty small space, and if it's too disruptive due to your lifestyle...'

'Only thing's my snoring. Think you can study while someone snores? Both my wives told me I snore like an 18-wheeler climbing a mountain.'

'I have my Walkman and earphones, so that should be fine. And I like to listen to classical music when I study—Mozart and Chopin mostly. It helps me concentrate.'

'Yeah, classical music is good, ain't it? I like classical, too. Mostly, though, I like country classical. You know some good country songs?'

'I don't believe so; there's not much of that back East.'

'Well, I get stuck on them country lyrics; can't keep those songs out of my head, especially the ones about love gone bad. Songs like *How Can I Miss You If You Won't Go Away*, or *I Keep Forgettin' I Forgot About You*. Then there's that one nasty one, *She Got the Ring and I Got the Finger*.

Cubby just stared at me for a minute and then began to look around *Cirrhosis* some more. 'Is there a place to hang clothes?' he asked.

'Well, I just piles mine up. But we can put up some hooks and maybe get one of them small cardboard hanging closets. Don't worry about the space; most of the time you'll have plenty of room 'cause I ain't even gonna be here that much. I'm working a line boat down south on the Illinois River these days; thirty days on and thirty days off. So you'll have the old *Cirrhosis* all to yourself half the time.'

'That's fine. I'll be fine here alone. Do you have a TV?'

'That's extra. A dollar an hour.'

'Oh.'

'I'm only kiddin'. We got a TV, though reception ain't too good down here, but we get the big channels. Also, we can head up to The Slough to watch a Vikings game.'

'The Slough?'

'That's the river bar and restaurant. Local hangout. Plus, we got The Waffle Palace right up the street. But, except for back when I cooked there, them waffles of theirs can kill you. You'll want to eat mine here on board *Cirrhosis*. Best waffles in the land.'

'I'm sure they're delectable, Mr. Bates.'

'Two things we got to get straight if we're gonna be roommates: Everyone on the river has a nickname; mine's Big Red, and now, with you being new on the river, you need one, too. Let me think on it a minute. Let's go with 'Cubby', okay? Cub pilots is young and new to the river. The other thing is you teach me some of them big college words, like 'delectable'. I figure the ladies is gonna like that. In return I'll show you all I know from being Big Red; important stuff like rivers, women, waffles.'

* * *

"So that's how me and Cubby got started, Toddy."

"Sounds like the script from The Odd Couple," Toddy said. "And *you* taught him all about women?"

"Yeah, him being most likely new to that species and all, I figured that I'd teach him about women, and all the snags, bends and deadheads you got to watch out for."

"Deadheads? You're calling women 'deadheads'?"

"No, no. I ain't really. But, like deadheads in the river, women can be trouble, Toddy; trouble that's hard to see coming. You need a damn manual."

"Is that so?"

"Well, teaching Cubby about women didn't work out so good anyway."

"I'm not surprised. What happened?"

"Along about October we was settled in pretty good. Cubby was studying most nights and no trouble at all. He said he was shooting for making something called 'magnum come loud' so he could get into this one particular law school he liked somewhere back East."

"*Magna cum laude.*"

"Yeah, that'd be it, Toddy. I bet you was one of them, too. Anyway, he studied hard. But Saturday nights I'd take him out to The Slough to get him a good feed and try to get him to unwind a little. Then this one Saturday he said he couldn't go. Said he had a 'study partner' coming over. So I figured I'd stay late at The Slough so as not to bother them none."

"That was thoughtful, Orca."

"Mebbe so, Toddy, but staying out long meant drinking too long. And drinking too long got me kinda cozy with Bonnie."

"Bonnie?"

"Bonnie was one of the function hostesses at The Slough; she'd been there for years. We called each other Big Red and Little Red, 'cause we both had long red hair, mine hanging down in a ponytail, and hers all piled up high. After her shift in the function area ended she came over and pulled herself up on the bar stool next to mine and we started kidding each other and laughing at stupid stuff. I thought Bonnie was looking particular good that night with that tight black top with them rhinestones and a bunch of glittering stuff on her eyes. I knew by daylight she weren't the prettiest flower in the garden, but after a few pitchers I got to looking at her through beer goggles. Bonnie was drinking Sex on the Beach, one of them girlie vodka drinks, and was keeping up with me, pushing down quite a few. I got to telling her about how I had to stay out late that night 'cause my new roommate, this nice young kid that was gonna be a lawyer, had a study partner with him on *Cirrhosis*. Then Bonnie starts kiddin' me again; 'Oh, big tough guy like you, afraid to go back to his own houseboat.'" So, next thing you know the two of us is staggering down the docks, singing that Frank Sinatra song "Fly Me to the Moon" and laughing away. I noticed the lights was low on *Cirrhosis*, so I figured that study partner was gone and Cubby was asleep. I gave Bonnie that 'shhhhhh' sign with my finger over my lips, but we couldn't stop laughing. I pushed open the door and there was Cubby on the couch next to this nervous little blond thing that I think we scared right out of her drawers. They must have been listening to us coming; she was sitting on the edge of the couch like she were some rare china tea cup about to fall off a shelf."

'Study hall's over, Cubby,' I said. 'This here's Bonnie. And you, little lady, must be the study partner.' She stood up and stuck out her hand to me and Bonnie.

'I'm Jennifer. Jennifer Obermueller.'

'Well, nice to meet you, honey,' Bonnie said, and then she started wandering and weaving around *Cirrhosis*, bumping and poking into this and that before she stopped and turned back to Jennifer. 'You one of the Obermueller family from Inver Grove Heights?' she asked.

'No, ma'am,' Jennifer said. 'I grew up on Summit Avenue here in St. Paul.'

'My, my, Red,' Bonnie said. 'We got the St. Paul aristocracy on board. From a high end neighborhood.' Then she looked over at Cubby. 'So, are you two an item?'

At this point Jennifer was looking toward the door like it was the gate to salvation. And Cubby weren't too comfortable either.

'I'll get us all a beer,' I said, trying to keep things from breakin' down.

'No, no,' Jennifer said. 'I really need to head back. I have to work in the morning.'

'It's Sunday tomorrow, honey,' Bonnie said, taking an open Grain Belt from me.

'I'm a church organist. That's one of my jobs. To help pay for school.'

'You gonna be a lawyer like your boyfriend here?' Bonnie asked.

'Danny and I are not...No, I'm a religion major.'

'Well then, you two can both swear on the same Bible,' Bonnie said, laughing. But nobody else was laughing. Bonnie just kept going. 'Get it? You know, lawyers swearing people in and all, and then religious folks having Bibles?'

'I'll get your coat, Jenn,' Cubby said. 'And walk you to your car.'

'Now, that boy's a real gentleman,' Bonnie said, taking a pull on her beer. 'Ain't he, Red? But, if you don't mind, honey, before you go I got just one question since I got myself a religious scholar right here in front of me. So, I been wondering about God's character. I mean, if he wants everybody to worship and follow him, and if they don't they burn in hell for all eternity, I mean, what's that attitude say about his character? And if he's so powerful, why did it take him six days to make everything? And what about them angels moving that big rock on the tomb?'

'I'll have to think on those, ma'am.'

'Okay, well, fair enough, honey. You think on 'em. Maybe talk to your professors.'

'I will ma'am. It was nice to meet you.'

'You take care, there, China Cup, and don't slip on them docks,' I said.

The next day Cubby was even quieter than usual. Like he was givin' me the silent treatment. It started to get to me, so finally I said, kind of laughing, 'You and your study friend probably ain't thinking of double dating with me and Bonnie any time soon.'

Cubby got up and put on his coat and headed for the door. Then he turned to me.

'I kind of liked her, Red. I really did. And do you think she'll *ever* want to come back here now? She was pretty put off, Red.'

'Oh, hell, Cubby, we didn't do nothing. Just a little fun. Maybe that girl's too sensitive. You know, breaks too easy. Like a china cup.'

'Well, you and Bonnie smashed my chances with that china cup, and that makes you a bull in a china shop, Red.' And then he was gone.

* * *

Toddy looked at me, real serious. "Do you see a pattern here, Orca? Because I do. You hurt people and then you save people. Let's get rid of the first part."

"Maybe it's that Assburgers, Toddy? You told me once it was maybe that Assburgers."

"I'm not so sure about that. I had said 'maybe', Orca. Even so, that's no excuse for hurting someone."

"Well, Toddy, I made it up to Cubby. Showed him stuff I knew. I made him waffles and showed him my secret recipe. I even showed him the sandstone cave up river, and he thought it was pretty cool, though I was kind of nervous going back there. Also taught him lots of stuff about the river and engines and how they run. Took him on the *Sully B* a couple times when I was piloting on her, switching barges down by Pig's Eye Lake. Even let him take the sticks a couple times. Kid had a real good feel for the water. He'd been floating most of his life, he told me, sailing with his grandfather on the ocean off the coast of Maine. Anyway, Toddy, I really wanted him around," I said. "I can't explain it. We was about as different as two people could be, not just in age and looks, but in smarts and stuff we liked. Everything. But I just kept feeling something. Can't explain it. It was the damnedest thing." I shook my head, and my eyes was gettin' watery as I thought about it, and about what finally happened that summer.

"Well, it must be kind of nice to have a young person around when you're suddenly alone again and in your—how old were you then Orca?—your mid-forties?"

"Yeah, more than twice Cubby's age. As days went by we got closer and closer, even though he still didn't talk much, except when he got to talking about sailing and the coast of Maine. That kid would get going about ghosting along in heavy fog with his grandfather on their old wooden boat, trying to feel their way into some harbor. Told me how his Grampy showed him about making a radar out of his voice, shouting 'boom, boom, boom' into a megaphone, and being able to tell by the echo where the closest land was."

"Sounds mystical," Toddy said, and shifted around on the couch, leaning forward with her hands on her chin.

"Yeah, that and what he called 'potato navigation'."

"Potato navigation?"

"Cubby weren't much of a kidder, but he got me on that one. 'Oh, yes,' he said, 'potato navigation was a real art. You'd go up to the bow of the boat in really heavy fog and throw potatoes out ahead of you as far as you could. If you couldn't hear the splash then you were about to crash into land.'"

"This young man sounds delightful."

"Funny, but most of the time he was pretty serious. But he got all upbeat and enthusiastic when he talked about his grampy," I said, "talking about life on that boat: cooking beef stew, playing chess and cribbage together, Grampy telling stories of the olden days."

"He must have really loved him."

"I never knew anybody who loved anybody nearly half that much, Toddy."

Me and Toddy got quiet for some time. Then Toddy said, "Orca, did it ever occur to you that you were doing the same thing with

Cubby as his grampy had done for him when he was a child: teaching and nurturing him as if he were your own. Anyway, it's wonderful how much he loved him. I hope his grampy lived a long life."

That got me quiet and things got to crawling out again, things I didn't want, and I put my head down.

"What is it, Orca?"

"It's a long, long story, what happened next, Toddy," I said, and figured I'd just bury it, push it back down with the other bad things. But then I looked over at Toddy and thought of that good brain of hers and all that wisdom packed in, and figured maybe she were the one person who could see my side of what I done.

Toddy pushed back the shades on the window behind the couch, and looked out at the deep and drifting snow. "I think we have the time for a long, long story," she said.

30
WHO STOLE GRAMPY'S SUNSETS?

The night it all started, even though it was late March, my truck had a tough time firing up when me and Cubby finally left The Slough. I'm telling you, it was cold enough to freeze the balls off a pool table.

'You packed the wood box real good on *Cirrhosis* when we left, right, Cubby?' I asked. It was mighty dark and slippery as we headed down the docks, which was still frozen in from one long winter—not like it was tonight, Toddy. They looked like some Alice in Wonderland thing, the old float sections all frozen at weird angles, bulging up and tilting down as we staggered down them toward the boat. That northwest winter wind give me the shivers in mind and body; rapping like a machine gun when it hit the plastic that was tacked over the outside of *Cirrhosis'* windows. That stove was almost out, and it was close to freezing on board. Cubby packed some more wood into the stove right quick, of course.

Then the phone rang. Cubby was busy poking the wood around, so he just answered by pushing the speaker phone button. I stood there, shivering and listening. I remember most every word.

Danny, you've got to get me out of here.

Grampy?

You said you'd take me sailing, Danny. I want to go sailing.

Grampy, it's still winter. As a matter of fact, it's freezing right where I'm standing. Let's start over. Grampy, it's about 2 am where you are, it's not summer and we can't go sailing right now. We'll have to wait until May or June. After I graduate and come back east I can get the sloop launched and we'll do that. Just stay in your nice warm house until we can go. Okay?

I can't see out the window, Danny. I'm used to seeing out the window. I'm used to seeing the sunsets. And the birds on the marshes off Ross Island. And, oh, that moon. Remember when we sailed down a moonbeam? Now I can't see any of these things.

You will in the morning, Grampy. You'll just have to wait. When Darcy comes in she'll help you get by the big window and she'll get your favorite tea.

There's no Darcy.

What do you mean, 'There's no Darcy'?

She's gone.

Gone where? Maybe she's in another part of the house right now.

No, the people who put me here didn't bring her. Got rid of her, I think.

What people?

Those same people who took away the sunsets and the sunrises.

These people put you where?

I don't know exactly, Danny.

Look around Grampy. What does it look like where you are?

Like a hospital.

Can you get someone to come to the phone and tell me more.

Can't. Strapped down.

What?

I'm strapped down, Danny.

Grampy, maybe you can just go back to sleep and we'll talk about it in the morning. Are you sure you weren't just having a bad dream?

I won't be right again in the morning..

You won't be right? What do you mean 'you won't be right?'

They'll be giving me that drink and I won't be right again. So it needs to be now.

Grampy, I can't think. I have to get warm. I'll call you at home in the morning, I promise.

But Danny, I'm not there.

Then give me the number where you are.

I don't know.

Look, Grampy, you can't be strapped down or you couldn't be using a phone. If you're strapped down, how can you use a phone?

I found this one here; someone left it on my bed.

How did a portable phone get in your bed?

I don't remember.

Grampy, I can't stand here much longer; it's too cold. It's really cold out here where I am. Look, let's talk tomorrow night instead, when you're 'right again' but earlier, like 10 pm. I'll be awake and warm with the stove really stoked up.

This is crazy, Danny. This is not right.

I know Grampy. Call me tomorrow night at 10, okay?

Danny?

Yes?

These people here; most of them are in chairs. And they're all almost dead. They're just not my type.

Tomorrow night then. We'll talk.

Danny?

Yes?

Trust me. This is not a dream.

Cubby turned to me and gave me a scared and confused kind of look.

"You gave him this houseboat number?"

"Yes, I sent it in a letter to him to his house on Ross Island in Seacasset about a week ago."

All I'm thinking is this: Grampy found that portable phone and he found and dialed our number. He ain't that out of it. Old or not, this guy's in a jam.

I think Cubby was up all night. And he weren't studying. There was no call from Grampy at 10 that next night, so Cubby called Grampy's house in Seacasset. No answer. Then the next morning he called Darcy, the lady who had been helping Grampy and doing the shopping. And that's when the shit hit the fan.

* * *

"Where was Cubby's mother during all of this, Orca?" Toddy asked.

"She died. Cancer. When Cubby was a teenager."

"Well what about his father?"

"See, Cubby was adopted. He never shared any details, only that it was one of them single parent adoptions, by a lady from out Boston way—his new mother—who wasn't married at the time, but always wanted children. So it was Grampy who really acted as Cubby's father after she adopted him. Oh, later on Cubby's mother married some shit named Steve, a guy who was never in it for being a father. He was no good, kind of like my old man; never cared a lick about anybody but himself. After Cubby's mother died, shit Steve just hit the road. I guess he knew he wasn't getting nothin', as far as money went. Everything Cubby's mom owned went to Grampy, and Grampy became Cubby's guardian."

"So Cubby's all that's left in the family?"

"Not exactly. That was a big problem by the name of Ashton, Cubby's uncle. Grampy's only son. I think Cubby came out here mostly to get away from Ashton. Cubby just said it was a bad scene, and he needed to get far away for a while."

"Oh, my. So what happened?"

"We're on our way downriver on a strange trip, Toddy, so hang on," I said. I pushed myself up from the rocker and went over to check on the wood stove, put a couple more logs in the wood box, and lowered myself back down into the chair.

"So this Darcy lady—good lady, Cubby said—she was all confused and really upset by what had happened. She told Cubby that Grampy was no problem, that he was sweet and easy and just loved being at home with his tea and looking out on the marsh. Then Ashton started coming around, asking where some of Grampy's things went and saying how Grampy didn't seem right, and things of his was missing, like he thought she was incompetent and a thief. And it weren't true. She said Ashton then came back a couple days later with a doctor; she said him and the doc seemed pretty cozy, and told her they had to ask Grampy a bunch of questions. And they wouldn't let her in the room with them when they did. Next thing she knows, she's fired. By Ashton. Then she hears from a nurse aide friend of hers that Grampy's been moved to the nursing home she's working at, and he's been a real handful, making a huge fuss about being kidnapped from his own house."

"Oh, dear, so what happened, Orca?"

"A lot, Toddy. Cubby found out the name of that nurse aide friend of Darcy's that worked at the nursing home, and called her to find out how Grampy was doing. I listened in on that call 'cause I had my suspicions. Well, she said Grampy was totally uncooperative and kept trying to 'escape' from the home.

After that call I told Cubby that I heard Grampy's voice loud and clear when he called that night. When a man's pleading, you got to listen, I said. Especially if he's been wronged. If you take away a man's freedom, you take away his life, 'specially at that age. I told Cubby we should head out there, yank him out, and put him back in his house.

It's so much more complicated than that, Cubby told me. He said there were legal issues. Told me that Ashton is now Grampy's guardian *and* his conservator.

Well, he's guardin' him alright but he won't be conserved for long the way this is going, I said. He'll die quick in one of them places.

I was getting pretty worked up, being that I don't do so well seeing people trapped like animals. I been on the muddy Miss long enough to know when it's time to open the lock gates, let that water flow free like it wants to. From everything I'd heard, that man weren't designed to be confined; there was too much life left in him. I told Cubby it was time we busted Grampy out before that place killed him and before this Ashton got Grampy signing over things. I told Cubby we should head East as soon as we could—get some time on the ground out there to straighten this thing out. I had a month on a line boat coming up that would take me to mid-

May, but then I'd be off for 30 days. You'll be graduated by then,
I told Cubby, and you'll need to move your stuff back East anyway. Plus, I ain't ever been out that way. It'll be a helluva road
trip, Cubby, I said. In my Dodge truck. Springing Grampy in the
spring! And I ain't coming back 'til we do."

31
OPENING PANDORA'S BOX

"How you doing, Toddy?" I asked, taking a break from telling my Cubby story. "That foot still hurting like it was?"

"Well, it's sore. Please, maybe some more ice and perhaps some more tea, if you wouldn't mind, Orca."

"At your service, little lady," I said, and pulled myself up. While I was heating more water, Toddy said some more stuff I never knew, though that ain't a surprise:

"I find it sad the way this country deals with its elders. You know, Orca, old age in this country seems to have turned into a stigma. Other countries aren't this way. Native Americans celebrate aging and respect their elders for their wisdom and life experiences. It's the same in Korea, in China, in India."

"Well, they got that right. All them places."

"And it sounds as if you and Cubby got it right, too, wanting to get Grampy out of that nursing home."

"Oh, we got Grampy out all right, Toddy. It was only after that when things got a little out of hand."

I passed Toddy the hot tea and new ice pack, along with a blanket I found folded up on the little bunk in Cubby's old room.

"My, my, I feel like a princess," Toddy said.

"Princess Toddy. Got a nice ring to it."

"You can't leave me hanging, Orca. What did happen? What was it that got out of hand?"

"If you'd have looked closer at my memories board back at the veterans' home, Toddy, you would have found out."

"Well, why don't you tell me now?"

"Look, maybe you can help me figure things out. I need to know if I done the right thing by this, the way it ended and all. You might remember seeing an old newspaper clipping on that cork board of mine. Whoa, I just thought of something!"

I moved aft by the little kitchen section and pulled up the floor-board hatch and sure enough, there was my big blue plastic box.

"I think I got another copy of that newspaper clipping and a bunch of other clippings right on board. It's probably with the other stuff I wanted to come back to get tonight."

Toddy leaned around the bulkhead, watching me as I hoisted it up and closed the hatch. I carried the box over between my rocker and Toddy on the couch, set it down, opened it up and looked in.

"Phew. Things do stink in there. Guess a damp bilge ain't a good place to store papers. Things is pretty soggy, Toddy," I said, shaking my head and pulling out a bunch of papers and setting them on the rug.

"Orca, could you please put a few more logs in the stove; it's still pretty chilly. Must have been when you opened that bilge door?"

While I was back aft doing that, Toddy leaned down from the couch and started separating the wet papers. "These look like a bunch of old AOL email printouts; should I keep them?"

"Oh, yeah. Those are Grampy's 'h-mails' to his dead wife."

"H-mails to his dead wife?"

"Yeah, he wrote to her 'bout every day after she died. To Cubby's mom, too, after she passed. Called them his h-mails, standing for 'heavenly emails'. Sent them from his old computer straight to heaven. Told his dear departed ones how things was going down on earth. He never heard back, though. But he kept sending them. When we was out East, me and Cubby printed out some of the important ones. That was how we found out....Anyway, that's a long story from way back."

Toddy kept pulling out papers while I was talking.

"Oh, dear, Orca, this has never been opened," she said, holding up an envelope with a green card attached to it. "It's to you and it's a certified letter from the IRS."

"Well, no sense opening a can of worms this late in the game Toddy. I paid my taxes; every once and a while anyway. But some years back, I figured I'd paid my share and they'd got enough from me. Besides, I needed to spread my money around, you know, to other causes."

"Yes, but Orca, you need to respond. And you should pay your fair share. After all, taxes pay for your roads, your river markers and locks, and, of course, now your veterans home."

I looked down for a bit. Then I looked up, straight into Toddy's eyes. "They pay for wars, too, Toddy."

"Well..."

"I don't want none of my money going to any war. So they ain't getting any of it from now on. Besides, what they gonna do, put me in jail? Hell, they'd have to feed me. I'd put 'em in the red just feeding me. In the red just for feeding Big Red. I ain't worth the government's effort, Toddy."

"Well, they might repossess your antique waffle iron collection."

That made me a little nervous. "You think they could do that, Toddy? Them things got some value on eBay, I bet."

"It's possible, Orca." Toddy put down the IRS envelope, and continued looking in the box. "There's a bunch of old maps here. Pretty ruined. And a plastic baggie with a picture."

"That's be Cubby on graduation day. Keep that out, will you Toddy? I need to put it up on my memories board."

"And here's some more papers. They look like old email print-outs. And there's a cookbook called *Never Eat Soggy Waffles*. Oh, and here's what looks like some legal papers in blue folders."

"That'd be courtesy of Denise and Lenore. My walking papers."

"And here's an old napkin from The Waffle Palace."

"It's got red lipstick on it, I bet," I said.

"Something reddish is smudged on there. Should I toss it?"

"No, don't toss it, Toddy. It's kind of special. Goes way back."

"There's another letter here, this one's been opened. It's from the Sullivans in Cleveland."

I came back over by the box. "Yeah, a lot of this stuff is important, Toddy. To me anyway." I took the picture and letter from her, stuffed them in my coat's big pocket, and lowered myself into Momma's rocker.

"You know, I been thinking. I know it ain't been a long time, you and me and all, but you're kinda all I got that's really important to me now and, well, when them injectors in this old heart of mine finally clog, it'd be good, somehow, if you know my story."

"What I bet, more than anything, Orca, is that the good would come from you telling it."

"I been writing things down in my notebook, Toddy, like you said to."

I leaned over the box. "Ain't much left in there," I said. "But here's the first things I was looking for, way down in the bottom." I pulled out two moldy newspaper clippings, leaned over them and looked close. Most of the words were as hard to see as them damned lobster buoys was in that dense Maine fog that me and Cubby and Grampy sailed into all them years ago.

I handed the articles to Toddy.

The Boston Globe
June 6, 1997

SEARCH BEGINS FOR THREE SAILORS

BOSTON - The Coast Guard is conducting a search for three men who left on a day sail from the harbor of Seacasset, Massachusetts on a dilapidated 28-foot wooden sailboat named Sarah *yesterday at around noon. One man, Joseph Roan, 87, was a resident of Sunny Gardens Nursing Home in Seacasset. His grandson, Daniel Roan, 21, and another unidentified person, described as a very large man with a red ponytail and in his mid-forties, left for a day sail and haven't returned. Anyone having seen or had contact with these individuals should...*

The Bangor Gazette
June 10, 1997

STRANGE JOURNEY OF LOST SAIL-ORS ENDS DRAMATICALLY BY A SMALL ISLAND OFF JONESPORT

JONESPORT – After four days of searching, the Coast Guard engaged in what they called a 'dramatic confrontation' with the sailboat Sarah *in the fog off remote Hard Harbor Island off Jonesport, Maine. One of the men...*

"Oh, no, the bottom parts of these stories are all blotted out," Toddy said. "My gosh, Orca, now I'm really left hanging! 'Dramatic confrontation...one of the men...?' Now, who on earth could that be? Not the great protector himself?"

"Well, your great protector's got a question for you, Toddy," I said. "It's about you saying 'He saves people. It's what he does,' to Walter and his wife back there at The Slough tonight. Maybe I scared a school bully to save a little kid a million years ago. And maybe me dragging old Gil out of that ravine was some kind of minor saving thing, but I think you got me overrated."

"I don't think so."

"You know something about me that I don't know you knows?"

Toddy looked up at me and put one hand under her chin.

"Yes."

I searched my brain in and out and around, and couldn't figure that there was any lick of a way Toddy knew about them things that happened in 'Nam. I just stared at her.

"Skid told me," she said finally.

"Skid?"

"When he took me down to the bathroom on the *Elsie*, we got to talking about you."

"Well, that ain't good. What'd he say?"

"He said it was something that happened before his time on the river, back when you were a young deckhand. He said the story was legendary, something that every river man heard and told."

"Skid's right about it being a long time ago. But I didn't do nothing legendary. It happened on the Ohio River. It'd been almost a week of heavy rain, which caused real high water. The river was running hard above the lock, about 11 miles per hour. We were on a tow headed upriver. We made it to the lock and was locking through with four loaded barges. As we powered out of the lock that nasty current above the dam hit us with full force and the captain lost control. The current broke us apart and them barges got carried over against the dam."

"Those big barges went over the dam?"

"Not the barges, Toddy. Somehow they just piled together against part of the dam and stayed put. The captain decided to go get them. Not a good idea. He drove the towboat over into the restricted area by the dam, thinking he was gonna corral them barges like some cowboy. I was standing on deck, forward by the pushing knees, hanging on tight 'cause that fast water was sweeping our whole towboat around pretty good while we was running sideways to that nasty current. The others was in the engine room and pilothouse. We were steaming so hard that water was flooding over the bow between the pushing knees, and I thought the captain might drive the towboat right under. I figured that even if we made it over to the dam, there was no way we could face up to and then control them loose barges in that current. I looked up at the pilothouse; the captain was leaning forward over the steering sticks and throttles with this crazed look on his face. I shook my head at him, but he was driving like a madman on a mission. Next thing you know the current is so strong it overpowers us, carrying us sideways into the dam and then the whole towboat gets swept over the dam and down into the river below. Then she turned over and sank. We all went under." I looked over at Toddy. "Two people drowned. Did Skid tell you that?"

"Yes. And he told me one survived. The one who repeatedly dove back down in the murky current trying to save the others."

"Didn't save nobody."

"You tried the impossible, Orca. The important thing is you tried. That's heroic."

"Heroes *save* people, Toddy."

"No, heroes are heroes because of their courage and caring for others. Because they try. Let me ask you this: Did you have anything to do with the towboat going over the dam? Could you have stopped that from happening? Could you see anything at all in that kind of churned-up river water when you dove down? Could you have found and pulled up a man's body to the surface in that kind of current? I'm willing to bet the answer is an absolute 'no' to everything. There is *absolutely* no reason to blame yourself."

"Yeah, Toddy, but..."

"I'm not done, Orca. I have one more question: How would you feel if you *hadn't* had the courage to dive down and try? How would you feel if you had never even tried? See, *that* is the true story. You tried. Guilt is a man-made emotion, Orca. It's often an untrue story passed down. We're going to change your story."

I got to thinking that I knew who the real hero was on board *Cirrhosis* right then, and that she was doing my heart plenty good. I figured what I was getting now was therapy—even though it was Toddy on the couch and not me—which was something I always thought was a bunch of mumbo jumbo. But this therapy was coming to me in one smart, pretty package, and I didn't want that to go away.

"Okay, Toddy, I'll tell you what's behind them newspaper stories."

32

TINY CAKES, INDEED

"To get the whole picture, Toddy, first you got to know about Cubby's graduation. There was no way I was gonna miss it. Especially with him not having any family coming. I knew those shits Steve and Ashton wouldn't show. And of course there'd be no Grampy. So I was it, and I wanted to make the day real special for Cubby; much as I could anyway. I was gonna sit in the front row at that graduation, sit there all proud and watch him come up to get his diploma and that magnum award. Then give him his graduation present. Then take him for a nice dinner at The Slough. Show him off to some of my river pals."

I looked over at Toddy, tucked under that blanket, those soft eyes looking real happy with me.

"That's nice, Orca."

"Yeah, it was gonna be a real special day. And I was planning on being the chauffeur for my little buddy, taking him to the graduation in style in my Dodge Power Wagon. When the big day came, I washed it up real good, cleaned up the inside. And I wrapped Cubby's present real nice."

"Wrapping. I'm impressed," Toddy said.

"First time for everything, Toddy. Didn't have no wrapping paper, so I used tin foil for the paper and duct tape for the ribbon. Held together pretty good. Real shiny, too."

"Well, I suppose that sent a more personal, handmade message."

"Yeah, but tying a bow with duct tape ain't easy. So here's the graduation story, Toddy."

* * *

When the big day came I put on my white shirt and my light blue necktie—buttoning my collar and tying that thing weren't no easy trick, believe me—and stepped into the best pants I had. I clipped on my good red suspenders, brushed and pulled back my hair and tied it in a tight ponytail, and I was ready to go. Right then Cubby came out of his little room wearing a blue suit, white shirt, yellow tie, and really shiny shoes. "Well, hell's bells, Cubby, what you looks like is a good decision," I said. Then Cubby looked me over.

"You, too, Red," he said, "but perhaps you could make your tie a little longer; it should come more than halfway down your stomach."

I grabbed my throat like I was being choked. "Jesus H., Cubby, I can't hardly breathe in this thing. Feels like I'm the featured poor bastard at a hangin' instead of a graduation guest."

"Or maybe a different tie, Red. That one has a stain on it."

I looked down and studied my tie. "This here stain must be from one of my weddings. That was the last time I wore it, I do believe. The stain looks like lasagna. That would have been my second wife, Lenore, most likely. That's what we had for the meal at that one."

I went to get my other tie and while I did Cubby said, "What about shoes?"

"I got my shoes on, Cubby."

"Those are work boots."

"All I got. Sorry. I'm a working man. Anyway, folks have to look up, not down, to talk to me, Cubby, so they'll never get to my feet."

"That's fine, I guess. We should go, Red, especially if you want to get a front row seat in the tent."

"Tent? "

"Yes, it's in a tent."

"I'm gonna be able to stand up in it, right?"

"Yes, it's big, Red. It's a big tent."

Well, I didn't make the first row or even the second. Those rows all had these 'reserved' signs on them, so I lowered myself down real carefully into one of them little folding chairs in the third row, and settled in for a long, long time. I got through the speeches all right, except for trying to understand this commencement speaker guy who said we ain't just seated under this tent, but we're all on a gigantic ball whirling around the sun at 67,000 miles per hour, in a galaxy shooting through space and time at 1.3 million miles per hour. I guess you need to go to college to figure what these speeches mean.

Then came the diplomas. I had forgotten to ask Cubby how many students was going to graduate, figuring if it was going to be in a tent there couldn't be that many. Well, those graduates came in from outside the tent, and how many there was I never found out, 'cause I lost count at student number 150. By then my feet was asleep, my legs was asleep, my ass was asleep, and the skinny old lady next to me with the pink dress and perfume that smelled like a bad memory was asleep. Cubby, his name way down the list 'cause it was beginning with "R", was number 175. Well, when he finally came up on the stage I got so proud I thought I was gonna burst. I started to stand up and cheer, but my lower half wasn't working too good by then so I figured I'd just give a little push on the back of that sleeping lady's chair to help myself up. Turned out that weren't a good idea. She was even lighter than I thought, and her chair flipped backward. She woke up pretty quick on the ground, staring straight up at me and the top of the tent. A few folks screamed and stood up. For me, it was all kind of slow motion, as my dead legs started losing the battle of trying to keep 290 pounds from crushing that 90-pound lady like a ten-pound sledge on a potato chip. But down I went, Toddy."

"Oh, my! Was she okay?"

"She was fine. I managed to get my good knee on the ground to keep from rolling onto her. A bunch of folks helped us back in our chairs—'Sorry about that; legs let go on me'—I said to the lady I almost squashed. It was okay. Hell, a few folks even kind of giggled when they saw we was all right. Then things got moving again."

"And poor Cubby, up there on the stage, his big moment, and then he sees this happen," Toddy said.

"But we got him all graduated. Then we had this tea in another tent, Toddy. I went over there, and headed right over to the food table, where they had the littlest pieces of cake you ever seen."

"Probably petit fours."

"Well, I had more than four. Two at a time, too. As number seven and eight was going down, some guy in a nice suit came by and smiled at me."

"Everything okay after that little incident?" he says to me.

"Yup. That little lady was tough, though; she just knocked me right over."

He laughed and stuck out his hand. "I'm Dean Oleander of the English department. You have a graduate here today?"

"Well, he ain't mine. Not exactly. I'm his landlord and his friend. His name's Cubby—well, Danny Roan."

"Oh, yes, I had him in several of my classes. A fine young man. So he's your tenant. Do you own in St. Paul?"

"Harriet Island area."

"Oh, down by the St. Paul Yacht Club."

"It'd be a little further downriver. More like under the Wabasha Street bridge."

"Sounds as if your abode floats."

"My abode's a boat: *Cirrhosis.*"

"*Cirrhosis?*"

"*Cirrhosis of the River* is her full name. A houseboat."

"Interesting."

"Not that interesting."

"Well, clever, I mean. The connotation is perhaps what's interesting."

"Perhaps," I said, acting all educated and all, though I didn't have a lick of an idea what one of them connotations was. I figured it might be close, like a cousin, to one of them medifors Cubby talked about, and I was gonna tell Dean Oleander that *Cirrhosis* was more of a medifor than a connotation, but I figured I was getting into shallow water on this stretch.

Right then Cubby came by. He was looking nervous about me and this Dean guy being left alone together. Dean stuck out his hand at Cubby, shaking it hard, saying, "Magna. Fine job. Fine job, Mr. Roan."

"Thank you, Dean Oleander."

"He sure studied his ass off," I chimed in.

"Indeed," said Dean.

"Yeah, indeed. That's what I been saying: indeed, indeed, indeed."

Things got quiet for a bit, then Dean said, "So what's next, Danny?"

"Law school, I hope. Back East."

Dean Oleander looked at me. "You'll be losing a fine tenant, no doubt."

"Indeed," I said. "But we're headed back east together. Got to bust somebody out of a particular institution where he's being held against his will."

Cubby shook his head and smiled. "Mr. Bates is always kidding around. Anyway, thank you for everything, Dean Oleander."

"Certainly. It was my pleasure."

And after I grabbed four more of those petty cakes, we headed back to the truck. As we were climbing aboard, I said to Cubby, "How come you called that Dean fellow by both his first and last names?"

"Dean is not his first name."

"Yeah, it is Cubby. He told me himself."

"No, Red, he *is* a dean."

"So, *I'm* an Orca? I don't get it, Cubby," I said as I fiddled for my keys. "Maybe I should've gone to college to understand this stuff." I fired up the Power Wagon. "Anyway," I said, "I know I liked you calling me 'Mr. Bates' back there—that made me feel pretty special."

"You are, Red," Cubby said.

As we were driving back, I made a turn and headed upriver, across the St. Paul High Bridge. "Why are we going this way, Red? I thought we were headed back to *Cirrhosis* and then going to dinner."

"It's nice going this way, Cubby. And a fine day out, a fine day for you and me both. So why not get a last view of the Miss," I said.

"Don't you ever get sick of the river, Red? I mean, you *live* on the river, you *work* on the river."

"This ain't for my benefit, Cubby," I said. "This might be..." But then my voice choked and my eyes wetted up. I turned my head away from Cubby and pretended to cough. "Might be *your* last good look at the Miss."

We was both quiet as we drove the rest of the way, crossing over the High Bridge and then down the river road, past the sandstone caves, until we came to Harriet Island Park. I pulled over by the picnic tables.

"Why are you stopping here, Red?" Cubby asked.

"This here's a nice quiet place and I figure you can open your present here."

"You got me a present? You didn't have to do that, Red. Driving me all the way back East, and then offering to help me with Grampy is more than enough of a present."

"Well, let's just say this gift is somethin' that's real special to me, 'cause it was given to me by someone real special."

"Well, I know it's not your gold bracelet, because it's right there," Cubby said, pointing to my wrist.

"Maybe someday, Cubby. But until then, this thing never comes off. No, this gift is something else, from someone who gave it to me 'cause I told her about something someone else real special told me. And now I'm passing it on to someone real special."

"I think I got it, Red. Special, right?"

"Special. Also, with you becoming a lawyer and all someday, well, this'll be a good reminder to keep on the right track."

"Well, you have me in suspense, Red."

"You head over to one of them tables and I'll grab it and my little cooler from the back and meet you there. We'll have our own little celebration."

I put the cooler and the present on the table and sat down real careful on the bench on the other side from Cubby. "First," I said, "we need to have a toast. You deserve a cold one, Cubby. And I do believe I'll join you." I opened the cooler and pulled out a couple of Grain Belts.

"You can't drink in the park, Red."

"Sure I can," I said. "It's easy. You just pops this tab and, watch carefully now, you pours it down your throat. See, you can drink in the park."

"I meant…"

"I knows what you meant Cubby. Look, we got to have a toast. And you can't toast without some kind of alcohol. And there ain't nobody around. It's your graduation, for chrissakes."

"I really appreciate all this. But I think I'll have to abstain. But thank you,"

"Okay. Objection abstained! That's what they always said on that Perry Mason show."

"It's 'sustained'. Who's Perry Mason?"

"He was a TV lawyer. Before your time. Good guy. Always got the bad guys and saved the good folks. Anyway, here's your present."

"Interesting wrapping, Red."

"Indeed. But be careful with the tinfoil; stuff's expensive and we can reuse it for our sandwiches on the road trip. Don't worry about the duct tape though; got plenty of that. So open the box, Cubby."

"'The Waffle Palace'. You gave me some waffles for graduation, Red?"

"That's just the box."

"I was beginning to wonder."

"Yeah, but save the box, okay? Or if you don't want the box, I'll take it. So open it up."

"It's a cricket wearing a top hat."

"Not just any cricket, Cubby."

"Jiminy Cricket from Disney, right? And he's wearing a sign: 'Always let your conscience be your guide'."

"Well, Cubby, I want you to be one of them good lawyers. Like Perry Mason."

"Thank you, Red. I intend to. This means a lot to me, and someday it will go right on my desk," Cubby said.

3 3

CLAIREBUOYANT

"You know, Orca," Toddy said after I finished the graduation story, "I think you have some spirit guide in you. You seem to be doing pretty well on your own. But, tell me, what was it about this small toy? Something you had when you were little?"

"Got it when I was a teenager. Got it as a gift from a real nice girl—my first real love, really—she gave it to me right after my momma's funeral."

And then it happened again; Toddy looked me in the eyes, brushed that long silky black hair back away from her face, took a deep breath, lifted her chin, and out came this voice from an angel:

I loved you then and ever shall
But there's no one here that's left to tell
The world has gone black before my eyes.

"Jesus H., Toddy, how the hell did you know about... You claire-buoyant or something?"

"No, I'm not. I just try to take everything in, and then put things together."

"Well, you better stay aboard as my spirit guide, little lady, 'cause with someone as clairebuoyant as you along, I ain't never gonna sink."

"And the word is 'clairvoyant'. It means..."

"I know you knows what it means, with you being clairvoyant and all. Sure could have used you sitting next to me in science. And history. And math. Not shop, though. I was okay in shop."

Toddy lifted the shade behind the couch and tried to look out. "Is it still snowing, Orca? I can't really see."

"I'll look out the back Toddy. Got to get more wood anyway. But don't worry, someone from Grouchy's Marina will shovel them docks clear at first light tomorrow."

"Tomorrow?"

"It ain't safe tonight on them docks. If the river was frozen, might be worth a try. But those docks are half under now from the weight of that snow. And falling off one is a ticket to heaven. Or in my case, hell. You got your cell phone, right? You need to call someone to say you won't be coming home?"

"No, I live alone. Are there enough blankets here for both of us?"

"I'm sure there are, and that good old wood stove, along with them electric heaters, should do fine. I'll make sure the stove's stoked up real good. Watch over things. You live alone, huh?"

"Yes. Now I do."

"You break somebody's heart Toddy?"

"Let's just say I could have used somebody who saves people."

"Seems to me that's *your* specialty."

"Not that time," Toddy said.

I looked across at her and for the first time that night she was looking down, and not at me. Everything got quiet. The wind stopped beating the windows. *Cirrhosis* stopped swaying. Then, when Toddy's head stayed down, I felt this big sadness, 'cause something seemed like it smothered that spirit of hers. I couldn't take that; couldn't add another sadness to that cage in the back of my head, 'cause that cage was already crowded. Back in there was when the doc told me about Momma's cancer; when Lil drove away after I got out of jail; when I bobbed to the surface for the last time under that Ohio River dam; what happened in 'Nam at Tan Son Nhut Air

Base, and when I left Sully on that woodsy trail near Long Binh. And then, years later, when Grampy left to row to Cloud 23. So I just stared at my feet, rocking away in my momma's chair.

"Are you all right, Orca?"

"You flat lined on me for a minute there, Toddy. You got all sad. Didn't know what to say. So I got sad. I'm wondering who *you* got to talk to? I mean, who guides the spirit guide?'

Then Toddy started sniffling, and it about broke me, but for once I didn't just sit there. I pushed out of that rocker and slid down on my knees by her, bad knee and all, and put my big arm around her neck.

"I lost someone, Orca. Someone that maybe I could have saved," she said.

"Can't be no fault of yours, Toddy. Can't be no fault of yours."

"His name was John Running Deer."

"Old boyfriend, huh?" I took my arm away, sat back on the rug, then pulled myself up into the rocker.

"We were close friends on the reservation when we were in high school. Then we reconnected as adults and it turned into something more."

"Well, I hope he appreciated what he had, Toddy," I said.

"I lost him, Orca. He was bipolar, which is a mental illness that brings severe high and low moods, even leading to suicide. He couldn't fix himself. And I couldn't fix him."

"Hard for me to wrap my arms around this, Toddy. I mean, why would somebody who had you in his life not fix himself?"

"It took me a long while to understand that it's hard, no matter who you are and no matter how hard you try, to get inside someone else's mind and soul. Sometimes the people on the outside, even if they're loved ones, can't get in."

"So it was like his brain and his soul was fighting with each other?"

"What's so sad is he had no control. His illness had taken over the controls."

"Not sure I'm seeing that."

"Well, I'll give you a metaphor."

"Good. I know them metaphors."

"Imagine you're on the river you love, pushing barges filled with gasoline, and it's night, and you're driving down river in a fast current like the one we went in earlier today, and you're headed under a narrow steel bridge in the middle of downtown St. Paul. And midway through the bridge span, you veer off on a collision course. Nothing makes sense. Your soul says it's wrong to hit the bridge, that it could cause a gasoline spill and even a huge explosion. But your brain has no control about steering the right way; there's something in the system, way out of sight, that's making this happen."

I thought on this for a while, rocking away and thinking about those tough, long nights on the river. Then I said to Toddy, "I think that mental disease thing is like when I was sleepwalking."

"I'm not sure what you mean, Orca. You were a sleepwalker?"

"It ain't anything I'm proud of, Toddy. But it might be some of this crazy brain stuff happening. Back when I was living with Denise—well, sort of living with her—we was in separate rooms by that time..."

"Because of your snoring?"

"Hell, no, Toddy. Denise could out-snore me anytime; hell, she could out snore a grizzly in hibernation; and when she woke up she was meaner than one coming out of hibernation. No, we just didn't like each other anymore. So some nights, after I'd had a week or so of long shifts on busy sections of the river, running through those narrow bridges like you just said, this sleepwalking thing happened. It was usually after the times I'd been driving blind."

"Driving blind?"

"Yeah, pushing empty grain barges that had their covers stacked so high on the barges in front of me I couldn't see nothing straight ahead and had to count on directions from a sketchy, stoned-out deckhand way out in front of me on the lead barge of my tow, using a handheld radio to talk me through the bridge span."

"You'd have to drive through bridges at night while not able to see straight ahead of you? Really? That would require a *lot* of trust."

"Yeah. So after these shifts I'd come home, push down a few beers, and hit the hay. But then I'd get up some hours later, being really still asleep, thinking I was still in the pilothouse and driving blind. I'd walk over to the little casement windows in my room and stare out over a side street with a street lamp and a few parked cars. Then I'd just lean my nose against the glass, grab the two crank handles on those windows and try to steer the house!"

"Oh, dear."

"Yeah, steering a house ain't easy, even for Big Red."

"You saw what? Cars? A street?"

"Nope, Toddy. I saw two steering arms, a pilothouse window, and stacked barge covers that *looked* like cars. I must have just scratched my head, standing there in my skivvies, wondering why the picture weren't making much sense. So I'm figuring that's what happens to these mental folks like John."

"What happened next?"

"I steered her right through, but it was mighty scary."

"Did this happen often?"

"You bet. Oh, I got suspicious about those cars, street lights, and even green grass out there ahead of the pilothouse. But the other part of my brain told me it was a trick—like you said with John—and I was really on the river, and it would be disastrous if I didn't steer through that bridge."

"Orca, I think this was just a case of your subconscious still at work, overtaking reality after too much stress."

"Well, Toddy, this got even sillier. As I said, I got real suspicious of myself. So one time before bed I taped a note to the window. It said: YOU ARE NOT AT WORK, ORCA BATES; YOU ARE IN A HOUSE AND DREAMING; **THERE AIN'T NO BRIDGE**. GO BACK TO BED; EVERYTHING IS FINE."

"So that solved the problem."

"Nope. I did it again. Walked over, grabbed the window handles, then read the note."

"And?"

"You'll think I'm paranoid, Toddy."

"You didn't believe the note, right? You crumpled it up and kept steering."

"How'd you know that, Toddy?"

"Because I've seen when the mind wasn't ready for something that made sense, Orca. I've seen when the brain gets separated from the soul," she said.

Toddy stared into my eyes, but wasn't seeing me. She was somewhere else.

"Sometimes people do crash into the bridge, or just drive off it," she said finally. "John Running Deer was one of those. On his motorcycle."

"He died?"

Toddy just nodded.

"Jesus God. I'm sorry Toddy," I said. "But it can't be your fault. Nothing's your fault. Nothing."

"I might say the same to you, Orca."

Right then I knew, like I felt a million years ago, back with Lil in The Waffle Palace days, that if anything ever happened to Toddy, this big balloon named Orca Bates was gonna pop for sure.

But Toddy just cheered up, and got all curious, like she always seemed to do, and said, "Orca, tell me what happened. Tell me what happened to Grampy and Cubby."

34

THE ROAD TRIP OF '97

Right after Cubby graduated, we sat down with some road maps and figured the best way East, which looked to be mostly the downstream route by those big cities like Chicago, Cleveland, Buffalo, and Albany. "How we gonna get through all them cities fast, Cubby?" I asked. "We don't want to waste no time."

"We drive through them. Maybe take some beltways if there's traffic."

"Or maybe get up a head of steam and shoot straight through. Like driving a bend."

"Well, we may have to slow down in congested areas."

"Maybe go through in the middle of the night; that way we can just hook her up and power right along."

"This isn't the river, Red."

"Well, I ain't spent much time in big cities, and I ain't gonna start now."

"You want to drive straight through to Boston?"

"Yeah, saves on motels. Motels is like these new cell phone services. You ever think about that?"

"No, that never came to mind."

"Well, both of them, you give them money and you don't get nothing back. That cell phone service gives you air and another voice, which you can't keep. That motel doesn't give you nothing either; the bed's there all the time anyway, don't matter whether anybody's in it or not. Same with that motel roof and the toilet and the rug and..."

"Okay, Red, we'll drive straight through. I don't mind doing half the driving."

So we got the Power Wagon loaded up with all Cubby's stuff and my duffle bag, said a few goodbyes, and headed out. We got a late start and left just before sunset. I stopped at one of them Holiday convenience stores and stocked up on the way out of town. "I made a list; should make shopping a breeze," I said, and handed it to Cubby as we pulled into the parking lot.

Sour gummie fruits, powdered downuts, twinkies, beef jerky, Big Man Coke

Bacon and cheddar cheeze Potatoe Skins, M&Ms (super size pack), Cheetos, Oreos, Bagel Bites, Dooreatos, cupcakes, pumpkin cheese cake bits

"God, Red, this food will kill us before we get to Boston," Cubby said.

"Why's that?"

"It's all pretty bad for you. Even *I* know that, and I'm a kid."

"Hell, I was gonna get an apple, too. That's good. Actually, I figure I got all them essential food groups fitted in that stuff, Cubby, like we learned in first grade: I got your fruits with them sour fruit slice gummies, I got your grains with them donuts and twinkies and bagel bites, I got your vegetables *and* your protein with the bacon and cheese potato skins, and I got your dairy with the pumpkin cheesecake bits."

"Yeah, but the sodium alone, Red..."

"Screw sodium. Let's get our provisions, Cubby, and hit the road."

Thanks to us not stopping 'cause we had all that food aboard, we made good time, staying on I-90, then I-94, and made it to Chicago in under six hours. I took that first shift, driving all the way while Cubby mostly slept. I'd about had it and was getting blurry right when we was in the middle of Chicago. That's when the good old Power Wagon started to pull to the right, then pulled real hard, and I knew the right front was gone flat. Well, I'll tell you something now that I found out later when I was havin' a beer with a towboat pilot from Chicago: big, white, pony-tailed Red and his little prep school-educated Asian friend Cubby had broken down at Halsted and 77th, one of the most dangerous neighborhoods in all of America. And it was two in the morning.

The smartest thing I could have done was keep driving on that dead tire. But I couldn't stand ruining that rim. So I found a spot with one dim, working street light, one that weren't broken or shot out, and pulled over under it. Cubby woke up and looked around, rubbing his eyes. "Where are we, Red?"

"A place where there ain't too many yacht clubs or private schools, Cubby. We got a flat and I had to pull off of 94 and we grounded out here. Stay in the car and keep the doors locked. I'm gonna go get the jack and change the tire."

"I'll come out with you. You'll need some help."

"Cubby, I don't need no help. Stay there. You be the lookout, okay?"

So I put on the parking brake, grabbed a flashlight from the glove box and went out and got the jack set up. Things was going pretty good; I got the truck jacked up and, holding the flashlight in my teeth and shining it on the wheel, was able to see to work off those lug nuts. Then I got the spare on. I was tightening the last lug nut when this admiring kind of whistle behind me made me jump. I dropped the lug wrench.

"Whoa momma, that is my-tee big and shiny. Real, real shiny, that bracelet. Don't you think? How much that worth, you figure?" one of the two guys behind me said.

Now I was real tired. Tired past really caring. I slowly pulled myself up, wiped my hands on my coveralls, and looked at them and said. "It's worth eight thousand bucks."

"Well, I got one more question, my man. What's gonna happen if I take that fancy thing off your wrist?"

I looked at the guy hard. There weren't no fear in my eyes. I didn't say nothing at first; didn't have to 'cause my face said it. Then I slowly shook my head and said: 'You know, young fella, I've seen more bad shit in the jungles of Vietnam than your skinny ass has produced in your whole life. So, unless you want some of that bad shit, well, if I was you, I'd head on home.'

He looked over at his buddy, then back at me. "I'm going to ask you one more time, my man: what's gonna happen if I take that fancy thing off your wrist?" he said.

I just gave a little smile. "Same thing that happened to the last guy who tried to take it off," I said. "Why don't you find out."

Right then the Power Wagon revved up really high and loud, the high beams started flashing on and off, and Cubby laid on the horn and held it there. I reached down for the lug wrench.

But when I stood up the enemy was gone, back into the jungles of Halsted and 77th.

"That scared the shit out of me," I said to Cubby as we headed back to calmer water on I-94.

"Oh my God, Red. Those guys had me shaking, too; and I was *inside* the car."

"No, not *them*, Cubby. That horn. You scared the shit out of me with that horn."

"Oh, you don't appreciate me doing that? Saving you. Scaring them away. That it?"

"Cubby, you can't blame them two guys."

"*What*???"

"From this neighborhood, where they come from and all, them seeing eight thousand bucks on my wrist was one more thing they didn't have; one more reminder about what they don't got, about what ain't a fair split."

"Are you serious?"

"Some folks is just lucky, born into it. What do they call that? Lucky sperm club. Or they just get lucky. Look at you, Cubby. Luck of the draw. You told me once you was a tiny baby in a dying country, then got adopted from the other side of the world, and next thing you got a wonderful momma in a fancy East Coast town in America. Things went your way on that. And you made the most of it. And I'm proud of you. But no hard feelings on those two guys back there; they just wanted a fair split."

"So what were you going to do if I didn't blow the horn?"

"This bracelet's a part of me for a real special reason. Part of my soul, really. I think they knew from the look in my eyes, and especially when they saw me smile a little, that they was in trouble. On the street, Cubby, when you smile right before a fight, the guys on the other side know you ain't afraid and you're not going down, and it probably ain't worth it for 'em."

"What *did* happen to the last guy who tried to take it off you?"

"You'll just have to use that good brain of yours to imagine that, Cubby."

Cubby took the next driving shift and as soon as he took the helm, I knew right quick that he weren't much at handling a Power Wagon. He kept speeding up and slowing down, sucking all that gas through my carbs. "You got to drive like you got an egg between the gas pedal and your foot, Cubby. Drive so you won't break that egg."

"I haven't driven in a while, Red. Haven't driven much at all in my life, really."

"Well, that don't make me real comfortable about taking a nap. But, hell, you'll find out real quick that I ain't done much sailing in *my* life when we get to sea. So we'll be even."

"When we get to sea?"

"Well, yeah, when we spring Grampy and take him sailing. He said he wanted to go sailing, remember?"

"Sure I do. But we have some obstacles. We don't know if they'll even let him out to go sailing; plus, I'm sure *Sarah* isn't ready for sailing. She's been wet stored in a little harbor on the Maine coast; been there quite a while. Grampy had her for sale."

"What's 'wet stored'?"

"It means being kept in the water in the winter instead of pulled out. It's better for wooden boats to stay in the water; it's their element; they need to float and breathe; need plenty of fresh air flowing through. Stagnant air and fresh water are the real enemies of a wooden boat. Otherwise they dry up; the seams between the planks open up. And they rot. Grampy taught me all this."

"Sounds like what happens to folks when they get put in a nursing home. You know, on the river, rot ain't a problem with our steel hulls, just rust. So these wood boats like salt? That right, Cubby? And that salt is good for not letting them rot?"

"Yes."

"Salt's sodium, right?"

"Well, yes."

"So I should keep on eating this sodium junk food, then. Keep the rot away."

"Come on, Red. Be serious. Anyway, I think we should discuss our plans for when we arrive."

"How we gonna take Grampy sailing if that boat is way up in Maine?"

"First we need to find out why he's in that place, and then if we *can* take him sailing."

"'Course we can. We'll just go get him. Bust him out," I said.

"I think we should first stop at Grampy's house on Ross Island, and try to use that as a base if we can. I still have my house key."

"How we gonna get out there if it's an island?"

"There's a permanent little bridge. It's barely an island at all, just separated from the mainland by a creek from the salt marsh."

"Good. We'll get a chance to sniff around. Case the joint. Maybe find a clue why he got taken away."

"I don't know. I'm not sure about anything anymore, Red. I'm not even sure if I'm allowed in his house."

"Your Grampy's house? Come on, Cubby."

"Well, there's this guardian and conservator thing now. And I'm not it."

"You talking about that Ashton guy?"

Cubby nodded.

"Don't worry about him; when we get out there on the island, I'll set up a perimeter defense to repel an attack from any direction."

"Red, this isn't a military exercise or a war."

"Maybe not, Cubby. Maybe not yet."

I did some navigating while Cubby was driving, and took us along by South Bend, Indiana on I-90 and then onto Route 31 when we got slowed down 'cause of some kind of accident. This got us on a nice quiet farm road right at sunrise, and pretty soon we were passing a few of these Amish folks with their funny black hats, clomping along in their black buggies pulled by a couple horses.

"We need gas pretty soon, Red," Cubby said.

"Well, I bet they ain't got much call for gas stations around here; we'll find some back near I-90, I figure." I looked back into one of the topless buggies when we went by. Sitting there at the reigns was a man and a woman dressed in plain black clothes; she had on one of them white caps that looked like an old-fashioned nurse bonnet and he had on a round black hat. "Those clothes and buggy, it's like looking back in time, ain't it, Cubby?"

"They dress that way to be practical and so no one stands out within the group or creates jealousy by having clothes that look better."

"Sounds like river men. Must be tough being a teenager."

"Around the age of fifteen the teens are allowed for a couple years to explore the world outside, like driving cars, drinking, and partying. But then they have to make a choice between staying Amish or leaving that world, their community, and family."

"As teenagers they get to choose between partying and driving cars or getting up at dawn to work these farms? Most of the ones I know can't even choose to wear a coat when it's freezing out."

"Well, from zero to fifteen they're raised to be responsible in a tight community. So leaving's not as easy as you think. That's what I understand, anyway."

"Cubby, how in hell you know all this stuff?"

"I did a book report on the Amish in eighth grade. I also learned that the Amish only go to school through eighth grade."

"Really? Hell, excepting for you, Cubby, that makes me one of the most educated folks in this area, me making it halfway through 11th grade and all."

"They learn plenty. It's not all about school."

"I know, but I wonder why they want to be stuck in the past? Clothing and buggies and all," I said.

"Most like it the way they have it," Cubby said. "You know, the simple life."

"Seems like feeding and taking care of horses and gardens ain't so simple when they could just pump in some high test in their trucks, if they had them, and stock up on food at the Holiday 24/7 stores," I said.

"I don't know, Red. I bet there's a lot more community and sharing going on than in many other places. I bet people pitch in; you know, like those old barn raisings. I'm sure the Amish do that. Probably families are a lot closer, spend much more time together. It sounds good."

Made a good hunk of sense to me, what Cubby said. I reached behind me and grabbed a new pack of Twinkies.

"Wish I had that brain of yours," I mumbled.

"What, Red?"

"Nothin."

I finally nodded off after Cubby started handling the Power Wagon pretty good, not being too jumpy on the accelerator. But I kept waking up and saying, 'You okay Cubby?' Cubby kept saying 'Fine, Red. Go back to sleep.' We worked our way toward Buffalo, going past Cleveland, moving along the south shore of Lake Erie. I sat up for good and started looking at the map. "Hell, Cubby, we'll be passing pretty close to Niagara Falls. Always wanted to see that place."

"You like waterfalls, Red?"

"Not especially, but that's where that guy drove his jet ski over the falls at full throttle. I read about it. Happened a couple years ago."

"What? That's suicide."

"Well, it weren't just a jet ski. He had a homemade rocket-parachute contraption attached that was going to shoot him clear of the falls, then the parachute was going to let him float down to the river below."

"What happened?"

"Rocket didn't ignite. Parachute didn't open. Met his maker."

We never did make it to Niagara Falls, but we did stop a few hours later for some chow because our supplies were running low.

"Let's get some real food, Red," Cubby said.

"Okay, Cubby, you watch the signs and we'll pull over when you see something you like," I said. Not five minutes later I couldn't believe my eyes. "Hey, Cubby, will you look at that! They got a Waffle Palace way out here in New York. We got to stop, Cubby. We got to stop."

"Come on, Red. You told me you hated their waffles."

"Hell, maybe they're different out this way. We need to find out."

"We do?"

"Well, yeah. Remember when I told you about my cooking days at the St. Paul Waffle Palace, when they finally used my recipe and suddenly folks was packed into the place? I always wondered if that recipe of mine ever made it out to the other franchises. I'll know in a minute when I taste one."

"It's not even breakfast time, Red."

"Any time's waffle time, Cubby. You can order something else."

We found the place not too far off the highway and went in. Things were more modern and colorful than the St. Paul spot, but they still had those wimpy looking one-legged red vinyl stools. We grabbed a booth and opened the menu. "Hell, Cubby, they ain't changed a thing," I said. "Still just plain and pecan waffles. None of my waffles. And look, nobody's in here."

"Red, it's almost four in the afternoon. This is a breakfast place."

"I had folks at all hours when I was cooking my special recipe."

Right then the waitress came over. One pretty waitress! Reminded me of an older version of Lil. I just looked up at her and smiled. "What's a nice looking broad like you doing in a place like this?" I asked.

She turned bright red. "ExCUSE me?" she said, narrowing her eyes at me.

"You should order, Red," Cubby said, jumping in.

"You got anything but plain or pecan waffles?"

"It's just the ones on the menu."

"Well, 'cause years ago I used to cook real special waffles in a Waffle Palace in St. Paul. Lots of kinds of waffles. People was lined up. Guess they didn't catch on here out East."

"That's nice. Now, would you like to order something?"

"I'll have coffee, two pecan double waffles, one plain waffle, and two eggs over easy, sausage and ham," I said.

"You get either sausage *or* ham."

"I do believe I would like sausage *and* ham. Charging me extra is fine."

She looked over at Cubby. "And you, sir?"

"May I please have the cheeseburger, fries and Coke special?"

After she left Cubby didn't look too happy. "God, Red, you can't talk like that, calling her a 'nice looking broad'."

"Why's that Cubby? That's a compliment."

"No, it's derogatory."

"What-a-tory"?

"You shouldn't do that."

"Calling somebody nice looking?"

"No, the 'broad' part."

"Hell, Cubby, that used to be a regular word for a woman."

"Maybe way in the past. It's not accepted now. Things change."

"Tell that to the Amish," I said.

35

GETTING MY FEET WET IN TASSELED LOAFER TERRITORY

"We must be almost to the ocean, Cubby. Pretty exciting for me," I said, jabbing a finger into my crumpled old map.

"You'll probably smell the salt air before you even see the ocean, Red. That's what happens to me."

"Let's first stop at the beach before we get to Grampy's, okay? I've never touched the Atlantic Ocean."

"You'll have plenty of time for that later," Cubby said.

"You know, you talk to me like I'm your kid sometimes. You ain't my father, Cubby. It should be more like the opposite."

"You sounded like a kid, that's all. Okay, we'll stop at Sandy Beach when we get into Seacasset."

"Sandy Beach? Clever name."

"Well, that's really what it's called."

We drove on, being quiet for a while, until we got onto Route 3A and then onto North Main Street in Seacasset. I looked over at Cubby, who was seeming kind of nervous. "You nervous about getting back?" I asked.

"Everything's going to be a lot different out here, Red."

"How's that?"

"The first thing is that people are much more reserved out here in the East than in the Midwest. They're not that open or trusting at first with strangers."

"What they got against strangers?"

"They're more cautious at first, that's all. Not as likely to initiate a dialogue."

"'Initiate a dialogue'? What kind of fancy talk is that? Why don't you just say 'they ain't likely to talk first'? You're sounding like that Dean guy from graduation."

"All I'm saying, Red, is you have to tone down your personality out here because people are more reserved."

"Indeed. Now you got me all curious about these East Coast folks. What's the difference?"

"Well, especially around where we're going, they're all pretty well off, and educated."

Right then my heart started to hurt a little, 'cause I was thinking maybe Cubby was figuring he was gonna be embarrassed by me in front of his people—Big Red, the guy who always says the wrong stuff at the wrong time. "Cubby," I said, "if you don't want me around your people, just say so."

"No, it's not that. Red, I know what it's like to be different. So don't take it that way. Look, imagine that you're suddenly sitting down to dinner with the Amish. You wouldn't want to pull out a six-pack at their dinner table. You have to adjust to their culture, that's all."

"So are they all going to have beards and black clothes and round hats?"

"No, more like Brooks Brothers button down Oxford cloth shirts, blue blazers, and tasseled loafers."

"That must be quite a rig. Why would somebody want to wear that stuff?"

"It's what they choose to wear."

"Not what I choose to wear. I don't choose."

"What?"

"Like most river men, I just put on the stuff I left on the floor the night before. Easy choice."

"You're not worried about color coordination?"

"You're pulling my leg now, Cubby. Hey, by the way, are these folks going to say 'indeed' a lot?"

"No, but they might say 'yes, quite'."

"I'll say 'yes, quite' a lot then, too."

"Not so much, Red. Not so much, okay?"

"So I'll be myself then."

"Not so much."

"Damn, Cubby, who you want me to be, anyway?"

"Diplomatic."

"Okay, I'll dress like one of them diplomats then," I said. And then I smelled it. "I smell the ocean, Cubby. I do believe I smell the ocean. We near that Sandy Beach?"

"Coming right up. We'll stop for a few minutes."

And there it was, the Atlantic Ocean. "You sure can't see across," I said. "Not like the river."

"If you could see across you'd be looking at Portugal."

"I'm just going to head down for a minute and touch the water. Be right back."

"There's usually quite a surge, Red, so be careful."

"Okay, Dad."

So I went down and stood by the edge, just staring out at those waves surging in, and thinking about when I flew over another big ocean to Vietnam, back when I was Cubby's age, and what a fool I was to think it was gonna be some great adventure instead of the mind fuck it was. I must have lost track of time, standing there, 'cause next thing I knew Cubby was standing behind me, laughing.

"Red, you're in up to your knees."

I looked down, then turned to look at him. "Got in pretty deep without knowing it," I said. "Story of my life." Cubby was standing there, smiling at me, shaking his head, hands on his hips. I don't know where it came from, but I remember thinking, *I love that kid.*

36
H - M A I L   D O N ' T   L I E

We drove by some mighty big homes on the way to Grampy's, and then stopped across from a little wooden bridge. "That's Ross Island across that bridge," Cubby said. It looked just wide enough for the Power Wagon. We got out and walked over to the bridge. "I sure love the look and smell of that salt marsh; the way it winds around reminds me of the bends on my river," I said.

"It is a river, really; a tidal river."

"They hardly need this bridge though, Cubby. Ain't much water in that little creek.'"

"Not now. But six hours from now that creek will be up right to the bottom of this bridge. Tides run about 9-11 feet around here."

"Glad we didn't have those tides on the river," I said. "The only times the tide changes on the river is during floods, droughts, and when the Corps of Engineers plays with the levels. But that reminds me; I did see the funniest instant high and low tide ever."

"Instant high and low tide?"

"Cubby, I sure wish I had this on film. Years ago we were coming up a real narrow section on the Minnesota River with a pretty big towboat for that stretch and probably too many barges out front, pushing a lot of water in every direction. Off to one side was a couple of guys fishing about twenty feet out from the bank in a small row boat. The guy on the oars was rowing pretty hard to get out of the way as we went by. I said to one of my deckhands as we went through, 'You watch those guys' faces; I think you might see something you'll never forget'. And sure enough, like Big Red getting into a bathtub, the water in that narrow stretch had no place to go but up, and those two fellas and their boat got lifted right up the side of the bank and into some bushes by the rising water we made. There they were, high and dry, one guy still at the oars and the other with his fishing line now hanging in a bush. Had to be the second funniest thing I ever seen."

"Okay, I'll bite; what was the funniest?"

"That was right *after* this happened. I looked back when our tow started to round the bend, and like magic all that water we'd pushed came right back in, refloating the fishing boat, washing it back down the bank and into the river, out to the spot where they'd first started fishing. I swear I saw one of them guys mouth the words 'What the fuck!' after this happened."

Grampy's house was a nice one-level place with lots of windows looking out over the salt marsh. We parked next to a wooden skiff that was half covered by an old canvas tarp. "Must have blown off," Cubby said. "Grampy wouldn't have covered it like that. He loves that skiff."

"Grass is pretty high. Looks like nobody's been keeping the place up," I said, moving a pot with some dead plants away from the path to the front door. Then I looked down at the footprints going up the walk to the front door and mailbox. "Mailman's been here. Or mail lady. There's big and little footprints in the muddy spots." We walked up the front path.

"Let's hope this key still works," Cubby said, as he tried it and opened the door.

I looked in the big wooden mailbox. It was empty.

"If somebody's been delivering the mail, somebody's also been taking the mail, Cubby," I said. "You think maybe the little feet is delivering it and the big feet is taking it?"

"I don't know, Red. Let's not get ahead of ourselves."

"Hell, I'm just taking a careful look at the crime scene."

"Crime scene? What crime?"

"Taking Grampy away."

"Red, take it easy. Come on in and I'll show you the house."

"Good. That should be real revealing."

When we got inside, Cubby went around opening windows to air the place out, and I started poking around. When I saw the boat model and later the train set I began to think I knew what Grampy was all about, wanting to be at home, and I knew I was on the right mission being out here. In the bay window looking out over the salt marsh was this wooden sailboat model, about three or four feet long and with a mast about four feet high. I leaned my nose in close and looked down into the cabin, which had glass over the top so you could see right in. Every little thing was in there, but tiny: in the head next to a tiny porcelain sink were tiny red towels the size of your fingernail with the name *Sarah* on them, in the galley was a tiny coal stove and next to it was a little sink with a brass water pump. There was even a chart the size of a matchbook cover on the chart table. Cubby came back into the room.

"Grampy made that. Every piece of it," Cubby said, all proud.

"I figured as much," I said. "Must have taken one hell of a long time."

"He had the time. In the two years while my grandma was bedridden at home before she died, Grampy took care of her almost all by himself; once in a while a home health aide came over, but Grampy said he knew Grandma best and how she liked to be treated and that she weighed so little now that he could lift her himself and take her into the bathroom and even put her in the bathtub. Once I asked him why he never complained about all this and he said, 'Danny, everybody has problems. It's the ones who think they're the only ones with problems that don't fare so well'. Grampy said that home was the place to die in, and that he and Grandma were going out feet first. So he was pretty much housebound and had a lot of time while my Grandma was sleeping, which was a lot. That's when he said to me, "I'm going to make a model of *Sarah*, the boat your Grandma and I spent our honeymoon on over fifty years ago. It's a good way to relive those wonderful times, only in miniature."

"Was he a model maker, Cubby?"

"Nope. He'd never done one before. But Grampy could do most anything. And he did things his way. All his life, it seems to me. Until now, I guess. Anyway, it didn't matter to him that he hadn't built a model boat before. He just began with seven blocks of wood stacked up and glued together, his chisels, and the templates he made to check the shape of the hull. I remember my first time going down to his basement workshop and seeing him getting started. "How are you going to make a model of a fully rigged sailboat from a pile of scape pine boards, Grampy?" He just winked at me. "It'll take forever, even if you figure out how to do it," I said.

"What'd Grampy say?"

"He said, 'That's fine'. Then he shaped and hollowed out the hull and it slowly began to turn into a boat. He built from scratch every piece you see here; every part: a miniature anchor, tiny clock and barometer, coal stove, winches and rigging, and a forward hatch."

Cubby and I looked down through the little hatch into the forward cabin. "I went aboard and got passed down through that hatch on the real *Sarah* when I was really little. Got wedged into the forward cabin in a basket for my first sail."

"What's that little silver thing? Looks like a sewing thimble."

"That's an urn for his ashes. He wants me to put some of his ashes in there when the day finally comes."

Cubby was getting choked up, so I moved things along. "So the big version of this is what I'll be on when we take Grampy sailing."

"We'll see. That sure would be nice."

Cubby said he wanted to show me Grampy's train set in the basement.

"The basement was Grampy's second home. Mine, too, I guess," Cubby said as we headed down the winding steps. "I loved being down here with him when I was little, watching him work all his tools, helping him make some of his weird gadgets. And I loved the mixture of smells: wood chips, furnace oil, and old sailing gear from *Sarah,* like tarred marlin, manila docking lines, and worn out canvas sails that he just couldn't throw away. Many of his ancient, worn-out power tools fascinated me, mostly because, with a little shake or twist of the cord, he could still manage to make them work. He made his band saw himself out of plywood. It's still down here."

"Why would anyone want a plywood band saw?" I asked.

"I asked him that, too. Plywood is strong and cheap, he told me. And he didn't have the tools to fashion a metal one, but the plywood frame was all he really needed for housing the band blade, a couple of pulleys and a place to attach the motor."

We made our way around behind the staircase to another part of the basement. I expected his train stuff to look like what kids had. But this was serious. Just like he did with that model of *Sarah,* Grampy had made another miniature world. This time it was the village of Seacasset, with Ross Island, his own house, a little down-town with some stores, and the harbor, with a tiny model of *Sarah* at anchor. All of this had train tracks running here and there and up and down through tunnels and over bridges.

About then I told Cubby that right now I needed to stretch out, catch a few winks for a while after having been sitting in the Power Wagon for 20 hours, and we headed upstairs. I found a big couch that looked mighty inviting and settled into it. Cubby went into the den, sat down at Grampy's desk, and started looking through stuff.

"You let me know if you find any clues, Cubby," I said, just before dozing off.

I don't know how long I was out, but I came to hearing this strange robot voice say "You've got mail!" I got up and went into the den and leaned over Cubby, who was sitting at Grampy's funny looking turquoise computer.

"I feel kind of sneaky about this, Red. Don't know if it's right, but I went into Grampy's email to look for clues. He told me the password before I came out to St. Paul for senior year, so I could help him from long distance if he needed it, so I guess it's okay for me to go in."

"So what's in there, Cubby?"

"H-mails. There must be hundreds of them." And he described all about Grampy writing them to his wife and Cubby's mom Ellie in heaven just about every day.

"I was going to try to go through them to find out what was going on in his life, at least through the ones that are dated fairly close to when he called us that night on *Cirrhosis* back in March. But his h-mails stop in late February."

"So he stopped sending them?"

"Why would he stop writing them all of a sudden?"

"Maybe his computer broke for a while or he got tired of using it?"

"No, there are other log-ins to the computer every week or so, right up into March; I checked the 'recent items' list. Other applications were being used during that time."

"So he was using his computer."

"Somebody was. And whoever that was deleted a bunch of his h-mails."

"Jesus, Cubby, I know you're smart and all, but how'd you know that?"

"Whoever did it didn't know about the 'recently deleted' folder. The whole bunch is still in there."

"Holy shit."

"Most of them are really touching and he sounds happy and fun loving and getting along just fine, except for a few quirks. But he doesn't seem the least bit out of it, and it's clear from his h-mails that his home is where he wanted to be and stay. Anyway, I'm printing out a couple copies of two of them, one set for each of us, to show a couple of things: that Grampy wasn't loony and that Ashton was pushing against his rights."

So Cubby printed these out; they're the ones I've still got today:

barbara&ellieoncloud23@hmail.com

June 14, 1996

I hope my two girls are happy and healthy up there. Here's my latest news from down here.

I read *The New York Times* today.

Always do.

It was a good day for me and the obituaries: I beat most of them in that section of the paper.

Guy named Stewart or Steward....forget exactly... doesn't matter.

He made it to 85.

That was close.

But I beat him just the same.

And I easily beat a couple of ladies too. (And they are supposed to live longer).

One named Hilary or Haley...doesn't matter.

67...an easy win.

She probably smoked...paper didn't say.

You smoked too, Barbara. Remember? Though I think it was your only bad habit. But how could you have known back then how bad it was. The magazines even made it sound glamorous!... something to aspire to – do you remember that slogan pushing cigarettes on women: 'You've Come a Long Way Baby!' Times do change. Wonder what they'll find out next that's been hurting us all the time. I hope it's not vanilla ice cream and chocolate sauce. I do love my ice cream. Sometimes in the middle of the night I'll wake up and go downstairs and grab the carton, a big spoon and the squirty Hershey's chocolate sauce and dive right in. No sense using a bowl. Only me. And you never would let me eat like that or even eat too much ice cream. Always worried about my heart. And instead it was you who left first. Someone always has to leave first. I so remember how I held you tighter and tighter each year as we both got older, as if trying to hold back time, or keep you from going first.

Anyway, you'd probably be here with me now in this lovely house instead of in heaven on Cloud 23 if you hadn't smoked.

And then I wouldn't have to send you all these "h-mails" as I like to call them. As I've said, stands for 'Heavenly Mail'. Goes right to your cloud from my old iMac computer. Pretty amazing. Remind me to write you soon and tell you about these computer things.

Oh, and these 'cell phones' too.

I hope you know that I have been sending h-mail to you both every day since you went up. Maybe you received them but just haven't written back yet (long distance to travel, I'm sure). But maybe they don't have computers up in heaven. (My letters to you keep getting returned by someone named "Mailer Demon" (the devil?); he says that the connection 'timed out'. I can see why!) Well, perhaps this one will get through, though I suppose it's very busy and crowded up there with all those people since Adam and Eve. (Some, I suppose, went to the other place.) Anyway, there must be some kind of system to get in touch with others. If there is, would you give my best to my mom and pop—good people, and I'm sure they're up there.

Ellie, your Danny has been wonderful—especially for a teenager—at keeping in touch from school and now that it's summer, he's stopping by and checking on me. We talk of going sailing to Maine again someday. Ha! Wouldn't that be something! Old *Sarah* is still up in Maine after being stored there for quite some time. Your brother Ashton is supposed to be checking on her, Ellie, but he keeps saying he's too busy. Danny may drive up on one of his days off. (Too long a trip for this old man—plus, Ashton took away my keys.) Also, I think I wrote you that Danny is transferring to a new college in St. Paul, Minnesota. He had a hard time with Steve after you went to heaven, and now it's the same with Ashton. Danny has a close pal going to school out in St. Paul who urged him to come out—said he even had a spare room—and Danny and I both think a change would be best right now (though I'll sure miss him).

Anyway, I want to keep telling you the news down here on earth and also how much I love and miss you. And I do want to keep telling you that I'll be along soon, but not just yet.

I do wonder if you are tired of waiting. I hope not.

Barbara, maybe you did get that one 'h-mail" when I told you to stay away from those handsome male angels. Maybe that's why you haven't written back.

Speaking of angels, the other day was quite a day for your Joe, especially now that the nice weather is here and I can be out and about. It was a long winter playing with that train set I made in the basement. Remember that? The most fun still is standing in the middle of the train set, wearing my engineer hat, and watching the cars go around and around. Oh, we've had a crash or two, mostly at the bend by the bridge, but so far the big locomotive has stayed intact.

Anyway, I've been able to walk down to the marsh by the ocean at least once a day. It's only about a quarter mile but it takes old Joe a long time. Then I must rest. Fortunately, there's a bench up on a little sand hill to sit on, the one in the tall grass with a view of the Boston skyline over the ocean. So, with a little rest I head back. Now the other day was the first hot day in June and I must confess that this old man got the thrill of his life! After I rested, I got up to walk a little closer to the water, down in a sandy hollow. There, alone and sunning herself, was a topless young woman! Well, I didn't want to startle her, so (after looking a while), I slowly backed away. That doesn't work for an old man in sand, and I fell. This got the attention of the young lady who pulled up her top and ran over to me. It was like staring up at an angel (though I'm sure that's old hat to you up there by now). Anyway, she was very concerned and quite attentive, which was fine by me. I told her I was okay but she insisted she drive me home, holding my arm and helping me through the sand and into her tiny sports car (that, too, was topless!).

I had no trouble getting in but worried how I would get out of the thing once we got home. When we got in the driveway, she helped me get out, pulling me up under my arms. She seemed to know what she was doing. Being gracious (and kind of lonely), I invited her in for some iced tea. We went out and sat in the screened porch and I learned she was one of those home health nurses and this was her day off. I invited her down to the basement and showed her the trains. Had her stand in the middle and even put on my engineer hat over her long red hair. Pretty girl, even in my old engineer hat. She seemed quite comfortable to be with an old man in his dark basement, so I thought, why not kid her a bit. "Would you like to go upstairs to my bedroom and view my etchings?" I asked. Wrong joke, I guess, and I haven't seen her since, though I do search that spot in the sand by the marsh each and every sunny day.

Well, time for supper. (I have some frozen meat-loaf, which I think I can slice nicely on the table saw in my workshop and then heat up. Then ice cream and chocolate sauce for dessert. Yum!)

As always, I love you both and I'll be up there soon...but not just yet.

Your Joe/Dad

"You think Ashton saw this and figured Grampy was crazier than a shithouse rat, him thinking he can email to heaven?" I said to Cubby.

"God, no. Grampy was always kidding like that, about all kinds of stuff. He's really light hearted and kind of like an old kid. Besides, I bet it made him feel good to pretend he had a way to talk to Grandma and my mom. He was really just writing down his thoughts, I think, and this gave him some sense they were going somewhere."

"Hey, Cubby, you should be one of them psychiatrists in addition to being a lawyer."

"Okay, Red. But check out this h-mail:

barbara&ellieoncloud23@hmail.com

June 22, 1996

Another day down here, dears.

I do still love our home; do you remember it? So full of memories. And I am so comfortable here. Everywhere I look reminds me of something: every shelf I built, all the books I've loved reading over the years, the chairs in the den where you and I discussed the world's problems, every picture we hung, and even every special picture lamp I wired. (This, I admit, was not the most legal wiring. I used old wiring stuff I had in the basement. Wouldn't want an inspector to see any of this, especially that burned spot on the wall from the special night light I wired for our bathroom. Somehow my splice shorted out. No problem though; the melting rubber smell gave it away. (The old ears are no good, but the nose still works fine). Anyway, if I was going to burn the house down, I'd do it with me <u>in</u> it. That way, everything's taken care of: the place is leveled, don't need the tear down, and I get buried (well, cremated) all at once."

Anyway, I sure hope Ashton doesn't try to put me in one of those 'homes' he keeps talking about. Storing me away like stale bread in a box. Ever since you went to heaven, Ellie, Ashton has been trying to be in charge of me. I question his motives. You were all love and caring, but Ashton—I'm not so sure. He keeps suggesting I should let him be in legal charge so he can help on things like finances and writing checks. Says he worries about my spending on the wrong things or signing the wrong thing. I keep telling him that Darcy, my helper, does the shopping and gets what I need. She even uses her checkbook, then brings back the receipts and I pay her back. I tell Ashton that I pay the few other bills I have myself, no problem. Like those for the water, heat, taxes, cable television and the computer. He keeps saying it could be a problem. Shaking his head.

I try very hard not to be a burden. Anyway, what I need to be is very CAREFUL and not FALL. If I fall, and Ashton finds out...well, I'm in trouble.

Well, dears, your old boy is getting tirred and some tyyping mistakks are happening now (see!?)

Oh, I'm also sending you the message (see below) from that Mailer Demon fellow I mentioned earlier (maybe this is the devil; you could ask around up there).

I love you both as always and I'll be up there soon...but not just yet.

Your Joe/Dad

From: Mail Delivery System <MAILER-DAEMON@ AOL.com>
To: joeroan
Subject: Undelivered Mail Returned to Sender.

*** ATTENTION ***
Your e-mail is being returned to you because there was a problem with its delivery. The reason your mail is being returned to you is listed in the section labeled: "----- The delivery status notification errors -----".
- Postmaster
----- The delivery status notification errors -----
barbara&ellieoncloud23@hmail.com>: connect to hmail.com[82.98.86.169]:25: Connection__**timed out**

I got to thinking about all this, and reading that last h-mail over and over. Finally I said, "Cubby, I bet Grampy deleted these h-mails himself."

"Really?"

"I don't think he was loony either. As a matter of fact, I think he was so *not* loony that he figured what he was writing could be found by Ashton, who would then think this proved he really *was* loony and so he could put him away."

"But why would he even *want* to do that to Grampy?"

"Let me ask you this, straight and simple, Cubby: who gets Grampy's money when he dies?"

"I don't know."

"Think maybe it's you?"

"I don't know."

"Think Ashton's getting any of it?"

"I don't know. It's weird, Ashton being his son and all, but Grampy never really liked him. Ashton was always figuring on ways to get money out of Grampy."

"You think Ashton thinks if you get Grampy's money you'll give any of it to him?"

"I don't know."

"You think Ashton is clever?"

"Well, yeah."

"You think Ashton all of a sudden became this caring guy that's now all worried about Grampy's welfare, worried about him living in his own house?"

"Doesn't make sense, Red."

"You think Ashton wants Grampy's money?"

"Of course."

"You think Ashton's in your mother's will or Grampy's will?"

"I don't know. Ashton must have gotten to be conservator and guardian maybe because I wasn't twenty-one at the time."

"You think that means he can change the legal stuff? How much power does this thing give him? Seems to me that in this h-mail we got here that Ashton's worried about Grampy spending his own money the wrong way, when maybe Grampy should be worried about how Ashton would spend it! I bet that conservator and guardian stuff gives him lots of control—maybe full control."

"Wow, Red, maybe *you're* the smartest one in the room," Cubby said.

"Biggest one in the room, anyway, Cubby. Always the biggest one in the room."

3 7

ME AND NURSE RATSHIT

The next morning we climbed into the Power Wagon and headed into this cutesy downtown to grab some chow at the nearest greasy spoon. Well, I found out soon enough that I was square in the middle of yuppiedom, and places like The Slough wouldn't make it long around here. We stopped at the little town square and parked next to this real fancy carved wooden sign that said Town Centre Directory. "Well, look at that, Cubby," I said, "I ain't the sharpest bulb in the shed, but I think they spelled 'Center' wrong. Too bad, this being such a nice sign and all."

"That's the British spelling, Red."

"Well, we come farther east than I thought, then."

"It's used in historic, colonial towns."

I started looking on the sign for some place to grab some grub.

"There's three or four spots around, Red. Take your choice. We can walk to all of them."

"I'm not sure if I'm looking at food places, poetry places, astrology places, or little houses."

"Huh?"

"What are these joints: A Brisket a Tasket? A Day Latte? Aroma Borealis? Banana Cabana?"

"They're our version of greasy spoons."

"You choose one, Cubby."

"Okay. And don't call the waitress a broad."

I looked back at the sign with the bad spelling. "I think we are abroad, Cubby. This is a new land to me."

* * *

"You pay a price for eating that stuff," I said to Cubby after we got done eating those tiny asparagus omelets at the Banana Cabana and began walking back to the truck.

"What do you mean, 'you pay a price'? I thought they were reasonable and they were good, Red."

"Yeah, but they're gonna make our pee smell. Wonder why that happens?"

"I don't know Red. I really don't know."

"You getting tired of me Cubby? Sounds like it."

"No, I'm just anxious about what we're going to find out about Grampy."

"You ever been in a nursing home?"

"No. This is a first."

"Me, too," I said. "Seems like everybody I know that died did it before they was old enough for one of those places. Momma finally died in the hospital. And Daddy, well, he just dropped dead from a heart attack. That's what they said anyway. They found him in the dead of winter, not far from his truck, just a big lump in the snow. I think he passed out, froze in his sleep. They say alcohol don't freeze easy — and he was mostly alcohol—but it froze in him."

"Sorry, Red."

"Don't be sorry. I had the world's best momma. One out of two ain't bad."

"I know what you mean."

We were quiet almost all the way to the nursing home, but as we got closer I said, "I'm thinking we got to have an action plan for this mission, Cubby."

"Well, my plan is to first find Grampy and ask him how he's doing and what's going on."

I parked the Power Wagon by the Sunny Gardens van and we headed up the steps to the main doors. The place looked more like the front of one of those Best Western hotels instead of an old folks home. Cubby introduced himself to the lady at the front desk, and said we were there to visit Grampy. The lady said that lunch was just ending and could we wait five or ten minutes.

So we sat down and waited. Nobody seemed to be around except the front desk lady. I leaned over and whispered to Cubby. "Maybe they don't have much business? Or maybe everybody died. I sure hope not."

"Relax, Red. We're out in the waiting area, not the inside. Why don't you watch that TV or read a magazine."

I looked up at the TV and there was that *Jerry Springer Show* playing with a couple of his guests screaming at each other. I heard one of them say, 'I'm pregnant by my brother' and that about did it for me. So I turned to the magazines. I didn't cotton to *Better Homes and Gardens* or *Today's Senior*, so instead I read this pamphlet they had on the table:

> *You, as the visitor, may feel anxious at the thought of visiting our nursing home, worried that what you will find will be a depressing place. The sight of so many elderly people who have suffered some form of disability may be upsetting. Imagine if it were you living in a nursing home, away from your familiar home and community, feeling lost and unsure of yourself in this new place. You might even feel that you've somehow been rejected. So it's key that you think of each resident as an important individual who has lived a long and full life, and whose uniqueness does not depend on physical appearance. You may be bothered by those who appear to be confused or disoriented. Keep in mind that these people can often be reached by simply holding their hands and looking into their eyes.*

"Cubby, maybe I'll go out and sit in the truck," I said. "I'm getting creeped out."

"What's the matter?"

"This pamphlet scares the hell out of me. It makes me feel like we're going into some alien world, like on the Twilight Zone."

"What?"

"You ever watch those old Twilight Zone shows on TV? You ever see the one where these nine-foot tall aliens come down and make friends with the earth folks, tell them their planet is paradise, then take some of them up to it, then come back empty and get more earth folks. Then they leave behind their special alien book about their mission, but all the earth folks can figure is how to translate the title: *To Serve Man*. So more people go up in the space ship to see paradise. Then, just as one more group is boarding, the translator finally cracks the code and yells, 'Get off of that ship! The rest of this book, *To Serve Man*, it's...it's a cookbook!' But it's too late."

"God, Red. What planet are *you* from? Do you think Sunny Gardens eats people?"

"No, Cubby, it's just something about this here pamphlet that gets me. I was using one of those medifors you told me about."

"No. No, that's not even close to what..."

Right then the desk lady came over and said we could go see Grampy in room 106. She gave us a little map of these long hallways and pointed off in the distance. There weren't no spaceship to paradise here. We had to walk and walk, down the longest and whitest hallways I ever saw. And once we got started, just like we was getting onto some freeway, there was traffic: walkers, wheelchairs, food carts, nurses, a doctor or two. I had to keep my wits about me so as not to crash. A lot of the folks in the wheelchairs were parked right in the middle, either asleep at the wheel, or crying, or just mumbling to themselves. I whispered to Cubby, "I can see why Grampy wants to go sailing."

Cubby moved on faster. I knew he was excited to see Grampy, and when we got there, I followed him in.

Grampy was in the corner, sitting in a wheelchair facing the window. He was thin with a big head of white hair and, even in the chair, I could tell by looking at his legs that he was probably as tall as me. Cubby walked around him slowly, put his hand on his shoulder, and leaned down and smiled. "Danny!" Grampy said, and let out a huge sigh.

"Grampy, don't do that!" Cubby said.

"Don't do what?"

"Sigh so hard."

"What so hard?"

"Sigh. Sigh so hard. It scares me."

Grampy let out a laugh. "Oh, rubbish, Danny. When I'm dying I'll let you know in a more articulate manner. Anyway, you came! You came! I knew you would. And you got her here safely, I bet."

"Got who here safely?" Cubby said.

"SHUT UP."

Cubby and I jumped a bit and looked at a woman in a wheelchair in the doorway of Grampy's room.

"Oh, that's Shut Up. She lives next door," Grampy said.

"SHUT UP."

"I'm making very little headway with that old girl. No one is, in fact. She keeps wandering into people's rooms, yelling 'shut up'. And speaking of old girls, I was hoping you got *Sarah* down here to Seacasset from Maine, so we could go sailing."

"SHUT UP."

Grampy leaned closer to Cubby. One of his eyes that didn't seem to work so good looked away into nowhere; the other one was fixed right into Cubby. "Danny, I have to get out of here. I *have* to. I'm a sailor and I don't belong here. This place is the doldrums." Right then he noticed me. "And who might this gentleman be?"

"He's my best friend," Cubby said. "Excepting for you, of course."

I stepped forward, feeling pretty damned special.

"Well, he must be a good man, then."

"He is. Grampy, this is Orca Bates."

"My friends call me Red, sir," I said. "And I'm mighty proud to know you."

"Well, I guess you know Danny is a fine young man."

"SHUT UP."

Right about then I'd reached my limit with Shut Up. I knew it wouldn't go down good if I just walked over and punched her lights out. Then I thought about that pamphlet: *"These people can often be reached by simply holding their hands and looking into their eyes"*. So I turned and walked slowly over to her chair, putting a big smile on my face. Then I leaned down, reached out, and gently picked up her left hand and looked into her eyes, just like the pamphlet said.

"My name is Orca Bates," I said. "And I just wanted to tell you that it is my absolute pleasure to have the good fortune to finally meet a woman of your beauty and quality." The room was quiet. Shut Up just stared at me. I stared back into Shut Up's eyes without blinking, telling myself I was some Richard Burton genius actor guy, and was just going to flood her with sincerity. Shut Up kept looking at me, staring right into my eyes, not saying nothing. Then I said, "You sit there quietly, young lady, and I'll be back real soon," and I moved back near Grampy and Cubby.

"Perhaps we could go outside for some fresh air," Grampy said. "The air is terrible in this place. Terrible *for* you, too. We're all shut in. Always overheated. No natural smells, like the salt marsh and sea air. All bad."

So right away we wheeled Grampy past the still silent Shut Up, and slowly out of the room. In the hall, Grampy said to me, "Are you a psychiatrist?"

Before I could answer, Cubby did. "I'm beginning to think so. Red is one of the finest river pilots you'll ever meet; also, he's starting to moonlight as a detective, and now maybe a therapist."

"A detective? How so?" Grampy asked.

"Let's wait until we get outside," Cubby said.

We pushed Grampy out into the bright sun and followed a path around the side of the building that the sign said led to a place called The Labyrinth. "Ain't that a place like a maze, where you get stuck?" I asked.

"There's a sign that does a decent job explaining it," Grampy said. "I get out here as much as they'll let me. It's up ahead." We pulled Grampy up to the sign and read it:

> The Labyrinth is not a maze. There are no tricks to it and no dead ends. It has a single circuitous path that winds its way into the center. The person walking it uses the same path to return from the center and the entrance then becomes the exit. The path is in full view, which allows a person to be quiet and focus internally.
>
> Generally there are three stages to the walk: releasing on the way in, receiving in the center and returning when you follow the path back out of the labyrinth. Symbolically, and sometimes actually, you are taking back out into the world that which you have received.
>
> To prepare, you may want to sit quietly to reflect before walking the labyrinth. Some people come with questions, others just to slow down and take time out from a busy life. Some come to find strength to take the next step. Many come during times of grief and loss.

It took me a while to get through the description, but when I got it I thought, 'This is a good place to take Shut Up'.

"Have you walked this, Grampy? I mean, been wheeled through it?" Cubby asked.

"You know, Danny, I didn't need a wheelchair until they put me in here," Grampy said. "Then I tripped on a stool and sprained my ankle. Things get moved around all the time in this place and I stumble. At home I knew every square inch and never tripped or fell. So they put me in this chair. I know my foot's better, but for some reason they want to keep me in it. Ashton's idea."

"How is Ashton?"

"He doesn't come around much, and when he does he's with his buddy, that Doctor Donogood?"

"That's his name?"

"That's what I call him. Does no good. Every time I see him I tell him I want to go home, that I'm fine, that I never wanted to leave my home in the first place. He just nods and says 'We'll see. We just want to do what's best.' And then he does what he wants to do, which is no good."

"What's that medicine they gave you, the one you told me on the phone didn't make you right."

"I don't know what it is. But it made me different. They kept saying I was being uncooperative, and that I kept trying to leave and walk home, so they were giving me this medicine to quiet me down. It did that all right; all I started to do from then on was mumble. So a few days later, at a point when I had half a brain working, I pretended to take the medicine but didn't swallow it. After that I started getting my old self back, Danny."

Right then I started thinking about *The Twilight Zone* show again. And also about how Shut Up must have not swallowed her drugs either. Maybe we need to spring Shut Up, too, I thought.

"Ashton is friends with the doctor?" Cubby asked.

"Seems so."

"Grampy," Cubby said, sounding real nervous, "I need to tell you something. First, Red and I are one thousand percent on your side. Second, I hope you don't mind, but I had to try to figure out what's going on here, so I went into your computer at the Ross Island house and read some of your emails. Well, your 'h-mails'. But it was all to help, to find out what's going on."

"I was only kidding, with all that heaven stuff. Just my way of talking to your grandma and mom. Who can blame me? It gets kind of lonely. You believe me Danny, right?"

"Of course I do. But why did you stop writing them all of a sudden?"

"I got worried about Ashton."

"Is that why you threw them in the computer's trash?"

Grampy glanced at me, looking pretty proud. "Smart young man. Smart young man. All that good schooling paid off."

"Red helped, too," Cubby said.

Right then I figured I'd lean into this conversation. "We're gonna get you out of this maze and take you sailing, Grampy. Don't you worry," I said.

"I'm going to find someone to talk with about all this," Cubby said. "Red, could you maybe push Grampy around the grounds while I do?"

So Cubby went inside to find the person in charge. I sat down on a bench next to the labyrinth. "Need to take a load off these feet," I said.

"I'm not surprised; you're a big man."

"Came out of my momma at nearly 13 pounds, they told me. Been big ever since."

"Well, you're a big help to Danny and to me, that's for certain. You've already helped me. Say, we couldn't quite hear you; what exactly did you say to Shut Up to get her to calm down?"

"Just a little love, Grampy. Just a little love."

"Well, I still need to get out of here, even if Shut Up stays quiet. I need to get back to my house, to the salt marsh, maybe to even sailing *Sarah* again on my own."

"So you're not thinking of going to Cloud 23 for a while yet."

"No, heaven goes on forever. Barbara, my wife—and also Ellie, Danny's mother—will be there waiting, bless them. I'll know when the time's right. And it will be right if I don't get out of here."

"Hell, Grampy, we could make a break for it right now. My truck's right over there."

"I'm not sure that's prudent at this point."

"Maybe Cubby, ah, Danny—Cubby's what I calls him—maybe he'll do some paperwork and get you out legitimate like."

"I do hope so. Have you ever sailed? You're in for a real treat if you haven't."

"I've got plenty of time on the water, but it's flat water, close to land. The Mississippi River."

"Well, you'll be just fine at sea; I bet you'll love the motion of the ocean swells and the quiet of pure sailing. Speaking of sailing, Danny never answered my question about where *Sarah* is. Is she still in Maine?"

"We're going up to Maine to get her. Sail her back and pick you up."

"Splendid. I'm so glad. So glad. And now, if you wouldn't mind, I need to find the rest room. The bladder is one of the problems of old age, though I do hate to go inside on such a gorgeous day."

"Hell, Grampy, I'll just wheel you over to them bushes, help you stand up, and you can take a leak right outside. There's nobody around."

"That would be a tad undignified."

"Yeah, maybe they'd throw you out."

"You are probably right. Let's do it."

Afterwards we sat for a while and he told me about sailing and I told him about tow boating. We took turns, 'cause each of us was really interested in the other's water world. But after a while it started to cloud up and Grampy needed a sweater; plus, Cubby had been gone a long time. So I wheeled Grampy inside.

As we headed to his room, I kept passing the lunch carts with all the dessert leftovers piled on and seeming like they were just going to waste. I pushed Grampy past some half-eaten pieces of lemon meringue pie, some pretty tasty looking sweet rolls, and even some ice cream that wasn't melted yet. Well, it seemed like a long time since that tiny asparagus omelet, and I didn't know how much longer we were going to be here in Sunny Gardens, so I wheeled us close to the next few carts, and throttled down to almost a dead stop. Couldn't find a fork, so I just grazed from the dessert remainders by hand—even dunked a sweet roll in the ice cream—then steamed forward. It all would have worked fine if I'd just looked astern before I ever got hooked up on this food drive. But this barge of a nurse—the one I named Nurse Ratshit—she was tailing me. She must have had on a full head of steam by the time I left the third food cart, 'cause she passed me on my port side out of nowhere, then turned back and blocked my headway.

"That food is for the residents, Sir," she said.

"I figured they didn't want it, since it was on the scrap carts."

"What's left goes to the homeless."

"You serve half-eaten scraps to the homeless? Hell, I'm almost homeless."

"May I ask how you are related to Mr. Roan?"

"He's my son."

"Sir, I have no time for humor. My job is to protect our residents."

"Well, you should let them loose then. And don't feed 'em bad drugs, lady."

I figured Ratshit was about to blow her steam safety valve, but right then Cubby came out of a room with a door marked 'Social Worker' and asked what was going on.

"This man was stealing food," Ratshit said.

Then Grampy spoke up. "No, that's my food. Partly paid for by me. And I wanted him to have it."

"And who are you?" Ratshit said, turning to Cubby.

"I'm his grandson."

"And who is he?" she said, glaring at me.

"That's Mr. Bates," Grampy said.

"And what is his role?"

"I'm really the county food inspector," I said. "And I needed to taste all that stuff."

Cubby got behind Grampy's wheelchair and started pushing it down the hall. "Come on, Red. Let's take Grampy back to his room and head out."

I started to follow along, but then I turned back to Ratshit. "Oh, and I took care of Shut Up for you. She don't need no drugs. Did it all with some love and attention. So you're welcome."

38
ANOTHER ALIEN WORLD: THE SEACASSET YACHT CLUB

Cubby was damned upset on the way home. He was sad for Grampy, confused about what to do, and steaming mad at Ashton. The phone rang in the Ross Island house just as we were coming in the door. Cubby picked it up and held it back from his ear 'cause the voice on the other end was so loud. I could hear every word.

"What the hell is going on, Danny? I just got a call from Sunny Gardens. The head nurse is bullshit."

'No, she's Ratshit,' I thought to myself.

"Gee, didn't see you at my graduation, Ashton," Danny said, ignoring the question.

"Yeah, well, I had this big deal that was closing. Would have made it if I could, you know. But somebody's got to work around here. Anyway, what's going on? Who was that big guy they said was with you? What happened in there?

"Grampy is miserable, Ashton. Why'd you put him in there?"

"Look, meet me at the club tonight around eight and we'll talk about it; I've got to run now. I'll be on the porch at that table way down toward the flagpole."

"All right," Cubby said, and hung up. He turned to me. "Red, you're going to a yacht club."

"A what?"

"The Seacasset Yacht Club."

"Sounds too fancy for me."

"We'll just be on the porch, not in the dining room; dress is smart casual."

"I can do casual, Cubby; don't know about the smart."

"Long pants, nice shirt, okay?"

So I put on my best Carhartt shirt, my chinos without the stain, hooked on my red suspenders, and topped it off with my Caterpillar Diesel cap.

"You can't wear your hat inside the club, Red. It's a rule," Cubby said.

Man, I thought, I *am* going to another planet. I put the hat in my back pocket.

* * *

"Don't they have any American cars out here?" I asked Cubby as we pulled into the yacht club parking lot, which was filled with fancy Mercedes and BMWs. "I bet the Power Wagon's got 'em all beat on horsepower, though" I said. I parked by the tennis courts, right next to a sign that seemed like it should be illegal nowadays. "Will you look at that, Cubby," I said. Ain't that kind of in-your-face racist?"

"What, Red?"

"That sign on the tennis court fence that says 'Whites Only'."

"That means tennis whites. You have to wear white clothes when playing tennis."

"Seems like it might mean something else to some other kind of folks."

"God, you're right, Red. It wasn't there last year. I guess they just assumed people all knew the meaning."

"Assuming ain't a safe way of thinking; that's what my momma always said to me when I was little. And anyway, why do you have to wear white clothes to play tennis?"

Cubby just shook his head and smiled. "I'm not sure they're ready for you here in the East, Red."

"Well, let's go in and find out."

A lot of folks said hello to Cubby as we made our way along the porch, and he introduced me to a few. He was in his home waters now, and I thought maybe that was good. Also, I figured I was doing pretty well myself, shaking hands and minding my manners and all. I began seeing a lot of them blue blazers and tasseled loafers that Cubby told me about, though I didn't hear anybody say 'yes, quite'.

Then this pretty young thing with blond hair in a pink headband and wearing a yellow flowered sundress gave Cubby a big hug. That got his attention real good, and I just stood there like a dummy until he finally introduced me to Jessica. Then they got back to ogling each other and I figured I'd slip away and do some exploring around this new planet called a yacht club. I made my way into a big room filled with silver trophies and model sailboats in glass cases. Above me, hanging from this high-beamed ceiling, was about four million flags. In the center of the room was a long, shiny wooden table covered with shrimp, cheese, and little pieces of roast beef. It all looked mighty good. I figured this spread was for anybody, so I looked around for a plate to load up on. Only ones I could find looked pretty fancy, leaning on a shelf under some of the trophies. They looked clean enough, so I grabbed one that maybe was for chowder, 'cause it said something about a chowder race on it.

Right then this little guy in a coat and tie popped up out of nowhere and said, "May I help you, sir?"

I said 'no, thanks', that I was fine, just grabbing a bite.

"Are you one of the new members? This is the welcoming food for our new members reception."

"No, I'm just passing through," I said.

"I see that."

"I'm here with Cubby, ah, Danny Roan."

"May I put that trophy plate back on the shelf for you, then?"

"Sure," I said, and handed it to him.

"You'll find some light snacks in the bar, sir."

So I backed out of that room and followed the sound of jabbering and cackling until I came to another room with more flags and some paintings of old sailing ships hanging in fancy gold frames around the fireplace. A bunch of folks was gabbing away in front of a big mahogany bar that had a brass rail on the floor to put your feet on. They were all men except for this one lady who was wearing this silly-looking white sailor costume with an anchor on her gold belt, stars over each boob, and a little white sailor hat with an anchor on it. There were three bartenders in red bowties. Sitting on a stand in the middle of the room, behind the folks that were lined up in front of the bar, was a giant glass bowl filled with about ten million of them cheese goldfish snacks. Right then a drink seemed like a real good idea, so I got in line and slowly wormed my way up to the bar. It was sure different from being at The Slough, and so was the talk; everybody was jabbering about stuff I never even heard of: short selling, index funds, windward mark protests, Mylar full batten mains. Finally I got up to the bar and ordered a pitcher of Budweiser. No Budweiser, the barkeep said. Then he rattled off some beer names I never heard of. "Your call," I said, and he poured me a glass of some yuppie beer called Stella Artois.

"Member number?" the barkeep asked.

"No number, paying cash," I said, and reached into my trousers.

"We don't take cash. Only charge, sir."

This made me nervous. "I'll have to get the number from the guy I'm with," I said, and started backing away from the bar. Right then somebody jostled me and I felt my CAT Diesel hat fall out of my back pocket. So I bent over to pick it up. But I must have gone too wide on my bend, 'cause my stern kicked out and slammed into the giant goldfish bowl, knocking it off its stand. This made the lady in the white sailor suit scream and then spill red wine all over herself while them ten million goldfish swam all over the floor. People on the porch, including Cubby and Jessica, came running in to see what all the commotion was about while I was backing out of the room and onto the porch, where I figured I'd find calmer waters.

"What happened in there, Red?" Cubby asked.

"Bunch of goldfish escaped, near as I can figure," I said.

"Well, I need to find Ashton. Can you come along? I could use your help."

We said goodbye to Jessica and I watched as she headed into the bar. "Bet there's a pot of gold under that yellow dress, Cubby. You should go prospecting for it."

"God, Red. Just stop."

We walked to the end of the porch where we found this guy with an eighty-dollar haircut who was wearing a pink shirt and bright green pants. The pants had these little red lobsters crawling all over them, looking like they was feeding on his legs. On his feet were them tasseled boat shoes with no socks. He was sitting with a woman at a round table.

"That Ashton?" I asked as we closed in.

"How'd you know?"

"Long shot."

As I got closer I realized the woman had a lot of miles on her, maybe built in 1940, but heavily reconditioned to look like a 1960's model—lots of body work and a new paint job.

"Ah, here's the new graduate," Ashton said.

"Hello, Ashton," Cubby said.

"Danny, may I introduce Shelby Wentworth."

"Hello. This is my friend Orca Bates."

"Danny, Shelby was just headed into the new members reception as she's on the nominating committee, you know," Ashton said, all proud, like she was the Queen of Siam or something.

After Shelby got up to go, I moved in to take her chair, but Ashton wasn't liking it.

"Perhaps your friend could grab a drink at the bar so we can have a private discussion, Danny."

"I tried doing that," I said. "It didn't work out too good."

"Red and I have been through a lot together; he's my friend and I'd like him to stay right here," Cubby said.

So that's what I did, but old Ashton pretty much ignored me.

"So what's going on Danny?" he asked.

"I should ask you."

"Whatever are you talking about?"

"I talked to the social worker today; she says Grampy feels like a prisoner. She says he keeps trying to go home."

"Home is not the best place for him."

"Why's that? Says who?"

"He's a vulnerable adult; he's a danger to himself, for one thing."

"Oh, so because of that he might die in his own home instead of dying while being locked away in some institution?"

"He's not locked away."

"So he's free to leave?"

"With supervision."

"They give him drugs, Ashton. To dumb him down. You know that?"

"He's anxious. When he was at home he was a danger to his house and to the neighborhood."

"Grampy was a danger to the neighborhood? You mean, he might have robbed somebody? Assaulted some kid?"

"No. I mean fire. He was likely to burn his house down and maybe destroy others along with it."

"There's not another home within a hundred yards."

"Also, he's losing his sense of reality. He thinks he can talk to heaven. He brings strange women into the house. He slices his frozen meat with his workshop table saw. Next thing he'll be writing checks to any scam artist who finds him. And there are plenty of those."

"He doesn't believe he can really talk to heaven; it's like a diary, a fun way for him to pretend to communicate with Grandma and my mom. And that lady he brought into the house was a healthcare worker he met down by the beach near the marsh. He was lonely. And he's always been really good with a table saw. So what if he cuts his hand off? He's 87. He's in his home. He wants to die there."

"Look, I know this is hard for you to accept, but…"

"It's not right. I'll take care of him then."

"Danny, I'm his son, and also his conservator and guardian. All this is up to me to decide now. You're only twenty-one. You've got a career to start. You want to be someone's nurse maid at twenty-one?"

"Grampy's not just 'someone'. Why don't we ask *him*?"

"Danny, I petitioned the court and outlined all these dangers."

"And was Grampy there?"

"Yes."

"And he agreed with you?"

"The court felt he was at the point where he needed a conservator and guardian, and I agreed to take it on."

"That's big of you. Why not get someone like Darcy to live with him full time in the house? Why fire her and then take him out of his home and lock him away?"

"Danny, there were lots of options discussed. I've put an enormous amount of time, money, and energy into this. It's done."

I watched Cubby really steam up, good old mild-mannered Cubby; no, that guy was gone now. He raised his voice at Ashton:

"You were *never* around when he was younger; you *never* showed any interest in being with him. You just went about your own stuff after Grandma and my mom died. My mom was *always* around and caring for him. Now you're suddenly so concerned about Grampy. What's with that?"

"I'm his son, for God's sake!"

"Sometimes I doubt it. Some son."

Ashton started turning red, and stared at Cubby. "You know, what I am is a *real* son with a real father," he said.

That was about the meanest thing I ever heard, and I churned up inside something awful. But Cubby made me proud; he didn't miss a beat, just stood up and stared Ashton down. "I'd rather be loved and wanted than a biological mistake," he said.

"Don't push me, Danny. I can make it very hard for you to even *see* your grandfather."

About here's where I just had to get aboard, 'cause I was burning, just burning and about to pop myself. "Mind if I ask you one question, Ashton?" I said. He looked at me like I was some strange, dirty, mean ol' dog that had wandered into his living room.

"Who *are* you, anyway? You from around here?"

"I ain't sure that matters. But I figure I got one question that could clear everything up, nice and tidy like, in me and Danny's minds."

Ashton lifted his chin and rolled his eyes. "The correct usage is 'Danny and my', but fire away."

"You ever seen Grampy's will? 'Cause I bet you ain't in it too much."

Ashton pushed his chair back. "You, sir, are one meddling asshole."

"Yes, quite indeed," I said. "That would be the correct usage. I'm the meddling asshole. But you're the scam artist."

And, by Jesus, if Ashton's face didn't get even redder under that eighty-dollar haircut. Then he just stood up and walked away.

Cubby stared at me, but I could tell that he'd put it all together.

"We got our work cut out for us, little buddy," I said. "And not a lot of time."

* * *

Me and Cubby headed off to the nearest Pizza Hut, where I pushed down a couple pitchers of Budweiser while we chowed on one of their Panormous pizzas (serves 4-6). "So what's the plan, Cubby?" I asked after a couple slices.

"Jessica's father is a lawyer. I think I should call him and get some advice."

"Good idea, I reckon. But what does he think of old Ashton? You might get some bad advice if those two guys are yacht club pals."

"You're right, Red. Maybe I should call one of those legal services offices that provides free legal advice."

So that's what Cubby did first thing the next morning. They told him it was this whole process: he'd have to gather evidence to show Ashton wasn't working in Grampy's best interest; then, if he couldn't find that stuff, he'd have to petition the court to get the accounting that Ashton's supposed to file; then he needed to get one of those probate attorneys to file a notice of appearance in court. The whole shebang sounded to me like it was gonna take longer than driving sixteen loaded barges from St. Paul to New Orleans. And all that time wasn't going to do Grampy any good, sitting in that nursing home, even if we finally won. Cubby and I talked it over. Then Cubby said,

"Well, let's at least go get *Sarah* right away then, get her back here, and then try to get Grampy that sail he's looking for. Then we can deal with this legal stuff. Let's grab what gear and supplies we need for the boat from the garage and basement, load the skiff into the truck, go tell Grampy we'll be back in a week or so, and head out."

39
MAINERS AND MASSHOLES

Me and Maine was a good fit, right from the start. First off, up there they don't waste no time on big words or long questions. I picked up their language pretty damned quick. For example, instead of asking 'What are you doing?' them Maine folks just say chuppta. And it seems like most everybody except Massholes—that's folks from Massachusetts—leaves their keys in their car. And they don't use blinkers 'cause everybody already knows where you're going. Plus, my Power Wagon fit right in with these folks. They took me as a character, which meant I was a regular.

Quimby's Boat Yard, like Grouchy's Marina, was frozen in time. We pulled up next to an old tin shed with a gas pump out front. I looked at the price per gallon: thirty-one cents. "I think I should fill up, Cubby," I said. "Thirty-one cents."

"They haven't sold gas for years, Red. That pump's been dead since I was a little kid."

I looked around. The place spoke to my heart; it was a putterer's paradise, filled with old lumber, bronze ship fittings, rusted engine blocks, propellers, a few old work vessels, and some fancy new yachts. I heard some grunts coming from one of the storage sheds and we watched as three yard workers picked up and slowly carried a sailboat mast from the shed past us toward the crane by the water. One of them looked twice at Cubby, then at me, and then back at my truck. "You boys out a staytahs?" he asked.

"Hi, Colby, I remember you. I'm Joe Roan's grandson," Cubby said. "And this is my friend, Red. He's from Minnesota."

"Real fine. Been a while. It's Danny, right? You was just a pup; got big since I last seen ya up this way. How's yer granddaddy?"

"He's in a nursing home, but we're up here to get *Sarah* ready to sail her back to where he is, so we can take him sailing."

"Mighty fine. But you boys got some work to do after we haul her. You got to change the zinc on her shaft, scrape her bottom, maybe caulk her garboards a bit. Then put plenty of paint on her, 'cause that's all that's holding things together down there. Then we'll splash her and bring her back to the dock, and with any luck old *Sarah* will be tighter than a gnat's arse and get ya home safe. Either that or you'll end up down there with the lobstahs."

We headed down to the dock. "Hey Cubby," I said, "what's an outastaytah?"

"He saw your license plate, Red. That's Maine talk for an out-of-state person. Lucky you had Minnesota plates and not Massachusetts ones."

"Why's that?"

"Because they don't like 'Massholes'."

"Why's that?"

"Grampy said it's because Massachusetts people have been buying up and tearing down old family homes on the Maine coast, putting fancy ones in their place, and slowly taking away the character of the community. Oh, and they don't like the way Massholes drive."

"But 'Minneholes' are okay?"

"What?"

"Nothing. Just making a joke, Cubby."

We walked down a rickety old gangway and stood on the dock. Cubby pointed out *Sarah*, hanging to a mooring just off the dock of the small cove. She looked pretty small to me. And low in the water. "Ice doesn't get in here?" I asked Cubby.

"Not bad ice; just slushy because of the salt water, and there's too much tide running in and out for things to freeze solid."

Real ice from a real winter—Minnesota ice—would have turned that boat to toothpicks, I thought as we headed back to the truck to get the skiff. As we were carrying it down to the dock, Cubby got to looking nervous. "You need to be careful getting into the skiff, Red. It's pretty tippy. You can't just step in, you know. You have to sit on the edge of the dock first, and then kind of slide in, making sure you stay in center as much as you can. This is cold water in Maine, and you don't want to go in. You'd probably freeze and drown before you could swim to shore."

"Can't swim anyway, so it won't matter how cold the water is. Anyway, I'd rather drown quick than slowly freeze my balls off."

"Oh, great. Well, we'll get a life jacket for you."

"They don't make 'em big enough for me; found that out years ago. Plus, I ain't afraid of any of that dying shit, if that's what you're worried about."

"Okay, but you should sit real still in the center of the stern seat. I'll row from the forward seat oarlocks, so we should balance out."

I just shook my head. "Yeah, right. Like you and me on a see-saw."

As soon as we came alongside, I could tell that Cubby was real sad about *Sarah's* condition. Even from the skiff, I could see she was an old lady now. Gettin' old, just like Grampy, I thought. The paint on the boat's sides was faded, and had bubbled, cracked and peeled all over. One side of the cabin trunk had a crack along the length of it that crossed through each old bronze porthole along the way. A forward porthole was gone, and the hole was covered with a scrap piece of de-laminated plywood, like some cheap patch over a wounded eye. The cockpit varnish had peeled away, leaving those nice mahogany seats gray with age. *Sarah* seemed to be crouching in the water, like some homeless old lady, ashamed that anyone would see her condition. Green, stringy, slimy algae was growing along what was left of her worn waterline.

I took a glance at Cubby; he was hunched over the oars with a look on his face like some young boxer against the ropes who just realized he's got no business in that ring. I knew his thoughts were all bigger than mine, what with all him and Grampy had done together on this little boat. Then I thought about me and my daddy, about how maybe it could have been different. Anyway, right about then this early summer breeze blew in through the narrow entrance of the cove, giving me a real shot of salt air. Seemed like that air was filled with smells of both life and death. I looked over at some low tide ledges covered with long brown kelp and seaweed, and thought, 'that stuff I'm smelling is just taking a break between tides, lying flat and quiet for a while, maybe getting some sunlight to sprout something new.' Then that sea breeze began to make those old manila ropes thump against *Sarah's* tall wood mast. A gull circled us, gliding silently, searching for something, I reckon. On the other side of the cove a lobster boat's engine revved in starting, and then settled down to a steady idle. A gas engine, not diesel. A Ford 302 maybe.

"She's got a lot of water in the bilge," Cubby said as he hauled himself aboard. "I can feel how sluggish she is."

"Wait 'til she feels me in her," I said as I tried to stand up in the skiff and climb aboard. But I couldn't figure out how to get from the skiff to *Sarah's* deck. Every time I stood up and tried to step out, the skiff slid out away from *Sarah*. My weight and bad knee weren't helping much either. "We might need that crane that's ashore to haul me up, Cubby," I said.

"Try sitting down on *Sarah's* rail and then lifting up and turning your legs onto the deck. That's how Grandma used to do it."

So Grandma Red made it aboard. *Sarah* settled down even more in the water; I swear I heard the old boat groan a little. Cubby slid the hatch and looked into the cabin. "Well, the first thing we need to do is pump," he said. "There's water over the floorboards. The electric bilge pump must not be working, or it's drained the batteries over the winter. There should be a pump handle under the port cockpit seat. Can you start with the pumping, Red, while I open things up and get some air in here? The handle goes in that manual pump hole in the cockpit under your legs. Please count the number of strokes so we can keep track of her leaking."

So that's what I did while Cubby opened the middle and forward hatches and all the portholes. "One, two, three, four, five, six, seven, eight..."

"Red, you don't have to say each stroke aloud."

"How am I going to keep track then?"

"What? Say each number to yourself."

"Won't work, Cubby. I have to count out loud or I forget."

"Seriously?"

"Jesus H, Cubby, I already forgot how many strokes I was at. See, it don't work."

"You were at eight."

"Nine, ten, eleven, twelve, thirteen, fourteen, fifteen..."

When I got to 116—or 160—I lost count, I stopped and went down into *Sarah*'s cabin to look around. It was about the coziest place I ever seen, not like the sleeping cabins on a towboat. Wood everywhere, not steel. No diesel smell. Quiet, too. No rattling and shaking. The cabin smelled musty, but mostly it had this cedar smell, 'cause the inside of the hull was lined with cedar strips. I couldn't stand up in there unless I put my head between the deck beams. But that was okay; little *Sarah* wasn't built for the likes of Big Red. There was an old coal stove in the galley. Across from it was a varnished oak counter with an old fashioned ice box next to a deep sink with a brass water pump that looked like a mini version from some farmer's well. Hanging here and there on the mahogany cabin trunk sides were old gimbaled kerosene lanterns. I sat down, patted one of the bunks, and leaned back. I could feel and smell the sea breeze coming through the open portholes. "Real fine, Cubby," I said. "Real fine."

"I knew you'd like it, Red. Being aboard an old wooden sailboat gets in your blood. There have been a lot of great conversations down in this cabin."

"Can't wait to see Grampy sittin' down here, that's for sure," I said. Just then a lobster boat roared by—sounded like straight eight, gas—and its wake slapped the hull. Old *Sarah* shot up, lifting with the wave, already feeling her oats again. "She's getting lively already, Cubby. Let's get her hauled and painted and head to sea."

"And don't forget the engine. That's your department, Red. It's under the cabin steps. Pretty old and temperamental."

"Don't you worry none. If man made it, Red can fix it."

"Well, Colby said we could tie up to the dock tonight to make things easier until they haul her out. But if the batteries are dead we won't be able to start the engine to get in there."

I got up and went to the engine hatch and opened it up. "Well, well, she's an old Atomic 4. Darned good motors. Universal started making 'em in the 40's."

"God, Red, how do you *know* that stuff?"

"My world relies on motors, Cubby. I know 'em better and trust 'em more than people," I said. I poked my finger in the hole in the flywheel. "You have the crank?" I asked.

"The crank?"

"Yeah, you can hand crank the Atomic 4 like an old Model T if you got no battery power, and she should fire up."

"Grampy told me something about that once. I'll hunt around in the tool locker."

Cubby found the crank pretty quick, along with some grease I asked for. "You need to grease the inside of the crank handle where it goes into the drive shaft, so when she kicks over this big iron handle lets go easy and doesn't kick back into your hands or face. And we'll need the choke fully closed so we get as rich a mixture as we can while cranking. And a big guy like me to crank."

"This is so cool," Cubby said.

I felt good. "See, I ain't so stupid."

"Red, I don't think you're stupid."

"I know, Cubby."

Anyway, when that Atomic 4 popped off you should've seen us: me and Cubby was smiles from ear to ear, high-fiving while that engine purred away.

The next two days we got a lot done, and I don't know when I ever enjoyed myself so much, pitching in here and there around the yard, spending half my time joking with these Mainer folks and the other half trying to understand them, like the time around midday when Colby looked over at me and said, "Jeetyet?"

"Jeet what, Colby?"

"Don't know yet. Haven't. Always a surprise. But I think today the wife packed a tuna roll. Joueatyet? 'Cause I'm breaking for lunch, Red."

Hauling *Sarah* out was real interesting to me. The yard had this marine railway, really just a couple of railroad tracks that, at high tide, looked like something out of that *20,000 Leagues Under the Sea* movie, disappearing mysteriously into the sea, and at low tide dead-ending in plain sight into the mud. When we was ready, one of the yard guys released the brake on the power winch that held a steel cable connected to a big wooden boat cradle sitting on a railway car, and down the tracks into the water slid the whole rig. Then me and Cubby motored *Sarah* over the partly submerged cradle, and waited for the tide to drop so she could settle into it. When the tide was right, they fired up this hiccupping, snorting donkey motor—probably named 'cause it replaced the donkey—which sat in a wooden shack at the head of the yard and powered the winch.

Once we were pulled out high and dry, Cubby worked on the boat bottom, scraping all the sea growth off, while I went through the engine completely, charging the batteries, gapping the plugs, checking distributor cap, rotor, condenser, and points, and changing oil and filters. Colby was right about the bottom needing caulking, and he did that himself; I learned that caulking is kind of an art. When he got done he said, 'I'm worried about that stahbahd gahboard plank. Don't sail her too hard, boys; if she works too much at sea she'll open up and you'll be bailing for your lives.' I felt like grabbing my balls as I thought about that cold Maine water.

About the time we were ready to launch *Sarah*, Colby came over while Cubby was tightening the new zinc on the propeller shaft. He was seeming kind of awkward, looking down and jabbing his toe in the dirt a few times. Cubby looked up. "What's up, Colby?"

Colby lifted his head and pointed at this hand-painted sign on the boat launch engine shack which read: NO CASH, NO SPLASH. "Quimby, the owner, sent me over, Danny. We had to do that there policy; got stuck too many times."

"Sure. I don't blame you. I thought Grampy always tried to pay you in advance."

"Every year, 'cept this last one, Quimby said."

I looked at Cubby, and we both nodded, thinking the same thing. "Ashton," I said.

"My uncle Ashton is supposed to pay the bills now," Cubby said.

"I'm really sorry, kid. Quimby said he sent bills all winter for last year. Didn't hear or get nothing," Colby said.

"What's the amount?" I asked. "Maybe I can take care of it."

"Red, that's really generous, but this isn't your problem," Cubby said. "I still have about $1700 in the college account Grampy had set up for me."

"You'll need that until you get a job," I said. "What's the total amount, Colby?" I asked again.

"'Oh, 'bout $3500."

"My Power Wagon's worth three times that. I even got the title in the glove compartment; always keep it with me in case I get in some trouble when I'm on the road and have to buy my way out. Tell Quimby when we sail I'll leave him the keys and even sign over the title if he wants 'til we get back with the money in a week or so. Then I'll just rip up the signed title, apply for a lost title replacement, and be back in business."

"Red, there must be some other way," Cubby said.

"Not right now, Cubby. We got to get rolling. Or sailing, I reckon."

So Colby checked with Quimby, who came out of his house/ office, took a look at the Power Wagon, came over to us and shook hands. "You drive a hard bargain," he said to me.

"I ain't sure about that, Quimby. You got the bargain. If we didn't do this deal and you didn't splash *Sarah*, then you'd be left with a pretty worthless old wooden boat taking up billable space in your yard and no $3500."

"Where you from, anyway?" Quimby asked.

"Minnesota."

"Where's that by?"

"West of here a ways," I said.

"Good folks out that way?"

"Some of the best."

"Okay. I'll be looking to see you with some cash when you come back for the truck."

"We'll be back if Colby caulked that seam good enough."

Cubby wanted me to stay aboard and pump while he took the Power Wagon into the IGA store for supplies. "Here's some cash and the keys," I said. "And you'll want my food list, Cubby."

"I know your list, Red."

"Well, get the same stuff as on our road trip, but add some beer."

"No beer at sea. Only at night, when we're at anchor. Okay?"

"Okay, and get some of them chocolate Hostess Ding Dongs instead of the Twinkies," I said. "Goes better with the beer."

"Don't forget to count when you pump," Cubby said as he headed to the truck. Then he turned back to me. "If it helps, Red, go ahead and count out loud."

And then he was gone.

4 0

SAILING: BEING TILTED WHILE SLOWLY GOING NOWHERE

After we said goodbye to Colby and the boatyard boys, we motored out into the channel. There was a little wind, so before he went forward to raise the sails, Cubby showed me how to keep *Sarah* into the wind by looking at this little red arrow at the top of the mast and then pointing the boat where that arrow was pointing. Then he went forward to raise the big sail and then the little one. We was tipped pretty good right away. "How 'bout just use the little one," I said.

"That's the jib, Red. You need to know the terms so we can communicate."

"Seems like we communicated fine. What's wrong with saying 'little one'? Seems clear enough."

"Okay, anyway, you need to fall off now."

"In this water? No way; I ain't falling off. I'm staying on the boat."

"It means 'fall off the wind'; to let the sails fill more with wind."

"Then I'll be headed out of this channel if I do that."

"We'll have to tack."

"Now what's that mean? Why don't we just use the motor for Chrissakes?"

"We need to sail when we can, Red. We don't carry much fuel. Plus, sailing's what it's all about."

"Sitting here hanging onto the seat, tipped over at thirty degrees and getting wet ain't what it's all about to me. You sure this boat ain't gonna tip over; a Mississippi River towboat would have capsized at this angle. I ain't afraid of drowning, but I do not want to freeze my balls off while doing it."

"There's six thousand pounds of lead in the keel."

"Well, that should sink us for sure," I said.

"No, imagine the physics."

"That subject was senior year in high school; never made it to senior year."

"Okay, imagine *Sarah* as a cork in a bath tub; the cork has a long pin pushed lengthwise down the center. Attached to the end of the pin, the part underwater, is a lead fishing weight. So you have a cork in the bathtub, floating upright with a weight at the end of the pin."

"Okay. One question. Am I in the bathtub with the cork?"

"Sure. Why not. That's an interesting image. So now blow on the cork; try to blow the cork over. What happens?"

"Cork blows over."

"Yes, but only until it's parallel to the water, then the wetted surface of the cork against the wind is decreased, and the counter-weight tries to pull the cork upright."

"I do believe there's one big difference, Cubby. A cork won't sink. A boat will."

"The cork's just to illustrate the concept. Anyway, we're not going to tip over, Red. It's against the laws of physics."

"Good, 'cause I don't want to break no laws—'cept the ones worth breaking."

Right then I looked up to the next buoy I was following in the channel, and it was gone, along with most everything else.

"We're going to get fogged in, Red, and right in the middle of this narrow channel," Cubby said. "You start the engine and I'll drop the jib. We'll keep the mainsail up in case we have an engine problem. Just hold the compass course you had. About 90 degrees, okay?"

"No problem. But don't you worry about this engine. She's a honey and she don't need no wind."

While I fired up the Atomic 4, Cubby got the little front sail down and then shot into the cabin to plot a course. He came up a couple minutes later.

"It's pretty much a straight line out between all the channel buoys, so we'll keep to that 90 degrees for 1.3 miles, which should put us at Green Bell 1. Then we'll head to 160 magnetic for 1.9 miles to the gong off of Hard Harbor Island. Then 240 for a quarter of a mile will take us straight in. We should be able to hear both the bell and gong fine since we're headed up wind."

"Did you write all this down, Cubby? Don't forget your helmsman here is the guy who can't even count pump stokes without forgetting."

"Yes. Don't worry."

"Hard Harbor Island don't sound too easy, with a name like that and all. Why we going in there?"

"I think we'll be fine; there's a couple of mean, outlying ledges that we had trouble with once years ago. But that's a story for later. Thanks to Grampy, I know the best approach. Anyway we're going in because that's where Machias Pike and his family live. We took *Sarah* in there almost every time when we brought the boat to and from Quimby's boat yard, and we got to be good friends. I hope they're still around. They're really unusual people, at least for this day and age. They live pretty much off the grid, making their living fishing and lobstering. Had a bunch of fish weirs and traps. Machias met his wife Nancy at an AA meeting in New Bedford. He had an old offshore lobster boat and together they hatched a plan to come up here, buy a small chunk of Hard Harbor Island, build a cabin, and start fishing.

Then they had a son named Oceanus, born right on the island. He was named after Oceanus Hopkins, who was the only child born on the Mayflower during the voyage that brought the Pilgrims to America. Pretty cool. Cool kid, too. Really tanned with big brown eyes and shoulder-length black hair; kind of like Mowgli from *The Jungle Book*. When we started hanging out as kids—first time was probably when I was eleven or twelve during our stops at their island on *Sarah*—I was kind of surprised by his use of words; he spoke really well. Then I went into their cabin and saw his book collection. He loved reading and had tons of paperback and hardback books. 'I read when I'm not fishing,' he said. 'And I don't fish much in the winter'. We talked about our favorite characters such as Huck Finn and The Artful Dodger, and books like *The Hobbit, Tom Sawyer,* and *Treasure Island.* We tried out new words on each other, ones we'd learned from the books we'd read. It was funny, here I was, this well-schooled kid born on the other side of the world—I bet Oceanus had never even seen an Asian— and this boy who had rarely been off the island. But it worked out great. We discussed the characters in the books we loved. I told him about my world, the bigger one of Boston and New York, and what I did and learned in the private school that Grampy and my mom sent me to. And he told me about his world of fishing and birds and how to spot bad weather. We even talked about how neat it would be if we changed worlds, and traded places for a year."

"Seems like the Pikes are some fiercely independent folks," I said. "They'd fit right in on the river. You think they're still there?"

"If we get through this fog, I guess we'll find out. You still headed 90 degrees, Red?"

"I thought you said ONE ninety."

"God, Red, are you serious!?"

"Just kidding, Cubby. Doing 90 degrees on the dot."

"Well, it's been about fifteen minutes now, so at four knots that would be about a mile we've done since that buoy where the fog dropped. I'll cut the engine soon and we'll listen for bell number one."

"Pretty smart math you did there. Right in your head. Pretty smart math."

"Not really, Red. Going about four knots for one quarter of an hour would make about a mile, so we should start looking."

"Okay, Einstein. All I know is I can't see shit."

We cut the engine and listened for Bell #1. Didn't take long. We both heard it at about the same time. Only problem was Cubby pointed one way into that dungeon of fog and I pointed about forty degrees from where he was pointing.

"Can't be both places," I said. "Want to flip for it?"

"The fog plays tricks on you out here. I learned that many times with Grampy. Your mind gets tired of seeing nothing and then you start imagining things that aren't there and hearing sounds that aren't coming from where they really are."

"Hey, over there! I think I see a Pizza Hut; sign in the window says you get a free pitcher of beer with each large pizza. Let's change course."

Cubby ignored me and held out his arm, pointing. "Let's try this way, going slow, then stop and see if the sound gets stronger. If not, we'll try your direction."

Cubby was right, and this big old green bell started to come into sight, first like a drunken ghost, just a swaying outline, then it got clearer and you could see the big 'I' on it.

"Now let's run 160 degrees at about four knots as before for about 20 minutes. Then we'll start all over again, stop the engine, and listen."

When we heard and found the gong buoy, Cubby said, "Now it gets tough."

"I got one question," I said. "Are we having fun yet?"

Cubby ignored me again, saying, "We'll run slow, about two knots, and then smell, feel, and listen."

"Pizza Hut? I can smell a pizza a mile away."

"No, spruce trees. Land. You should smell the trees, feel the warmth of the land, and hear the breakers. The entrance is hard to spot, even in good visibility. But there are bold hills on both sides and the water's deep going into the cove."

"Starting to see why they named it Hard Harbor. Too bad we don't have radar."

"We do. Sort of," Cubby said, and headed into the cabin. He came back with an old brass megaphone in his hand.

"You calling for help?"

"Same principle as electronic radar, really. It will let us measure the echo distances."

"Jeez, Cubby, I wish I had just a small piece of your brain."

"It's not me, Red. Grampy showed me this years ago."

And so as we eased in closer we tried to smell, feel, and listen. I didn't smell the trees, but it did feel a little warmer. Cubby put the megaphone to his lips: "Boom...boom...boom," he shouted over and over in different directions. "Seems as if the much longer return echo is right about there," he said, pointing into the fog while looking down at the compass. "Right at our 240 degrees. We're near those ledges, so listen very carefully for surf, okay? I'm going forward to keep as close a lookout as I can. If I point, Red, *don't* ask questions, just head where I'm pointing. And do it right away."

Cubby was getting real tense, but then—though I sure never saw or heard nothing change—he started looking relieved, and said 'cause of the calmer water and warmth now we'd probably made it past the ledges to the beginning of the entrance. Then he went down into the cabin again, and popped up with what looked like a giant fishing drop line with a huge lead sinker on it.

"Maybe not the best time for fishing, Cubby," I said. "Not just yet, anyway."

"It's a lead line. The old fashioned way to tell the depth before they had electronic echo sounders."

He unwound it to three knots, told me each knot was a fathom of depth, went up forward on the deck, swung the lead forward into the water and let it drop as we moved ahead. "No bottom," he said. And he swung again. "Still no bottom." Then, "Got bottom! Three fathoms, Red. Eighteen feet. We're in!" Then he came back to the cockpit, and we high-fived.

"Screw electronics. Nice work, Cubby."

"We're a team, Red. Nice steering. We'll anchor right here," he said.

"Then my beer, right? You said after we anchor, beer's okay. That's the rule."

After we were settled in good, and I'd popped my third cold one, I heard an outboard motor start up. Sounded like an old two-stroke; small, maybe ten horse. Then out of the fog came a beat up-looking skiff with a young man standing up in the back. He motored slowly around behind us and looked at the stern of *Sarah*. Cubby popped up on deck. "Oceanus!" he shouted. The black-haired kid just nodded and shut down his outboard.

He looked at us both. "Grampy there with you, Danny?"

"No, he's in a nursing home in Seacasset. But we're bringing *Sarah* back to Seacasset to get him out and take him sailing."

Oceanus put his hands on his hips and looked around at the fog. Then he said, "She's some thick today. Glad you made it over the ledges and got in here okay."

"Not without a little trepidation."

"Well, a little trepidation is a good thing in the fog. My folks will be real happy to see you."

I whispered to Cubby, "You guys ain't gonna start using big words now, are you?"

"No, mostly diminutive ones. Don't worry."

"You're messing with me, Cubby. You're messing with me."

"Oceanus, this is my good friend, Orca Bates, but everyone calls him Red."

"Howdy. Welcome to the special world of Hard Harbor. Your timing's good for dinner; my dad and I just brought in a couple of hundred pounds of halibut. We've got to eat some; can't sell it all! I'll check with my folks, but if I don't come back out, why don't you row ashore in an hour or so."

"Sounds fine," Cubby said.

After he left I asked Cubby if I could bring some beer ashore.

"His parents are alcoholics, Red."

"Well, that'd be three of us then."

"Not a good idea, Red. You've already had three anyway."

I jabbed at my stomach. "Putting three beers in here is barely coating the bottom of the tank, Cubby. Barely enough fuel to fire me up."

Cubby just shook his head and opened a seat locker.

"You know," I said. "I ain't real thrilled with the idea of rowing ashore in that little skiff of ours."

"That's why you're wearing this," Cubby said, and handed me this old orange life jacket.

"I'm *not* wearing that. I told you. I ain't afraid of the drowning part, and all that life jacket is gonna do is keep me alive while I slowly freeze my balls off. No, I'm going straight to the bottom if we swamp. I know I'll be a hell of a meal for them lobsters down there—fatten them up for some lucky lobsterman—but I'll make sure I'm drowned and dead before they get to me."

"Suit yourself, Red. I'm not your father."

"More like a son acting like a father," I said, and pulled myself up off the cockpit seat.

We made it in okay, though getting out of the skiff and stepping onto all those ledges covered with seaweed got me nervous about my bad knee. Cubby led me down the path to the Pike cabin. Making our way along the winding, foggy trail, I could smell the spruce, the sea air, the seaweed on the ledges. Ahead of us I heard a dog bark. And somewhere out in that foggy bay came the faint sound of an engine, gas or diesel; couldn't tell. We came to a much darker part of the trail, narrower and real woodsy. It began to make me mighty nervous. Then, somewhere close but out of sight a couple gulls started fighting over something, making awful screeching sounds that knocked me back to some real bad times. Those demons slipped right out from where I'd shoved them away; and there, at the top of the stairs, was that little kid, hands over his ears, listening to his daddy yelling and screaming and sometimes whacking his momma after a drunken night at The Slough; and then, there he was again, a big kid now, in 'Nam, right after Sullivan got it. Sully's torn wide open, shrieking in pain, calling for his own momma—and the big kid's kneeling next to him, trying to hold his guts together, saying, "You'll be fine, Sully. Trust me. You'll be fine."

I stopped walking on that island trail, looked down at the big gold bracelet that's always on my wrist—the one that was Sully's, the one he wanted me to have if he didn't make it—and I started getting dizzy and staggered a bit, wandering off the path.

"Where you going, Red?" I heard Cubby ask. I turned toward him. Then that dog bark got louder and pretty soon, racing around the bend came this big pointer hunting-type beast. I hit the dirt.

"That's Cujo," Cubby said, holding out his arms. "Don't worry."

"Hope he ain't the Cujo from that Stephen King movie," I said, getting up. But he sure looked glad to see Cubby.

"I think he still knows me," Cubby said, all happy.

"That's good. Tell him I'm with you, okay?"

The first thing I noticed as we came into the clearing by the cabin was what looked like a cross between a wrecked car and a giant tool of some sort. I wandered over to it. Right then the door to the cabin popped open and out walked a tall, thin, bearded fellow in blue overalls. "Hope you like halibut, boys" he said. He sauntered over to us and stuck out his hand to Cubby. "Good to see you, Danny," he said. Then he turned to me. "Name's Machias. Pleased to meet a friend of Danny's."

I stuck out my hand. "Proud to know ya. I'm Orca Bates. But everyone calls me Red." Then I turned to the contraption. "I like this," I said, looking at the car/tool contraption, "though I ain't sure where you're going with it."

"Used to be my old Chevy van. Brought it out on a flat barge though there wasn't much need for a car out here on the island, plus the body was rusted out. But the drive train and engine were still good, and I knew I needed a sawmill to make this house when we bought the land. Plenty of hardwood and softwood out here; just needed to make it into lumber. The idea I had was to use the existing hubs and drive train from the vehicle, then build the bed and carriage, modify the drive shaft, and fashion a blade tensioner. A lot of work and improvising, but in the end we had ourselves a saw mill!"

"I'll bet General Motors never had this in mind. That's about the cleverest damned thing I ever seen," I said.

"Well, come in and meet a clever cook, my wife Nancy," he said.

"You're in for a treat, Red," Cubby said, reaching down to pat Cujo. We all went in to meet Nancy and get some dinner. Nancy was as wide as Machias was tall. First thing I thought of was what would happen if the both of us was in that skiff of Grampy's. She was as cheerful a sort as you'd ever want to meet. The house smelled of butter and lemon, and I followed Nancy into the kitchen, real curious about what was cooking. "You a cook yourself?" she asked.

"Mostly waffles, ma'am. But the best waffles you ever tasted."

"Well, you'll have to give me the recipe."

"I'll trade you for what's going on here," I said, looking in and putting my nose over the stove.

"It's sautéed halibut steak. I like the sauté method, so I can make a quick sauce in the same cooking skillet. To begin, I marinate the steaks in lemon juice. Then I sauté the fish in olive oil and capers. While the halibut is cooking, I roast asparagus in the oven to bring out the sweetness in the stalks, then put it in the pan with the fish for a little while to grab more flavor. A little lemon butter finishes the dish."

"Ain't much beats my special raised waffle recipe, but I think you got me here, ma'am."

Before dinner, Oceanus gave me the tour of the house while his folks and Cubby chatted in the kitchen. He showed me the big stone fireplace that his dad had built from rocks on the island, then he took me up the roughly finished central stairs leading to the sleeping loft areas. He showed me his space, and there was that huge collection of books that Cubby had mentioned. "Keep on reading," I said. "Wish I did."

"I plan on it. These books take me back and forward in time. And around the world. Right from this cabin."

"You ever want to see the real world? I mean, the world for real? You know, women and all."

"Someday maybe. I get to wondering about things once in a while. People do come by, and I like it when they come; but I also like it when they go. No, I figure I've got the real world I need right here. Also, from what I've read, travelers say most places don't live up to their imagination."

"But this ain't the real world," I said.

"Really? I'm not sure about that. What does that mean, 'the real world', anyway? I think right here is as real as any other place."

"You got me on that. I'll shut up," I said.

"I'd love to hear about your world. Danny told us you're a river pilot. Very cool. I've read *Huck Finn* and *Tom Sawyer*, but not too much about today's Mississippi River. Maybe during dinner."

"Well, the short version is that I live on a cramped, broken down houseboat surrounded by nobodies and real cold winters. And when the river's thawed, I go to work, pushing barges around here and there, and up and down. That's my world."

At dinner, which was around a big pine table in the end of the kitchen, there was plenty of talk while I pushed down about four helpings of halibut. I learned a lot about fishing. And I learned more than I ever needed to know about lobsters from both Machias and Oceanus.

"Native Americans used them as fertilizer and fish bait. And in Colonial times they were considered poverty food, and fed to prisoners," Machias told me.

"Fish eating fish, huh," I said, laughing.

Oceanus piped in. "Actually, a lobster is an arthropod, closely related to the insect. They're more like a grasshopper or mosquito than a fish or mammal."

"I'll bet them fancy restaurants don't share that information," I said, smiling. Then I had another thought: "So they don't scream when you put 'em in boiling water."

"No, because they're invertebrates they don't have a complex nervous system, so they don't feel pain like mammals," Oceanus said.

I looked over at Cubby and the Pikes. All these years in the pilothouse I should have been reading stuff, I thought. Maybe I could have been smart, too.

"Tell me how Grampy's doing," Machias asked Cubby.

"Not so good. He's pretty upset. He's cooped up in a nursing home and he doesn't want to be there. Shouldn't be there, actually. It's a long story, but his son, my Uncle Ashton, put him in there pretty much against his will some months ago, while I was away at college. I'm trying to figure out how to get him out legally. Somehow Ashton was able to become his guardian and conservator, and has control. Grampy wants to get back into his house and he wants to be on *Sarah* and go sailing again. The least I can do is take him for a day sail. I'm sure they'll let us do that."

I had my doubts. But I didn't say nothing.

"Well," Nancy said, shaking her head, getting teary, and looking over at her son. "you know we owe him so much, so if there's anything, anything at all that we can do, you just say the word."

Machias put his hand over hers at the table. Then he looked over at me. "Pretty hairy for you coming by those ledges in the fog, I bet," he said. "Must be all new to you, coming from inland and all."

"I didn't tell you, Red," Cubby said, "but years ago Grampy and I misjudged the entrance, and ended up on one of the ledges in a bad cross sea. I was little and pretty terrified. Grampy got on the VHF radio and called for help."

"Lucky we were fishing close by," Machias said. "I think *Sarah* would have sprung a plank before long, the way she was twisting and pounding in that swell rolling over the ledge. Water's too cold to last long and I don't figure you'd even know which way to swim in that fog."

Cubby nodded. "I still get scared thinking about it," he said.

Right then I felt real proud of Cubby. I felt real proud because what he didn't do was run away. Instead he came back, faced up to his fears, and came back to that same entrance in the fog and brought *Sarah* through it. Without Grampy. Real proud is what I was.

It was a fine dinner together, and when we came outside the wind had shifted to the northwest and cleared out the fog. I was feeling pretty good, like I had some real comrades out here now. Cujo followed us down the trail to the water and stood by the shore watching me work my way into the skiff. He started whining a little, getting nervous, I figure. "I know," I said, looking back at him. "It ain't easy. If I go in, you come get me, Cujo, before one of them giant inverted braces gets to me."

Cubby looked at me from the forward seat of the skiff. "*What* did you say Red?"

"Them lobsters."

He laughed and shook his head. "Oh, invertebrates. The word is 'invertebrates'."

"Whatever. After what I learned about them tonight, I ain't eating one of them insects and I ain't gonna let one eat me."

"They actually will eat each other. Did you know that? They're cannibals."

"Just row carefully, Cubby. Let's get back to the boat. I need more beer."

We sat in *Sarah*'s cockpit and watched the sunset, me slurping my beer and Cubby just leaning back and looking at the sky. I don't know what he was thinking, but I was wishing I had myself a little family like the Pikes, with a nice jolly wife like Nancy and a son like— well, like Cubby. Too late now, I figured, with me pushing fifty and all. Wives never worked out for me anyway. Too much spaghetti!

"What are you thinking 'bout?" I asked Cubby after a time.

"I'm thinking that with this northwest wind we're going to have good weather, no fog, and a steady breeze. We'll be headed 190 degrees, almost south, so we'll have a broad reach home. About twenty-eight hours if we can hold five knots of speed."

"Reaching for a broad sounds pretty good right about now."

"Anyway, because of this good weather, I think we should do a straight shot, offshore, overnight. No stops. That'll mean you being alone at the tiller while I'm sleeping when I can. You okay with that?"

"Sure, but how am I gonna see that little arrow at the top of the mast when it's dark?"

"You should be fine just following the compass course if this wind stays steady. Northwest winds usually hold for a while. If there's a wind shift, and you have to adjust the sails, you can wake me."

"Maybe I'll just sail by one of them stars."

"You know how to do that, Red?"

"Hell, Cubby, I'm kidding. I thought you was smart! If I followed a star we'd be sailing right up to heaven."

Cubby just shook his head. "Anyway, Red, I'm going to go below and lay a course on the chart and measure our distance to Seacasset." He headed down into the cabin to sit at the chart table. Then he turned back to me. "You know, this won't take long, and it's still kind of early, Red. How about a game of chess? I'm sure Grampy's board is down here somewhere."

"Chess is for smart people. Hell, took me years to figure out checkers."

"Chess is a wonderful game, and I can teach you. Grampy and I played a lot, even when I was little. I even beat him a couple of times when I was a kid."

"Figures."

After Cubby got done at the charts, he put down the little eating table that folded from the cabin bulkhead, lit the lamps, and set up the chess board, putting all these pieces on black and white squares. We sat down on the bunks on each side of the table. He told me I had the black army, and the aim of the game was for my army to capture the enemy king.

"I don't know, Cubby. I've had enough war in my life," I said. "How about checkers?"

"Let me just explain how chess works. It's really great for the mind, and kind of a mirror of life, rich in metaphors for human experience. Even though it's a battle between opposing armies, it's completely non-violent. And you've got to use both primitive instinct and sophisticated calculation. You learn from experience, memorize common patterns, build your position, set traps, analyze variations, and finally move in for the kill."

"Can I win on just primitive instinct? 'Cause I'm kinda weak on sophisticated calculation and analyzing variations."

And so he started explaining how important the king is, and that if he gets captured the game is lost. And how the queen is the most powerful. And the rooks are good for attacking the enemy. And bishops are good attackers, too. And knights can jump over other pieces. And pawns are foot soldiers.

"That's what I was," I said. "A pawn. And the rest of this all sounds real familiar. I was in a real chess game, Cubby. And it weren't no fun."

"I know. How come you never talk about that, Red?"

"'Cause I don't. So how about telling me more about the Pike family? I'd like to know more. I like them folks. First off, I was wondering why Nancy said their family owes Grampy so much. I thought they was the ones who saved you and Grampy, not the other way around."

"There's one more part," he said, getting up to adjust the kerosene lamp on the bulkhead. "It was a day after Grampy and I had stopped by Hard Harbor and had our usual good visit with the Pikes on our way to leave *Sarah* at Quimby's yard for the winter. We'd said our goodbyes and left Hard Harbor that next morning, making it to the boatyard in good time and tying to Quimby's dock. We slept aboard that night, figuring we'd unload the boat and take the bus back to Massachusetts that next day. What woke me in the morning was the sound of a helicopter. I remember thinking how odd that was, as we never saw or heard planes this far Downeast. Certainly not a helicopter. About then Colby from the yard came down to the dock. 'There's been an accident at Hard Harbor,' he said. 'The Pike boy fell from the top of the wharf ladder at low tide. A rotten step let go. I heard all this on the VHF. His dad found him; called for help. The boy was unconscious, lying in the mud and rocks at the base of the ladder. Guess he fell about fifteen feet. Anyway, that there's the chopper going to airlift him now.'

"Then Grampy said, 'Colby, do you have a fast outboard? We should get out there and lend a hand.'"

'Nothing to do. Heard on the VHF that both his parents are going with him to the hospital on the chopper,' Colby said."

"That's mighty frightening," I said to Cubby. "Good news, I guess. It's clear from what I seen today that Oceanus is okay and still has plenty of brains left."

"He had a bad concussion, a severe neck sprain, and a broken collarbone. And, being unconscious there in the mud, he would have drowned when the tide came in if his dad hadn't found him. He ended up in Mass General in Boston. Great hospital. We went to visit him, of course."

I told Cubby I was glad it all came out okay. Then I had one of them profound thoughts: "We're all just hanging from a thread, I guess," I said. "Hey, is that one of them 'medifors' I just did? Pretty good, huh?"

"Good one, Red. Maybe we should hit the hay. I'm not sure chess is in your future. At least not tonight."

"You never did answer me about why the Pike family is so grateful to Grampy."

"Grampy paid Oceanus' hospital bills. They had no insurance. Grampy tried to remain anonymous, but the Pikes found out."

I just shook my head slowly. "That Grampy of yours. He's a real king; just the best, ain't he, Cubby?"

Cubby nodded.

That's all I said. But what I thought was: I may just be the pawn, but I'm the toughest pawn I know. And Grampy *will* be leaving that nursing home, even if I have to flatten Nurse Ratshit and Ashton on the way out the door.

* * *

I must've taken a leak over the side three times that night 'cause of all that beer I drank. Cubby kept waking up every time I did. Captains are light sleepers by trade, and he was captain on this vessel. In the morning, while I was wrestling with *Sarah*'s stove and making coffee and Cubby was pumping the bilge, I told him I was sorry I had to pee so much.

"Two things woke me and kept me awake, Red: the boat heeled over pretty good while you were up on deck leaning over the side, and then I wondered why you didn't come right back into the cabin. I kept thinking you'd fallen overboard. By then I was wide awake."

"Hell, Cubby, me falling over would've made a splash big enough to cause a tidal wave. It would have waked up you and the folks on the mainland."

"Then what were you doing up there?"

"Looking at the stars. Thinking back about some stuff."

Cubby was right about the northwest wind holding steady, and we headed out in clear weather under both sails. Didn't even need to start the motor. When I heard Cujo bark, I looked back to the island, and there was all three of the Pike family waving and slowly getting smaller. After a while the land disappeared and all we had was empty horizon and water. Old *Sarah* just gurgled along, rolling gently through them ocean swells.

"I could get used to this," I said to Cubby. "I guess this sailing business is pretty easy."

"I think it's best for you to watch and learn and then practice your steering and sailing in these good conditions, Red, so why don't I take the first four-hour morning watch so you can observe. Then when you take over at ten, I'll make some more coffee and cereal and grab a couple muffins for us."

So I watched Cubby sail for four hours, asking a few stupid questions. Then it was my turn, and I settled in to this sailing business. Steering a compass course was no problem for a river man, even though most of the time on the river we were fine just steering by line of sight. But out here, with no land, that compass was everything. Same with that little arrow at the top of the mast telling me what to do. I wished my life came with an arrow like that. Before Cubby went below deck, he looked around.

"We're on a nice beam reach now, Red."

"No more broads, huh? Now we got beamy ones."

"Just keep that arrow pointing at ninety to one hundred degrees from our heading. If the wind backs or heads you, you'll have to adjust the sails."

"Sailing just got complicated," I mumbled.

"What, Red?"

"Nothin'."

I did okay on my ten to two watch, then had some more chow—two Hostess Ding Dongs—and took a nap before my next watch, which was from six to ten at night. We were sailing real slow then, and there still weren't nothing to look at but that red arrow and empty water ahead, behind, and on either side. And when it got dark, I couldn't even see that arrow and had to just hope that wind stayed the same while I stared into the red lighted binnacle and sailed by the compass until it was Cubby's watch from ten to two a.m. When he came on deck, I told him it was so nice up here, I was gonna sleep right in the cockpit, and grabbed a blanket and fell asleep in about eight seconds, dreaming that I was sailing *Sarah* through the trees in some jungle and getting tangled up in giant vines like the arms of an octopus. I felt Cubby rubbing my arm, saying 'Red, you're having a bad dream'. By then his watch was over and my two to six dawn watch was starting; but Cubby was nice enough to heat me some coffee before he hit the hay.

Those next four hours were some of the best of my life. Even though I'd spent plenty of nights alone in the pilothouse driving tows on the river, this was different. I was out at sea for the first time in my life, far from land, no sound except *Sarah's* gurgling through the water and that little skiff right astern, making its own happy sounds, like some toddler behind his momma. I felt a peace I'd never known, like I was one of those happy, chubby Buddhist guys instead of some big lug with a messed up life who'd seen too much of the wrong side of human nature. You know, Red, I thought, maybe you got your little family at last. Right here. You got Cubby, down below tucked away sleeping, and you got good old *Sarah* and the little skiff all moving along, with just the wind taking you home to Grampy. Peace. A big wide sea of peace. None of them bad thoughts here trying to push their way in. Just the wave sounds, with that rolling sea cradling us. No pain. Just peace.

When dawn came and the good old sun peaked over the horizon behind us, that little red arrow returned. Still no land around. This got me to thinking about that Columbus guy and those other early sailors being real scared 'cause they figured the earth was flat and they might sail right over the edge. I kept wondering about that and got so curious I let go of the tiller for a minute and climbed up on the top of the cabin house for a higher look at the horizon, which I figured might start to curve since the earth was really round and all. While I was standing up there, looking ahead, I heard a giant whooshing sound just behind me and turned back. I think right then I must've had me one of them spiritual experiences, because, twenty feet away, I was eye to eye with a giant whale, only this eye I was looking into was the size of a grapefruit.

I swear to this day that whale spoke to me. Maybe it knew I was named Orca. Or maybe it could relate, me being such a big creature of my species. I was surprised that I was so calm, like I was just meeting someone new, and I just started making conversation: "Morning, Big Guy. Wish I had a blowhole like that in my head so I could let off steam," I said. Then Big Guy dunked down under, and I figured he weren't interested in my problems. But soon enough he popped up again. "Anyway," I continued, "glad you're back. Name's Orca. It's great to meet someone else kind of big for this world. You got family around? Where you headed? Us? Well, we're going to get Grampy in Massachusetts; he's trapped in a nursing home, and we're going to get him out. He needs to be free and living large like you."

Just then Cubby shouted out from the cabin.

"Red, who are you *talking* to?"

"Shhhhhh. I'm talking to Big Guy," I whispered.

"What?"

"Big Guy. The whale."

Cubby came up on deck and looked around. But Big Guy was gone. Must have been something I said. As usual.

"You were talking to a whale, Red? If he talked back that's a bad sign. You need some sleep."

I just shook my head. "You scared him away. We was communicating."

"I bet," he said. He leaned over the binnacle and checked the compass. "All good on your course? Looks like it. Nice job."

"I didn't do nothing but stare at that little red arrow and the compass. Then the whale came. But before that I did get to wondering if we'd sail over the edge, you know, like that Columbus guy was afraid of doing."

"Grampy and I talked about that once when we were at sea. He told me it was probably a myth that most sailors thought that, all except for perhaps a few superstitious ones. Certainly Columbus didn't believe that. Any experienced seaman or officer could have figured it out after watching the land drop below the horizon on outbound voyages. You know, our ancestors had eyes and common sense, just like us. Plus, since the time of the Greeks it had been known that the earth was round."

"Maybe the Greeks didn't tell nobody," I said. And then I thought for a minute. "I still don't know why the water at the bottom of the earth don't fall off."

"That would have been in your physics course, Red."

"If somebody told me how good this physics stuff was, I might've stuck around for senior year in high school."

"You can always take a physics course; it doesn't have to be when you're in high school. Anyway, you should get some sleep. I'll take her now. Wind's starting to pick up. Oh, by the way, Red, the place to sleep at sea is right on the cabin floor. Put one of the bunk cushions down there and stretch out. You'll find it's better than being up in a bunk."

"Why's that?"

"It's where there's the least amount of motion, plus you can't fall off the floor, but you can fall out of your bunk."

"Physics again, right?"

"You got it."

So down into the cabin I went. I moved one of the bunk cushions onto the narrow cabin floor like Cubby said, stretched myself out, and tried to doze off while listening to that water gurgle by the wooden sides and bottom planks of *Sarah*, as we heeled over pretty good in that new wind. That got me to thinking about how there was only those old one-inch thick mahogany planks between me and eternity; or, worse, between me and those lobsters and sea creatures a couple of hundred feet below. I must have fallen asleep thinking about that 'cause I started dreaming that my feet were wet, and then my legs. Well, it weren't no dream. I shouted up to Cubby in the cockpit. "Hey, Houston, we got a problem down here!" I said.

"Like what Red?"

"Like we're fucking sinking!"

Cubby shot down into the cabin, his feet landing in four inches of water that was over the floorboards. "Shit. Start pumping, Red," he yelled. "Fast. I'm going to see if it's coming in through the engine shaft or a thru hull fitting."

"Want me to count?"

"NO! Just pump!"

"Good. That'll be faster then."

I got the water out after about ten minutes of pumping, but it came right back so I kept pumping her dry again while Cubby tried to find the leak.

"It's not the shaft opening or a thru hull; it must be along a garboard plank down by the keel, like Colby was worried about," he said. "But it's not getting worse. We'll just have to keep pumping."

"What's this 'we' shit?" I said as I wiped my sweaty face on my favorite tee shirt, the one that said *I Got this Shirt for my Wife - Great Trade!*, and started pumping again.

"You'll be pumping because what I'm going to be doing is dropping the sails so we can start motoring, which, if the problem is one of the garboards, will reduce the strain from the sails down through the mast step and onto that bad plank. I hope we have enough gas to just power. *Sarah's* obviously working too hard, even in this amount of wind."

"Me, too," I said, still pumping away.

When Cubby came back to the cockpit after lowering the sails, and turned to go down into the cabin, I caught a good look at his back side. "Looks like you shit your pants, Cubby," I said. "This leaking making you that nervous?"

"What?"

"Something brown all over your back side there."

Cubby reached back and touched it, then looked at it on his fingers, then smelled it.

"It's chocolate."

"Shit, Cubby, you must have sat on my last pack of Ding Dongs," I said, laughing.

Cubby snapped. "Fuck you, Red. *You're* a Ding Dong. None of this is funny. You leave your shit all over the boat. You're a pig, you know that? And I'm sick of it."

My heart hurt. My little family was falling apart. "Sorry Cubby," I said.

"Just pump, okay?"

"Got it. Pumping away keeps them lobsters away."

And that's pretty much what I did, hour after hour, for the next thirteen hours. I didn't say this to Cubby, but after about ten of those hours I kinda hoped we might sail off the edge of the earth and be done with it. At least if we sailed off the edge we wouldn't be sinking, and I could cheat them ugly lobsters out of a good meal.

4 1
SPRINGING GRAMPY

"So what's the plan?" I asked Cubby after we picked up Grampy's overgrown mooring in Seacasset Harbor.

"We'll get a good meal, and have a long hot shower at Grampy's. I just listened to the VHF marine weather. It calls for a great day tomorrow for us to take Grampy sailing. And the sooner the better before word gets to Ashton that we're here with *Sarah*."

"You think they'll let you take him out of that place?" I asked.

"Red, he's my *grandfather*. Why couldn't I?"

"You ain't in charge of him. Your Uncle Ashton is."

"So?"

"So maybe he'll say you're unsuitable or some other lie to keep you away from being alone with Grampy."

"You think so?"

"I think Ashton is a dickhead is what I think."

"Let's go to the Ross Island house and get settled," Cubby said.

"How far is it? I ain't walking. I ain't even sure if I can walk on level ground after all this rocking."

"I'll call Jessica, and see if she can give us a lift."

"The girl in the little yellow sundress from the yacht club? Hell, she already gave me a lift."

"God, Red. Will you stop it?"

We made it ashore in the little skiff, and tied up to the town dock. "I feel like a drunken sailor; the whole ground just keeps rocking," I said as I stepped on dry land.

"You are a drunken sailor."

"Will be soon, I hope."

"The rocking problem comes from your inner ear," Cubby said.

"No, the problem comes from the ground under my feet. It's moving."

"Your ears have little fluid-filled tubes in them. When you lean one way, the fluid stimulates one side of the tube, and it gives you the sense of motion. On a boat the tubes are constantly stimulated in the same pattern, so your body gets used to this and then anticipates it. That's why you keep rocking for a while even though you're on stable ground. Grampy told me. You should be fine tomorrow."

"It feels like my brains are just sloshing around in my head."

"Maybe you need to expand your brain, Red."

"Might be easier to make my head smaller."

"Just kidding, you know."

"I know, Cubby."

Cubby couldn't reach Jessica on the pay phone, so he called a cab which took us to Ross Island, but only after I had the driver make a quick stop for a twelve-pack of beer. We got the cabby's card before he left, 'cause we figured we'd need him again when we picked up Grampy. Cubby's house key still worked and we went in to Grampy's house and took long hot showers. I let Cubby go first, so I could push down a few beers just to get stable and level-headed. I figured the booze would likely counteract that ear fluid tube business or make my brain float level again. When I did take a shower though, I had to brace myself, one hand on each of the shower walls to keep from falling over. After my shower I stretched out on one of the beds in the guest room on the second floor, and was just dozing off when Cubby came in and told me he was headed over to the nursing home to arrange a sail for the next day. He said it would be better if I stayed at the house due to my relationship with Nurse Ratshit. I couldn't argue that, and off Cubby went after calling that taxi. I passed out right after that. What woke me was a screen door slamming, then some footsteps, then what sounded like a bunch of desk drawers opening and closing, like somebody was madly searching for something. Now, other than maybe lobsters, I ain't afraid of much. But I figured if that guy down there was Ashton, and even though I was drooling over the idea of coming down and squishing the little twit 'til his tasseled loafers popped off, it was better for Grampy if Ashton didn't know we were here. So I just listened, hoping he didn't see any of our gear and my empty beer bottles in the laundry room, until finally I heard the screen door slam again and a car start and speed down the gravel driveway.

"We had a visitor," I said to Cubby when he returned. "The guy stayed downstairs; sounded like he was looking for something. Didn't know I was here."

"It must have been Ashton; I locked the door behind me when I left, so it had to be someone with a key. Anyway, there's good news and bad news. The good news is Grampy was thrilled we made it back here with *Sarah*. He said that's all he's been thinking about since we left last week. The bad news is he's getting disoriented and seems really depressed. But he's more determined than ever to get out of the nursing home permanently and back to his house. I told him to keep it to himself about us going sailing, that I was just going to tell the social worker we were taking him home to quietly sit by the marsh; and that's not a lie because he wants to go home first before we go to the boat. That seemed to have worked with the social worker, but then as I was leaving, the director of the home, a man named Barnes, stopped me. He said that he was sorry, but he had a written order from Grampy's guardian and conservator— Uncle Ashton—that he had to notify Ashton first for permission if anyone wanted to take Grampy out of the home."

"What'd you say?"

"I said, 'my own grandfather?'"

"What'd he say?"

"He said that was what he had to comply with, and he couldn't risk any potential litigation over this. I just said I'd check with Ashton, and then I left."

"Cubby, I got to sit down right now in the middle of the room, or I'm gonna put my fist through the nearest wall I'm so burned up. Then I'm going to get another beer to cool down. Then I'm going to think."

"Red, what I think is that you should stay out of this."

"Like I'm not already deep into it?" I said. "No, I think it's *you* who should stay out of this. You got the future. Mine's done with. You need to keep clean about all this—not break them nursing home rules, so you don't wreck your future for becoming a lawyer and all—and also, so you got the best chance of getting this legal guardian stuff straightened out with Grampy when we get done sailing. So it's gotta be me that springs him. You gotta look innocent and keep a clean record."

Cubby didn't say nothing, and I sat there in the chair in the middle of the room and cooled down and thought a little longer. Finally I said, "First thing we got to do is pay off that cabby; by the looks of him, I think he can be bought cheap."

"God, Red, what are you *talking* about?"

"Here's the plan: you bring *Sarah* to the dock, and me and the cabby will drive to the nursing home to get Grampy, then just the cabby will go in to get him, carrying this fake note from Ashton saying it's okay to pick him up and take him to his house for the day. Then the cabby will drive me and Grampy to the boat instead. We'll spend the whole day sailing, and the cabby will bring him back to the nursing home. Piece of cake. And if anything goes wrong, I'll swear the whole thing was my idea."

"Red, I'll be complicit. And a plagiarized letter? It's fraud. That will be easy to show."

"Complicit? What's that mean?"

"It means 'knowingly involved with others in an illegal activity or wrongdoing'."

"This is all bullshit," I said. But deep down I knew Cubby was right. So I got to thinking again, thinking hard, which almost busted my little brain out my ears. But finally, I had it. "Me and Ashton is going to have a little chat," I said to Cubby.

"What?"

"A special Big Red chat. It's worked before; and it'll work this time, too."

"Red, you're freaking me out."

"No problem. Nobody's going to get hurt."

"God, Red," Cubby said, and he started pacing around the room.

"Trust me, Cubby. That's all I can tell you now, so that you don't know nothing and you don't become compliant."

"Complicit."

"Yeah. Complete shit. That's what this is. But you'll be the clean good guy when I get done. Anyway, what's Ashton's address?"

"No, Red."

"Cubby, I'm just going to *talk* to him. Tell him some stuff."

"What stuff?"

"About something I found when I was snooping around the house today, that's all. I was saving it for later, for after our sail with Grampy, but now I need it 'cause of my new plan. Anyway, you can't know about it 'cause of this complicit business."

"You need to tell me, Red." Cubby walked over to the window and just stared out for a while.

"You'll find out soon enough," I said. "Cubby, you got to trust me on this."

"Okay. It's 415 Nightingale Avenue, here in Seacasset. But I don't even know if he's home."

"No problem. I'll wait."

And then I called the cabby, who took me to 415 Nightingale Avenue, which weren't no dump, believe me.

"You want me to wait?" the cabby asked.

"No, I'll just call you later."

"How long?"

"As long as it takes. Why? You planning on retiring soon?"

"No, just asking, buddy."

So I went up on the porch to the front door, which had this brass door knocker shaped like a mermaid, lifted up her tail, and banged away. Nothing. So I sat down on one of the rockers on the porch and waited, worried that if he didn't show soon I was gonna miss dinner, which would be a first in my life. Finally, a BMW pulled into the driveway, and out popped Ashton, dressed in one of them silly whites-only tennis outfits. He didn't see me right away, but went to the mailbox and pulled out his mail and started looking through it.

"Why do they make you tennis folks always wear white?" I asked from my porch rocker. Ashton jumped a bit, then turned and stared at me.

"Get the fuck off my porch, or I'll have you arrested for trespassing."

"For knocking on your door? How am I supposed to knock on your door if I don't go up on the porch?"

"What do you want?"

"Just want to have a little chat."

It was getting clear that Ashton didn't want to get any closer or have a chat. He started to fiddle with his car keys while looking around, probably for a cop.

"I heard you rustling through Grampy's drawers earlier," I said.

"What are you talking about?"

"I was upstairs, having a nap when you came by Grampy's house."

"I could have you arrested for being in that house; it's under my jurisdiction."

"You didn't find it, did you?"

"Find what?"

"Find what I got now instead of what you don't got."

"I suggest that you remove yourself from my property this moment, and go back to whatever planet you come from."

"Indeed."

"Good."

"But not 'til you write and sign a letter that Cubby—I mean, Danny—can take your father sailing tomorrow."

"Why would I put him in jeopardy and do such a thing?"

"'Cause of what I got now instead of what you don't got."

"You're an idiot."

"Not today."

"And on what boat do you propose to sail."

"His boat, *Sarah*."

"It's in Maine."

"Not anymore. Me and Cubby sailed that boat, Grampy's boat, down here."

"Okay, look, why don't you just tell me what you have against me?"

"Let's just call it proof of what you're up to. Why don't you come up on the porch and see? I ain't gonna bite. There ain't nothing to be afraid of. No physical threat. No need to keep a tight asshole, Ashton. All I got is some pieces of paper."

"You're as vulgar as you are fat, you know that?"

"Vulgar, fat and sitting here holding the h-mails that make you— what's that word—oh, yeah, 'complicit' in a criminal conspiracy."

"I won't participate in this perpetuation of false allegations."

"I don't care what you want to call it, but let me just ask you why you won't let your nephew take his grandfather out of the nursing home?"

"Look, this is not a big deal. It's only a sail. Drop all this non-sense and I'll write that letter saying he can go for a sail with Danny, okay?"

"You need to write 'go for a sail with Danny and I'."

"Danny and *me*."

"No, you ain't going."

"No...it's 'Danny and *me*'. Wrong usage. Jesus. Look, never mind. You forget all this h-mail stuff and I'll write the letter."

"That's swell. I just happened to bring along this nice lined notepad and a pen. If you don't want to get too close to me you can sit on the steps and write and sign and date it. Make it to the attention of Mr. Barnes at the Sunny Gardens Nursing Home, saying that it's okay for Danny Roan and Orca Bates to take Joseph Roan out for the day tomorrow for a sail on his boat."

Ashton wrote and signed and dated the letter that said just that. It looked fine. I asked Ashton if I could use his phone to call a cab, but that didn't fly. So I left and started walking until I found a pay phone, and finally got back to Ross Island. Then, all proud like a bird dog with a duck, I brought Cubby the letter.

"How'd you do that, Red?" Cubby asked after he read it.

"Had a nice Big Red chat, mixed in with some of that complicit stuff."

"What?"

"Can't say. Need to protect you."

"God, Red, this letter from Ashton does look good. Nice work on that."

"Right. And now we need to call Pizza Hut. Fast."

"Sounds good."

* * *

The next morning since we had that letter, I figured it was fine for me to go right in with Cubby to get Grampy, but Cubby said we shouldn't push things, so I waited in the cab. When they didn't show after about twenty minutes, I got pretty antsy, and started shifting around in the back seat. The cabby looked back at me and said, "They coming out or what? I ain't gettin' any younger."

"You're gettin' paid for sitting there. Seems like a pretty good deal to me," I said.

"You from around here, mister?"

"No, Midwest."

"Figured you was from away."

"Why's that?"

"Don't know. Just figured."

"Just figured how?"

"Don't know. Well, you know, you being like you are and all, going in my cab to those two big houses and you with that Oriental kid and all. Just didn't add up."

"What are you, Sherlock Holmes?"

"Just figuring, that's all."

"You know what I figure?"

"What's that?"

"I figure you should mind your own fucking business. And my friend's Asian. Not Oriental. Orientals are rugs."

The cab got real quiet after that.

After about fifteen minutes they came out, Cubby holding a small bag and helping Grampy along in his walker. I got out of the cab and went over to help. Man, it looked like Grampy had gone downhill in just the week or so that we was away, but then he looked up at me, and I knew there weren't nothing wrong with his mind. "My, my, Mr. Bates, we do have a day for it, don't we? Perfect sailing day."

"At your service, Grampy," I said, opening the back door of the cab. "You look happier than a convict getting out of the clink."

Grampy stopped at the cab door, reached up and put one hand on the cab's rear window to steady himself, looked back at the nursing home, and shook his head. Then he looked up at the sky and lifted his nose, like he was trying to smell the sea, and said,

> *...and all I ask is a windy day with the white clouds flying,*
> *And the flung spray and the blown spume, and the sea-gulls crying.*

"We got all that stuff for you, Grampy. Plus, I even learned a little about sailing since I seen you, though your grandson is the real sailor. I'm just ballast."

"Well, sailboats need ballast, Mr. Bates. Oh, but I do need to get a few things at the house before we sail," Grampy said as we helped him into the back seat. I got in with him, and Cubby jumped in the front. Just before we took off, out of the corner of my eye, I caught this flash of white headed toward us. It was Ratshit. "Let's flush this toilet. Quick," I said to Cubby. But as soon as I said the word 'toilet', I knew Ratshit had us in her sights. She walked over, leaned into Cubby's window, and then looked into the back seat at Grampy. "I know you have permission, but in my professional opinion I have to say that he's in no condition for this sailing business," she said to Cubby. Before Cubby could respond, Grampy leaned forward, looked at Ratshit, and said, "Then what, pray tell, do you deem me in condition for?"

"Well, Mr. Roan, we'll plan to see you at suppertime. I believe we're having your favorite chicken pot pie," Ratshit said. Then she aimed at me and gave me a look that could stop a clock. I knew I had to fire back right away before she said something. So I smiled and said, "No food inspection this morning, ma'am, but if you have any leftover desserts later today, can you hold a few for me to inspect when we get back?"

Right then Cubby did the smart thing and told the cabby to move on out, and we were off to the free world. I patted Grampy on the shoulder. "That was a nice line of yours, Grampy. I think maybe you did some good, got that nurse thinking," I said.

"Your line wasn't so bad either," Grampy said, staring out the window. Then, after us driving a bit, he said more poetry stuff,

> *Do I dare*
> *Disturb the universe?*
> *In a minute there is time*
> *For decisions and revisions which a minute will reverse.*
> *For I have known them all already, known them all:*
> *Have known the evenings, mornings, afternoons..."*

"I don't know about them lines, Grampy," I said, "but I think I liked that 'white clouds flying' one better."

"It's *Prufrock*. T.S. Eliot."

"Oh."

Grampy continued to stare out the window all the way to Ross Island, looking at the world going by as if he'd never seen it before, like a little puppy going outside for the first time, sniffing and curious about everything. We drove by the marsh and sandy dunes and turned up the drive onto Ross Island.

"I saw a topless woman there once. Even took her home with me for a while. Didn't work out, though. Still, quite a thrill for an old man," he said.

"Quite a thrill for any man," I said. "I see them topless ones along the woodsy banks of the Mississippi in the parks up toward Lock One when it's hot. Always a treat for me and my deckhands."

"You'll have to tell me all about the river life when we're at sea," Grampy said as we pulled into his driveway.

We helped Grampy out, took his walker out of the trunk, and told the cabby we'd be just a few minutes. Grampy took in the whole scene.

"Oh my, it's good to be home," he said, and started working his way up the front walk. "I'll just be grabbing a few things. Won't take long."

Cubby went into the house with him, and I walked down by the salt marsh. I didn't feel like making small talk with the cabby, and I was beginning to take a real liking to the tidal marsh and that seaweed smell. 'Pungent' smell, Cubby said it was. New word for me. Good word, I figure. About ten minutes later they came out, with Cubby carrying a canvas bag. "What's that?" I asked.

"It's Grampy's old sea bag," he said. "Probably just a sweater and windbreaker and hat. He packed it himself while I cleaned up after last night's pizza and beer."

"Yeah, I was planning to do cleanup."

"Sure you were, Red, sure you were."

* * *

We stopped at the market and loaded up with plenty of snacks for the day, though Cubby kept me on a short leash regarding Ding Dongs and my other Hostess favorites, mostly getting stuff that's healthy for you. Grampy wanted us to buy a lot more food than we needed. I weren't complaining about that.

When the cabby pulled into the town landing, Grampy spied *Sarah* right away. "You got her here, you really did, boys! You got her here. How wonderful," he said, already pulling on the door handle of the cab. Cubby popped out first to help him, asking the cabby to open the trunk to get Grampy's walker.

While Cubby rowed the skiff out to *Sarah* to bring her into the dock to pick us up, me and Grampy sat on a bench by the pier and stared out at his boat. "Grace and dignity," Grampy said. "Don't you think so, Mr. Bates."

"You should call me Red, Grampy. I should be the one calling you Mister, being respectful and all."

"I know there's a lot of you to respect as well, Mr. Bates."

"Well, there's a lot of me, anyway."

"So we'll stick to Mr. Bates. But you stick with Grampy—much more endearing."

"What's that you said about grace and dignity?"

"Look out there at *Sarah*. See how she floats and lifts to the swell? How she carries herself after all these years? She's so old, but it's still there: the grace and dignity. In that nursing home we were treated like little children, as if the staff thought we had no history, no pride, no accomplishments. No dignity."

I just nodded—didn't know what to say. I rubbed my eyes and stared out at Cubby in the skiff, headed to *Sarah*. Then Grampy started reciting this poem:

> *To finally finish gobbling pieces*
> *Of wealthy incident*
> *To compile and KNOW*
> *And then to stand*

With cracking voice and outstretched arms
And say
What wisdom comes from all those years.
That would be your fulfillment.
Oh, Grandfather
Master of antiquity
Where's that brow-stuck star
That you deserve?

"You got yourself one good memory," I said.

"I must have read it twenty times last night. I will *never* forget that poem or the person who wrote it."

"Some great poet, huh?"

"My grandson Danny wrote that. He gave it to me yesterday, when he came to the home."

"That kid's really got brains, don't he?"

"And soul."

"Yeah, that too."

We sat there quiet for a while, watching Cubby get aboard *Sarah*, tie off the skiff to the stern, rig the dock lines and fenders, start the motor, and let go the mooring line. I was about to get up and grab Grampy's walker, so we could head down the pier when he said, "Mr. Bates, I should tell you something. I won't be going back to that place. I can't do it to myself. And I can't do it to Danny. It's a fight he doesn't need, getting me out of there. He needs to get on with his life. I've lived mine. And it's been a good one. But also— and Danny can't know about this—I don't have a lot of time left. Of that I'm certain; I won't go into why. So, for all of this I ask your indulgence."

I didn't know what to say, plus I weren't sure what 'indulgence' meant. Finally, I said, "So where you going if you ain't headed back there?"

"Sailing."

"Yeah, but after that?"

Grampy looked at me and smiled. Then he looked up at the sky.

"Hell, Grampy, that's a good enough answer for me," I said. "Let's go have one great sail."

I was worried about getting him aboard, but Grampy practically floated onto *Sarah*. He sat right down in the cockpit and patted the top of the cabin. "Good girl," he said. Then he looked up at that little red arrow at the top of the mast. "We do have a day for it, don't we? Breeze is northwest. Can't beat a northwest wind. Clear air. Fair winds. No fog or rain coming for at least 24 hours." He looked over at us both, sitting across from him in the cockpit. "Well, boys, I'm not getting any younger. Let's head out."

"Why don't you take the tiller, Grampy," Cubby said. "I'll get the mainsail up while we're motoring out of the harbor."

"Danny, with this wind direction, we can sail right off the dock. No sense spoiling the morning with the sound of the engine."

"Sounds fine, Grampy."

I watched him at the helm—it was like he was listening to *Sarah* and feeling what she wanted. It reminded me of the great towboat pilots on the river, just a light touch on the steering sticks, letting the vessel speak to you, never over steering. He sat on the lee side and later, as we got offshore and the northwest wind stiffened a bit, he settled in even more—his arm draped over the cockpit coaming, sea foam rushing by his elbow, his canvas hat cocked on his head just enough so he could look at that wind arrow at the top of the mast. He was in another world. And he looked like he could stay that way forever.

After three or four hours, we must have sailed close to twenty miles out to sea. Cubby and I offered to take over the helm, but Grampy said he was fine. "No thank you, boys; I've waited a long time for this," he said, and he just kept sailing east in that northwest wind, *Sarah* boiling along. The seas were pretty flat, with that wind coming off the land, and *Sarah* was steady. But I could see a worried look on Cubby's face. He went below and checked the bilge. When he came up on deck, he looked less worried and said, "The bilge is dry. I'm really kind of surprised, Grampy. She opened up and we took a lot of water sailing here from Maine. We pumped a lot."

"Red pumped a lot," I corrected.

"Yeah. But now she's tight."

"Tighter than Spandex on a fat woman," I said.

"God, Red."

"That's a good one, Mr. Bates. I'll have to remember that."

"See, Grampy liked it, Cubby."

"Anyway, Grampy, what's with that leak? How could a leak just go away? Colby at the boat yard said it was probably one of the garboard planks."

"It may not be the garboards. In this breeze we'd still have that leak if it were. It may be a stopwater, perhaps up where the stem joins the keel, that hadn't swelled or settled in properly after launching, and has since somehow settled in to do its job."

"Well, when we haul her out we'll find what's wrong, and we'll get her fixed for good," Cubby said.

Grampy looked at Cubby and smiled. "You think that will be the end of it?" he asked.

"Why not?"

"Danny, *Sarah* is very old, and when you try to get at the stem, you'll find the fastenings on her planks weak and deteriorated, and the planks will be soft and punky around the fastenings. And the stopwater between the stem and the keel may be deteriorated, but that, by then, will be inconsequential. She's old, Danny. Nothing lasts forever."

Grampy shook his head, like some Buddha guy giving a lesson on life, then leaned back and glanced at the sky.

"Well, I think we should think about coming about and heading back," Cubby said after a bit, standing up and reaching for the jib sheet.

"I'm not going back," Grampy said.

"What are you talking about, Grampy? We're supposed to get you back by dinner."

"Sit down, Danny." Grampy looked at him, all serious. "Look, it's time for you to get on with it."

"Get on with *what*?"

"Get on with your life. I can't stand it in there and I can't stand you worrying about me stuck in there."

"What choice do we have? Keep sailing around the world 'til we run out of food or the boat sinks?" Cubby looked over at me, his eyes wide. "Red, help me out here."

"I'm just ballast, Cubby. But the way I figure it, it's Grampy's boat, he's the captain now, so it's his call. And you don't want to start being like Ashton and Ratshit, telling him what to do with his life."

"Red, this is different."

"Well, we'll vote on it then," I said. "But it'll be two to one, 'cause I'm with Grampy. But before you jump all over me, I have to tell you that I think I got a plan."

"You think you got a plan? A plan? Okay, Red, let's hear your plan."

"See, it's like this—nobody knows which way we're headed. We're about twenty miles at sea. It'll be dark before anyone figures to look for us, and by the time they do we'll be long gone."

"Oh, my God. Long gone to where, Red?"

"To Hard Harbor Island."

Last time I saw Cubby this mad was when me and Bonnie scared that china cup Jennifer girl right off my houseboat. "You're both out of your minds," he said. "This will trigger a missing person search. Plus, it borders on being criminal," he said.

Me and Grampy just smiled at each other.

"IT'S NOT FUNNY!" Cubby yelled.

"Your grandfather committing a crime by taking his own boat sailing *is* kind of funny Cubby," I said.

"So what's after Hard Harbor, huh? What then?"

Grampy just looked up at that little red arrow or the clouds or the sky. I couldn't tell which. Then he said, "It'll work out, Danny.

But it won't work out if we go back. I don't want either of you in any trouble, so I'm keeping a log of all of this, showing that this is all my doing. As vessel master, I abrogate you both of any and all responsibility regarding the outcome of this voyage."

"Abrogate," I said. "Jesus, Grampy, where do you learn a fifty-cent word like that? That one of them medifors?"

"No, Mr. Bates. It means you two won't be responsible. That's my wish and command."

Then I had a great thought, and looked at Cubby and Grampy, all excited. "You know what we are boys? We're the seagoing Three Musketeers. And we're off on a great adventure. Hell, maybe there'll even be some kind of seafaring duel at the end."

"Do you like Dumas, Mr. Bates?" Grampy asked.

"Who? He one of the Three Musketeers?"

"No, Alexandre Dumas is the author."

"Huh? I thought it was a cartoon and a movie. Saw the movie three times."

"Will you two listen!" Cubby said. "I was the one to arrange and request this 'day sail'. So we're going back."

Then Cubby stood up and headed for the tiller. I put out my arm.

"This some kind of mutiny, Cubby?" I said. "'Cause maybe you ain't Christian Fletcher and this ain't that *Bounty* movie."

"It's Fletcher Christian, Red, not Christian Fletcher," Cubby said, shaking his head. I swear I saw the start of a smile on his face before he sat back down on the cockpit seat.

"Whatever. Anyway, we'll be fine," I said, and stood up and moved to the tiller. "I'll take the watch until it gets dark, Grampy. You need a break. We ain't going back. Don't worry. You two should try to grab some shut-eye, 'cause I ain't much good at sailing once I can't see that little red arrow."

"But we're going to talk some more later. Okay?" Cubby said.

They both went down below, and I settled in looking up at that arrow and trying to remember my new sailing skills. *Sarah* was just gurgling along, the northwest wind steady just like Grampy said. All was going good, but I sure was getting hungry, so I leaned down the hatch to ask Cubby to toss me up something to eat, even one of those healthy sandwiches he bought. Cubby was busy getting Grampy settled into his bunk, helping him off with his sneakers and tucking one of them old wool blankets around him like he was putting his own kid to bed, a kid he'd probably have some day, I figured. I'll probably never get to put a kid to bed, I thought. Made me sad to think about it. So I started looking back at the sea around *Sarah* hoping to spot Big Guy 'cause I wanted to ask that whale a couple things, figuring that anybody that big that's been around that long must know some pretty wise stuff. I wanted to ask: 'Why are we here?" and "What's going to happen to us?" But he didn't show. Probably down there chowing down on the whale version of Ding Dongs. Then I wondered about his whale lady, which got me thinking about when I was ten, and Momma told me how ladies are like spaghetti. I figured lady whales is probably the same, and Big Guy's lady was down there wrapped up in all her responsibilities, teaching her baby whale how to fish, and how to be safe, and how to dodge harpoons and stuff. Kind of a giant Jiminy Cricket.

Sometime later I got to wondering myself what would happen to us Three Musketeers. I got to thinking about that TV show lawyer, Perry Mason, defending us if we really got charged with something. Couldn't be kidnapping, 'cause we didn't ask for a ransom. Couldn't be theft, 'cause it's Grampy's boat. I wondered if we could get charged with a broken promise, which was the only thing we done wrong, I figured, since we said we'd have Grampy back by supper. Then that head of mine started bringing me down. I knew it was those two words, 'broken promise' that did it.

Certain thoughts is triggers that let the dragons out. Hard to push them back in—'bout as hard as putting toothpaste back in the tube—so usually I try booze. Or I do something crazy on the river to distract them, something that takes all my concentration, like driving a bend, pushing a big tow when I should be flanking it.

Well, this time, on *Sarah*, it was a boat on the horizon coming toward us that did it—did it by distracting me, that setting sun reflecting on its pilothouse windows. I watched it for some time, figuring no sense bothering Cubby and Grampy until I knew it was looking for us, and then, well, I didn't know what I'd do. How would a Musketeer handle it? Maybe fire a warning shot across their bow. It was around eight p.m., so I figured maybe word had gotten out by then, and the Coast Guard got called to look for us. But soon I could tell it was a fishing boat, one of them draggers like I'd seen on TV. It was rolling from side to side, its big fishing arms sticking way out on each side like a big insect, one of them praying mantises maybe. But they just steamed by, paying us no mind. After that I figured we could listen to the VHF radio, channel 16, to see if the Coast Guard had issued a Pan Pan alert, telling all listeners to be on the lookout for a missing boat, or one in distress, or some other emergency.

The wind calmed down some at sunset, and Cubby and Grampy came up on deck to take over. I went below and found my favorite spot on the cabin floor, but only after I grabbed the last of my Ding Dong stash from my secret hiding spot behind the life jackets. I settled in on a bunk cushion that I slid onto the floor, chowed down, and then tried to doze off. It was calm enough now that I could hear Grampy and Cubby talking in the cockpit.

"Seems like a fine man, that Mr. Bates. Quite a character, too. It must have been interesting living with him on that houseboat."

"'Interesting' is one word you could use, Grampy."

"And he came to your graduation, you said?"

"He certainly did. Made a big impression."

"Well, fine. That's pretty special. I wish I'd been there."

"I wish you had, too. You deserved to be there, Grampy. More than anyone."

"Except your mother. If she could have lived to see what a fine young man you've grown into that would have been such a joy to her. But Mr. Bates came. Substitute parent, really. And then to drive you out East after graduation. Quite an effort. Did he want to see New England? The ocean?"

"That's one reason, I guess. But he was really upset about your situation."

"But he didn't even know me. I bet he saw how upset *you* were about it."

"I told him all about you, Grampy. How you raised me, really. And how we sailed in Maine. We shared a pretty small space on *Cirrhosis*, so we did a lot of talking."

"Cirrhosis?"

"*Cirrhosis of the River.* The name of Red's houseboat."

Right then I heard Grampy let out a laugh that almost shook the boat.

"Marvelous. Absolutely marvelous," he said. I could hear him slapping his knee.

"Anyway," Cubby said, "he wanted to get you out as much as I did."

"Sounds as if he's the kind of man who needs to right a wrong."

"I guess, but he can drive me crazy sometimes, Grampy."

"Well, I bet it's not because he doesn't care, Danny. I'm sure you'll miss him when he returns to Minnesota."

"It's just that, with Red, I'm never quite sure what's going to happen next. I mean, look at us, Grampy. We're offshore in a leaky old wooden boat, headed for an island almost in Canada, leaving behind all kinds of people thinking we're probably drowned. That's all Red's doing! It drives me crazy!"

"It's my doing. Not his. He's just following my wishes. If I'd have told anyone I wouldn't be coming back, we never could have done this."

"But you have to go back sometime, Grampy. Right?"

A minute passed.

"Could you let out the mainsail a tad, Danny? I can feel the wind backing a bit. Let's just enjoy this glorious sail."

Then it got quiet, and I drifted off, trying not to think of them lobsters waiting for me 150 feet below.

I don't know what they talked about while I was sleeping, but when I poked my head out of the cabin the sun was just coming up. *Sarah* was still slipping along pretty good. Grampy was still at the tiller, and Cubby was stretched out on the other cockpit seat, a worried look on his face. I knew why he was worried. Then I got an idea that I figured might make everybody satisfied, and I pulled myself up on deck.

"Hey, Musketeers," I said. "I been thinking about their saying; you know: 'One for All and All for One'. Well, that gave me an idea. Why don't *we* call *them*?—call the Coast Guard real quick so they can't trace us like they do on them bad guy movies—tell them we ain't coming back, but we're okay so don't worry. That way we ain't making anyone sad like we was dead or something."

Grampy looked at me. "Mr. Bates, they'll be able, in a few seconds, to triangulate the signal and get our location."

"So we got to maintain radio silence then?"

"It's a small world, Mr. Bates," Grampy said, "and getting smaller all the time. Hard to hide anymore."

"Small world," I said, shaking my head. "Spinning around and you can't get off."

Grampy smiled at that. Then he looked up at the sky, kind of not focused at all, looking nowhere, like he was having one of them out-of-body experiences. "Hard Harbor is a small world of its own," he said finally. "Perhaps that will be enough."

Nobody said much for a while, and we just kept sailing on into that rising sun.

* * *

Right after we spotted Hard Harbor Island, just like it were some script from a movie, this fog bank dropped down on us in the late afternoon, giving us the cover we needed. With Cubby and now Grampy on board this time, I knew I was with a boatload of local knowledge and, even though we couldn't see nothing, Cubby and Grampy did their usual homemade radar, listening, and using that lead line, and we was in that harbor slicker than shit through a Mississippi swamp. We dropped anchor in what that lead line said was three fathoms, and we figured we were in the right spot in the little anchorage.

"Beer's all right, now? Right boys?" I said, after we got *Sarah* shipshape. "We got to celebrate landfall."

"I happen to have placed a fine Venezuelan rum in my sea bag to celebrate the day, Mr. Bates. Perhaps you might go below and grab it."

I looked at Grampy and grinned. God, I love this guy, I thought, as I headed below and up to the forward cabin. When I poked around in Grampy's sea bag, my hand landed on a bunch of stuff: some papers, something that felt like a small jewelry box, something heavy like a lead weight, and then the bottle of rum. That stuff made me curious and almost made me stop and poke around some more, but the rum got the better of me.

"Well, Grampy," I said as I came up on deck with the bottle, "you got to abrogate me when I get into this rum—can't be responsible for my actions."

Even Cubby had a sip as we sat there in the fog and waited. For what, I weren't sure.

"So what happens now?" Cubby asked.

Grampy smiled. "Of course we see the Pikes," he said.

"And then what?" Cubby asked, shaking his head. "And what after that?"

"There's always something after anything," Grampy said. "Always will be. Let's just enjoy this moment. What an adventure we've just had, Danny! What a glorious sail that was!"

"That's fine, but now it's over, so I want to call the Coast Guard to let them know we're all right," Cubby said. He headed into the cabin, turned on the VHF and grabbed the microphone. 'Coast Guard, Coast Guard, this is sailing vessel *Sarah*. Come in. Come in.'

I reached down to the wiring panel and flipped off the 12-volt power switch, then came down the cabin steps and sat down in front of the switch, putting 290 pounds of barricade between Cubby and the power supply.

"That's it, Red. That's it. I'm done! I'm done with you and this whole thing. I'm rowing ashore to find the Pikes. I'll call from there."

Cubby shot up the cabin steps, slid over the side into the skiff, untied the bow line, set the oars, and started rowing into the fog.

"I hope you ain't gonna be cavorting with the enemy, Cubby," I said as he began to disappear.

The splashing of his oars stopped for a few seconds, and all was quiet. Then the oars started splashing again, and Cubby yelled: "And it's 'consorting', Red. Not 'cavorting'. God!" And then he was gone.

4 2
ROWING TO CLOUD 23

"He know where he's going?" I asked Grampy. "I can't barely see my own feet in this fog."

"Oh, yes. Danny always had a great fog nose. He'll feel his way to the Pike's pier just fine, I'm willing to bet."

"Well, we got to fortify, Grampy," I said after another swig of rum.

"Excuse me, Mr. Bates?"

"You know: 'One for All and All for One'. They're going to be coming for us. We got to defend ourselves. Can't go down without a fight."

Grampy didn't say anything to that. Instead he said, "Tell me your thoughts about the river and what it means to you, Mr. Bates."

"Well, I ain't thought about it too deep. I guess it's a pretty slow motion kind of life, pushin' barges up and down. Kind of like being an ant, just working away, shoving around one piece of bread crumb after another just to survive. The river's your whole world when you're on it. And when you're not on it, you're thinking about it, talking about it, and figuring when you're gonna get back on it."

"So true, I bet. Hermann Hesse said, 'The river is everywhere at the same time, and that there is no such thing as time."

"Huh. Who's Hermann Hesse?"

"He wrote *Siddhartha*, among other works. A German writer and poet."

"Who's Siddhartha?"

"He's a young man who leaves his family to find the meaning of life. He comes to a river and hears a sound that signals the true beginning of his life—the beginning of suffering, rejection, peace, and, finally, wisdom."

"I been through the first two. Need to get to the peace and wisdom part, though. Maybe I should read the book. Or see the movie if they made one."

"Or you could listen to the river for the answers."

"I'll try that when I get back, Grampy. Anyway, how do you know all this book stuff? Were you one of them college professors? One of them deans maybe?"

"No, but in truth I wanted to be. My career was in medical devices—as an engineer and inventor."

"That's really something. What'd you invent?"

"It was a right ventricle assist heart device. Thankfully, the patent that was granted allowed for a very comfortable life financially, including paying for Danny's college... and often bailing out Ashton."

"You know, it ain't none of my business, but what's the deal with Ashton? I mean, seems like all this is 'cause of him."

"I don't know where we went off course with him, honestly. My dear wife Barbara and I did the best we could, but it's as if Ashton had no moral compass. It's puzzling. My daughter Ellie, Danny's mother, was always kind and thoughtful from her early childhood right through the agonizing last weeks of her life."

"River men would call him a bad seed," I said. "My daddy was one of them. Sometimes I wonder if I got some of that."

"Quite the opposite, Mr. Bates. Quite the opposite."

"Well, thanks. Anyway, we need a plan right now, Grampy."

"Well, we'll just let things flow like the river."

"That ain't much of a plan if you don't mind me sayin' so."

Right then I heard an outboard—sounded like that small two-stroke one that Oceanus had on his skiff, but you couldn't see nothin', that fog bein' thicker than fleas on a dog. Finally I made out the outline of a skiff and then that head of long black hair, and I knew it was Oceanus.

"Grampy, it's Oceanus Pike," I said.

Grampy pulled himself up, hanging onto the boom to steady himself from the wake that came from Oceanus' skiff. "Wonderful. Just wonderful," he said. Oceanus pulled alongside, cut his motor, and grabbed onto *Sarah's* rail.

"Whole world's looking for you, Grampy," he said. "It's all over the VHF, and folks on the mainland say it's all over the news."

"I suppose so. Wonderful to see you, Oceanus. Have you been well?"

"Just fine. But what about you?"

"Couldn't be better. How's the head? Still no after-effects from that concussion, I trust?"

Oceanus shook his head. "I saw Danny on our wharf. He's pretty upset. Says he was going to call the Coast Guard from our VHF."

"I suppose so," Grampy said. "Why don't you come aboard and we'll fill you in."

Oceanus climbed aboard and gave Grampy a hug, and I shook his hand. Oceanus looked at us both. "So what's up?" he said.

"Grampy ain't going back to the nursing home no matter what. That's what's up," I said. "So we're staying right here." I could hear Cujo barking ashore, and the sound of a lobster boat's engine revving somewhere outside the ledges. "They had Grampy trapped in there like some caged dog. Drugged him, too."

"Thank you, Mr. Bates," Grampy said, "but it's more than that. At any rate, I'm right where I want to be right now, so that's enough, though perhaps you might give me an estimate of what time the Coast Guard might arrive if Danny's called them."

"Most likely, they'll be sending a 41-footer out from Jonesport. They'll have to go real slow in this fog, so it'll probably take an hour and a half or so."

"Think they'll find us?" I asked.

"Those guys are pretty good. You're the only boat in here besides my dad's lobster boat. They'll pick both boats up on radar and probably nose in to see if one is *Sarah*," Oceanus said. "Nothing 'cept maybe a minefield is going to keep them out." Then he looked at Grampy. "Will they take you away, Grampy? I mean, right off your own boat? Back to that place?"

Grampy nodded.

"Well, I don't see how this is fair."

"Did you say 'minefield'?" I asked.

Oceanus nodded, and ran his fingers through that long black hair, which was now pretty soaked from the fog, and stringing down his forehead. "I'll do most anything you want, Grampy, after what you did for me, but I can't make a minefield."

Then from somewhere in the back of my little brain came a really smart idea. "How about a mine field that won't hurt nobody?" I said. They both looked at me. I kept going. "You got lobster trap buoys all around us. What about stringing some heavy poly rope between some of them, maybe sink the poly down a few feet with some fishing weights."

"Polypropylene?" Oceanus asked.

"Yeah, that heavy plastic rope. It'll melt right onto them 41's props."

They both stared at me.

"Well, there ain't no law against stringing some lines in the water," I said.

"I doubt that would work," Oceanus said. "And besides, there's not enough time. And even if we foul their props or rudders, eventually they'll get free. And there'll be other boats. And the fog will eventually lift."

Grampy chimed in. "Once again, thank you, Mr. Bates, for your loyalty. But right now I need to talk to Danny before the Coast Guard gets here. That's what's most important."

Oceanus stood up. "I'll head in, get Danny, and send him back out here, Grampy. Then I'll talk to my dad and see what he thinks about all this. It'll be dark before long, and it'll really be a black hole in here if this fog stays too. Maybe the Coast Guard won't even come out until dawn."

"Do have Danny come out as soon as you can," Grampy said.

Oceanus nodded and slipped over the side into his skiff.

Me and Grampy just sat there in the cockpit for a while, saying nothing. I got to wondering what Grampy wanted to talk to Cubby about but figured, for once, I'd keep my mouth shut. Then, out of nowhere, Grampy said, "Do you know about Cloud 23, Mr. Bates?"

"Yes, sir. From them h-mails of yours."

"Well, I'm planning on going there tonight. But I really shouldn't tell Danny. He would never understand and would most likely try to stop me. So I need you to indulge me one last time. I need your confidence and your cooperation if you'd be good enough to oblige."

"I ain't the sharpest bulb in the tool shed, Grampy, so maybe you could enlighten me on how you plan on getting up there to Cloud 23."

"I'll be rowing."

"Huh? Might be better to take Oceanus' skiff; it's got an out-board."

"No, I greatly prefer to row. You do know what I'm doing, Mr. Bates?"

"Got it. Goin' to heaven. Just taking the long way."

"You're much more perceptive than you think."

"Well, when you see your wife and Cubby's mom up there, tell them Cubby is damn good for this screwed-up planet of ours. And that he should stick around down here for a good long while to fix things. And that they should be real proud."

"I'll add you to that list, Mr. Bates. You stick around too. Both of you."

* * *

Cubby felt his way toward *Sarah* a little later, just before dark. I figured he was a little bit lost when I heard him yell, "Hey, you guys, say something loud so I can find you." So we both yelled "Over here!" and soon heard the splash of his oars and then picked up the outline of the skiff. Once Cubby got aboard, Grampy said, "Let's go below, dry out a bit, and talk, Danny."

So that's what we did. That old fog-damp cabin warmed up in no time under those four kerosene lanterns hanging on the bulkheads and cabin sides. Me and Grampy sat on one side of the little cabin table, across from Cubby, outlined kind of like ghosts in that dim light as *Sarah* rocked gently in the swell that rolled in over the ledges at the entrance to Hard Harbor. All of us was quiet, each one of us listening, I figured, for the sound of the throaty exhausts of those Cummins diesels pushing some Coast Guard 41- footer through the fog. But all we could hear was the sound of a bell buoy out by the ledges.

"I called the Coast Guard, Grampy," Cubby said finally.

"I understand."

"So you're okay with that?"

"Certainly. You did what you felt was right, Danny. And now I want to give you some things. Perhaps you could grab my sea bag from up forward."

So Cubby fetched Grampy's faded canvas sea bag and put it on the table next to the rum bottle. Grampy fiddled with the zipper for a while and finally opened the bag. One at a time, like it was a Christmas stocking, he pulled out a little felt bag, a small jewelry case, and a white envelope, and handed each to Cubby. "These are some things I was able to put aside and save for you," Grampy said.

"I don't know what to say. Why are you giving me these things now, Grampy?"

"No time like the present. Go ahead, take a look."

So Cubby opened the small felt bag, and slid out a pretty hefty gold bar.

"That should get the boat yard bill paid and Mr. Bates' truck out of hock, with some left over," Grampy said.

"This is amazing, Grampy. But how'd you know about the truck?" Cubby asked.

"Mr. Bates told me when I asked him about how Quimby and Colby and the boatyard were doing and if Ashton had us squared up with *Sarah's* storage bill."

Grampy turned and nodded at me. "You're a fine man, Mr. Bates. And I'm sure you'll have your truck back soon."

Then Grampy looked back at Cubby. "Go ahead, open the rest."

So Cubby opened the jewelry case, lifted up an old watch, and put it up to the lantern. "Wow, this is a really nice watch, Grampy."

"1951. Rolex. An extremely rare automatic triple calendar watch with moon phases and tropical dial. I used to love watches. And this was my special investment, a treat to myself I guess, after the heart device patent went through. No pun intended, but it's time-less."

"Must be worth something," I said. "That's the year I was born."

"Sure looks old, Grampy."

"Age has its value, Danny."

"It's really valuable, huh?"

"Save it, Danny. Lock it up in a safe deposit box. It's inflation proof. Really sought after. It will only get more valuable. Should you need to auction it to, let's say, pay for law school, take it to Sotheby's or Christie's auction houses. They'll know what to do." Grampy pushed the white envelope over toward Cubby. "This last thing is a $15,000 certificate of deposit. It's in your name. It will be a good start for you. If you do get things straightened out with my estate, that's fine. But otherwise, you're bright enough to make your own way in the world."

Cubby looked across at us. Then he started choking up.

"Aw, come on, Cubby," I said, leaning over the table and patting his arm.

"It's just that now we're going to be right back where we started; back to that nursing home," he said, rubbing the back of his hand over each eye.

"No we ain't. We'll hold 'em off. Put up a good fight," I said. Then I turned to Grampy, "You got a flare gun on board?"

Cubby looked up at me; now there was real anger in those eyes. "Will you get real, Red. God, what do you think this is, one of your action movies? Don't make it even worse." He got up from the table, moved aft, and stared out the main hatch into the fog for a minute or two. Then he turned back to me. "You know, I don't know why you're even here, Red. Why are you out here with us at all, sticking *your* neck out? I can't understand why a person like you, so much older and from a completely different world, would even be friends and hang around with me. This is bad stuff right now, Red. Don't you get that?"

I shook my head slowly. Didn't get excited. More like calm and sad. "Hell, this ain't bad stuff, Cubby," I said. "Not when you've seen what I've seen. In the real bad stuff, made by the devil himself, there's more evil and more sadness than most folks can ever imagine. Puts everything in perspective." I took a good gulp of that rum. "No, this ain't sticking my neck out. This is about making up for that bad stuff. It's about springing Grampy. It's about freedom for Grampy. He's my friend now, too. And I pick my friends and stands up for what riles them and what riles me. I'm doing what's right. Maybe someday you'll understand. Maybe someday you'll see what I'm seeing."

"If all that 'stuff' happened over there, Red, then *talk* about it. Let it out. You *never* talk about Vietnam. Every time it comes up you change the subject."

"No use sharing that, ruining someone else's day and all. Why share something that the other person can't even imagine? No, Cubby, only one good thing, far as I can tell, ever come out of that war. The rest was all bad; no good for nothing. Hell, now that we're into this, Cubby, I ain't once heard *you* talk about your bad stuff either. Why should I talk about my bad stuff when you don't ever talk about yours? You know, stuff about you being adopted and all, your real mother giving you up, and what that all means."

"For your information, Red, my 'real' mom will *always* be my real mom. She's as real as Grampy. She's as real as this table. Yes, I lost her, just like I lost my birth mother. And that's real hard to talk about. Do you know how terrifying it is to lose *two* mothers, Red? To be from *two* worlds? To not know who you really are or if you'll ever find a place where you really belong?"

Cubby turned his back to us again and looked out the main hatch into that nothingness for a long time. Then, without moving, almost like he was talking to that fog, he said, "Do you know how it feels to be a white person living in an Asian body?"

My heart hurt, 'cause I remembered what I thought when Cubby first showed up at my houseboat door. I reached for the rum bottle and poured us all a good shot. We was quiet for some time. Finally I pulled myself up from the table and walked aft. I stood over Cubby, resting my hands on his shoulders. "I know what loss feels like, Cubby," I said.

Right then Grampy stepped in. "Have a seat you two, and let's hear about this one good thing of yours, Mr. Bates. I think we could use something like that right now."

"Okay. Maybe you're right," I said. I squeezed back onto a seat at the table. Cubby sat down next to Grampy.

"It was at the end of the war, in '75, when they was evacuating orphaned war babies out of the country before the fall of Saigon."

"Operation Babylift?" Grampy asked.

"You know about that, Grampy?"

"I certainly do," he said, and looked at Cubby.

"Huh. Well, I was crew on a chopper during this time. We was headed to a Saigon airfield to meet a flight inspector when this giant Lockheed C-5 Galaxy, chock full of babies, crashed close by. We landed near it, jumped out, and ran toward the pieces of that plane."

I stopped—took a deep breath. "What I seen then was like having my heart sliced open and cut out," I said, shaking my head. And right then those demons I kept locked away in the back of my brain escaped, and I was back there, in the middle of the fire, the smoke, the burning grass, and the screaming. And then, just like it did that day, my throat clenched up, my nose and eyes streamed. I looked at Cubby and Grampy, staring at them. I must have been one scary sight. But somehow I kept going, just like I did that day of the crash. "Way worse than the worst I'd seen in 'Nam," I said. "'Cause this time...this time it was *babies*. A bunch of us ran back and forth, into that open piece of the plane, grabbing one baby after another and putting them down out of reach of the fire and smoke. Most was like rag dolls, with bracelets on their tiny wrists, their little arms hanging, not moving. And they just piled up. 78! Jesus God—there was 78 dead babies that day. And we just picked them up, piled them in heaps." The memory made me clench my fists, then shake them, over and over, before opening my hands, holding my palms up in front of me, like some priest at the altar. I leaned over the table, almost sobbing now. "You know what it feels like to hold a dead baby?" Then I sobbed away. Grampy put his hand on my shoulder 'til I settled down. Then, real gently, he said, "The good thing, Mr. Bates. The one good thing. Tell us about that."

"I don't know how many trips I made but on one of the last ones, when I was in the forward part of the passenger deck, I heard crying, looked around, and saw a pile of blankets move a little. Under that pile I found a little baby. Alive. I remember looking at its bracelet when that tiny hand was grabbing the hair on my wrist. One part of the name was 'Ha'. Can't remember the rest. Anyway, I reckon I saved that baby." I rubbed the wet from my eyes. "So that was the one good thing," I said.

Nobody said nothing for a long time after that. It was real quiet around that table, no noise except for the creaking of *Sarah's* hull when that ocean swell lifted her now and then. Grampy and Cubby just looked at each other like they both knew what each was thinking.

Finally, Cubby said, "'Ha' means 'river', Red."

"No shit. River, huh? Ain't that something. How'd you know that, Cubby?"

"Because it was my surname. My Vietnamese name."

"Well, if that don't send me the shivers," I said.

Grampy put his rum glass down carefully on the table. "Danny was one of the babies on that plane," he said.

I sank down into the bunk cushion, looked up at the cabin top for a few seconds, then sat up straight, like I was waking from a dream. Then I realized it weren't no dream; it was something I'd always wondered about, even fantasized about, ever since I first met Cubby. I cocked my head and looked at Grampy and Cubby. "Can you just replay that last line?" I asked.

Right then came that throaty rumble we knew was coming. "They're here," I said, pulling myself up from the table. "Them's Cummins diesels. Coast Guard. I'm headed up to the cockpit; see what's going on." I grabbed the rum bottle. Then I turned to Grampy, "Where's that flare gun?"

"It should be in the locker behind you."

"You're going to signal them? Right, Red?" Cubby asked.

"Hell, no. I'm going to defend us. Defend my comrades. That flare gun will have to do, since I ain't got no Musketeer musket," I said, and reached around in the locker until I found that flare pistol and a packet of three shells. Then I started to head up on deck.

"Oh, my God, Red. You're totally nuts," Cubby screamed. He put his head in his hands, leaned over that little table, and just started shaking. Grampy reached out and put his hand on Cubby's arm.

"It's fine, Danny," Grampy said, "Nothing violent is going to happen. Stay down here and I'll go up and talk to Mr. Bates. It's best for your future that you stay uninvolved."

Then Grampy worked his way up the companionway steps and sat next to me in the cockpit. Man, it was darker than a moonless night in the Minnesota woods.

"I think I see their running lights," Grampy said.

"Yeah. But they sure ain't moving much."

"Maybe now's the time for me," Grampy said.

"You sure about this, Grampy? I mean, what with all that just happened down in the cabin about me and Cubby..."

Right then we heard voices. Excited-sounding voices. It sounded like someone said 'Cut your engines', and sure enough that engine rumbling stopped. Even though we still couldn't see them, or even see the outline of their boat except for the red and green running lights, we could hear them pretty good now: 'Something's on the rudder, Chief; helm's not responding' somebody said. I couldn't make out exactly what came after that, but there was a lot of back and forth words and some yelling coming out of that fog.

"Jesus, Grampy, you think Oceanus actually put some of that poly rope out there underwater?" I whispered.

Grampy didn't answer. I looked over at him. He had his sea bag in his lap and was staring into the fog, looking away from the Coast Guard boat, and out toward the sound of that bell buoy. "What you got left in there?" I asked, pointing to the bag.

"Just some mementos; some old love letters from Barbara and some pictures from our wedding."

"Oh."

Then we heard this megaphone-powered voice come out of the fog. "Ahoy *Sarah*. Sailing vessel *Sarah*. This is the United States Coast Guard. We're temporarily disabled, but we're here to ensure the safety of Mr. Joseph Roan and are proceeding to follow our orders to bring him to shore."

I stood up in the cockpit. "Why don't you boys go do some real rescuing or crime fighting, and just leave us be."

"Again, we're following orders, sir."

"You want to keep America free? Well, start with Grampy's freedom. He ain't broke no laws. He's on his own boat. It's a United States Coast Guard-documented vessel, I might add. He's a U.S. citizen. And all he wants is to be left alone. He don't want to get off."

"We'll be coming alongside as soon as we're operational, sir."

"Well, I hear the folks on most of this planet is watching what will happen, now that the news is out. You try to take this old gentleman by force and the whole country will be hating you Coasties. You won't be no heroes, that's for sure. So, you know, now that you're disabled and all, seems like this is a good time to abort your mission. Save face while you still can. You got the best excuse in the world, boys."

Right then Grampy stood up, grabbing the boom to steady himself, and whispered to me.

"We all need to know when to let go, Mr. Bates. I've had a good life that finished up with a splendid sail with two splendid people. And for that I thank you. But you and Danny have more life to live," he said, and put his hand on my shoulder. Then he took one last look into the cabin before turning back to me. "My work is done, and I'm done being a burden, and I won't go back to that nursing home" he said. "And besides, I have a feeling that Danny has the father he always needed. I think he knows that now." He leaned even closer to me. "So please allow me one last request: Bring the skiff alongside and help me and my sea bag get aboard. And do it before Danny comes on deck. He'd never let me go. He's too young to understand what I want to do, which is to go rowing—head out to sea—in this lovely dense fog. Then maybe up and away, to join my dear Barbara on Cloud 23."

III

43
BACK TO 2014: ME AND TODDY— MORNING ON CIRRHOSIS AND AT THE WAFFLE PALACE

"So that's the story, Toddy," I said, and pulled myself up from that rocker and walked over to one of *Cirrhosis'* snowed-up windows. I leaned my head against the glass, trying to see out through the plastic that was tacked over the outside. "Maybe we should get some shut-eye, Toddy. In a few hours Grouchy will be firing up that big snowblower of his and starting to clear off the docks."

"Orca?"

"Yeah, Toddy?"

"FOR GOD'S SAKE: WHAT HAPPENED TO GRAMPY?"

"Well, they found the skiff a couple days later, empty, out by the ledges. Never found Grampy. Nope, he was long gone. Even took his sea bag with him."

Toddy pulled herself up from the couch slowly, being careful with her bad ankle, and hopped over to where I was standing by the window. We stood there trying to look out, but really just looking at nothing. Finally, she said, "Did Cubby understand?"

"Not so much, Toddy. He blamed me. Kept asking me why I let Grampy go. I told him it was what Grampy wanted, but Cubby didn't get it. Anyway, when the fog finally lifted and the search for Grampy was going on, we was asked about a zillion questions by the Coast Guard, so we gave them Grampy's log of the trip. That cleared us and we was free to go. But Cubby wanted to stay and search on his own, on *Sarah*, so I said I'd stay with him.

We poked around along the rocks and in the open ocean around Hard Harbor Island. He barely said a word to me. I knew we'd never find Grampy, 'cause I knew where he was headed. Finally, Cubby just gave up, and we took *Sarah* into Quimby's boatyard. Cubby wrote him a check dated for a week later, so he had time to cash something in to cover it, and I got my truck back. I offered to take Cubby back to Seacasset, but he said he'd rather take the bus and that it would be better if I stayed away. So I drove back to St. Paul. Never heard from him again."

"He never re-connected with you? I mean, my God, that plane crash in Vietnam! You probably saved his life! There is no such thing as a coincidence, Orca. That is fate. Fate that it was *you* who pulled him from that plane, and then years later fate connecting you randomly like that on this very houseboat."

"I know, Toddy. When I was dropping him off at that bus station in Maine after we got my truck back, I wanted to tell him just that. Then that Greyhound bus pulled up and I knew time was gettin' away from me. Finally, as Cubby started to pick up his sea bag, I said, "You need to understand, Cubby, it was Grampy's choice.""

"He was all I had, Red. He was all I had left. And now he's gone. You should've stopped him," he said.

"But what about that plane crash?" I said. "You and me and that plane crash. I mean, ain't that a sign about something?"

"There were lots of babies on that plane, Red. And lots of them probably had 'Ha' as part of their name. It's a real common name in Vietnam," he said.

"Yeah, but it *coulda* been you."

Cubby looked down at the dusty sidewalk. 'Look, I've got to go, Red,' he said, And then he got on that bus.

"Did you try to connect with him ever again?" Toddy asked.

"Wrote him a letter couple of years later, trying to explain. And I sent a few postcards from scenic places along the river when I was driving tows. Sent them all to that Ross Island address. Never heard back. Maybe he'd just had enough of me."

"Oh, Orca, so many years have gone by, I think he understands now that what you did was right. I really do."

"You think so, Toddy?"

"Yes, I'm sure he does."

"No, I mean, do *you* think so, Toddy? Do you think what I done was right, letting Grampy go?"

Toddy turned to me; looked straight at me. "You know, I'll bet Cubby's mom told him what I'm sure she felt: that his birth mother also let him go, let him be put on that plane, because it was best for her baby. She made the ultimate sacrifice, relinquishing her child in hopes of a safer life for him."

I just looked down and shook my head. Toddy put her hand on my wrist and squeezed. "Indians have a saying, 'Today is a good day to die'. It means we are ready in our mind, heart and spirit to enter the never-ending and timeless River of Spirit to float forever. I don't think Grampy ever feared death, Orca; in fact, I bet he truly wanted his body to change to vapor in the eternal circle. Into spirit. And that's what you helped him do. You gave Grampy a new life, Orca."

I thought about that for a while. Didn't get too far on that vapor and eternal circle stuff, but damn if it didn't make me feel a whole lot better just the same. "Well, Toddy," I said, "after we get some shut eye, maybe it's time to get off *this* particular river for a while, especially since I think I'm going to turn to vapor if I don't recharge soon. How about we stop at The Waffle Palace and push down a few of their waffles before we head back to the veterans' home? Haven't been back to the Palace in some time. Their waffles gotta be better by now."

I made sure Toddy was set up good and warm on the couch with plenty of blankets, and I headed to my old bunk room to grab a few hours' sleep. And, at dawn, as sure as water's wet, came the sound of Grouchy's snow blower, and me and Toddy got up and ready to leave. I pushed open the door hard to shove away all that drifted snow; then Toddy held my arm and hopped out onto the front deck. We waited 'til Grouchy cleared a path and started to turn the snow blower around. When he saw us, he shut it down, lifted up his snow goggles, smiled and then shook his head. He looked down at all the snow. "You believe this? And it's only mid-November. Global warming, my ass!"

"Mornin', Grouchy," I said. Then I picked up Toddy and stepped down carefully onto the dock. It felt real good. Didn't even feel my bad knee as I stood there holding Toddy in my arms and smiling back at Grouchy. "She hurt her ankle on your dock last night," I said. "But she ain't gonna sue you or nothin'."

Grouchy grinned at me and shook his head. "You certainly are sumphin', Orca Bates. That was quite a storm last night, huh? You two stay warm enough?"

"Just toasty," Toddy said. Then she leaned her head on my shoulder and gave Grouchy a big smile just before I put her down.

When we got to Toddy's car, I scooped off the snow while she warmed up that Subaru's little four-banger engine, and we headed out to get some breakfast.

"Thanks for that, Toddy," I said, as we turned up Wabasha Street.

"For what?"

"For keeping Grouchy guessin', I reckon."

"Why, whatever do you mean, Orca?"

"You're playin' with me, Toddy. I know you're playin' with me," I said, and looked over at her. I don't notice much, but what I did see was this little smile. It was just a little smile, but it squeezed my heart all the same.

Kind of like the level of my schooling, not much had changed at the old Waffle Palace over the years. Even those one-legged little chrome-backed stools with the red vinyl seats were still there, along with those booths that was always a squeeze for me. Even though I knew it was some forty-plus years since my teenage days in there with Lil, when I walked in the door with Toddy that early morning I pictured everything just the way it was when I first came in: there was Art Schloggle, same skinny guy in the cheap shiny suit, sitting by the cash register at the end, flirting with the waitress. I saw that waitress turn and nod to me. I saw the pen tucked over her right ear, and around it some of the longest and prettiest wavy red hair I'd ever seen. I saw her turn to me and give me a smile, one aimed at a nobody who just came out of nowhere. A smile that was sweeter than anything you could pour on a waffle.

"Let's sit at my favorite old booth, Toddy," I said, "if I can squeeze into it." Toddy took my arm and hobbled over. I helped her off with her coat. The waitress, a girl with half the side of her head shaved and a little diamond stuck in the side of her nose, came over with some menus, which looked different from the old ones. I hoped this meant the waffles was going to be different, too. "Coffee?" she asked. We nodded and off she went.

"Seems like she missed a big spot shaving," I said. "I guess they don't make waitresses like they used to."

Toddy looked down at the menu and then back at me. "That's a style, Orca."

I just shook my head.

"So here we are. At The Waffle Palace at last," Toddy said.

"Yup. Another fine dining experience, Toddy. First, The Slough last night, now the Palace. Nothing too good for you." I looked at my menu. "Well, I'll be damned. They got raised waffles, Toddy. Something to live for. We'll see, anyway."

So I ordered a couple and Toddy ordered one. She sat there looking at me. "I feel as if I've known you my whole life, Orca" she said finally.

"I reckon you know me better than anybody after last night, Toddy. It's like you picked me up, took off the top of my head, and shook out all that stuff I was keeping in."

"You are not your mind, Orca."

"Excuse me, Toddy?"

"Most of life is imaginary."

"I'm going to try to stay aboard here, Toddy, wherever you're going with this."

"You know, Mark Twain said, 'I've been through some terrible things in my life, some of which actually happened.' Nobody can deal with the past or the future because they only exist as thoughts in the present. So remember, you only have to deal with the present, which is only one thought at a time. Only one. That's the reality."

Toddy looked down at her coffee, and didn't say nothing for a long time. Then she looked up at me, right into me. "You're big, you're strong, you're smart," she said. "And every day, Orca, you can have control. You can choose who you are."

I was glad Toddy said I was smart, but trying to get a line around this imaginary life business was giving me a headache. I was going to speak up, but right then the waffles came out, and I dove right in.

"Jesus H, Toddy," I said after my first bite, "these are *my* waffles. They're still using my recipe. If that ain't the most flattering thing." After I pushed them both down, I told Toddy I wanted to stick my head in the kitchen, and got up to find the cook. I pushed open that swinging door next to the food pickup window and leaned into the kitchen. The cook, a little guy about forty, wearing glasses and a backwards Minnesota Twins hat, looked up at me. "Help you, Mister?"

"Used to cook here. Just got one quick question: them raised waffles, that your own recipe?"

"No, we been using it for a long time, all the time I been here anyway, which is about seven years. Folks can't get enough of 'em. Can't give it out though—it's a Waffle Palace secret."

"That's my recipe."

"Don't know about that, Mister. Who are you?"

"Name's Orca Bates."

"Don't know. Huh. Man, that name's familiar."

"Well, thanks. Glad that recipe is selling."

The cook looked up at his order board, which was next to the old cork bulletin board that I remember we tacked schedules and cartoons on. He pulled down a couple order slips, looked at them, and then looked back at the cork board. "Hell, I know why that name's familiar," he said, and reached up to grab an old yellowed envelope. "This is for you, I guess. Been tacked up there for some time." He handed it to me. Sure enough, it was addressed to Orca Bates, c/o The Waffle Palace, Wabasha Street, St. Paul, Minnesota.

"Thanks," I said, and headed back to our booth where Toddy was sipping her coffee.

"Did you meet the cook, Orca?" she asked as I lowered myself down behind my empty plate. "And it looks as if you have mail."

I turned the letter over. There was a return address from a place I wanted to hear from for a long, long time. "God, Toddy, it's from Cubby," I said. I tore it open and handed it to her. "Read it to me," I said.

8/8/13

Dear Red,

I hope this letter gets to you. Since getting mail was always a long shot at your marina, and thinking maybe you'd moved, I figured I'd have a better shot sending it to The Waffle Palace.

*I did get your letter and postcards. I still have them. It was hard not responding and just leaving things hanging, but I needed this time to come to terms with what happened with Grampy. I still struggle with many things in my life, mostly a deep sense of loss: my mother, my birth mother, and of course Grampy. But there's another big loss. It's the loss of the father I almost had. I struggled so much and for so long with why you let go of Grampy that night. But why did **I** let go of you?*

Probably because I couldn't risk any more loss. But I know now that I can't live that way.

So here's the Cubby update: I have a wonderful wife named Sasha and a beautiful little girl named Mai Linh. I did become a law-yer—probate law—and I'm still sailing, though Sarah's *long gone to firewood. A few years ago we bought a cruising sailboat, a Maine Friendship sloop. Like you and Grampy, it's a true classic. I named her after Grampy: the Joseph P. Roan. We love to sail the coast of Maine every summer. I've lost track of the Pike family, but I heard they moved inland. I hope that's not so. I'd love to hear from you, Red. I hope you are happy.*
Your old roommate and friend,
Cubby

P.S.

We also bought a big, sturdy skiff to tow astern in case we get into trouble. I named it Mr. Bates. *Painted the name right on the stern in big red letters. We get more questions from folks about that name! 'It's a long story,' I always reply, and just leave it at that. We'd love to have you aboard in Maine someday, Red. Sasha and Mai Linh are really curious to meet the skiff's namesake. And I'll be sure to have the big boat loaded up with Ding Dongs and beer, and after 'pushing down a few' (as you would say), perhaps we'll both share our thoughts and stories of our lives since I headed back to Seacasset on that bus sixteen years ago. I'm ready to do that now; I hope you are, too.*

I just sat there, big old head in my hands, sobbing away while Toddy squeezed my arm. Finally, I raised my head, wiped my eyes, and looked at her. Her eyes were as wet as mine. "How'd you know, Toddy? How'd you know he'd come around? You said he would."

"It doesn't matter, Orca. What matters is right now. It's always about right now."

"You really are one of them shamans, ain't you?"

"Let's go home, Orca. Back to the veteran's home. We need you there. We need your spirit. We need your soul. And we need your waffles."

44

A Few Weeks Later: Back at the Home

Keep it to yourself—and especially don't tell no one on the River—but I'm settled in here pretty good. I been writing like crazy in this notebook; I think Toddy was right about it being good for me. Plus, now I got Toddy wearing these tight new winter fleece white yoga pants with little green pine trees on 'em, watching me pretty close, making sure I take my pills and all. She worries about me getting exercise—I still won't do her yoga class—and I like having her worry. But I don't like worrying her, if that makes any sense. So when I get these chest pains, I just pop a nitro and keep the whole thing to myself.

Best thing now, next to Toddy herself, of course, is that she finally convinced me to try to find Cubby's number and call him; then we're gonna be picture talking, using that Facetime thing on that iPhone of hers. With that gadget I'll get to see and chat with Cubby and maybe even his wife and that little girl of theirs. Oh, and I plan on scheming with him to figure a way to get me back East. I even floated that idea by Toddy, us doing the trip together. "Just look at it as another great outing, Toddy," I said. "Just a little longer, that's all."

"We'll see," she said.

"When Momma used to say that, it meant 'no'," I said.

"We'll see," she said again, smiling and shaking that long silky black hair.

I figured that was good enough for now. Just take one step at a time, Red, I thought. Be patient. Toddy will come around.

Third best thing in here now is my cookin'. The whole place waits for my waffles every morning. I'm thinking of making some special-shaped waffles if I can get my hands on some molds. Might make one shaped like a river, and maybe I'll make one shaped like the veterans' home. I was also thinking of making one shaped like a bird for our blind bird-watching resident, Jim Gillson, but I figure, him being blind and all, he might not appreciate it. I been hanging around with him lately, listening and learning about bird calls. Finally, I thought I'd make a Toddy waffle: real nice shape, soft all over, and deep, like Toddy—deep squares to hold a lot of good topping—and extra nourishing 'cause I'll be adding some of that healthy yogurt to my batter. Yup, those will get gobbled up mighty quick, I figure.

Today was my birthday, the day that sixty-three years ago Momma pushed my nearly thirteen pounds out into this strange world. I'd been sitting in my room, thinking that about the saddest thing in the world is to live sixty-three years and be all alone 'cause nobody remembers or cares, when in danced Toddy, singing happy birthday. She was carrying a white box with a red ribbon around it and a big bow on top. There was a card slid under the bow. It made me think of that day years ago by the river with Lil, opening that Jiminy Cricket present. Toddy put the box on my lap. I just looked down at it for a long time.

"Well, go ahead Orca. Open it," Toddy said.

"Open the card first?" I asked.

"Yes, that's the usual procedure."

The front of the card was a picture of a man by a river, and it said,

> Time is but the stream I go 'a-fishing in.
> H.D. Thoreau

"Thanks Toddy, but I ain't much of a fisherman anymore," I said.

"It's a transcendentalist message."

"Oh. Is that like one of them medifors?"

"Not exactly. You should open the card."

Inside, in Toddy's flowery handwriting, was this note:

> *Happy Birthday to a river man*
> *Who carried me downstream and around a bend*
> *On a day and then night I'll never forget,*
> *And taught me the lesson that's*
> *Emblazoned on this shirt.*
> *Forever with you in spirit,*
> *Toddy*

I opened the box. Inside was an XXXL white T-shirt. I held it up and read the big red letters on the front:

HEROES COME IN ALL SIZES

I pushed myself up from my chair, caught my breath for a minute, and pulled it on. Toddy looked at me and smiled—a real big smile that went right to my heart.

Damn, but you know what? That shirt fit me pretty good, I do believe.

* * *

ACKNOWLEDGEMENTS

Thanks to my friends who saw me through the four years of writing <u>Rounding the Bend</u>. There are so many of you and I'm terrified to miss someone. But you know who you are; you provided support, talked things over, read, wrote, offered comments, allowed me to steal your good ideas, and assisted in the editing, proofreading and design. Most of all, you helped Big Red, Toddy, Lil, Cubby, and Grampy come to life and hopefully endure in readers' minds.

I do want to specifically thank my 12 advance readers: Natalie Borden, Dick Buckley, Stan Collinson, Peter Gradjansky, Davis Griffith, John Halter, Peter Maroney, Spencer Moore, Daisy Nell, Chris Roper, Mary Kay Roper, Margo Steiner, and Lynn Sweezy.

I'm especially thankful for having such a wonderful wife and brilliant critic in Mary Kay, who set the bar so high that Big Red and I barely cleared it.

I always love to hear from readers, so please reach out.

davidroper00@gmail.com
facebook.com/davidhroperauthor/
davidhroper.com

Made in the USA
Middletown, DE
15 June 2017